LUKE RHINEHART

THE DICE MAN

HarperCollins*Publishers*

HarperCollins*Publishers*
77–85 Fulham Palace Road,
Hammersmith, London W6 8JB

www.**fireandwater**.com

This paperback edition 1999
7 9 8 6

First published in Great Britain by
Talmy, Franklin Ltd 1971

Previously published in paperback by HarperCollins 1994
Reprinted six times

Previous paperback edition published by Grafton 1972
Reprinted twenty-seven times

ISBN 0 00 651390 5

Set in Times

Printed and bound in Great Britain by
Clays Ltd, St Ives plc

THE DICE MAN

Since *The Dice Man*, Luke Rhinehart has written four other acclaimed novels, *Matari, Long Voyage Back, Adventures of Wim* and the long-awaited sequel to *The Dice Man, The Search for the Dice Man*. His latest work is *The Book of the Die*. Luke Rhinehart lives in the United States.

Praise for *The Dice Man*:

'Touching, ingenious and beautifully comic'
                                            ANTHONY BURGESS

'Brilliant ... very impressive'   COLIN WILSON

'Hilarious and well-written ... sex always seems to be an option'   *Time Out*

'I find *The Dice Man* very funny indeed and sometimes almost terrifying in its accurate evocation of the amount of nonsense American psychoanalysts talk and believe in!'
                              PROFESSOR H. J. EYSENCK

to A.
   J.
   M.
without any of whom,
no Book.

In the beginning was Chance, and Chance was with God and Chance was God. He was in the beginning with God. All things were made by Chance and without him was not anything made that was made. In Chance was life and the life was the light of men.

There was a man sent by Chance, whose name was Luke. The same came for a witness, to bear witness of Whim, that all men through him might believe. He was not Chance, but was sent to bear witness of Chance. That was the true Accident, that randomizes every man that cometh into the world. He was in the world and the world was made by him, and the world knew him not. He came unto his own, and his own received him not. But as many as received him, to them gave he power to become the sons of Chance, even to them that believe accidentally, they which were born, not of blood, nor of the will of the flesh, nor of the will of men, but of Chance. And Chance was made flesh (and we beheld his glory, the glory as of the only begotten of the Great Fickle Father), and he dwelt among us, full of chaos, and falsehood and whim.

– from *The Book of the Die*

Preface

'The style is the man,' once said Richard Nixon and devoted his life to boring his readers.

What to do if there is no single man? No single style? Should the style vary as the man *writing* the autobiography varies, or as the past man he writes about varied? Literary critics would insist that the style of a chapter must correspond to the man whose life is being dramatized: a quite rational injunction, one that ought therefore to be repeatedly disobeyed. The comic life portrayed as high tragedy, everyday events being described by a madman, a man in love described by a scientist. So. Let us have no more quibbles about style. If style and subject matter happen to congeal in any of these chapters it is a lucky accident, not, we may hope, soon to be repeated.

A cunning chaos: that is what my autobiography shall be. I shall make my order chronological, an innovation dared these days by few. But my style shall be random, with the wisdom of the Dice. I shall sulk and soar, extol and sneer. I shall shift from first person to third person: I shall use first-person omniscient, a mode of narrative generally reserved for Another. When distortions and digressions occur to me in my life's history I shall embrace them, for a well-told lie is a gift of the gods. But the realities of the Dice Man's life are more entertaining than my most inspired fictions: reality will dominate for its entertainment value.

I tell my life's story for that humble reason which has inspired every user of the form: to prove to the world I

7

am a great man. I shall fail, of course, like the others. 'To be great is to be misunderstood,' Elvis Presley once said, and no one can refute him. I tell of a man's instinctive attempt to fulfil himself in a new way and I will be judged insane. So be it. Were it otherwise, I would know I had failed.

We are not ourselves; actually there is nothing we can call a 'self' any more; we are manifold, we have as many selves as there are groups to which we belong . . . The neurotic has overtly a disease from which everybody is suffering . . .

— J. H. VAN DEN BERG

My aim is to bring about a psychic state in which my patient begins to experiment with his own nature — a state of fluidity, change and growth, in which there is no longer anything eternally fixed and hopelessly petrified.

— CARL JUNG

The torch of chaos and doubt — this is what the sage steers by.

— CHUANG-TZU

I am Zarathustra the godless: I still cook every chance in my pot.

— NIETZSCHE

Anybody can be anybody.

— THE DICE MAN

Chapter One

I am a large man, with big butcher's hands, great oak thighs, rock-jawed head, and massive, thick-lens glasses. I'm six foot four and weigh close to two hundred and thirty pounds; I look like Clark Kent, except that when I take off my business suit I am barely faster than my wife, only slightly more powerful than men half my size, and leap buildings not at all, no matter how many leaps I'm given.

As an athlete I am exceptionally mediocre in all major sports and in several minor ones. I play daring and disastrous poker and cautious and competent stock market. I married a pretty former cheerleader and rock-and-roll singer and have two lovely, non-neurotic and abnormal children. I am deeply religious, have written the lovely first-rate pornographic novel, *Naked Before the World*, and am not now nor have I ever been Jewish.

I realize that it's your job as a reader to try to create a credible consistent pattern out of all this, but I'm afraid I must add that I am normally atheistic, have given away at random thousands of dollars, have been a sporadic revolutionary against the governments of the United States, New York City, the Bronx and Scarsdale, and am still a card-carrying member of the Republican Party. I am the creator, as most of you know, of those nefarious Dice Centers for experiments in human behavior which have been described by the *Journal of Abnormal Psychology* as 'outrageous', 'unethical', and 'informative'; by *The New York Times* as 'incredibly misguided and corrupt'; by *Time* magazine as 'sewers', and by the *Evergreen*

Review as 'brilliant and fun'. I have been a devoted husband, multiple adulterer and experimental homosexual; an able, highly praised analyst, and the only one ever dismissed from both the Psychiatrists Association of New York (PANY) and from the American Medical Association (for 'ill-considered activities' and 'probable incompetence'). I am admired and praised by thousands of dicepeople throughout the nation but have twice been a patient in a mental institution, once been in jail, and am currently a fugitive, which I hope to remain, Die willing, at least until I have completed this 543-page autobiography.

My primary profession has been psychiatry. My passion, both as psychiatrist and as Dice Man, has been to change human personality. Mine. Others'. Everyone's. To give to men a sense of freedom, exhilaration, joy. To restore to life the same shock of experience we have when bare toes first feel the earth at dawn and we see the sun split through the mountain trees like horizontal lightning; when a girl first lifts her lips to be kissed; when an idea suddenly springs full-blown into the mind, reorganizing in an instant the experience of a lifetime.

Life is islands of ecstasy in an ocean of ennui, and after the age of thirty land is seldom seen. At best we wander from one much-worn sandbar to the next, soon familiar with each grain of sand we see.

When I raised the 'problem' with my colleagues, I was assured that the withering away of joy was as natural to normal man as the decaying of his flesh and based on much the same physiological changes. The purpose of psychology, they reminded me, was to decrease misery, increase productivity, relate the individual to his society, and help him to see and accept himself. Not to alter necessarily the habits, values and interests of the self, but

12

to see them without idealization and to accept them as they are.

It had always seemed to me a quite obvious and desirable goal for therapy but, after having been 'successfully' analyzed and after having lived in moderate happiness with moderate success with an average wife and family for seven years, I found suddenly, around my thirty-second birthday, that I wanted to kill myself. And to kill several other people too.

I took long walks over the Queensborough Bridge and brooded down at the water. I reread Camus on suicide as the logical choice in an absurd world. On subway platforms I always stood three inches from the edge, and swayed. On Monday mornings I would stare at the bottle of strychnine on my cabinet shelf. I would daydream for hours of nuclear holocausts searing the streets of Manhattan clean, of steamrollers accidentally flattening my wife, of taxis taking my rival Dr Ecstein off into the East River, of a teen-age baby-sitter of ours shrieking in agony as I plowed away at her virgin soil.

Now the desire to kill oneself and to assassinate, poison, obliterate or rape others is generally considered in the psychiatric profession as 'unhealthy.' Bad. Evil. More accurately, *sin*. When you have the desire to kill yourself, you are supposed to see and 'accept it,' but *not*, for Christ's sake, to kill yourself. If you desire to have carnal knowledge of a helpless teeny-bopper, you are supposed to accept your lust, and not lay a finger on even her big toe. If you hate your father, fine – but don't slug the bastard with a bat. Understand yourself, accept yourself, but do not be yourself.

It is a conservative doctrine, guaranteed to help the patient avoid violent, passionate and unusual acts and to permit him a prolonged, respectable life of moderate

13

misery. In fact, it is a doctrine aimed at making everyone live like a psychotherapist. The thought nauseated me.

These trivial insights actually began to form in the weeks following my first unexplained plunge into depression, a depression ostensibly produced by a long writing block on my 'book,' but actually part of a general constipation of the soul that had been a long time building up. I remember sitting at my big oak desk after breakfast each morning before my first appointment reviewing my past accomplishments and future hopes with a feeling of scorn. I would take off my glasses and, reacting to both my thoughts and the surrealistic haze which became my visual world without my glasses, I would intone dramatically, 'Blind! Blind!' and bang my boxing-glove-sized fist down on the desk with a dramatic crash.

I had been a brilliant student throughout my educational career, piling up academic honors like my son Larry collects bubblegum baseball cards. While still in medical school I published my first article on therapy, a well-received trifle called 'The Physiology of Neurotic Tension.' As I sat at my desk, all articles I had ever published seemed absolutely as good as other men's articles: blah. My successes with patients seemed identical to those of my colleagues: insignificant. The most I had come to hope for was to free a patient from anxiety and conflict: to alter him from a life of tormented stagnation to one of complacent stagnation. If my patients had untapped creativity or inventiveness or drive, my methods of analysis had failed to dig them out. Psychoanalysis seemed an expensive, slow-working, unreliable tranquilizer. If LSD were really to do what Alpert and Leary claimed for it, all psychiatrists would be out of a job overnight. The thought pleased me.

In the midst of my cynicism I would occasionally daydream of the future. My hopes? To excel in all that I had been doing in the past: to write widely acclaimed articles and books; to raise my children so they might avoid the mistakes I had made; to meet some technicolor woman with whom I would become soulmate for life. Unfortunately, the thought that these dreams might all be fulfilled plunged me into despair.

I was caught in a bind. On the one hand I was bored and dissatisfied with my life and myself as they had been for the past decade; on the other, no conceivable change seemed preferable. I was too old to believe that lounging on the shores of Tahiti, becoming a wealthy television personality, being buddy-buddy with Erich Fromm, Teddy Kennedy or Bob Dylan, or entertaining Sophia Loren and Raquel Welch in the same bed for a month or so would change anything. No matter how I twisted or turned there seemed to be an anchor in my chest which held me fast, the long line leaning out against the slant of sea taut and trim, as if it were cleated fast into the rock of the earth's vast core. It held me locked, and when a storm of boredom and bitterness blew in I would plunge and leap against the line's rough-clutching knot to be away, to fly before the wind, but the knot grew tight, the anchor only dug the deeper in my chest; I stayed. The burden of my self seemed inevitable and eternal.

My colleagues, and even myself, mumbling coyly by our couches, all asserted that my problem was absolutely normal: I hated myself and the world because I had failed to face and accept the limitations of my self and of life. In literature this refusal is called romanticism; in psychology, neurosis. The assumption is that a limited and bored self is the unavoidable, all-embracing norm. And I was beginning to agree until, after a few months of wallowing in depression (I furtively had purchased a .38 revolver and nine cartridges), I came washing up on the shore of Zen.

For fifteen years I had been leading a rather ambitious,

driving, driven sort of life; anyone who opts for medical school and psychiatry has to have a pretty healthy neurosis burning inside him to keep the motor going. My own analysis by Dr Timothy Mann had made me understand *why* my motor was racing away but hadn't slowed it. I now cruised consistently at sixty miles per hour rather than oscillating erratically between fifteen and ninety-five, but if anything blocked my rapid progress along the speedway I became as irritable as a cabby waiting for a parade to pass. When Karen Horney led me to discover D. T. Suzuki, Alan Watts and Zen, the world of the rat race, which I had assumed to be normal and healthy for an ambitious young man, seemed suddenly like the world of a rat race.

I was stunned and converted – as only the utterly bored can be. Seeing drive, greed and intellectual aspiration as meaningless and sick in my colleagues, I was able to make the unusual generalization to myself; I too had the same symptoms of grasping after illusions. The secret, I seemed to learn, was in not caring, in accepting limitations, conflicts and ambiguities of life with joy and satisfaction, in effortless drifting with the flow of impulse. So life was meaningless? Who cares. So my ambitions are trivial? Pursue them anyway. Life seems boring? Yawn.

I followed impulse. I drifted. I didn't care.

Unfortunately, life seemed to get more boring. Admittedly I was cheerfully, even gaily bored, where before I had been depressedly bored, but life remained essentially uninteresting. My mood of happy boredom was theoretically preferable to my desire to rape and kill, but personally speaking, not much. It was along about this stage of my somewhat sordid road to truth that I discovered the Dice Man.

Chapter Two

My life before D-Day was routine, humdrum, repetitious, trivial, compulsive, disordered, irritable – the life of a typical successful married man. My new life began on a hot day in the middle of August, 1968.

I awoke a little before seven, cuddled up to my wife Lillian, who was accordioned up into a Z in the bed beside me, and began pleasantly caressing her breasts, thighs and buttocks with my big gentle paws. I liked to begin the day this way: it set a standard by which to measure the gradual deterioration that succeeded from then on. After about four or five minutes we both rolled over and she began caressing me with her hands, and then with her lips, tongue and mouth.

'Nnn morning, sweetheart,' one of us would eventually say.

'Nnnn,' would say the other.

From that point on the day's dialogue would all be downhill, but with warm, languid hands and lips floating over the body's most sensitive surfaces, the world was as near perfection as it ever gets. Freud called it a state of ego-less polymorphous perversity and frowned upon it, but I have little doubt that he never had Lil's hands gliding over him. Or his own wife's either for that matter. Freud was a very great man, but I never get the impression that anyone ever effectively stroked his penis.

Lil and I were slowly advancing to the stage where play is replaced by passion when two, three, four thumps resounded from the hall, our bedroom door opened and sixty pounds of boy-energy exploded onto our bed in a graceless flop.

'Time to wake up!' he shouted.

Lil had instinctively turned away from me at the sound of the thumps and, although she arched her lovely behind against me and squirmed intelligently, I knew from long experience that the game was over. I had tried to convince her that in an ideal society parents would make love in front of their children as naturally as they would eat or talk, that ideally the children would caress, fondle and make love to the parent, or both parents, but Lillian felt different. She liked to make love under sheets, alone with her partner, uninterrupted. I pointed out that this showed unconscious shame and she agreed and went on hiding our caresses from the kids. Our girl, a forty-five-pound variety, was by this time announcing in slightly louder tones than her older brother:

'Cock-a-doodle-do! Time to get up.'

Generally, we were up. Occasionally, when I don't have a nine o'clock patient, we encourage Larry to fix himself and his sister some breakfast. This he is happy to do, but the curiosity aroused by the sound of shattering glassware or the *lack* of sound of anything from the kitchen makes our extra minutes in bed unrewarding: it is difficult to enjoy sensual bliss while certain that the kitchen is on fire. This particular morning Lil arose right away, modestly keeping her front parts turned away from the children, slipped on a flimsy nightgown that may have left them in ignorance, but left nothing to my imagination, and slouched sleepily off to prepare breakfast.

Lil, I should note here, is a tall, essentially slender woman with sharp and pointed elbows, ears, nose, teeth and (metaphorically) tongue, but soft and rounded breasts, buttocks and thighs. All agree she is a beautiful woman, with natural wavy blonde hair and statuesque dignity. However, her lovely face has a peculiarly pixyish expression which I'm tempted to describe as mousy except that then you'll picture her with beady red eyes, and they're actually beady blue. Also, mouses are rarely five feet ten and willowy, and rarely attack men, as Lil does. Nevertheless, her pretty face, in some perceivers, calls up the image of a mouse, a beautiful mouse to be sure, but a mouse. When during our courtship I remarked upon this phenomenon it cost me four weeks of total sexual abstinence. Suffice it to say, my friends, that this mouse analogy is strictly between you and me.

Although young Evie had scrambled talkatively away to follow her mother toward the kitchen, Larry still lay sprawled next to me on the large king-sized bed. It was his philosophical position that our bed was large enough for the whole family and he deeply resented Lil's obviously hypocritical argument that Mommy and Daddy were so big that they needed the entire area. His recent strategy was to plop on the bed until every last adult was out of it; only then would he triumphantly leave.

'Time to get up, Luke,' he announced with the quiet dignity of a doctor announcing that he's afraid the leg will have to come off.

'It's not eight o'clock yet,' I said.

'Un-nn,' he said, and pointed silently at the clock on the dresser.

I squinted at the clock. 'It says twenty-five before six,' I said and rolled away from him. A few seconds later I felt him nudging me in the forehead with his fist.

'Here are your glasses,' he said. 'Now look.'

I looked. 'You changed the time when I wasn't looking,' I said, and rolled over in the opposite direction.

Larry climbed back onto the bed and with no conscious intention, I'm sure, began bouncing and humming.

And I, with that irrational surge of fury known to every parent, suddenly shouted 'Get OUT of here!'

For about thirteen seconds after Larry had raced to the kitchen I lay in my bed with relative content. I could hear Evie's unending chatter punctuated by Lil's occasional yelling, and from the Manhattan streets below, the unending chatter of automobile horns. That thirteen-second involvement in sense experience was fine; then I began to think, and my day was shot.

I thought of my two morning patients, of lunch with Doctors Ecstein and Felloni, of the book on sadism I was supposed to be writing, of the children, of Lillian: I felt bored. For some months I had been feeling – from about ten to fifteen seconds after the cessation of polymorphous perversity until falling asleep at night – or falling into another session of polymorphous perversity – that depressed feeling of walking up a down escalator. 'Whither and why,' as General Eisenhower once said, 'have the joys of life all flown away?' Or, as Burt Lancaster once asked: 'Why do our fingers to the grain of wood, the cold of steel, the heat of the sun, the flesh of women, become calloused?'

'BREAKFAST, DADDY!'

'EGGS, hon.'

I arose, plunged my feet into my size-thirteen slippers, pulled my bathrobe around me like a Roman preparing for the Forum, and went to the breakfast table, with, I supposed, a superficial sunniness, but deeply brooding on Lancaster's eternal question.

We have a six-room apartment on the slightly upper, slightly East, slightly expensive side, near Central Park, near the blacklands, and near the fashionable upper East Side. Its location is so ambiguous that our friends are still not certain whether to envy us or pity us.

In the small kitchen Lil was standing at the stove

20

aggressively mashing eggs in a frying pan; the two children were sitting in whining obedience on the far side of the table. Larry had been playing with the window shade behind him (we have a lovely view from our kitchen window of a kitchen window with a lovely view of ours), and Evie had been guilty of talking without a break in either time or irrelevance since getting up. Lil, since we don't believe in corporal punishment, had admonished them verbally. However, Lil's shrieks are such that were children (or adults) ever given a free choice, I'm sure they would prefer that rather than receive 'verbal admonitions' they be whipped with straps containing metal studs.

Obviously Lil does not enjoy the early morning hours, but we found that having a maid at this hour was 'impractical.' When, earlier in our marriage, the first full-time live-in maid we hired turned out to be a beautiful, sex-oozing wench of a mulatto whose eyes would have stiffened a Eunuch, Lillian intelligently decided that a daytime, part-time maid would give us more privacy.

As she brought the plates of scrambled eggs and bacon to the table she glanced up at me and asked:

'What time will you be back from Queensborough today?'

'Four-thirty or so. Why?' I said as I lowered my body delicately into a small kitchen chair across from the kids.

'Arlene wants another private chat this afternoon.'

'Larry took my spoon!'

'Give Evie her spoon, Larry,' I said.

Lil gave Evie back her spoon.

'I imagine she wants to talk more of the "I have to have a baby" dream,' she said.

'Mmmm.'

'I wish you'd talk to Jake,' Lil said as she sat down beside me.

21

'What can I tell him?' I said. '"Say, Jake, your wife desperately wants a baby: anything I can do to help?"'

'Are there dinosaurs in Harlem?' Evie asked.

'Yes,' Lil said. 'You could say precisely that. It's his conjugal responsibility; Arlene is almost thirty-three years old and has wanted a baby for – Evie, use your *spoon*.'

'Jake's going to Philadelphia today,' I said.

'I know; that's one reason Arlene's coming up. But the poker is still on for tonight, isn't it?'

'Mmm.'

'Mommy, what's a virgin?' Larry asked quietly.

'A virgin is a young girl,' she answered.

'Very young,' I added.

'That's funny,' he said.

'What is?' Lil asked.

'Barney Goldfield called me a stupid virgin.'

'Barney was misusing the word,' Lil said. 'Why don't we postpone the poker, Luke? It's – '

'Why?'

'I'd rather see a play.'

'We've seen some lemons.'

'It's better than playing poker with them.'

Pause.

'With lemons?'

'If you and Tim and Renata were able to talk about something besides psychology and the stock market, it would help.'

'The psychology of the stock market?'

'And the stock market! God, I wish you'd open your ears for just once.'

I forked my eggs into my mouth with dignity, and sipped with philosophical detachment my instant coffee. My initiation into the mysteries of Zen Buddhism had taught me many things, but the most important was not to argue with my wife. 'Go with the flow,' the great sage

22

Oboko said, and I'd been doing it for five months now. Lil had been getting madder and madder.

After about twenty seconds of silence (relatively speaking: Larry leapt up to put in toast for himself; Evie tried a brief burst of monologue on dinosaurs which was smothered with a stare), I (theoretically the way to avoid arguments is to surrender before the attack has been fully launched) said quietly, 'I'm sorry, Lil.'

'You and your damn Zen. I'm trying to *tell* you something. I don't like the forms of entertainment we have. Why can't we ever do something new or different, or, revolution of revolutions, something I want.'

'We do, honey, we do. The last three plays – '

'I had to drag you. You're so – '

'Honey, the children.'

The children in fact looked about as affected by our arguments as elephants by two squabbling mosquitoes, but the ploy always worked to silence Lil.

After we'd all finished breakfast she led the children into their room to get dressed while I went to wash and shave. Holding the lathered brush stiffly in my raised right hand like an Indian saying 'How!', I stared glumly into the mirror. I always hated to shave a two-day growth of beard; with the dark shadows around my mouth I looked – potentially at least – like Don Giovanni, Faust, Mephistopheles, Charlton Heston, or Jesus. After shaving I knew I would look like a successful, boyishly handsome public relations man. Because I was a bourgeois psychiatrist and had to wear glasses to see myself in the mirror I had resisted the impulse to grow a beard. I let my sideburns grow, though, and it made me look a little less like a successful public relations man and a little more like an unsuccessful, out-of-work actor.

After I'd begun shaving and was concentrating particularly well on three small hairs at the tip of my chin Lil came, still wearing her modest, obscene nightgown, and leaned against the doorway.

'I'd divorce you if it wouldn't mean I'd be stuck with the kids,' she said, in a tone half-ironic and half-serious.

'Nnn.'

'If you had them, they'd all turn into clownish Buddha-blobs.'

'Unnnn.'

'What I don't understand is that you're a psychiatrist, a supposedly good one, and you have no more insight into me or into yourself than the elevator man.'

'Ah, honey – '

'You don't! You think loving me up, apologizing before and after every argument, buying me paints, leotards, guitars, records and new book clubs must make me happy. It's driving me crazy.'

'What can I do?'

'I don't *know*. You're the analyst. You should know. I'm bored. I'm Emma Bovary in everything except that I have no romantic hopes.'

'That makes me a clod doctor, you know.'

'I know. I'm glad you noticed. It's no fun attacking unless you catch my allusions. Usually you know about as much about literature as the elevator man.'

'Say, just what is it between you and this elevator man?'

'I've given up my yoga exercises – '

'How come?'

'They just make me tense.'

'That's strange, they're supposed – '

'I *know*! But they make me tense – I can't help it.'

I'd finished shaving, taken off my glasses, and was grooming my hair with what I fear may have been greasy kid stuff; Lil moved into the bathroom and sat on the wooden laundry basket. Crouching now quite a bit in order to see the top of my hair in the mirror, I noticed

24

that my knee muscles were already aching. Moreover, without my glasses I looked old today, and in a blurred sort of way, badly dissipated. Since I didn't smoke or drink much, I wondered vaguely if excessive early morning petting were debilitating.

'Maybe I should become a hippie,' Lil went on absently.

'That's what a few of our patients try. They don't seem overly pleased with the result.'

'Or drugs.'

'Ah Lil, sweet precious – '

'Don't touch me.'

'Ah – '

'No!'

Lil was backed up against the tub and shower curtain as if threatened by a stranger in a cheap melodrama, and I, slightly appalled by her apparent fear, backed meekly away.

'I've got a patient in half an hour, hon, I've got to go.'

'I'll try infidelity!' Lil shouted after me, 'Emma Bovary did it.'

I turned back again. She was standing with her arms folded over her chest, her two elbows pointing out sharply from her long slender body, and with a bleak, mousy, helpless look on her face; at the moment she seemed like a kind of female Don Quixote after having just been tossed in a blanket. I went to her, and took her in my arms.

'Poor little rich girl. Who would you have for adultery? The elevator man? [She sobbed.] Anyone else? Sixty-three-year-old Dr Mann, and flashy, debonair Jake Ecstein [she detested Jake and he never noticed her]. Come on, come on. We'll go out to the farmhouse soon; it'll be the break you need. Now . . .'

Her head was still nestled into my chest, but her breathing was regular. She'd had just the one sob.

'Now . . . chin up . . . bust out . . . tummy in . . .' I said. 'Buttocks firm . . . and you're ready to face life again. You can have an exciting morning: talking with Evie, discussing avant-garde art with Ma Kettle [our maid], reading *Time*, listening to Schubert's *Unfinished Symphony*: racy, thought-provoking experiences all.'

'You . . . [she scratched her nose against my chest] . . . should mention that I could do coloring with Larry when he gets home from school.'

'And that, and that. You've absolutely no end of home entertainments. Don't forget to call in the elevator man for a quick one when Evie is having her rest time.'

My right arm around her, I walked us into our bedroom. While I finished dressing, she watched quietly, standing next to the big bed with arms folded and elbows out. She saw me to the door and after we had exchanged a farewell kiss of less than great passion she said quietly with a bemused, almost interested expression on her face:

'I don't even have my yoga anymore.'

Chapter Three

I shared my office on 57th Street with Dr Jacob Ecstein, young (thirty-three), dynamic (two books published), intelligent (he and I usually agreed), personable (everyone liked him), unattractive (no one loved him), anal (he plays the stock market compulsively), oral (he smokes heavily), non-genital (doesn't seem to notice women), and Jewish (he knows two Yiddish slang words). Our mutual secretary was a Miss Reingold. Mary Jane Reingold, old (thirty-six), undynamic (she worked for us), unintelligent (she prefers Ecstein to me), personable (everyone felt sorry for her), unattractive (tall, skinny, glasses, no one loved her), anal (obsessively neat), oral (always eating), genital (trying hard), and non-Jewish (finds use of two Yiddish slang words very intellectual). Miss Reingold greeted me efficiently.

'Mr Jenkins is waiting in your office, Dr Rhinehart.'

'Thank you, Miss Reingold. Any calls for me yesterday?'

'Dr Mann wanted to check about lunch this afternoon. I said "yes".'

'Good.'

Before I moved off to my patient, Jake Ecstein came briskly out of his office, shot off a cheerful 'Hi, Luke baby, how's the book?' the way most men might ask about a friend's wife, and asked Miss Reingold for a couple of case records. I've described Jake's *character*; his *body* was short, rotund, chubby: his *visage* was round, alert, cheerful, with horn-rimmed glasses and a piercing, I-am-able-to-see-through-you stare; his *social front* was used-car salesman, and he kept his shoes shined with a finish so bright that I sometimes suspected he cheated with a phosphorescent shoe polish.

'My book's moribund,' I answered as Jake accepted a fistful of papers from a somewhat flustered Miss Reingold.

'Great,' he said. 'Just got a review of my *Analysis: End and Means* from the *AP Journal*. They say it's great.' He began glancing slowly through the papers, placing one of them every now and then back onto his secretary's desk.

'I'm glad to hear it, Jake. You seem to be hitting the jackpot with this one.'

'People are seeing the light – '

'Er . . . Dr Ecstein,' Miss Reingold said.

'They'll like it – I may convert a few *analysts*.'

'Are you going to be able to make lunch today?' I asked. 'When are you leaving for Philadelphia?'

'Damn right. Want to show Mann my review. Plane leaves at two. I'll miss your poker party tonight.'

'Er . . . Dr Ecstein.'

'You read any more of my book?' Jake went on and gave me one of his piercing, squinting glances, which, had I been a patient, would have led me to repress for a decade all that was on my mind at that instant.

'No. No, I haven't. I must still have a psychological block: professional jealousy and all that.'

'Er . . . Dr Ecstein?'

'Hmmm. Yeah. In Philly I'm gonna see that anal optometrist I've been telling you about. Think we're about at a breakthrough. Cured of his voyeurism, but still has visual blackouts. It's only been three months though. I'll bust him. Bust him right back to twenty-twenty.' He grinned.

'Dr Ecstein, sir,' said Miss Reingold, now standing.

'Seeya, Luke. Send in Mr Klopper, Miss R.'

As Jake, still carrying a handful of forms, exited briskly

into his inner office, I asked Miss Reingold to check with Queensborough State Hospital about my afternoon appointments.

'Yes, Dr Rhinehart,' she said.

'And what did you wish to communicate to Dr Ecstein?'

'Oh, Doctor,' she smiled doubtfully. 'Dr Ecstein asked for the case notes on Miss Riffe and Mr Klopper and I have him by mistake the record sheets of our last year's budget.'

'Don't worry, Miss Reingold,' I replied firmly. 'This may mean another breakthrough.'

It was 9.07 when I finally settled into my chair behind the outstretched form of Reginald Jenkins on my couch. Normally nothing upsets a patient more than a late analyst, but Jenkins was a masochist: I could count on him assuming that he deserved it.

'I'm sorry about being here,' he said, 'but your secretary insisted I come in and lie down.'

'That's quite all right, Mr Jenkins. I'm sorry I'm late. Let's both relax and you can go right ahead.'

Now the curious reader will want to know what kind of an analyst I was. It so happens that I practised non-directive therapy. For those not familiar with it, the analyst is passive, compassionate, non-interpretive, non-directing. More precisely, he resembles a redundant moron. For example, a session with a patient like Jenkins might go like this:

JENKINS: 'I feel that no matter how hard I try I'm always going to fail; that some kind of internal mechanism always acts to screw up what I'm trying to do.'

[Pause]

ANALYST: 'You feel that some part of you always forces you to fail.'

JENKINS: 'Yes. For example, that time when I had that date with that nice woman, really attractive – the

29

librarian, you remember – and all I talked about at dinner and all evening was the New York Jets and what a great defensive secondary they have. I *knew* I should be talking books or asking her questions but I couldn't stop myself.'

ANALYST: 'You feel that some part of you consciously ruined the potential relationship with that girl.'

JENKINS: 'And that job with Wessen, Wessen and Woof. I could have had it. But I took a month's vacation in Jamaica when I knew they'd be wanting an interview.'

'I see.'

'What do you make of it all, Doctor? I suppose it's masochistic.'

'You think it might be masochistic.'

'I don't know. What do you think?'

'You aren't certain if it's masochistic but you do know that you often do things which are self-destructive.'

'That's right. That's right. And yet I don't have any suicidal tendencies. Except in those dreams. Throwing myself under a herd of hippopotamuses. Or 'potami. Setting myself on fire in front of Wessen, Wessen and Woof. But I keep goofing up *real* opportunities.'

'Although you never consciously think of suicide you have dreamed about it.'

'Yes. But that's normal. Everybody does crazy things in dreams.'

'You feel that your dreaming of self-destructive acts is normal because . . .'

The intelligent reader gets the picture. The effect of non-directive therapy is to encourage the patient to speak more and more frankly, to gain total confidence in the non-threatening, totally accepting clod who's curing him, and eventually to diagnose and resolve his own conflicts, with old thirty-five-dollars-an-hour echoing away through it all behind the couch.

And it works. It works precisely as well as every other

tested form of psychotherapy. It works sometimes and fails at others, and its success and failures are identical with other analysts' successes and failures. Of course at times the dialogue resembles a comedy routine. My patient the second hour that morning was a hulking heir to a small fortune who had the build of a professional wrestler and the mentality of a professional wrestler.

Frank Osterflood was the most depressing case I'd had in five years of practice. In the first two months of analysis he had seemed a rather nice empty socialite, worried half-heartedly about his inability to concentrate on anything. He tended to drift from job to job averaging two or three a year. He talked a great deal about his jobs and about a mousy father and two disgusting brothers with families, but all with such cocktail-party patter that I knew we must be a long way from what was really bothering him. If *anything* was bothering him. The only clue I had to indicate that he was anything but a vacuous muscle was his occasional spitting hissing remarks – usually of a general nature – about women. When I asked one morning about his relations with women he hesitated and then said he found them boring. When I asked him how he found fulfillment for his sexual needs, he answered neutrally, 'Prostitutes.'

Two or three times in later sessions he described in detail how he liked to humiliate the call girls he hired, but he would never make any effort to analyze his behavior; he seemed to feel in his casual man-of-the-world way that humiliating women was good, normal, all-American behavior. He found it more interesting to analyze why he left his last job; the office he worked in 'smelled funny.'

About halfway through the session that August day he interrupted his seemingly pleasant recollections of having single-handedly destroyed an East Side bar by sitting up on the couch and looking intensely but, in my professional opinion, dumbly, at the floor. Even his face seemed bulging with muscles. He sat there in the same position for several minutes, grunting quietly to himself with a sound like a noisy refrigerator. Finally he said:

'I get so tied up inside I just have to . . . to do something or I'll explode,' he said.

'I understand.'

[Pause]

'Do something . . . *sexually* or I'll explode.'

'You get so tense you feel you must express yourself sexually.'

'Yes.'

[Pause]

'Don't you want to know how?' he asked.

'If you'd like to tell me.'

'Do you want to know? Don't you need to know to help me?'

'I want you to tell me only what you feel like telling me.'

'Well, I know you'd like to know, but I'm not going to tell you. I've told you about the fuckin' women I've fucked and how they make me want to puke with their snaky wet orgasms, but I guess I'll keep this to myself.'

[Pause]

'You feel that although I'd like to know, you've already told me about your relations with women and so you won't tell me.'

'Actually, it's sodomy. When I get tense – it might be right after I've fucked some white-satin slut, I get . . . I need . . . I want to ram the Goddam insides out of some woman . . . some girl . . . young . . . the younger the better.'

'When you're very keyed up you want to ram the insides out of some woman.'

'The *Goddam* insides. I want to sink my prick up that

32

intestine into that belly through the esophagus up that throat and come right out the Goddam top of her head.'

[Pause]

'You'd like to penetrate through her whole body.'

'Yeah, but up her ass. I want her to scream, to bleed, to be horrified.'

[Pause. Long pause]

'You'd like to penetrate her anus and make her bleed, scream and be horrified.'

'Yeah, but the whores I tried it with chewed gum and picked their nose.'

[Pause]

'The whores you tried it with were neither hurt nor horrified.'

'Shit, they took their seventy-five bucks, shot their ass into the air and chewed gum or read a comic book. If I tried to get rough some guy six inches taller than me would appear in the doorway with a sledgehammer or something. [Pause] I found sodomy, *per se* [he smiled awkwardly], didn't end my tenseness.'

'You were unable to release your tension by relations with prostitutes when the women seemed to experience no pain or humiliation.'

'So I knew I had to find someone who would scream.'

[Pause]

[Long pause]

'You sought other alternatives to relieve your tensions.'

'Yeah. Fact is I began raping and killing young girls.'

[Pause]

[Long pause]

[Longer pause]

'In an effort to relieve these tense feelings you began raping and killing young girls.'

'Yeah. You're not allowed to tell, are you? I mean you

33

told me professional ethics forbid your telling anything I say, right?'

'Yes.'

[Pause]

'I find the raping and killing of girls helps relieve the tension quite a bit and makes me feel better again.'

'I see.'

'My problem is that I'm beginning to get a little nervous about getting caught. I sort of hoped maybe analysis might help me find a little more normal way to reduce my tensions.'

'You'd like to find a different way to reduce tensions other than raping and killing girls.'

'Yeah. either that or help me to stop worrying about getting caught . . .'

The alert reader may now be feeling that this stuff is slightly too sensational for a typical day at the office, but Mr Osterflood really exists. Or rather existed – more of that later on. The fact is that I was writing a book entitled *The Sado-Masochistic Personality in Transition*, a work which was to describe cases in which the sadistic personality developed into a masochistic one and vice versa. For this reason my colleagues always sent me patients with a markedly strong sadistic or masochistic bent. Osterflood was admittedly the most professionally active sadist I'd treated, but the wards of mental hospitals have many like him.

What is remarkable, I suppose, is Osterflood's walking around loose. Although after his confession I urged him to enter an institution, he refused and I couldn't *order* his being committed without breaking professional confidence; moreover no one else apparently suspected that he was an 'enemy of society.' All I could do was warn my friends to keep their little girls away from Harlem playgrounds (where Osterflood obtained his victims) and try hard for a cure. Since my friends all kept their children out of Harlem playgrounds because of the danger of Negro rapists even my warnings were unnecessary.

After Osterflood left that morning I brooded a little on my helplessness with him, made a few notes, and then decided I ought to work on my book.

I dragged myself to it with the enthusiasm of a man with diarrhea moving toward the toilet: I had a compulsive need to get it out but had some months earlier come to the conclusion that all I was producing was shit.

My book had become a bore: it was a pretentious failure. I had tried a few months before to get Random House to agree to publish it when it was finished, imagining that with extensive advertising the book would achieve national and then international fame, driving Jake Ecstein to fury, women and reckless losses in the stock market. Random House had hedged, hawed, considered and reconsidered . . . Random House wasn't interested. This morning, as on most recent mornings, neither was I.

The flaw in the book was small but significant: it had nothing to say. The bulk of it was to be empirical descriptions of patients who had changed from primarily sadistic behavior patterns to masochistic ones. My dream had been to discover a technique to lock the behavior of the patient at that precise point when he had passed away from sadism but had not become masochistic. If there were such a point. I had much dramatic evidence of complete crossovers; none of 'frozen freedom,' a phrase describing the ideal mean state that came to me in an explosion of enlightenment one morning while echoing Mr Jenkins.

The problem was that Jake Ecstein, car-salesman front and all, had written two of the most rational and honest books about psychoanalytic therapy that I'd ever read, and their import essentially demonstrated that none of us knew or had any likelihood of knowing what we were doing. Jake cured patients as well as the next fellow and then published clear, brilliant accounts demonstrating that the key to his success was accident, that frequently it was his failure to follow his own theoretical structure which led to a 'breakthrough' and the patient's improvement. When I ended my early-morning dialogue with Miss Reingold joking that Jake's reading the 1967 budget record sheets might lead to a breakthrough I was partly serious. Jake had shown again and again the significance of chance in therapeutic development, perhaps best dramatized in his famous 'pencil-sharpening cure.'

A female patient he'd had under treatment for fifteen months with so little success in changing her neurotic aplomb that even Jake was bored, achieved total and complete transformation when Jake, absentmindedly confusing her with his secretary, ordered her to sharpen his pencils. The patient, a wealthy housewife, went into the outer office to obey and suddenly, when about to insert a pencil into the sharpener, began to shriek, tear her hair and defecate. Three weeks later, 'Mrs P.' (Jake's choice of pseudonyms is only one of his unerring talents) was cured.

I, then, was coming to feel that my elaborate writing efforts were only idle, pretentious playing with words for publication.

I thus spent the hour before lunch: (a) reading the financial section of *The New York Times*; (b) writing a page-and-a-half case report of Mr Osterflood in the form of a financial and budget report ('bearish outlook for prostitutes'; 'bull market in Harlem playground girls'), and (c) drawing a picture on my book manuscript of an elaborate Victorian house being bombed by motorcycle planes piloted by Hell's Angels.

Chapter Four

I lunched that day with my three closest colleagues: Dr Ecstein, whom I mock because he's so intelligent and successful; Dr Renata Felloni, the only female Italian-born practicing analyst in recent New York history; and Dr Timothy Mann, the short, fat, disheveled father figure who had psychoanalyzed me four years before and been mentoring me ever since.

When Jake and I arrived, Dr Mann was hunched over the table chewing heavily on a roll and blinking benevolently at Dr Felloni seated opposite him. Dr Mann was a big wheel: one of the directors at Queensborough State Hospital, where I worked twice a week; a member of the executive committee of PANY (Psychiatrists Association of New York) and the author of seventeen articles and three books, one of them the most frequently used text on existentialist therapy in existence. It had been considered an extraordinary honor to be psychoanalyzed by Dr Mann and I had appreciated it greatly until my increasing boredom and unhappiness had deluded me into believing that analysis had done me no good. Dr Mann was concentrating on his eating and may or may not have been listening to the dignified discourse of Dr Felloni.

Renata Felloni resembles a spinsterish dean of women at a Presbyterian all-girls college: she has gray hair always neaty coiffured, spectacles and a slow, dignified, Italian-cum-New England twang that makes her discussions of penises, orgasms, sodomy and fellatio seem like a discussion of credit hours and home economics. Moreover, she had, as far as anyone knew, never been married and, with

37

less certainty, had never in the seven years we had known her given any indication of ever having *known* a man (biblical 'know'). Her dignity acted to prevent any of us from either direct or indirect investigations into her past. All we felt free to talk with her about were weather, stocks, penises, orgasms, sodomy and fellatio.

The restaurant was noisy and expensive, and, except for Dr Mann, who loved every trough he had ever fed in, we all hated it and went there because every other restaurant we had tried in the convenient area was also crowded, noisy and expensive. I usually spent so much nervous energy trying to hear what my friends were saying over the clattering of voices, dishes and 'soft' music and trying to avoid watching Dr Mann eating that I never remembered whether the food was good or not. At any rate I rarely got sick on it.

'Only ten percent of our subjects believe that masturbation is "punished by God eternally",' Dr Felloni was saying as Jake and I sat down opposite each other at the tiny table. She was apparently talking about a research project she and I were jointly directing, and she smiled formally and equally to her left at Jake and to her right at me, and continued: 'Thirty-three and a third percent believe that masturbation is "punished by God finitely"; forty percent that it is physically unhealthy; two and one-half percent believe that there is danger of pregnancy, seventy-five per – '

'Danger of pregnancy?' Jake broke in as he turned from accepting a menu.

'We use the same multiple choices,' she explained smiling, 'for masturbation, kissing, petting, premarital and postmarital heterosexual intercourse, homosexual petting, and homosexual sodomy. So far, subjects have indicated that there is danger of pregnancy only with masturbation, petting to orgasm, and heterosexual intercourse.'

I smiled to Jake, but he was squinting at Dr Felloni.

'Well,' Jake asked her, 'what's the question you're reeling off these percentages for?'

'We ask, "For what reasons, if any, do you believe that sexually exciting yourself through fantasy, reading, looking at pictures or manual excitation is bad?"'

'Do you give them a choice of reasons for why masturbation is good?' Dr Mann asked, wiping his lower lip with a piece of roll.

'Certainly,' Dr Felloni replied. 'A subject can answer that he approves of masturbation for any of six options: (1) It is enjoyable; (2) it releases tension; (3) it is a natural way of expressing love; (4) it is something one should experience to be complete; (5) it procreates the race; (6) it is the social thing to do.'

Jake and I now began laughing. When we quieted she assured Jake that only the first two choices had been chosen for masturbation, except for one person who had indicated that masturbation was valuable as a way of expressing love. She had determined in a recent interview, however, that the subject had checked that item in a cynical frame of mind.

'I don't know why you ever got involved in this thing,' Jake said, turning to me suddenly. 'Social psychologists have been turning out studies like yours for decades. You're digging in sterile ground.'

Dr Felloni nodded politely at Jake's words as she did whenever someone was uttering anything which might vaguely be construed as criticism of her or her work. The more vigorous and direct the criticism the more vigorously she nodded her head. It was my hypothesis that were a prosecuting attorney ever to attack her for a full hour there would be no need for a guillotine: her neck would have melted away, and her head, still nodding, would be rolling on the floor at the prosecutor's feet. She replied to Jake:

'Our plan to evaluate the validity of the multiple choice answers by in-depth interviews of every subject is, however, a genuine contribution.'

'You'll spend – my God – a hundred and twenty hours verifying the obvious: namely, multiple-choice attitude tests are unreliable.'

'Yes, but remember we got a foundation grant,' I said.

'So what? Why didn't you request it for something original, something worthwhile?'

'We wanted a foundation grant,' I answered ironically.

Jake gave me his I-see-into-your-soul squint and then laughed.

'We couldn't think of anything original or worthwhile,' I added, laughing too, 'so we decided to do this.'

Dr Felloni managed to nod and frown, both vigorously.

'You'll discover that sexual intercourse is more frequently approved after marriage than before,' said Jake, 'that homosexuals approve of homosexuality, that – '

'Our results,' Dr Felloni said quietly, 'may not fulfill conventional expectation. We may discover from our in-depth interviews that subjects misrepresent their attitudes and experiences in a way that previous experimenters did not guess.'

'She's right, Jake, I agree the whole thing seems a mammoth bore and may lead to the verification of the obvious, but it might not.'

'It will,' Dr Mann said.

'What?' I said.

'It will verify the obvious and nothing more.' He looked up at me for the first time. His jowls were a Santa Claus pink, either from alcohol or anger. I couldn't tell.

'So?'

'So why do you waste your time? Renata could do the whole thing herself without your help.'

'It's an entertaining time-filler. I often daydream of publishing embellished results to parody such experiments. You know: "Ninety-five percent of American youth believe that masturbation is a better way of expressing friendship and love than intercourse."'

'Your experiment is a parody without embellishment,' Dr Mann said.

There was a silence, if you can exclude the cacophony of voices, dishes and music of the surrounding hubbub.

'Our experiment,' Dr Felloni finally said with a gallop of nods, 'will offer new insight into the relations between sexual behavior, sexual tolerance and personality stability.'

'I read your letter to the Esso Foundation,' Dr Mann said.

'I know a teen-age girl that could run intellectual rings around most of us here,' Jake said, changing the subject without blinking an eye. 'She knew everything, brains coming out of her ears. I was within weeks of a major breakthrough. But she died.'

'She died?' I asked.

'Fell from the Williamsburg Bridge into the East River. I must confess I see her as one of my two or three possible failures.'

'Look, Tim,' I said turning back to Dr Mann. 'I agree our experiment borders on nonsense, but in an absurd world, one can only go with the flow.'

'I'm not interested in your metaphysical speculations.'

'Or my scientific ones. Maybe I'd better stick to talking about the stock market.'

'Oh come off it now, you two,' Jake said. 'Ever since Luke wrote his paper on "Taoism, Zen and Analysis",

Tim has been acting as if he'd been converted to astrology.'

'At least with astrology,' said Dr Mann, looking coldly at me, 'one still tries to predict something important. With Zen one drifts into Nirvana without thought or effort.'

'One doesn't drift into Nirvana,' I said helpfully. 'The drifting is Nirvana.'

'A convenient theory,' Dr Mann said.

'All good theories are.'

'Gold stocks and General Motors have risen an average of two points a week so far this month,' Dr Felloni said, nodding.

'Yeah,' said Jake, 'and you'll notice that Waste Products, Inc., Dolly's Duds and Nadir Technology are all rising.'

Dr Mann and I continued to look at each other, he with warm red face and chill blue eyes, and I with what I intended to be cheerful detachment.

'My stock seems rather low these days,' I said.

'Perhaps it's gravitating to its natural level,' he replied.

'It may yet rally.'

'Drifters don't rally.'

'Yes, they do,' I said. 'You just don't understand Zen.'

'I feel blessed,' Dr Mann said.

'You've got eating, let me have my Zen and sex experiments.'

'Eating doesn't interfere with my productivity.'

'I rather imagine it increases it.'

He flushed even more and pushed back his chair.

'Oh shit,' said Jake, 'Will you two stop it. Tim, you're sitting there like a fat Buddha attacking Luke's Buddhism, and Lu –'

'You're right,' Dr Mann said, sitting now as stiffly in his chair as his lumpy clothing and body would permit. 'I apologize, Luke. The rolls were cold today and I had to attack something.'

'Sure,' I said. 'I apologize too. My martini was diluted and I had to hit back.'

The waitress was at the table again and Jake was getting ready to order dessert, but Dr Felloni spoke loudly to the general table:

'My own portfolio has risen fourteen percent in the last three months despite a market decline of two percent.'

'Pretty soon you'll found your own foundation, Renata,' Dr Mann said.

'Prudent investment,' she replied, 'is like prudent experimentation: it sticks to the obvious.'

For the rest of the lunch, the conversation was all downhill.

Chapter Five

After lunch I paid my ransom at the local parking lot and drove off through the rain for the hospital. I drove a Rambler American. My colleagues drive Jaguars, Mercedes, Cadillacs, Corvettes, Porsches, Thunderbirds and (occasional slummers) Mustangs: I drove a Rambler. At that time it was my most original contribution to New York City Psychoanalysis.

I went east across Manhattan, up over the Queensborough Bridge and down onto the island in the East River where the State Hospital is located. The ancient buildings appeared bleak and macabre. Some looked abandoned. Three new buildings, built of cheerful yellow brick and pleasant, shiny bars, make the hospital appear, together with the older horror houses, like a Hollywood movie set in which two movies, 'My Mother Went Insane' and 'Prison Riot', are being filmed simultaneously.

I went directly to the Admissions Building, one of the old, low, blackened buildings which, it was reliably reported, was held together solely by the thirty-seven layers of pale green paint on all the interior walls and ceilings. A small office was made available to me there every Monday and Wednesday afternoon for my therapy sessions with select patients. The patients were select in two senses: one, I selected them, and two, they were actually receiving therapy. I normally handled two patients, meeting each for about an hour twice a week.

A month before this, however, one of my two patients had attacked a hospital attendant with an eight-foot-long bench and, in being subdued, had received three broken ribs, thirty-two stitches and a hernia. Since this was slightly less than he had inflicted upon the five attendants doing the subduing, no charges of hospital brutality seemed justified, and after his wounds healed, he was to be sent to a maximum-security hospital.

To replace him, Dr Mann had recommended to me a seventeen-year-old boy admitted for incipient divinity: he showed a tendency to act as if he were Jesus Christ. Whether Dr Mann assumed all Christs to be masochistic or that the boy would be good for my spiritual health was unclear.

My other QSH patient was Arturo Toscanini Jones, a Negro who lived every moment as if he were a black panther isolated on a half-acre island filled with white hunters armed with Howitzers. My primary difficulty in helping him was that his way of seeing the world seemed to be an eminently realistic evaluation of his life as it had been. Our sessions were usually quiet ones: Arturo Toscanini Jones had very little to say to white hunters. Although I don't blame him, as a non-directive therapist I was a little handicapped; I needed sounds for my echo.

Jones had been an honors student at City College of New York for three years before disturbing a meeting of the Young Conservatives Club by throwing in two hand grenades. This act would normally have earned long tenure in a penitentiary, but Jones's previous history of 'mental disturbance' (marijuana and LSD user, 'nervous breakdown' sophomore year – he interrupted a political science class by shouting obscenities at his professor) and the failure of the two hand grenades to maim anything more valuable than a portrait of Barry Goldwater, earned him instead an indefinite stay at QSH. He had become my patient under the questionable assumption that anyone who throws hand grenades at Young Conservatives must be sadistic. That afternoon I decided to let myself go a bit and see if I couldn't provoke a dialogue.

'Mr Jones,' I began (fifteen minutes had already passed in total silence), 'what makes you think that I can't or won't help you?'

Sitting sideways to me in a straight wooden chair, he turned his eyes at me with serene disdain: 'Experience,' he said.

'That nineteen consecutive white men have kicked you in the balls doesn't necessarily mean the twentieth will.'

'True,' he said, 'but the brother who came up to that next Charlie with his hands not protecting his crotch would be one big stupid bastard.'

'True, but he could still talk.'

'No suh! We Niggahs gotta use our *hands* when we talk. Yessuh! We're *physical*, we are.'

'You didn't use your hands then when you spoke.'

'I'm *white*, man, didn't you know that? I'm with the CIA investigating the NAACP to see if there's any secret black influence on that organization.' His teeth and eyes glittered at me, in play or hatred I didn't know.

'Ah then,' I said, 'you can appreciate my disguise: I'm *black*, man, didn't you know that? I'm with – '

'You're not black, Rhinehart,' he interrupted sharply. 'If you were, we'd both know it and only one of us would be here.'

'Still, black or white, I'd like to help you.'

'Black they wouldn't let you help me; white, you can't.'

'Suit yourself.'

'That'll be the day.'

When I lapsed into silence, he resumed his. The last fifteen minutes were spent with us both listening to the regular rhythmic shrieks from a man someplace in the Cosmold Building.

After Mr Jones left I stared out the gray window at the

rain until a pretty little student nurse brought me the folder on Eric Cannon and said she'd bring the family to my office. After she left, I mused for a few seconds on what is called in the medical profession the 'p' phenomenon: the tendency of starched nurses' uniforms to make it seem as if all nurses were bountifully blessed in the bosom and thus shaped like the letter 'p'. It meant that doctors surveying the field could never be sure that a nurse they were flirting with was proportioned like two grapefruit on a stick or two peas on an ironing board. Some claimed it was the very essence of the mystery and allure of the medical profession.

Eric Cannon's folder gave a rather detailed description of a latter-day sheep in wolf's clothing. Since the age of five the boy had shown himself to be both remarkably precocious and a little simpleminded. Although the son of a Lutheran minister, he argued with his teachers, was truant from school, disobedient to teachers and parents, and a runaway from home on six separate occasions since the age of nine, the last episode occurring only six months before, when he disappeared for eight weeks before turning up in Cuba. At the age of twelve he began a career of priest baiting, which culminated in the boy's refusal to enter a church again. He also refused to go to school. He was caught possessing marijuana. He was stopped in what appeared to be the act of trying to immolate himself in front of the Central Brooklyn Selective Services Induction Center.

Pastor Cannon, his father, seemed to be a good man – in the traditional sense of the word: a conservative, restrained defender of the way things are. But his son had kept rebelling, had refused to be treated by a private psychiatrist; refused to work, refused to live at home except when it suited him. His father had thus decided to

47

send him to QSH, with the understanding that he would receive therapy with me.

'Dr Rhinehart,' the pretty little student nurse was saying suddenly at my elbow. 'This is Pastor Cannon and Mrs Cannon.'

'How do you do,' I said automatically and found myself grasping the chubby hand of a sweet-faced man with thick graying hair. He smiled fully as he shook my hand.

'Glad to meet you, Doctor. Dr Mann has told me a lot about you.'

'How do you do, Doctor,' a woman's musical voice said, and I turned to Mrs Cannon. Small and trim, she was standing behind the left shoulder of her husband and smiling horribly: her eyes kept flickering off to a line of female hags who were oozing noisily through the hallway outside our door. The patients were dressed with such indescribable ugliness they looked like character actors who had been rejected for *Marat-Sade* for being overdone.

Behind her was the son, Eric. He was dressed in a suit and tie, but his long long hair, rimless glasses and sparkle in the eyes which was either idiotic or divine made him look anything but middle-class suburbanite.

'That's him,' said Pastor Cannon with what honestly looked like a jovial smile.

I nodded politely and motioned them all toward the chairs. The pastor and his wife pushed past me to sit down, but Eric was staring out at the last of the women passing in the hall. One of them, an ugly, toothless woman with dish-mop hair, had stopped and was smiling coyly at him.

'Hi ya, cutie,' she said. 'Come down and see me sometime.'

The boy stared a second, smiled and said, 'I will.'

Laughing, he darted a bright-eyed look at me and went to take a chair. A juvenile idiot.

I plumped my big bulk informally on the desk opposite the Cannons and tried my 'gee-it's-wonderful-to-be-able-to-talk-to-you' smile. The boy was sitting near the window to my right and slightly behind his parents, looking at me with friendly anticipation.

'You understand, Pastor Cannon, I hope, in committing Eric to this hospital you are surrendering your authority over him.'

'Of course, Dr Rhinehart. I have complete confidence in Dr Mann.'

'Good. I assume also that both you and Eric know that this is no summer camp Eric is entering. This is a state mental hospital and – '

'It's a fine place, Dr Rhinehart,' said Pastor Cannon. 'We in New York State have every right to be proud.'

'Hmmm, yes,' I said, and turned to Eric. 'What do you think of it all?'

'There are groovy patterns in the soot on the windows.'

'My son believes that the whole world is insane.'

Eric was still looking pleasantly out the window. 'A plausible theory these days, one must admit,' I said to him, 'but it doesn't get you out of this hospital.'

'No, it gets me in,' he replied. We stared at each other for the first time.

'Do you want me to try to help you?' I asked.

'How can you help anyone?'

'Somebody's paying me well for trying.'

The boy's smile didn't seem to be sardonic, only friendly.

'They pay my father for spreading the Truth.'

'It may be ugly here, you know,' I said.

'I think I'll feel right at home here.'

49

'Not many people here will want to create a better world,' his father said.

'Everyone wants to create a better world,' Eric replied, with a hint of sharpness in his voice.

I eased myself off the desk and walked around behind it to pick up Eric's record. Peering over my glasses as if I could see without them I said to the father: 'I'd like to talk with you about Eric before you leave. Would you prefer that we talk privately or would you like to have Eric here?'

'No difference to me,' he said. 'He knows what I think. He'll probably act up a bit, but I'm used to it. Let him stay.'

'Eric, do you want to remain or would you like to go to the ward now?'

'Full fathom five my father lies,' he said looking out the window. His mother winced, but his father simply shook his head slowly and adjusted his glasses. Since I was interested in getting the son's live reaction to his parents, I let him stay.

'Tell me about your son, Pastor Cannon,' I said, seating myself in the wooden desk chair and leaning forward with my sincere professional look. Pastor Cannon cocked his head judiciously, crossed one leg over the other and cleared his throat.

'My son is a mystery,' he said. 'It's incredible to me that he should exist. He's totally intolerant of others. You . . . if you've read what's in that folder you know the details. Two weeks ago though – another example. Eric [he glanced nervously at the boy, who was apparently looking out or at the window] hasn't been eating well for a month. Hasn't been reading or writing. He burned everything he'd written over two months ago. An incredible amount. He doesn't speak much to anyone anymore. I was surprised he answered you . . . Two weeks ago, at

50

the dinner table, Eric playing saint with a glass of water, I remarked to our guest that night, a Mr Houston of Pace Industries, a vice-president, that I almost hoped sometimes that there would be a Third World War because I couldn't see how else the world would ever be rid of Communism. It's a thought we've all had at one time or another. Eric threw the water in my face. He smashed his glass on the floor.'

He was peering intently at me, waiting for a reaction. When I merely looked back he went on:

'I wouldn't mind for myself, but you can imagine how upset my wife is made by such scenes, and this is typical.'

'Yes,' I said. 'Why do you think he did it?'

'He's an egomaniac. He doesn't see things as you and I do. He doesn't want to live as we do. He thinks that all Catholic priests, most teachers and myself are all wrong, but so do many others without always making trouble about it. And that's the crux. He takes life too seriously. He never plays, or at least never when most people want him to. He's always playing, but never what he's supposed to. He's always making war for his way of life. This is a great land of freedom but it isn't made for people who insist on insisting on their own ideas. Tolerance is our byword and Eric is above all intolerant.'

'Sorry about that, Dad,' Eric suddenly said, and with a friendly smile got up and took a position directly behind and between his parents with a hand resting on the back of each of their chairs. Pastor Cannon looked at me as if he were trying to read by the expression on my face exactly how much longer he had to live.

'Are you intolerant, Eric?' I asked.

'I'm intolerant of evil and stupidity,' he said.

'But who gives you the right,' his father said, turning partly around to confront his son, 'to tell everyone what's good and evil?'

'It's the divine right of kings,' Eric replied, smiling.

His father turned back to me and shrugged. 'There you are,' he said. 'And let me give you another example. Eric, when he was thirteen years old, mind you, stands up in the middle of my church during a crowded midmorning Communion and says aloud above the kneeling figures: "That it should come to this," and walks out.'

We all remained as we were without speaking, as if I were the concentrating photographer and they about to have their family portrait taken.

'You don't like modern Christianity?' I finally said to Eric.

He ran his fingers through his long black hair, looked up briefly at the ceiling and screamed.

His father and mother came out of their chairs like rats off an electric grid and both stood trembling, watching their son, hands at his side, a slight smile on his face, screaming.

A white-suited Negro attendant entered the office and then another. They looked at me for instructions. I waited for Eric's second lungful scream to end to see if he would begin another. He didn't. When he had finished, he stood quietly for a moment and then said to no one in particular: 'Time to go.'

'Take him to the admissions ward, to Dr Vener for his physical. Give this prescription to Dr Vener.' I scribbled out a note for a mild sedative and watched the two attendants look warily at the boy.

'Will he come quietly?' the smaller of the two asked.

Eric stood still a moment longer and then did a rapid two-step followed by an irregular jig toward the door. He sang: 'We're OFF to see the Wizard, the Wonderful Wizard of Oz. We're OFF . . .'

Exit dancing. Attendants follow, last seen each reaching to grasp one of his arms. Pastor Cannon had a comforting arm around his wife's shoulder. I had rung for a student nurse.

'I'm very sorry, Dr Rhinehart,' Pastor Cannon said. 'I was afraid something like this would happen but I felt that you ought to see for yourself how he acts.'

'You're absolutely right,' I said.

'There's one other thing,' said Pastor Cannon. 'My wife and I were wondering whether it might be possible if . . . I understand it is sometimes possible for a patient to have a single room.'

I came around my desk and walked up quite close to Pastor Cannon, who still had an arm around his wife.

'This is a Christian institution, Pastor,' I said. 'We believe firmly in the brotherhood of all men. Your son will share a bedroom with fifteen other healthy, normal American mental patients. Gives them a feeling of belonging and togetherness. If your son feels the need for a single, have him slug an attendant or two, and they'll give him his own room: the state even provides a jacket for the occasion.'

His wife flinched and averted her eyes, but Pastor Cannon hesitated only a second and then nodded his head.

'Absolutely right. Teach the boy the realities of life. Now, about his clothing – '

'Pastor Cannon,' I said sharply. 'This is no Sunday school. This is a mental hospital. Men are sent here when they refuse to play our normal games of reality. Your son has been sucked up by the wards: you'll never see him the same again, for better or worse. Don't talk so blithely about rooms and clothes; your son is gone.'

His eyes changed from momentary fright into a cold glare, and his arm fell from around his wife.

'I never had a son,' he said.

And they left.

Chapter Six

When I got home, Lillian and Arlene Ecstein were collapsed side by side on the couch in their slacks and both were laughing as if they'd just finished splitting a bottle of gin. Arlene, by the way, always seems permanently eclipsed by the brilliant pinwheeling light of her husband. A little short from my six-foot-four point of view, she usually looked prim and prudish with thick horn-rimmed glasses like Jake's and undistinguished black hair tied back in a bun. Although there were unconfirmed rumours that on her otherwise slender body she owned two marvelously full breasts, the baggy sweaters, men's shirts, loose blouses and over-sized smocks she always wore resulted in no one's noticing her breasts until they'd known her for several months – by which time they'd forgotten all about her.

In her own sweet, simpleminded way I think she may once have given me a housewifely come-on, but being married, a dignified professional man, a loyal friend and having already forgotten all about her, I had resisted. (As I recall she spent one whole evening asking me to take pieces of lint off her smock: I spent the evening taking pieces of lint off her smock.) On the other hand, vaguely, late at night, after a hard day at the mental hospital, or when Lil and the children all had the flu or diarrhea or measles, I would feel regret at being married, a dignified professional man and a loyal friend. Twice I had daydreamed of somehow engulfing one entire Arlene breast in my mouth. It was clear that were fate ever to give me a reasonable opportunity – e.g. she were to climb naked into bed with me – I would yield; we would have one fine quick fire of first fornication and then settle into some dull routine of copulation on the q.t. But as long as the initiative were left to me *I* would never do anything about it. The two-thirds married professional man friend would always dominate the bored animal. And, as you, my friend, know, the combination would be miserable.

Although Lil's laugh was loud, even raucous, Arlene's was like a steady muffled machine-gun; she slumped lower on the couch as she laughed, while Lil stiffened her back and chortled at the ceiling.

'Well, what have you two been doing lately?' I asked, sliding my briefcase under the desk and hanging my raincoat neatly in a puddle on the floor just inside the kitchen.

'We've just been splitting a bottle of gin,' Lil said happily.

'It was that or dope and we couldn't find any dope,' Arlene added. 'Jake doesn't believe in LSD and Lil couldn't find yours.'

'That's strange. Lil knows I always keep it in the boy's toy cabinet.'

'I was wondering why Larry went off to school without a fuss this morning,' Lil said, and, having said something amusing, she stopped laughing.

'Well, what's the occasion? Is one of you getting divorced or having an abortion?' I asked, fixing myself a martini from the still two-thirds full bottle of gin.

'Don't be silly,' Lil said. 'We'd never dream of such high points. Our lives ooze. Not ooze excitement or sex appeal, just ooze.'

'Like vaginal jelly from a tube,' Arlene added.

They sat slumped on the couch looking grief-stricken for half a minute and then Lil perked up.

'We might form a Psychiatrists' Wives Invitational Club, Arlene,' she said. 'And not invite Luke and Jake.'

'I would hope not,' I said and pulled a desk chair around and, straddling it theatrically, drink in hand, faced the females with fatigue.

'We could be charter members of PWIC,' Lil went on, scowling. 'I can't quite figure out what good it will do us.' Then she giggled. 'Perhaps, though, our PWIC will grow bigger than yours,' and both women, after staring at me pleasantly for a few seconds, began giggling stupidly.

'We could have our first social project by changing husbands for a week,' said Arlene.

'Neither of us would notice any difference,' Lil said.

'That's not true. Jake brushes his teeth in a very original way, and I bet Luke has abilities I don't know about.'

'Believe me,' Lil said, 'he doesn't.'

'Sssss,' said Arlene. 'You shouldn't show public contempt for your husband. It will bruise his ego.'

'Thank you, Arlene,' I said.

'Luke's an in-tell-i-gent man,' she managed to get out. 'I'm not even a liberal arts woman, and he's studied . . . he's studied . . .'

'Urine and stools,' completed Lil, and they laughed.

Why is it that I can lead my life of quiet desperation with complete poise, dignity and grace, while most women I know insist on leading lives of quiet desperation which are *noisy*? I was giving the question serious thought when I noticed Lil and Arlene crawling toward me on their knees, their hands clasped in supplication.

'Save us, O Master of the Stools, we're bored.'

'Give us the word!'

It was good to be back in the quiet of home and fireside after a trying day with the mentally disturbed.

'O Master, help us, our lives are yours.'

The effect of two crawling, begging, drunken women

56

wiggling their way toward me was that I got an erection, not professionally or maritally the most helpful response, but sincere. Somehow I felt that more was expected of a sage.

'Rise, my children,' I said gently and I myself now stood up before them.

'O Master, speak!' Arlene said, on her knees.

'You wish to be saved? To be reborn?'

'Oh, yes!'

'You wish a new life?'

'Yes, yes!'

'Have you tried the New All with Borax?'

They collapsed forward in groans and giggles, but straightened quickly with a 'We have, we have, but still no satori' (from Lil), and 'even Mr Clean' (from Arlene).

'You must cease caring,' I said. 'You must surrender everything. EVERYTHING.'

'Oh, Master, here, in front of your wife!' and they both giggled and fluttered like sparrows in heat.

'EVERYthing,' I boomed irritably. 'Give up *all* hope, *all* illusion, *all* desire.'

'We've tried.'

'We've tried and still we desire.'

'We still desire not to desire and hope to be without hope and have the illusion we can be without illusions.'

'Give *up*, I say. Give up *everything*, including the desire to be saved. Become as weeds that grow and die unnoticed in the fields. Surrender to the wind.'

Lillian suddenly stood up and walked to the liquor cabinet.

'I've heard it all before,' she said, 'and the wind turns out to be a lot of hot air.'

'I thought you were drunk.'

'The sight of you preaching is enough to sober anyone.'

Arlene, still on her knees, said strangely, blinking

57

through her thick glasses, 'But I'm still not saved. I want to be saved.'

'You heard him, give up.'

'That's salvation?'

'That's all he offers. Can Jake do better?'

'No, but I can get a family discount with Jake.'

And they laughed.

'Are you two really drunk?' I asked.

'I am, but Lil says she wants all her faculties intact to stay one up on you. Jake's not home so I've given my faculty a vacation.'

'Luke never loses any of his faculties: they've all got tenure,' Lil said. 'That's why they're all senile.' Lil smiled a first bitter and then pleased-with-herself smile and raised a fresh martini in mock toast to my senile faculties. With slow dignity I moved off to my study. There are moments even a pipe can't dignify.

Chapter Seven

The poker that evening was a disaster. Lilian and Arlene were exaggeratedly gay at first (their bottle of gin nearly empty) and, after a series of reckless raises, exaggeratedly broke thereafter. Lil then proceeded to raise even more recklessly (with my money), while Arlene subsided into a sensually blissful indifference. Dr Mann's luck was deadening. In his totally bored, seemingly uninterested way, he proceeded to raise dramatically, win, bluff people out, win, or fold early and miss out on only small pots. He was an intelligent player, but when the cards went his way his blandness made him seem superhuman. That this blubbery god was crumbling potato chips all over the table was a further source of personal gloom. Lil seemed happy that it was Dr Mann winning big and not I, but Dr Felloni, by the vigor with which she nodded her head after losing a pot to him, also seemed vastly irritated.

At about eleven Arlene asked to be dealt out, and, announcing drowsily that losing at poker made her feel sexy and sleepy, left for her apartment downstairs. Lil drank and battled on, won two huge pots at a seven-card-stud game with dice that she liked to play, became gay again, teased me affectionately, apologized for being irritable, teased Dr Mann for winning so much, then ran from the table to vomit in the bathtub. She returned after a few minutes uninterested in playing poker. Announcing that losing made her feel a frigid insomniac, she retired to bed.

We three doctors played on for another half-hour or so, discussing Dr Ecstein's latest book, which I criticized brilliantly, and gradually losing interest in poker. Near midnight Dr Felloni said it was time for her to leave, but instead of getting a ride crosstown with her, Dr Mann said he'd stay a little longer and take a taxi home. After she'd left, we played four final hands of stud poker and with joy I won three of them.

When we'd finished, he lifted himself out of the straight-backed chair and deposited himself in the over-stuffed one near the long bookcase. I heard the toilet flush down the hall and wondered if Lil had been sick again. Dr Mann drew out his pipe, stuffed and lighted it with all the speed of a slow-motion machine being photographed in slow motion, sucked in eternally at the pipe as he lit it and then, finally, boom, let loose a medium-megaton nuclear explosion up toward the ceiling, obscuring the books on the shelves beside him and generally astounding me with its magnitude.

'How's your book coming, Luke?' he asked. He had a deep, gruff, old man's voice.

'Not coming at all,' I said from my seat at the poker table.

'Mmmmm.'

'I don't think I'm on to much of value . . .'

'Un . . . Un. Huh.'

'When I began it, I thought the transition from sadistic to masochistic might lead to something important.' I ran my finger over the soft green velvet of the poker table. 'It leads from sadism to masochism.' I smiled.

Puffing lightly and looking up at the picture of Freud hung on the wall opposite him, he asked:

'How many cases have you analyzed and written up in detail?'

'Three.'

'The *same* three?'

'The same three. I tell you, Tim, all I'm doing is

uninterpreted case histories. The libraries are retching with them.'

'Nnnn.'

I looked at him, he continued to look at Freud, and from the street below a police siren whined upward from Madison Avenue.

'Why don't you finish the book anyway?' he asked mildly. 'As your Zen says, go with the flow, even if the flow is meaningless.'

'I am going with the flow. My flow with that book has totally stopped. I don't feel like pumping it up again.'

'Nnnn.'

I became aware that I was grinding a die into the green velvet. I tried to relax.

'By the way, Tim, I had my first interview with that boy you had sent to QSH for me. I found him – '

'I don't care about your patient at QSH, Luke, unless it's going to get into print.'

He still didn't look at me, and the abruptness of the remark stunned me.

'If you're not writing, you're not thinking,' he went on, 'and if you're not thinking you're dead.'

'I used to feel that way.'

'Yes, you did. Then you discovered Zen.'

'Yes, I did.'

'And now you find writing a bore.'

'Yes.'

'And thinking?'

'And thinking too,' I said.

'Maybe there's something wrong with Zen,' he said.

'Maybe there's something wrong with thinking.'

'It's been fashionable among thinkers lately to say so, but saying, "I strongly think that thinking is nonsense," that seems rather absurd to me.'

'It *is* absurd; so is psychoanalysis.'

He looked over at me; the crinkles around his left eye twitched.

'Psychoanalysis has led to more new knowledge of the human soul than all the previous two million years of thinking put together. Zen has been around a long time and I haven't noticed any great body of knowledge flowing from it.' Without apparent irritability he let out another vigorous mushroom cloud toward the ceiling. I was fingering one of the dice, nervously pressing my fingers into the little dots; I still looked at him, he at Freud.

'Tim, I'm not going to argue the merits and demerits of Zen again with you. I've told you that whatever I've gained from Zen is not something I've been able to articulate.'

'What you've gained from Zen is intellectual anemia.'

'Maybe I've gained sense. You *know* that eighty percent of the stuff in the psychoanalytic journals is crap. Useless crap. Including mine.' I paused. 'Including . . . yours.'

He hesitated, and then bubbled up a chuckle.

'You know the first principle of medicine: you can't cure the patient without a sample of his crap,' he said.

'Who needs to be cured?'

He turned his eyes lazily into mine and said:

'You do.'

'You analyzed me. What's the matter?' I shot back stare for stare.

'Nothing the matter that a little reminder of what life is all about won't cure.'

'Oh, piss,' I said.

'You don't like to push yourself, and along comes Zen and tell you to "go with the flow".'

He paused and, still looking at me, dropped his pipe in an ashtray on the small table beside him.

'Your flow is naturally stagnant.'

62

'Makes a good breeding ground,' I said and tried a short laugh.

'For Christ's sake, Luke, don't laugh,' he said loudly. 'You're wasting your life these days, throwing it away.'

'Aren't we all?'

'No, we're not. Jake isn't. I'm not. Good men in every profession aren't. You weren't, until a year ago.'

'When I was a child. I spoke like a child –'

'Luke, Luke, listen to me.' He was an agitated old man.

'Well – ?'

'Come back to analysis with me.'

I rubbed the die against the back of my hand and, thinking nothing clearly, answered:

'No.'

'What's the matter with you?' he said sharply. 'Why have you lost faith in the significance of your work? Will you please try to explain?'

Without premeditation I surged up from my chair like a defensive tackle at the sight of a shot at the quarterback. I strode across the room in front of Dr Mann to the big window looking along the street toward Central Park.

'I'm bored. I'm bored. I'm sorry but that's about it. I'm sick of lifting unhappy patients up to normal boredom, sick of trivial experiments, empty articles –'

'These are symptoms, not analysis.'

'To experience something for the first time: a first balloon, a visit to a foreign land. A fine fierce fornication with a new woman. The first paycheck, or the surprise of first winning big at the poker table or the racetrack. The exciting isolation of leaning against the wind on the highway hitchhiking, waiting for someone to stop and offer me a lift, perhaps to a town three miles down the road, perhaps to new friendships, perhaps to death. The rich glow I felt when I knew I'd finally written a good paper, made a brilliant analysis or hit a good backhand lob. The excitement of a new philosophy of life. Or a new home. Or my first child. These are what we want from life and now . . . they seem gone, and both Zen and psychoanalysis seem incapable of bringing them back.'

'You sound like a disillusioned sophomore.'

'The same old new lands, the same old fornication, the same getting and spending, the same drugged, desperate, repetitious faces appearing in the office for analysis, the same effective, meaningless lobs. The same old new philosophies. And the thing I'd really pinned my ego to, psychoanalysis, doesn't seem to be a bit relevant to the problem.'

'It's totally relevant.'

'Because analysis, were it really on the right track, should be able to change me, to change anything and anybody, to eliminate all undesired neurotic symptoms and to do it much more quickly than the two years necessary to produce most measurable changes in people.'

'You're dreaming, Luke. It can't be done. In both theory and practice it's impossible to rid an individual of all his undesired habits, tensions, compulsions, inhibitions, what-have-you.'

'Then maybe the theory and practice are wrong.'

'Undoubtedly.'

'We can perfect plants, alter machines, train animals, why not men?'

'For God's sake!' Dr Mann tapped his pipe vigorously against a bronze ashtray and glared up at me irritably. 'You're dreaming. There are no Utopias. There can be no perfect man. Each of our lives is a finite series of errors which tend to become rigid and repetitious and necessary. Every man's personal proverb about himself is: "Whatever is, is right, in the best of all possible people." The whole tendency is . . . the whole tendency of the human personality is to solidify into the corpse. You don't change

64

corpses. Corpses aren't bubbling with enthusiasm. You spruce them up a bit and make them fit to be looked at.'

'I absolutely agree: psychoanalysis rarely breaks this solidifying flow of personality, it has nothing to offer the man who is bored.'

Dr Mann harrumphed or snorted or something and I moved away from the window to look up at Freud. Freud stared down seriously; he didn't look pleased.

'There must be some other . . . other secret [blasphemy!] some other . . . magic potion which would permit certain men to radically alter their lives,' I went on.

'Try astrology, the *I Ching*, LSD.'

'Freud gave me a taste for finding some philosophical equivalent of LSD, but the effect of Freud's own potion seems to be wearing off.'

'You're dreaming. You expect too much. A human being, a human personality is the total pattern of the accumulated limitations and potentials of an individual. You take away all his habits, compulsions and channeled drives, and you take away *him*.'

'Then perhaps, perhaps, we ought to *do* away with "him".'

He paused as if trying to absorb what I'd said and when I turned to face him, he surprised me by booming two quick cannon shots of smoke out of the side of his mouth.

'Oh Luke, you're nibbling on that Goddam Eastern mysticism again. If I weren't a consistent self, a glutton at the table, sloppy in dress, bland in speech and rigidly devoted to psychoanalysis, to success, to publication – and all of these things *consistently* – I'd never get anything done, and what would I *be*?'

I didn't answer.

'If I sometimes smoked one way,' he went on, 'sometimes another, sometimes not at all, varied the way I dressed, was nervous, serene, ambitious, lazy, lecherous,

65

gluttonous, ascetic – where would my "self" be? What would I achieve? It's the way a man chooses to limit himself that determines his character. A man without habits, consistency, redundancy – and hence boredom – is not human. He's insane.'

With a satisfied and relaxed grunt he placed his pipe down again and smiled pleasantly at me. For some reason I hated him.

'And accepting these self-defeating limitations is mental health?' I said.

'Mmmmm.'

I stood facing him and felt a strange rush of rage surge through me. I wanted to crush Dr Mann with a ten-ton block of concrete. I spat out my next words:

'We must be wrong. All psychotherapy is a tedious disaster. We must be making some fundamental, rock-bottom error that poisons all our thinking. Years from now men will look upon our therapeutic theories and our techniques as we do upon nineteenth-century bloodletting.'

'You're sick, Luke,' he said quietly.

'You and Jake are among the best and as humans you're both nothing.' He was sitting erect in his chair.

'You're sick,' he said. 'And don't feed me any more bull about Zen. I've been watching you for months now. You're not relaxed. Half the time you seem like a giggly schoolboy and the other half like a pompous ass.'

'I'm a therapist and it's clear I, as a human, am a disaster. Physician, heal thyself.'

'You've lost faith in the most important profession in the world because of an idealized expectation which even Zen says is unrealistic. You've gotten bored with the day-to-day miracles of making people slightly better. I don't see where letting them get slightly worse is much to be proud of.'

'I'm not proud of – '

'Yes, you are. You think you've got absolute truth or at least that you alone are seeking it. You're a classic case of Horney's: the man who comforts himself not with what he achieves, but with what he dreams of achieving.'

'I am.' I stated it flatly: it happened to be true. 'But you, Tim, are a classic case of the normal human being, and I'm not impressed.'

He stared at me not puffing, his face flushed, and then abruptly, like a big balloon bouncing, arose from his chair with a grunt.

'I'm sorry you feel that way,' he said and chugged toward the door.

'There must be a method to change men *more* radically than we've discovered – '

'Let me know when you find it,' he said.

He stopped at the door and we looked at each other, two alien worlds. His face showed bitter contempt.

'I will,' I said.

'When you find it, just give me a ring. Oxford 4–0300.'

We stood facing each other.

'Goodnight,' I said.

'Goodnight,' he said, turning. 'Give my best to Lil in the morning. And Luke,' turning back to me, 'try *finishing* Jake's book. It's always better to criticize a book after you've read it.'

'I didn't – '

'Goodnight.'

And he opened the door, waddled out, hesitated at the elevator, then walked on to the stairwell and disappeared.

Chapter Eight

After closing the door I walked mechanically back into
the living room. At the window I stared at the few lights
and at the empty early-morning streets below. Dr Mann
emerged from the building and moved off toward Madison Avenue; he looked, from three floors up, like a
stuffed dwarf. I had an urge to pick up the easy chair he
had been sitting in and throw it through the glass window
after him. Distorted images swirled through my mind:
Jake's book lying darkly on the white tablecloth at lunch;
the boy Eric's black eyes staring at me warmly; Lil and
Arlene wriggling toward me; blank pieces of paper on my
desk; Dr Mann's clouds of smoke mushrooming toward
the ceiling; and Arlene as she had left the room a few
hours earlier; an open, sensuous yawn. For some reason I
felt like starting at one end of the room and running full
speed to the other end and smashing right through the
portrait of Freud which hung there.

Instead I turned from the window and walked back and
forth until I was looking up at the portrait. Freud stared
down at me dignified, serious, productive, rational and
stable: he was everything which a reasonable man might
strive to be. I reached up and, grasping the portrait
carefully, turned it around so that the face was toward the
wall. I stared with rising satisfaction at the brown cardboard backing and then, with a sigh, returned to the
poker table and put away the cards, chips and chairs. One
of the two dice was missing but when I glanced at the
floor it was not to be found. Turning to go to bed, I saw
on the small table next to the chair Dr Mann had been

lecturing me from, a card – the queen of spades – angled as if propped up against something. I went over and stared down at the card and knew that beneath it was the die.

I stood that way for a full minute feeling a rising, incomprehensible rage: something of what Osterflood must feel, of what Lil must have been feeling during the afternoon, but directed at nothing, thoughtless, aimless rage. I vaguely remember an electric clock humming on the mantelpiece. Then a fog-horn blast groaned into the room from the East River and terror tore the arteries out of my heart and tied them in knots in my belly: if that die has a one face up, I thought, I'm going downstairs and rape Arlene. 'If it's a one, I'll rape Arlene,' kept blinking on and off in my mind like a huge neon light and my terror increased. But when I thought if it's not a one I'll go to bed, the terror was boiled away by a pleasant excitement and my mouth swelled into a gargantuan grin: a one means rape, the other numbers mean bed, the die is cast. Who am I to question the die?

I picked up the queen of spades and saw staring at me a cyclopean eye: a one.

I was shocked into immobility for perhaps five seconds, but finally made an abrupt, soldierly about-face and marched to our apartment door, opened it and took one pace outside, wheeled, and marched with mechanical precision and joyous excitement back into the apartment, down the hall to our bedroom, opened the door a crack and announced loudly: 'I'm going for a walk, Lil.' Turning, I marched out of the apartment a second time.

As I walked woodenly down the two flights of stairs I noticed rust spots on the railing and an abandoned advertising circular crumpled into a corner. 'Think Big,' it urged. On the Ecstein floor I wheeled like a puppet, marched to the door of their apartment and rang. My next clear thought swept with dignified panic through my mind: 'Does Arlene really take the pill?' A smile colored my consciousness at the thought of Jack the Ripper, on his way to rape and strangle another woman, and worrying whether she was protected or not.

After twenty seconds I rang again.

A second smile (my face remained wooden) flowed through at the thought of someone else's already having discovered the die and thus now busily banging away at Arlene on the floor just on the other side of the door.

The door unlatched and opened a crack.

'Jake?' a voice said sleepily.

'It's me, Arlene,' I said.

'What do you want?' The door stayed open only a crack.

'I've come downstairs to rape you,' I said.

'Oh,' she said, 'just a minute.'

She unlatched and opened the door. She was wearing an unattractive cotton bathrobe, possibly even Jake's, her black hair was straggling down her forehead, cold cream whitened her face, and she was squinting at me without her glasses like a blind beggar woman in a melodrama of the life of Christ.

Closing the door behind me I turned toward her and waited, wondering passively what I was going to do next.

'What did you say you wanted?' she asked; she was groggy with sleep.

'I've come downstairs to rape you,' I replied and advanced toward her, she continuing to stand there with a widening and perhaps wakening look of curiosity. Feeling for the first time a faint hint of sexual desire, I put my arms around her, lowered my head and planted my mouth on her neck.

Almost immediately I felt her hands pushing hard against my chest and soon a long-drawn-out 'Luuuu-

UUke,' part terror, part question, part giggle. After a good solid wet arousing kissing of her upper dorsal region I released her. She stepped back a step and straightened her ugly bathrobe. We stared at each other, in our differently hypnotized states, like two drunks confronting each other, knowing they are expected to dance.

'Come,' I found myself saying after our mutual moment of awe, and I put my left arm around her waist and began drawing her toward the bedroom.

'Let go of me,' she said sharply and pushed my arm away.

With the mechanical swiftness of a superbly driven puppet my right hand slammed across her face. She was terror-stricken. So was I. A second time we faced each other, her face now showing a blotch of red on the left side. I mechanically wiped some cold cream off my fingers onto my trousers, then I reached out and took hold of the front of her robe and pulled her to me.

'Come,' I said again.

'Get your hands off Jake's bathrobe,' she hissed uncertainly.

I released her and said: 'I want to rape you, Arlene. Now, this moment. Let's go.'

Like a frightened kitten she hunched down away from me with her hands tugging her robe at the throat. Then she straightened.

'All right,' she said, and with a look which I can only describe as righteous indignation, began to move past me down the hall toward the bedroom, adding, 'But you leave Jake's bathrobe alone.'

The rape was then consummated with a minimum of violence on my part, in fact with no great amount of imagination, passion or pleasure. The pleasure was primarily Arlene's. I went through the appropriate motions of mouthing her breasts, squeezing her buttocks, caressing her labials, mounting her in the usual fashion and, after a longer time bucking and plunging than customary (I felt through the whole act like a puppet trained to demonstrate normal sexual intercourse to a group of slow teenagers), finished. She writhed and humped a few too many seconds longer and sighed. After a while she looked up at me.

'Why did you do it, Luke?'

'I had to, Arlene, I was driven to it.'

'Jake won't like it.'

'Ah . . . Jake?'

'I tell him everything. It gives him valuable material, he says.'

'But . . . this . . . have you been . . . raped before?'

'No. Not since getting married. Jake's the only one and he never rapes me.'

'Are you sure you have to tell him?'

'Oh yes. He'd want to know.'

'But won't he be tremendously upset?'

'Jake? No. He'll find it interesting. He finds everything interesting. If we'd committed sodomy that would be even more interesting.'

'Arlene, stop being bitter.'

'I'm not bitter. Jake's a scientist.'

'Well, maybe you're right but – '

'Of course, there was that once . . .'

'What once?'

'That a colleague of his at Bellevue caressed one of my breasts with his elbow at a party and Jake split open his skull with a bottle of . . . bottle of . . . was it Cognac?'

'Split his skull?'

'Brandy. And another time when a man kissed me under mistletoe, Jake, you remember, you were there, told the guy – '

'I'm remembering – so look, Arlene, don't be silly, don't tell Jake about tonight.'

She considered this.

'But if I don't tell him, it will imply I've done something wrong.'

'No. I've done something wrong, Arlene. And I don't want to lose Jake's friendship and trust just because I've raped you.'

'I understand.'

'He'd be hurt.'

'Yes, he would. He wouldn't be objective. If he'd been drinking . . .'

'Yes, he would . . .'

'I won't tell him.'

We exchanged a few more words and that was that. About forty minutes after arriving, I left. Oh, there was one other incident. As I was leaving and Arlene and I were tonguing each other affectionately at the door to her apartment, she in a flimsy nightgown with one heavy breast plunging out and cupped in my hand, and I more or less dressed as when I entered, the sound of a key in the door suddenly split through our sensuality, we leapt apart, the apartment door opened and there stood Jacob Ecstein.

For what seemed like sixteen and a half minutes (possibly five or six seconds) he gave me that scrutinizing look through his thick glasses and then said loudly:

'Luke, baby, you're just the guy I want to see. My anal optometrist? He's cured. I did it. I'm famous.'

Chapter Nine

Back upstairs in my living room I stared dreamily at the exposed one on the die. I scratched my balls and shook my head in dazed awe. Rape had been possible for years, *decades* even, but was realized only when I stopped looking at whether it were possible, or prudent, or even desirable, but without premeditation did it, feeling myself a puppet to a force outside me, a creature of the gods – the die – rather than a responsible agent. The cause was chance or fate, not me. The probability of that die being a one was only one in six. The chance of the die's being there under the card, maybe one in a million. My rape was obviously dictated by fate. Not guilty.

Of course I could simply have broken my verbal promise of following the dictates of the die. True? True. But a promise! A solemn promise to obey the die! My word of honor! Can we expect a professional man, a member of PANY, to break his word because the die, with the odds heavily against it, determined rape? No, obviously not. I am clearly not guilty. I felt like spitting neatly into some conveniently located spittoon in front of my jury.

But on the whole it seemed a pretty weak defense, and I began vaguely hunting for a new one when I became ablaze at the thought: I am right: I must always obey the dice. Lead where they will, I must follow. All power to the die!

Excited and proud, I stood for a moment on my own personal Rubicon. And then I stepped across. I established in my mind at that moment and for all time, the

74

never-to-be-questioned principle that what the die dictates, I will perform.

The next moment was anticlimactic. I picked up the die and announced: 'If it's a one, three or five, I'll go to bed; if it's a two I'll go downstairs and ask Jake if I can try to rape Arlene again; if it's a four or a six I'll stay up and think about this some more.' I shook the die violently in the cup of my two hands and flipped it out onto the poker table, it rolled to a stop: five. Astonished and a bit let down, I went to bed. It was a lesson I was to learn many times in subsequent casts; the dice can show almost as poor judgment as a human.

Chapter Ten

By training I have learned to look for the casual insignificance of every overt cause. In the morning, after a careless, buttockless period before breakfast, lukewarm coffee and Lil's hungover imprecations, I wandered into the living room to recreate the scene of the crime. Pacing back and forth I tried to demonstrate to myself that I would have gone down to Arlene whether the die had been a one, a four, or a box of matches. I remained unconvinced. I knew in my big hard-pumping heart that only the die could have pushed me down those stairs and into Arlene's entranceway.

I tried then to prove that I had seen the die that was on the side table before it had been covered with a card or at any rate before I made my solemn vow to commit holy rape if it turned out to have a one face up. I tried to determine who had left the card and die there and guessed it must have been Lil during her headlong flight to the bathroom. It seemed thus that I couldn't have known that it was a one. Had I seen from the angle of my chair the *sides* of the die and thus unconsciously known that the die must have turned upward either a one or a six? I walked over to the little table and tumbled a die onto it and, without looking at what came face up, covered the die with the queen of spades more or less as it had been covered the night before. I went back and sat at the poker table. From there, staring through my glasses, squinting, straining, trying with superhuman effort, I managed to make out the table and the slightly humped playing card. If there was a die under the card it was unpublished news

as far as my eyes were concerned. For me to have seen
the die from my chair at the poker table I would have had
to have an unconscious with telescopic sight. The case
was clear: I couldn't possibly have known what was under
the queen of spades; my rape was determined by fate.

'What happened to the picture of Freud?' asked Lil,
who had come in from the kitchen after turning the kids
over to the maid.

Seeing that Freud's portrait was still facing the wall, I
said:

'I don't know. I assumed you did that last night as you
went to bed. A symbolic rejection of me and my
colleagues.'

Lil, her messed blonde hair, reddish eyes and uncertain
frown making her look unusually like a mouse approaching cheese in a trap, looked at me suspiciously.

'I did it?' she asked, her mind stumbling over the events
of last night.

'Sure. Don't you remember? You said something like
"Now, Freud can look into the bowels of the house," and
staggered off to the john.'

'I did not,' she said. 'I strode with great dignity.'

'You're right. You strode with great dignity in a variety
of directions.'

'But essentially I moved east.'

'True.'

'East and johnward.'

We laughed and I asked her to bring another cup of
coffee and a doughnut to my study. Evie and Larry
momentarily escaped from the clutches of the maid and
swooped through the living room like two desperadoes
shooting up a town and disappeared back toward the
kitchen. I retreated to my home within my home: my old
oaken desk in the study.

For a while I sat there throwing the two green dice

77

across its scarred face and wondering what the events of the night before meant for me. My legs and loins felt heavy, my mind light. Last night I had done something I had vaguely felt like doing for two or three years. Having done it I was changed, not greatly, but changed. My life for a few weeks would be a little more complex, a little more exciting. Searching for a free hour to play with Arlene would while away time that in the recent past had been spent not being able to work on my book, not being able to concentrate on my cases and daydreaming about stock market coups. The time might not be *better* spent, but I would be better entertained. Thanks to the die.

What else might the dice dictate? Well, that I stop writing silly psychoanalytic articles; that I sell all my stock, or buy all I could afford; that I make love to Arlene in our double bed while my wife slept on the other side; that I take a trip to San Francisco, Hawaii, Peking; that I bluff every time when playing poker; that I give up my home, my friends, my profession. After giving up my psychiatric practice I might become a college professor . . . a stockbroker . . . a real estate salesman . . . Zen master . . . used-car salesman . . . travel agent . . . elevator man. My choice of profession seemed suddenly infinite. That I didn't want to be a used-car salesman, didn't respect the profession, seemed almost a limitation on my part, an idiosyncracy.

My mind exploded with possibilities. The boredom I had been feeling for so long seemed unnecessary. I pictured myself saying after each random decision, 'The die is cast,' and sloshing stoically across some new, ever wider Rubicon. If one life was dead and boring, so what? Long live a new life!

But what new life? During the last months nothing had seemed worth doing. Had the die changed that? What specifically did I want to do? Well, nothing *specific*. But

78

in general? All power to the dice! Good enough, but what
might they decide? Everything.
   Everything?
   Everything.

Chapter Eleven

Everything didn't turn out to be too much at first.

That afternoon the dice scorned all sorts of exciting options and steered me instead to the corner drugstore to choose reading matter at random. Admittedly, browsing through the four magazines chosen – *Agonizing Confessions*; *Your Pro-Football Handbook*; *Fuck-it* and *Health and You* – was more interesting than my usual psychoanalytic fare, but I vaguely regretted not having been sent by the dice on a more important or absurd mission.

That evening and the next day I seemed to avoid the dice. The result was that two nights after my great D-Day I lay in bed brooding about what to do with Arlene. I wanted, no doubt about it, to press her to my bosom once again, but the dangers, complications and comedy seemed almost too much to pay. I tossed and turned in indecision, anxiety and lust until Lil ordered me to take a sedative or sleep in the bathtub.

I rolled out of bed and retreated to my study. I was halfway through a complicated imaginary conversation with Jake in which I was explaining with great clarity what I was doing under his bed and pointing out the legal complications involved in homicide, when I realized with a rush of relief that I'd simply let the dice decide. Indecisive? Uncertain? Worried? Let the rolling ivory tumble your burdens away. $2.50 per pair.

I took out a pen and wrote out the numbers one to six. The first option to occur to my essentially conservative nature was to chuck the whole thing: I'd ignore my brief affair and treat Arlene as if nothing had happened. After

80

all, the sporadic screwing of another man's wife might provide complications. When the woman is the wife of your Best Friend, nearest Neighbor, and closest Business Associate, the intrigue and betrayal are so complete that the end hardly seemed worth the effort. Arlene's end wasn't so different from Lil's that it justified painful hours of scheming as to how one might enter it in dice-dictated ways and painful hours of brooding about whether one should brood about having entered it. Nor were the convolutions of her soul likely to offer any more originality than those of her body.

Arlene and Jake had married seventeen years before when they were both juniors in high school. Jake had been a highly precocious teen-ager and after seducing Arlene one summer, he found himself sexually inconvenienced in the fall when they were separated by his being away at Tapper's Boarding School for Brilliant Boys. Masturbation drove him to a fury of frustration since no daydream or self-caress remotely approached Arlene's round breasts cupped in his hands or filling his mouth. At Christmas he announced to his parents that he must either return to the public high school, commit suicide or marry Arlene. His parents brooded briefly between the last two of these options and then reluctantly permitted marriage.

Arlene was quite happy to leave school and miss her algebra and chemistry finals; they were married over the Easter holiday and she began working to help support Jake through his schools. Arlene's education had thus come from life, and since her life had been spent clerking at Gimbel's, girl-Fridaying at Bache and Company, typing at Woolworth's and controlling a switchboard at the Fashion Institute of Technology, her education was a limited one. In the seven years since she'd stopped working, she had devoted herself to philanthropic causes of which no one had ever heard (The Penny Parade for

Puppies, Dough for Diabetes, Help Afghanistanian Sheepherders!), and reading lurid fiction and advanced psychoanalytic journals. It's not clear to what degree she understood any of her activities.

The day of his marriage was apparently the last time Jake had bothered to give a thought to the pursuit of women. He seemed to have acquired Arlene in the same spirit with which in later life he acquired a lifetime supply of aspirin, and, a little after that, a lifetime supply of laxatives. Moreover, just as the aspirin and laxative were guaranteed not to produce any annoying side effects, so too he saw to it that periodic use of Arlene would be free of such effects also. There was an ill-intended rumor that he had Arlene take the pill and use an inter-uterine device, a diaphragm and a douche, while he used a contraceptive, always used her anus anyway and then always practiced *coitus interruptus*. Whatever his methods, they had worked. They were childless, Jake was satisfied and Arlene was bored and longed to have a baby.

So my first option was clear: no more affair. Feeling rebellious I wrote as number two option, 'I'll do whatever Arlene says we ought to do' (rather courageous in those days), number three, I would attempt to re-seduce Arlene as soon as possible. Too vague. I'd try to re-seduce her, hummm, obviously Saturday evening. (The Ecsteins were having a cocktail party.)

Number four, I – I seemed to have exhausted the three obvious courses of action – no, wait, number four, I would say to her whenever I could get her alone that although I loved her beyond words, I felt that we should keep our love Platonic for the sake of the children. Number five, I would play it by ear and let my impulses dictate my behavior (another chicken's squawk). Number six, I would go to her apartment Tuesday afternoon (the next time I knew her to be alone) and more realistically rape her (i.e. no effort at softness or seduction).

I looked at the options, smiled happily and flipped a die: four: Platonic love. Platonic love? How did that get in there? I was momentarily appalled. I decided that it was understood by number four that I might be dissuaded from Platonism by Arlene.

That Saturday evening Arlene greeted me at the door wearing a lovely blue cocktail dress I'd never seen before (neither had Jake) with a glass of Scotch and with a wide-eyed stare: representing awe, fright or blindness from being without her glasses. After handing me the Scotch (Lil was upstairs still dressing), Arlene fled to the other side of the room. I drifted over to a small group of psychiatrists led by Jake and listened to a consecutive series of monologues on methods of avoiding income taxes.

Depressed, I drifted after Arlene, poetry poised like cookie crumbs on my lips. She was yo-yoing from the kitchen-bar to her guests, smiling bigly and blankly, and then rushing away in someone's midsentence on the presumed pretense of getting someone a drink. I'd never seen her so manic. When I finally followed her into the kitchen one time she was staring at a picture of the Empire State Building, or rather at the calendar beneath it with all the banking holidays squared in orange.

She turned and looked at me with the same wide-eyed awe, fear or blindness and asked in a frightening loud, nervous voice:

'What if I'm pregnant?'

'Shhhh,' I replied.

'If I'm pregnant, Jake will never forgive me.'

'But I thought you took the pill every morning.'

'Jake tells me to but for the last two years, I've substituted little vitamin C tablets in my calendar clock.'

83

'Oh my God, when, er, when . . . Do you think you're pregnant?'

'Jake'll know I cheated on him and didn't take the pill.'

'But he'll think he's the father?'

'Of course, who else could be?'

'Well . . . uh . . .'

'But you know how he detests the thought of having children.'

'Yes, I do. Arlene . . .'

'Excuse me, I've got to serve drinks.'

She ran out with two martinis and returned with an empty highball glass.

'Don't you dare to touch me again,' she said as she began preparing another drink.

'Ah Arlene, how can you say that? My love is like . . .'

'This Tuesday, Jake is going to spend all day at the Library annex working on his new book. If you dare try anything like last night I'll phone the police.'

'Arlene . . .'

'I've checked their number and I plan to always keep the phone near me.'

'Arlene, the feelings I have for you are . . .'

'Although I told Lil yesterday that I'm going to Westchester to see my Aunt Miriam.'

She was off again with a full whiskey and two pieces of cheesed celery, and before she returned again Lil had arrived and I was trapped in an infinite analysis with a man named Sidney Opt of the effect of the Beatles on American culture. It was the closest I came to poetry that night. I didn't even talk to Arlene again until, well, that Tuesday afternoon.

'Arlene,' I said, trying to rope in a scream as she pressed the door convincingly against my foot, 'you must let me in.'

'No,' she said.

'If you don't let me in I won't tell you what I plan to do.'

'Plan to do?'

'You'll never know what I'm going to say.'

There was a long pause and then the door eased open and I limped into her apartment. She retreated decisively to the telephone and, standing stiffly with the receiver in her hand with one finger inserted into presumably the first digit, she said:

'Don't come any nearer.'

'I won't, I won't. But you really should hang up the phone.'

'Absolutely not.'

'If you keep it off the hook too long they'll disconnect the phone.'

Hesitantly she replaced the receiver and sat at one end of the couch (next to the telephone); I seated myself at the other end.

After looking at me blankly for a few minutes (I was preparing my declaration of Platonic love), she suddenly began crying into her hands.

'I can't stop you,' she moaned.

'I'm not trying to do anything!'

'I can't stop you, I know I can't. I'm weak.'

'But I won't touch you.'

'You're too strong, too forceful . . .'

'I won't touch you.'

She looked up.

'You won't?'

'Arlene, I love you . . .'

'I knew it! Oh and I'm so weak.'

'I love you in a way beyond words.'

'You *evil* man.'

'But I have decided [I had become tight-lipped with annoyance at her] that our love must always be Platonic.'

She looked at me with narrowed, resentful eyes: I suppose that it was her equivalent of Jake's penetrating squint, but it made her look as if she were trying to read subtitles on an old Italian movie.

'Platonic?' she asked.

'Yes, it must always be Platonic.'

'Platonic.' She meditated.

'Yes,' I said, 'I want to love you with a love that is beyond words and beyond the mere touch of bodies. With a love of the spirit.'

'But what'll we do?'

'We'll see each other as we have in the past, but now knowing we were meant to be lovers but that fate seventeen years ago made a mistake and gave you to Jake.'

'But what'll we do?' She held the phone to her ear.

'And for the sake of the children we must remain faithful to our spouses and never again give in to our passion.'

'I know, but what will we do?'

'Nothing.'

'Nothing?'

'Er . . . nothing . . . unusual.'

'Won't we see each other?'

'Yes.'

'At least say we love each other?'

'Yes, I suppose so.'

'At least reassure me that you haven't forgotten?'

'Perhaps.'

'Don't you like to touch me?'

'Ah Arlene yes yes I do but for the sake of the children . . .'

'What children?'

'My children.'

'Oh.'

She was sitting on the couch, one arm in her lap and

the other holding the telephone to her right ear. Her low-cut blue cocktail dress which for some reason she was wearing again was making me feel less and less Platonic.

'But . . .' she seemed trying to find the right words. 'How . . . how would your . . . raping me hurt your children?'

'Because – how would my raping you hurt my children?'

'Yes.'

'It would . . . were I to touch the magic of your body again I might well never be able to return to my family. I might have to drag you off with me to start a new life.'

'Oh.' Wide-eyed, she stared at me.

'You're so strange,' she added.

'Love has made me strange.'

'You really love me?'

'I have loved you . . . I have loved you since . . . since I realized how much there was hiding beneath the surface of your outward appearance, how much depth and full-ness there is to your soul.'

'I just don't understand it.'

She put the phone down on the arm of the couch and raised her hands again to her face, but she didn't cry.

'Arlene, I must go now. We must never speak of our love again.'

She looked up at me through her glasses with a new expression – one of fatigue or sadness, I couldn't tell.

'Seventeen years.'

I moved hesitantly away from the couch. She continued to stare at the spot I had vacated.

'Seventeen years.'

'I thank you for letting me speak to you.'

She rose now and took off her glasses and put them next to the telephone. She came to me and put a trembling hand on the side of my arm.

'You may stay,' she said.

87

'No, I must leave.'

'I'll never let you leave your children.'

'I would be too strong. Nothing could stop me.'

She hesitated, her eyes searching my face.

'You're so strange.'

'Arlene, if only . . .'

'Stay.'

'Stay?'

'Please.'

'What for?'

She pulled my head down to hers and gave me her lips and mouth in a kiss.

'I won't be able to control myself,' I said.

'You must try,' she said dreamily. 'I have sworn never to go to bed with you again.'

'You what?'

'I have sworn on my husband's honor never to get into bed with you again.'

'I'll have to rape you.'

She looked up at me sadly.

'Yes, I suppose so.'

Chapter Twelve

During the first month the dice had rather small effect on my life. I used them to choose ways to spend my free time, and to choose alternatives when the normal 'I' didn't particularly care. They decided that Lil and I would see the Edward Albee play rather than the Critic's Award play, that I read work x selected randomly from a huge collection; that I would cease writing my book and begin an article on 'Why Psychoanalysis Usually Fails'; that I would buy General Envelopment Corporation rather than Wonderfilled Industries or Dynamicgo Company; that I would not go to a convention in Chicago; that I would make love to my wife in Kama Sutra position number 23, number 52, number 8, etc.; that I see Arlene, that I don't see Arlene, etc.; that I see her in place x rather than place y and so on.

In short the dice decided things which really didn't matter. Most of my options tended to be from among the great middle way of my tastes and personality. I learned to like to play with the probabilities I gave the various options I would create. In letting the dice choose among possible women I might pursue for a night, for example, I might give Lil one chance in six, some new woman chosen at random two chances in six, and Arlene three chances in six. If I played with two dice the subtleties in probability were much greater. Two principles I always took care to follow. First: never include an option I might be unwilling to fulfill; second: always begin to fulfill the option without thought and without quibble. The secret of the successful dicelife is to be a puppet on the strings of the die.

Six weeks after sinking into Arlene I began letting the dice diddle with my patients: it was a decisive step. I began creating as options that I comment aggressively to a patient as my insights arose; that I restudy some other standard analytic theory and method and adopt it for a specified number of hours with a patient; that I preach to my patients.

Eventually I began also to include as an option that I give my patients assigned psychological exercises much as a coach gives his athletes physical exercises: shy girl assigned to date make-out artist; aggressive bully assigned to pick a fight with nine-eight-pound weakling and purposely lose; studious grind assigned to see five movies, go to two dances and play bridge a minimum of five hours a day all week. Of course, most meaningful assignments involved a breach of the psychiatrist's code of ethics. In telling my patients what to do, I was becoming legally responsible for any ill consequences which might result. Since everything a typical neurotic does eventually has ill consequences, my giving them assignments meant trouble. It meant, in fact, the probable end of my career, a thought which for some reason I found exhilarating. I was like a professional psychiatrist, the very jockstrap of my basic self; I was becoming belly to belly with whim.

In the first few days the dice usually had me express freely my own feelings toward my patients – to break, in effect, the cardinal rule of *all* psychotherapy: do not judge. I began overtly condemning every shabby little weakness I could find in my sniveling, cringing patients. Great gob of God, that was fun. If you remember that for four years I had been acting like a saint, understanding, forgiving and accepting all sorts of human folly, cruelty and nonsense; that I had been thus repressing every normal reactive impulse, you can imagine the joy with which I responded to the dice letting me call my patients sadists, idiots, bastards, sluts, cowards and latent cretins. Joy. I had found another island of joy.

My patients and colleagues didn't seem to appreciate my new roles. From this date my reputation began to decline and my notoriety to rise. My college professor of English at Yale, Orville Boggles, was the first troublemaker.

A big, toothy man with tiny dull eyes, he had been coming to me off and on for six months to overcome a writing block. He hadn't been able to do more than sign his name for three years, and in order to maintain his academic reputation as a scholar he had been reduced to digging out term papers he had written as a sophomore at Michigan State, making small revisions and getting the articles published in quarterlies. Since no one read them past the second paragraph anyway, he hadn't been caught; in fact, on the basis of his impressive list of publications he had received tenure the year before he came to me.

I had been unenthusiastically working on his ambivalent feelings toward his father, his latent homosexuality and his false image of himself, when under the impetus of the dictates of the dice I suddenly found myself one day exploding.

'Boggles,' I said after he arrived one morning (I had always previously addressed him as Professor Boggles), 'Boggles,' I said, 'what say we cut the shit, and get down to basics? Why don't you consciously and publicly decide to quit writing?'

Professor Boggles, who had just lain down and hadn't yet said a word, quivered like a huge sunflower leaf at the first breath of a storm.

'I beg your pardon?'

'Why try to write?'

'It is a pleasure I have long enjoyed – '

'Merde.'

He sat up and looked toward the door as if he expected Batman to break in any moment and rescue him.

'I came to you, not because I am neurotic, but in order to cure a very simple writing block. Now – '

'You are a patient who came with a cold and who is dying of cancer.'

'Now that you seem unable to cure the block you try to convince me not to write. I find this – '

'You find this uncomfortable. But just imagine all the fun you could be having if you gave up trying to publish? Have you looked at a tree in the last six years?'

'I've seen many trees. I want to publish, and I don't know what you think you're doing this morning.'

'I'm letting down the mask, Boggles. I've been playing the psychiatrist game with you, pretending we were after big things like anal stage, object cathexis, latent hetero-sexuality and the like, but I've decided that you can only be cured by being initiated into the mysteries behind the façade, into the straight poop, so to speak. The straight poop, that's symbolism. Boggles, that's – '

'I have no desire to be initiated – '

'I know you don't. None of us do. But I'm letting you pay me thirty-five dollars per hour, and I want to give you your money's worth. First of all, I want you to resign from the university and announce to your department chairman, the board of trustees and to the press that you are going to Africa to re-establish contact with your animal origins.'

'That's nonsense!'

'Of course it is. That's the point. Think of the publicity you'll get: "Yale professor resigns to seek Truth." It'll get a lot more play than your last article in the *Rhode Island Quarterly* on "Henry James and the London Bus Service." Moreover – '

'But why Africa?'

'Because it has nothing to do with literature, academic advancement and full professorships. You won't be able to fool yourself that you're gathering material for an article. Spend a year in the Congo, try to get involved with a revolutionary group or a counter-revolutionary group, shoot a few people, familiarize yourself with the native drugs, let yourself get seduced by whatever comes along, male, female, animal, vegetable, mineral. After that, if you still feel you want to write about Henry James for the quarterlies, I'll try to help you.'

He was sitting on the edge of the couch looking at me with nervous dignity. He said, 'But why should you want me to stop wanting to write?'

'Because as you are now, Boggles, and have been for forty-three years, you're a dead loss. Absolutely. I don't mean to sound critical, but absolutely. Deep down inside you know it, your colleagues know it and at all levels I know it. We've got to change you completely to make you worth taking money from. Normally I'd recommend that you have an affair with a student, but with your personality the only students who might open up for you would be worse off than you and no help.'

Boggles had stood up but I went serenely on.

'What you need is a more extensive personal experience with cruelty, with suffering, hunger, fear, sex. Once you've experienced more fully these basics there might be some hope of a major breakthrough. Until then none.'

Old Boggles had his overcoat on now and with a toothy grimace was backing toward the door.

'Good day, Dr Rhinehart, I hope you're better soon,' he said.

'And a good day to you, Boggles. I wish I could hope the same for you, but unless you get captured by the Congolese rebels, or get sick in the jungle for eight months or become a Kurtzian ivory trader, I'm afraid there's not much hope.'

I rose from behind my desk to shake hands with him, but he backed out the door. Six days later I got a polite letter from the president of the American Association of Practicing Psychiatrists (AAPP) noting that a patient of mine, a Dr Orville Boggles of Yale, had paranoic hallucinations about me and had sent a long, nasty, highly literary complaint to the AAPP about my behavior. I sent a note to President Weinstein thanking him for his understanding and a note to Boggles suggesting that the length of his letter to the AAPP indicated progress vis-à-vis his writing block. I also gave him permission to try to have his letter published in the *South Dakota Quarterly Review Journal*.

Chapter Thirteen

'Jenkins,' I said one morning to the masochist Milquetoast of Madison Avenue, 'have you ever considered rape?'

'I don't understand,' he said.

'Forced carnal knowledge.'

'I . . . don't understand how you mean that I should consider it.'

'Have you ever daydreamed of killing someone or of raping someone?'

'No. No, I never have. I feel almost no aggression toward anyone.' He paused. 'Except myself.'

'I was afraid of that, Jenkins, that's why we'd better give serious consideration to rape, theft or murder.'

Jenkins lay neatly and quietly on the couch through this whole interview, not once raising his voice or stirring a muscle.

'You . . . you mean daydream about such actions?' he asked.

'I mean commit them. As it is, Jenkins, you're becoming just another dirty old man, aren't you?'

'P-p-pardon?'

'Spend most of your time lying on your crumb-filled bed reading porno and fantasizing about lovely girls who need you to save them. After they've narrowly missed being crushed by the landslide, or cut in two by the cultivator, or stabbed by the lunatic or burnt by the fire, you rescue them and they give you a spiritual kiss on the fingertips, right? But when do you reach a climax, Mr Jenkins?'

'I . . . I don't know what . . . I don't understand?'

'Does the final pleasure come when you're comforting the rescued girl or when the flames are licking at her face, the knife scraping along her veins, the cultivator about to mash her potatoes . . .? When?'

'But I want to help people. I feel no aggression. Ever.'

'Look, Jenkins, I'm sated with your passivity, your day-dreaming. Haven't you ever done anything?'

'No opportunity has ever – '

'Have you ever hurt another human?'

'I can't. I don't want to. I want to save – '

'First you've got to save yourself and that you can only do by breaking your inertia. I'm giving you an assignment for our Friday session. Will you do it for me?'

'I don't know. I don't want to hurt people. My whole soul is based on that principle.'

'I know it is. I know it is, and your soul's sick, remember? That's why you're here.'

'Please, I don't want to rape any – '

'You've noticed I have a new receptionist. I mean a second one?' [She was a middle-aged call girl I had hired expressly to date Mr Jenkins.]

'Er, yes, I have.'

'She's lovely, isn't she?'

'Yes, she is.'

'And she's a nice person, too.'

'Yes,' he said.

'I want you to rape her.'

'Oh no, no, I, no, it would not be a good idea.'

'All right then, would you like to date her?'

'But . . . is it ethical?'

'What are you planning to do to her?'

'I mean . . . she's your receptionist . . . I thought – '

'Not at all. Her private life is her own business. [It certainly was.] I want you to date her. Tonight. Take her to dinner and invite her back to your apartment and see what happens. If you get the urge to rape her, go ahead. Tell her it's part of your therapy.'

'Oh, no, no, I'd never want to do anything to hurt her. She seems such a lovely person.'

'She is, which makes her all the more rapable. But have it your own way. Just do your best to feel aggression.'

'Do you really think it might help if I got a little aggressive?'

'Absolutely. Change your whole life. With hard work you might even make it to murder. But don't brood if at first all you can do is swear under your breath at pedestrians.' I stood up. 'Now go. You'll need a couple of minutes to wheedle Rita into accepting a date.'

It took him twenty, despite Rita's trying to say 'yes' from the moment he told her his name. After three and a half weeks of Jenkins-style courting he finally managed to seduce her in the front seat of his Volkswagen, much to the relief of all concerned. To the further relief of the principals, they shifted to Jenkins's apartment for further indoor work. The only evidence I was able to garner that Jenkins was trying to express aggression was that once he accidentally bumped her nose with his elbow and didn't say he was sorry. Rita tried the old game of 'Oh, you're so masterful, hit me,' but Jenkins responded by assuring her that no matter how masterful he was he would never hit anyone. She urged him to bite her breasts, but he said something about having weak gums. She tried to irritate him into anger by using her body to arouse him and then deny the desires she had aroused, but Jenkins sulked until she gave in.

Meanwhile he was trying every trick in the masochist's trade to try to make Rita break off with him. He stood her up on two occasions (Rita sent a bill for her time), accidentally broke her wristwatch (I got the bill) and as a lover usually had his orgasm when she was least expecting

97

it and in the middle of a yawn. Nevertheless, Rita clung lovingly – three hundred dollars a week – on.

At the end of a month of solid success with her, Jenkins was definitely more comfortable with women; he even flirted for five minutes with Miss Reingold. But he was also perilously close to a total nervous breakdown. Being unable to contract a venereal disease, make Rita pregnant, infuriate her, cause her to leave him or fail in any other obvious way, he was desperate. Of course, he'd compensated by accelerating the rate of failure in all other areas of his life. Twice he lost his wallet. He left the water in the bathtub running while he was out and flooded his apartment. Finally, one day he told me he'd lost so much money on the stock market since taking over his own investing, that he'd have to drop therapy.

I urged him to continue, but that afternoon he managed to get hit by a bulldozer while watching some construction and was hospitalized for six weeks. A few months later the dice told me to send him a bill for Rita's services and, I regret to report, he promptly paid it. I've tentatively listed his case as a failure.

Other cases didn't work out too well either. With a woman plagued by compulsive promiscuity I tried the William James method number three for breaking habits: oversatiation. I convinced her to work at a busy Brooklyn brothel for a week, figuring that would be enough to drive anyone to chastity, but she stayed a month. With the money she earned she hired one of her male customers to accompany her on a vacation to Puerto Vallarta. I haven't seen her since, but have tentatively listed her case as a failure also.

My analytic sessions became role-playing sessions without the dice. But instead of restricting such role playing to drama and play as in Moreno-like drama therapy, I restricted it to real life. Everything had to be done with real people in real life.

In most cases over the next five months I assigned my patients to quit their jobs, leave their spouses, give up their hobbies, habits and homes, alter their religions, upset their sleeping, eating, copulation, thinking habits: in brief, to rediscover their unexpressed desires; to achieve their unfulfilled potential. But all this without telling them about the dice.

Without introducing the patients to the use of the dice as in my later dice therapy, the results, as you have begun to see, were generally disastrous. In addition to two lawsuits, one patient committed suicide (thirty-five dollars an hour out of the window), one was arrested for leading to the delinquency of a minor, and a last disappeared at sea in a sailing canoe on his way to Tahiti. On the other hand, I had a few distinct successes.

One man, a highly paid advertising executive, gave up his job and family and joined the Peace Corps, spent two years in Peru, wrote a book on faking land reform in underdeveloped countries, a book highly praised by everyone except the governments of Peru and the United States, and is now living in a cabin in Tennessee writing a book on the effects of advertising on underdeveloped minds. Whenever he's in New York he drops in to suggest I write a book about the underdeveloped psyches of psychiatrists.

My other successes were less obvious and immediate.

There was Linda Reichman, for example. She was a slender, young rich girl who had spent her last four years living in Greenwich Village doing all the things rich, emancipated girls think they're expected to do in Green- wich Village. In four weeks of treatment prior to my own emancipation, I had learned that this was her third analysis, that she loved to talk about herself, particularly

99

her promiscuity, with indifference to and cruelty toward men, and their stupid ineffectual efforts to hurt her. Her monologues were occasionally flooded by literary, philosophical and Freudian allusions and as abruptly empty of them. Each session she usually managed to say something intended to shock my bourgeois respectability.

It was only three weeks after letting the dice dictate anarchy that I had a rather remarkable session with her. She'd come in even more keyed up than usual, swivel-hipped her rather swivelable hips across the room and flopped aggressively onto the couch. Much to my surprise she didn't say a thing for three minutes; for her, an all-time record. Finally, with an edge to her voice, she said: 'I get so sick and tired of this . . . shit. [Pause] I don't know why I come here. [Pause] You're about as much help as a chiropractor. Christ, what I'd give to meet a MAN someday. I meet nothing but . . . ball-less masturbators. [Pause] What a . . . stupid world it is. How do people get through their crumby lives? I've got money, brains, sex – I'm bored stiff. What keeps all those little clods without *anything*, what keeps all those little clods *going*? [Pause] I'd like to blast the whole thing . . . fucking city to pieces. [Long pause.]

'I spent the weekend with Curt Rollins. For your info, he's just published a novel that the *Partisan Review* calls – and I quote – "as stunningly poetic a piece of fiction as has appeared in years." Unquote. [Pause] He's got talent. His prose is like lightning: cutting, darting, brilliant; he's a Joyce with the energy of Henry Miller. [Pause] He's working on a new novel about fifteen minutes in the life of a young boy who's just lost his father. Fifteen minutes – a whole novel. Curt's cute, too. Most girls throw themselves at him. [Pause] He needs money. [Pause] It's funny, he doesn't seem to like sex much. Wham-bam,

100

back to the old writing board. Wham-bam. [Pause] He liked the way I sucked him off though. But . . .

'I'd like to chop his hands off. Chop, chop. Then he could dictate his novel to me. [Pause] Chop his hands off: I suppose that means I want to castrate him. Could be. I don't think it would bother him much. I think he'd consider it gave him more time for his precious writing, his all-important fifteen minutes in the life of a little prick. [Pause] "Stunning novel" – Jesus, it had the grace of late Herman Melville and the power of a dying Emily Dickinson. You know what it was about? A sensitive young man who discovers that his mother is having an affair with the man that's teaching him to love poetry. Sensitive young man despairs. "Oh Shelley, why has thou forsaken me?" [Pause] He's another ball-less masturbator. [Pause]

'You sure are quiet today. Can't you even throw in a few uh-huhs or yesses? I'm paying you forty bucks an hour, remember? For that I should get at least two or three yesses a minute.'

'I don't feel like it today.'

'You don't feel like it today? Who cares? You think I feel like spilling out my garbage three days a week? Come on, Dr Rhinehart, you've gotta like it. The world is built on the principle that all humans must eat shit regardless of taste. Come on, speak up. Act like a psychiatrist. Let's hear that faithful echo.'

'Today I'd like to hear what you'd like to do if you could recreate the world to suit your own . . . highest dreams.'

'Cut the crap. I'd turn it into a great big testicle, what else?'

[Pause] [Longer pause]

'I'd . . . I'd eliminate all the human beings first . . . except . . . eh . . . maybe for a few. I'd destroy everything man has ever made, EVERYTHING, and I'd put – all

101

the animals would still be there – No. No, they wouldn't. I'd eliminate all of them too. There'd be grass though, and flowers. [Pause]

'I can't picture the humans. [Pause] I can't even picture me. I must have got wiped out. Ha! Woo. My highest dream is of an empty world. Boy, that's something. The little lays at Remo's would love that. But where are they in this world of mine? They're gone too. An empty, empty, empty world.'

'Can you imagine a human being that you would like?'

'Look, Doctor, I detest humans. I know it. Swift detested them, Mark Twain detested them. I'm in good company. It takes clods to appreciate clods, herd to appreciate herd. Whatever I am, I've got enough on the ball to realize that the best of humans is either weak or a phoney. You too, obviously. In fact, you psychiatrists are the biggest phonies of all.'

'Why do you say that?'

'Your phoney code of ethics. You hide behind it. I've sat here for four weeks telling you about my stupid, cruel, promiscuous, senseless behavior and you sit back there nodding away like a puppet and agreeing with everything I say. I've twitched my butt at you, flashed a little thigh, and you pretend you don't know what I'm doing. You acknowledge nothing except what I put into words. All right; I'd like to feel your prick. [Pause] And now the good doctor will say with his quiet asinine voice, "You say you'd like to feel my prick," and I'll say, "Yes, it all goes back to when I was three years old and my father . . ." and you'll say, "You feel the desire to feel my prick goes back . . ." and we'll both go right on acting *as if the words didn't count*.'

Miss Reichman briefly paused and then raised herself on her elbows and without looking at me, spat, clearly and profusely, in a high arc, onto the rug in front of my desk.

'I don't blame you. I've been acting like an automaton. Or, more concretely, an ass.'

Miss Reichman sat up on the couch and turned from the waist to stare at me.

'*What* did *you* say?'

'You feel you don't know what I said?' But as I said this I put on a mock psychiatrist face and tried to grin intimately.

'Holy shit, there's a human being in there after all. [Pause] Well. Say something else. I've never heard you say anything before.'

'Well, Linda, I'd say it was time to end non-directive therapy. Time you heard some of my feelings about you. Right?'

'That's what I just said.'

'First, I think we'd better acknowledge that you're outstandingly conceited. Second, that sexually you may offer much less than many women, since you are thin, with, to judge by superficial appearances only, a smallish bosom necessitating falsies [she sneered], and you probably bring the male racing to a climax before he's got his fly totally unzipped. Thirdly, that intellectually you are extremely limited in the depth and breadth of your reading and understanding. In summation, that as human beings go you are mediocre in all respects except in the quantity of your fortune. The number of men you've slept with and who've proposed as well as propositioned, is a reflection of the openness of your legs and of your wallet, not of your personality.'

Her sneer had expanded until it had nowhere else to go on her face and so spread to her shoulders and back, which writhed theatrically away from me in disdain. By the time I finished, her face was flushed and she spoke with an exaggerated slowness and serenity.

'Oh poor poor Linda. Only big Lukie Rhinehart can save cesspool soul from hardening into concrete shit. [She abruptly changed pace] You conceited bastard. Who do you think you are sounding off about me? You don't know me at all. I haven't told you anything about myself except a few sensational superficialities. And you judge me by these.'

'Do you want to show me your breasts?'

'Fuck you.'

'Do you have some essays, or stories or poems, or paintings that you can show me?'

'You can't judge a person by measurements or by essays. When I make love to a man they don't forget it. They know they've had a woman, and not some fluffed-up iceberg. And you'll hide behind your precious ethics and feel superior because all you see is the surface.'

'What other good qualities do you have?'

'I call a spade a spade. I know. I'm not perfect and I say so, and I've learned that you psychiatrists are priggish little voyeurs and I tell you, and that's why you all end up attacking me. You can't stand the truth.'

'My ethics kept me from making love to you?'

'Yes, unless you're a fairy, like another headshrinker I knew.'

'Let me then formally announce that in my future relations with you I will not seek to maintain the traditional patient–doctor relationship and I will *not* abide by the standard of ethics set down in the code of the American Association of Practicing Psychiatrists. From now on I shall respond to you as human to human. As psychiatrist human I will advise you, but no more. How's that?'

Linda shifted her feet to the floor and looked over at

104

me with a slow smile, meant to suggest sexiness? She was, in fact, reasonably sexy. She was slender, clear-complexioned, full-lipped. As long as she had been my patient, however, I had not responded to her sexually one millimeter, or to any other female patient in five years, despite writhings, declarations, propositions, strippings and attempted rapes – all of which had occurred during one session or another. But the doctor–patient relationship froze my sexual awareness as completely as doing fifty push-ups under a cold shower. Looking at Linda Reichman smile and perceptibly arch her back and project her (true or false?) bosom, I felt my loins, for the first time in my analytic history, respond.

Her smile slowly curled into a sneer.

'It's better than you *were*, but that's not saying much.'

'I thought you wanted to feel my prick.'

'I can't be bothered.'

'In that case, let's get back to you. Lie down again and let your mind go.'

'What do you mean, lie down again. You just said you were going to be human. Humans don't talk to each other with their backs to each other.'

'True. So go ahead, we'll talk . . . eyeball to eyeball.'

She looked at me again and her eyes narrowed slightly and her upper lip twitched twice. She stood up and faced me. The light from my desk picked up a light perspiration on her face, which revealed this time no suggestive smile – although one may have been intended – but rather a tense grimace. She roved slightly toward me, unbuttoning her skirt at the side as she approached.

'I think maybe it would be good for both of us – if we got to know each other physically. Don't you?'

She came to the chair and let her skirt fall to the floor. Her half-slip must have gone with it. She had on white silk bikini-panties but no stockings. Sitting down in my

105

lap (the chair tipped back another three inches with an undignified squeak), her eyes half-closed, she looked up into my face and said drowsily, 'Don't you?'

Frankly, the answer was yes. I had a fine erection, my pulse was forty percent, my loins were being activated by all the requisite hormones and my mind, as nature intended it in such cases, was functioning vaguely and without energy. Her lips and tongue came wetly against and into my mouth, her fingers along my neck and into my hair. She was role-playing Brigitte Bardot and I was responding accordingly. After a prolonged, satisfactory kiss, she stood up, and with a set, drowsy, mechanical half-smile removed, item by item, her blouse, bra (she hadn't needed falsies), bracelet, wristwatch and panties.

Since I continued to sit with a blissfully unplanned and idiotic expression, she hesitated, and sensed that somewhere about now was my cue to embrace her passionately, carry her to the couch and consummate our union. I decided to miss the cue. After this brief hesitation (her now wet upper lip twitched once), she knelt down beside me and fingered my fly. She undid the belt, a hook and lowered the zipper. Since I didn't move one millimeter (voluntarily) she had trouble extricating her desired object from my boxer undershorts. When she had succeeded in freeing him from his cage, he stood with dignified stiffness, trembling slightly, like a young scholar about to have a doctoral hood lowered over his head. (The rest of me was cold and immobile as the code of ethics of AAPP encourages us.) She leaned forward to put her mouth over it.

'Did you ever see the movie, *The Treasure of Sierra Madre*?' I asked.

She stopped, startled, then closing her eyes completely, drew my penis into her mouth.

She did what intelligent women do in such cases.

Although the warmth of her mouth and the pressure of her tongue produced predictable feelings of euphoria, I found I was not much mentally excited by what was happening. That mad scientist dice man was looking at everything too hard.

After what began to seem like an embarrassingly long time (I sat mute, dignified, professional through it all), she rose up and whispered, 'Take off your clothes and come.' She moved nicely to the couch and lay down on her stomach with her face to the wall.

I felt that if I sat immobile any longer she would snap out of it and become angry, get dressed and demand her money back. I had seen her in two roles, sex kitten and intellectual bitch. Was there some sort of third Linda? I walked over (my left hand pants clutching) to the couch and sat down. Linda's white, nude body looked cold and babyish against the formal brown leather. Her face was turned away but my weight on the side of the couch let her know I had arrived.

Whatever limitations Linda might have as a human being seemed adequately compensated for by a round and apparently firm posterior. Her instinct – or probably her well-learned habit – of stuffing her buttocks at an obviously aroused man seemed correct. My hand actually arrived within two and one-quarter inches of that flesh before the mad scientist in the London fog got the message through.

'Roll over,' I said. (Get her best weapon aimed elsewhere.)

She rolled slowly over, reached up two white arms and pulled my neck down until our mouths met. She began to groan authoritatively. She pressed first her mouth hard against mine and then, somehow getting me to lift my legs up on the couch beside hers, pressed her abdomen hard into mine. She tongued, writhed, groaned and clutched

107

with intelligent abandon. I just lay, wondering not too acutely what to do.

Apparently I had missed another cue, because she broke our kiss and pushed me slightly away. For an instant I thought she might be abandoning her role, but her half-closed eyes and twisted mouth told me otherwise. She had parted her legs and was reaching for potential posterity.

'Linda,' I said quietly. (No nonsense about movies this time.) 'Linda,' I said again. One of her hands was playing Virgil to my Dante and trying to lead him into the underworld, but I held Dante back. 'Linda,' I said a third time.

'Put it in,' she said.

'Linda, wait a minute.'

'What's the matter, put it in.' She opened her eyes and stared up, not seeming to recognize me.

'Linda, I've got my period.'

Now why I said that Freud certainly knows, but searching for absurdity I had said it, and, realizing its psychoanalytic meaning, I felt quite shamed.

Linda either hadn't read Freud or didn't care; she was, I saw regretfully, on the verge of passing from Bardot to bitch without any intermediate third Linda.

She blinked once, started to say something which came out as a snort, twitched her upper lip three, four times, half-closed her eyes again, groaned and said, 'Oh come, please come into me, now. Now.'

Although her hands weren't pulling, my stallion responded to those words with enthusiasm and had galloped to within one and one-eighth inches of the valley of the stars when the mad scientist pulled the reins.

'Linda, there's something I'd like you to do, first,' I said. (What? What? For God's sake, what?) This was, in fact, the perfect statement: she couldn't tell whether it was something sexual I wanted her to do, in which case she could revel in her Bardot role, or something impractical having to do with my being a psychiatrist. Curiosity, stronger than Bardot or bitch, looked out of fully open eyes.

'What?' she asked.

'Lie here just as you are without moving, and close your eyes.'

She looked at me – our bodies were separated by only three or four inches and one of her hands was still pulling me toward the great melting pot – and again she was neither Bardot nor bitch. When she sighed, let go of me and closed her eyes, I eased myself to a seat on the edge of the couch again.

'Try to relax,' I said.

Her eyes shot open and her head jerked up like a doll's.

'What the hell do I want to relax for?'

'Please, for me, do this . . . one thing. Lie there in your full beauty and let your arms, legs, face, everything relax. Please.'

'What for? You're not relaxed.' And she laughed coldly at my denied, deprived, but still unbending middle leg.

'Please, Linda, I want you. I want to make love to you, but first I want to caress you and kiss you and I want you to receive my love without – with complete relaxation. I know it's impossible, so I'll suggest a way you might do it. I want you to think of a little girl picking flowers in a field. Can you do that?'

Bitch glared up at me.

'Why?'

'If you do it, you may – if you follow my instructions you may be in for a surprise. If I come into you now, neither of us will learn anything.' I brought my face dramatically down to within a few inches of hers. 'A little girl picking flowers in a totally lush, green, beautiful but deserted field. Do you see that?'

She glared a moment longer, then lowered her head to the couch and closed her legs together. Two or three minutes passed. Very distantly I could hear Miss Reingold's typewriter tit-tatting away.

'I see a little kid picking tiger lilies near a swamp.'

'Is the little girl a pretty girl?'

[Pause]

'Yeah, she's pretty.'

'Parents – what are this little girl's parents like?'

'There are little field daisies too, and lilac bushes.'

[Pause]

'The parents are bastards. They beat the kid . . . the little girl. They buy long necklaces and they whip her with them. They tie her up with linked bracelets. They give her poison candy which makes her sick, and then they force her to drink her own vomit. They never let the girl be alone. Whenever she goes to the fields, where she is now, they beat her when she comes home.'

(I didn't say a word, but the impulse to say 'and they beat her when she comes home' had the strength of Hercules.) There was a long pause.

'They beat her with books. They hit her on the head again and again with books. They stick pins and pencils in her. And tacks. When they're done with her they throw her in the cellar.'

Linda was not relaxed; she wasn't crying; she seemed her bitchy self essentially, complaining against the parents but not able to feel sorry for the little girl. She felt only bitterness.

'Look very closely at the little girl in the fields, Linda. Look very closely at her. [Pause] The little girl – ?' [Pause]

'The little girl . . . is crying.'

110

'Why is the little . . . does she have . . . does the girl have any flowers?'

'Yes, she has . . . It's a rose, a white rose. I don't know where . . .'

[Pause]

'What is she . . . how does she feel toward the white rose?'

'. . . The white rose is the only . . . thing in the world which she can talk to, the only thing that . . . loves her . . . She holds the flower in front of her eyes by the stem and she talks to it and . . . no . . . she doesn't even hold it. It floats to her . . . like magic, but she never, not once ever, touches it, and she never kisses it. She looks at it and it sees her and in those moments . . . in those moments . . . the little girl . . . is happy. The white rose, with the white rose . . . she is happy.'

After another minute Linda's eyes blinked open. She looked over at me, at my wilted penis, at the walls, the ceiling. At the ceiling. A buzzer sounded for what I now realized may have been the third or fourth time and I started.

'The hour's up.' she said dazedly and then added: 'What a funny, stupid story,' but without bitterness, dreamily.

Except for the silent restoration of our clothing, the session was over.

111

Chapter Fourteen

During these first months of diceliving I never consciously decided to let the dice take over my whole life or to aim at becoming an organism whose every act was determined by the dice. The thought would have frightened me then. I tended to restrict my options so that Lil and my colleagues wouldn't begin to suspect that I was into anything slightly unorthodox. I kept my shimmering green cubes hidden carefully from everyone, consulting them surreptitiously when necessary. But I found myself adapting quickly to following the die's sporadic whims. I might resent a particular command, but like a well-oiled automaton I went and did the job.

The dice sent me to bars scattered throughout the city to sit, sip, listen, chat. They picked out strangers to whom I was sent to talk. They chose roles that I played with these strangers. I would be a veteran outfielder with the Detroit Tigers in town for a Yankee series (Bronx bar), English reporter with the *Guardian* (the Barbizon Plaza), playwright homosexual, alcoholic college professor, escaped criminal and so on. The dice determined that I try to seduce stranger chosen at random from the phone book of Brooklyn (actually Mrs Anna Maria Sploglio was the lucky lady and she totally repulsed me. Thank God); that I try to borrow ten dollars from stranger 'X' (another failure); that I give twenty dollars to stranger 'Y' (he threatened to call the police, then took the money and ran, not walked, away). In bars, restaurants, theaters, taxis, stores – whenever out of sight of those who knew me – I was soon never myself, my old 'normal self.' I went bowling. I signed up at Vic Tanny's to muscle my middle. I went to concerts, baseball games, sit-ins, open parties; anything and everything that I had never done, I now created as options, and the dice threw me from one to the other – and rarely the same man from day to day.

New places and new roles forced me into acute awareness of how others were responding to me. When a human is being himself, flowing with his inner nature, wearing his natural appropriate masks, integrated with his environment, he is normally unaware of subtleties in another's behavior. Only if the other person breaks a conventional pattern is awareness stimulated. However, breaking my established patterns was threatening to my deeply ingrained selves and pricked me to a level of consciousness which is unusual, unusual since the whole instinct of human behavior is to find environments congenial to the relaxation of consciousness. By creating problems for myself I created thought.

I also created problems.

Although I tried to act so I would always give Lil a 'rational' explanation for my eccentricities, I let the dice increasingly determine what kind of a father and husband I would be, especially during the three weeks Lil, Larry, Evie and I (for three-day weekends) spent in our rented farmhouse on eastern Long Island.

Now historically, my friends, I had been a withdrawn, somewhat absentee father. My contacts with my two children had consisted primarily of: (a) yelling at them to stop yelling when I was on the telephone in the living room; (b) yelling at them to go play someplace else when I wanted to make love to Lil during the day; (c) yelling at them to obey their Mommy when they were most blatantly disobeying their Mommy; (d) yelling at Larry for being stupid when trying to do math homework.

There were times when I would not yell at them, it is

true. Whenever I was daydreaming about something ('Rhinehart Discovers Missing Link in Freudian Theory!' 'Sophia Loren to Divorce Ponti for NY Psychiatrist,' 'Incredible Stock Market Coup by MD Amateur'), or thinking about something (how to discover missing link, win Miss Loren, make a coup) I would talk calmly to the children about whatever it was they felt like talking about ('That's a beautiful painting, Larry, especially the chimney.' Lil 'That's a ballistic missile.'), and even, upon occasion, play with them. ('Bam bam, I got you, Daddy.' I collapse to the floor. 'Oh, Daddy, you're only *wounded*.')

I liked my kids but primarily as potential Jungs, Adlers and Anna Freuds to my Sigmund. I was much too wrapped up in being a great psychiatrist to compete in the game of being a father. My paternal behavior manifested flaws.

Among the alternatives which I gave the dice to consider were some which expressed the fond father buried deep within, and others which gave full rein to the not so benevolent despot.

On the one hand the dice twice determined that I pay extra attention to my children, that I spend a minimum of five hours a day with them for each of three days. (Such devotion! Such sacrifice! Mothers of the world, what would you give to spend *only* five hours a day with your children?)

In September one day, after breakfast in the big old kitchen with white cupboards and built-in sunshine in the big old farmhouse on the big plot surrounded by big trees and bright, flowing fields of poison ivy, I asked the children what they wanted to do that day.

Larry eyed me from his seat by the toaster. He had short red pants, white (in places) T-shirt, bare feet, built-

114

in scratches and scabs on both chubby legs and bleached yellow hair hiding most of his suspicious frown.

'Play,' he answered.

'Play what?'

'I already took out the garbage yesterday.'

'I'd like to play with you today. What do you plan to do?'

From her seat Evie looked at Larry wondering what they were going to do.

'You want to play with us?'

'Yes.'

'You won't hog the dump truck?'

'No. I'll let you be the complete boss.'

'You will?'

'Yep.'

'Hooray, let's go play in the sand.'

The sand was actually the farmer's plowed field, which rectangled the farmhouse on three and a half sides. There, winding in an intricate maze among the green explosions of cabbage, was a road system to put Robert Moses to shame. For an hour I traveled in a 1963 pickup truck (Tonka, 00 h.p., .002 c.c. engine, needed new paint job) over these roads. There was frequent criticism that I wrecked too many secondary roads while maneuvering my bulk down tertiary roads, and that tunnels that had been standing for years through cyclones and hurricanes (three and a half days through one brief shower) had collapsed under the weight of my one errant elbow. Otherwise the children enjoyed my presence, and I enjoyed the earth and them. Children are really quite nice once you get to know them.

They're more than nice.

'Daddy,' Larry said to me later that day when we were lying in the sand watching the surf of the Atlantic come rolling onto Westhampton Beach, 'why does the ocean make waves?'

I considered my knowledge of oceans, tides and such, and decided on

'Wind.'

'But sometimes the wind doesn't blow, but the ocean always makes waves.'

'It's the god of the sea breathing.'

This time he considered.

'Breathing what?' he asked.

'Breathing water. In and out, in and out.'

'Where?'

'In the middle of the ocean.'

'How big is he?'

'One mile tall and as fat and muscley as Daddy.'

'Don't ships bump his head?'

'Sometimes. Then he makes hurricanes. That's what's called an "angry sea".'

'Daddy, why don't you play with us more?'

It was like dropping a heavy sea anchor into my stomach. The phrase 'I'm too busy' came into my mind and I flushed with shame. 'I'd like to but – ' entered and the flush got deeper.

'I don't know,' I said and huffed down to the surf and bulldozed my way in. By floating on my back just beyond the breakers all I could see was the sky, rising and falling.

Both the dice and my own desires permitted me to be with the children more in August and September. The dice once dictated that I take them to a Coney Island Amusement Park for a day, and I look back on that afternoon as one of the two or three absolute islands of joy in my life.

I brought toys home to them spontaneously a couple of times and their gratitude at this unexplained, unprecedented gift of the god was almost enough to make me give up psychiatry and the dice and devote myself to fulltime fatherhood. The third time I tried it, Larry's crane wouldn't work and the children fought solidly for three days over the other one. I considered vacationing in Alaska, the Sahara, the Amazon, anywhere, but *alone*.

The dice made me a very unreliable disciplinarian. They willed that in the first two weeks in September I should never yell, scold or punish the children for anything. Never had the house been so quiet and peaceful for so long. In the last week of September (school had begun) the dice ordered that I be an absolute dictator regarding homework, table manners, noise, neatness and *respect*. Fifteen hard spanks were to be administered for all transgressions. By the sixth day of my trying to enforce my standards Lil, the maid and the children locked themselves in the playroom and refused to let me enter. When Lil chastised me for my sudden week-long spasm of tyranny I explained that I'd been overwhelmed by a speech by Spiro Agnew on the evils of permissiveness.

Events like these strained, to say the least, my relations with Lil. One does not live seven years with a person – an intelligent, sensitive person who (periodically) shows you great affection – without forming certain emotional ties. You do not father two handsome children by her without strengthening that bond.

Lil and I had met and mated when we were both twenty-five. We formed a deep, irrational, obviously neurotic need for one another: love – one of society's many socially accepted forms of madness. We got married: society's solution to loneliness, lust and laundry. We soon discovered that there is absolutely nothing wrong with being married which being single can't cure. Or so, for a while, it seemed to us.

I was in medical school earning nothing, and Lil, the

117

spoiled daughter of Peter Daupmann, successful real estate man, went to work to support me. Lil, sole support of Lucius Rhinehart, MD to be, became pregnant. Lucius, practical, firm (except at confining sperm to their quarters), urged abortion. Lil, sensitive, loving, female, urged child. Practical man sulked. Female fed foetus, foetus left female: handsome son Lawrence: happiness, pride, poverty. After two months, spoiled child Lil works again for dedicated, practical, impoverished Luke, MD (but under analysis and interning and not practicing). Lil soon develops healthy resentment of work, poverty and dedicated, practical MD. Our bond to each other grows, but the intense pleasurable passion of yesteryear diminishes.

In brief, as the alert reader has concluded long before this, we were *typically* married. We had happy moments which we could share with no one; we had our insider jokes; we had our warm, sensual, sexual love as we had our mutual concern for (well, Lil anyway), interest in and pride in our children; and we had our two increasingly frustrated, isolated private selves. The aspirations we had for these selves did not find fulfillment in marriage, and all the twisting and writhing on the bed together couldn't erase this fact, although our very dissatisfaction united us.

Now the dice treated everything and everyone as objects and forced me to do the same. The emotions I was to feel for all things were determined by the dice and not by the intrinsic relationship between me and the person or thing. Love I saw as an irrational, arbitrary binding relationship to another object. It was compulsive. It was an important part of the historical self. It must be destroyed. Lillian must become an object: an object of as little intrinsic effect upon or interest for me as . . . Nora Hammerhill (name picked at random from Manhattan phone book). Impossible, you say? Perhaps. But if a human being can be changed, this most basic of relationships must be susceptible to alteration. So I tried.

The dice sometimes refused to cooperate. They commanded me to show her concern and generosity. They bought her the first piece of jewelry I'd given her in six years. She accused me of infidelity. Reassured, she was very pleased. The dice sent us to three dramas on three consecutive nights (I had averaged three plays a year, two of which were inevitably musicals with record short runs); we both felt cultured, avant-garde, unphilistine. We swore we'd see a play a week all year. The dice said otherwise.

The dice one week requested that I give in to her every whim. Although she twice called me spineless and at the end of the week seemed disgusted with my lack of authority, I found myself listening and responding to her at times where normally I wouldn't have known she existed, and at times I touched her with my thoughtfulness.

Lil even enjoyed the dice's sudden passion for awkward sexual positions, although when the dice ordered me to penetrate her from thirteen distinctly different positions before reaching my climax, she became quite angry as I was trying to maneuver her into position eleven. When she wondered why I was getting so many strange whims these days, I suggested that perhaps I was pregnant.

But the medium is the message, and the dice decisions, no matter how pleasant they might sometimes be to Lil or Arlene or others, acted to separate me from people. Sexual dice decisions were particularly effective in destroying natural intimacy (try convincing a woman that one awkward sexual position is all that will satisfy you when she feels otherwise). Such dice commands obviously involved my being able to manipulate (both psychologically *and* physically) the woman as well as myself. They once perversely chose that 'I not partake of sexual

119

intercourse for one week with any woman,' and thus caused considerable internal conflict; a serious matter of conscience and principle: precisely what was denoted by 'sexual intercourse'?

By the end of the first week I was desperate to know: did the dice intend to leave me free to participate in everything except penetration? Or except ejaculation? Deep down inside had the dice intended me to steer clear of all sexual activity?

Whatever the die's intentions, on the seventh day I found myself on a couch, dressed conservatively in a T-shirt and two socks, beside Arlene Ecstein, dressed fetchingly in a lovely brassiere dangling around her waist, one stocking rolled up to midshin, two bracelets, one earring and one pair of panties modestly covering her left ankle. As part of her iron-clad code she had not been in a bed with me since D-Day, but her iron-clad code had said nothing about cars, floors, chairs or couches, and the various parts of her body were being used against the various parts of mine with unmistakable intentions. Since I had permitted her caresses, indeed abetted them, I realized that I had reached the point when if she said, 'Come into me,' and I said, 'I don't feel like it,' she'd laugh me onto the rug. The decibel count of her groans indicated that in thirty-five seconds she would request my physical presence in her playroom.

To postpone the seemingly unavoidable act I shifted around and placed my head between her legs and began articulate oral communication. Her response was equally articulate and her message was well-received. However, I knew that Arlene found such communication, while pleasant, a relatively poor substitute for orthodox toe-to-toe talk.

My course of action became clear. My conscience had decided with remarkable facility that the dice had

120

intended only that I abstain from genital intercourse, and although Arlene had once told me that she'd read that semen was fattening and didn't want to try it, it had become a matter of her code or that of the dice man. In another half-minute the dice man's honor was intact. I was sexually satisfied and Arlene was looking up at me wide-eyed and wiping her mouth with the back of her hand.

Although I apologized for what I called my 'incontinence' ('Is that what it's called?' she asked), Arlene cuddled up affectionately, apparently proud that she had so overexcited me that my passion had overflowed against my will. I redeclared my passionate Platonic love, stuck my fingers in her, kissed her breasts, her mouth . . . in another few minutes I would have been facing the same dilemma a second time with no escape possible, but remembering, I jumped off the couch and began conscientiously increasing my outer decor.

Chapter Fifteen

I was Christ for a day. As a pattern-breaking event, being a loving Jesus certainly qualified, and I was surprised how humble and loving and compassionate I began to feel. The dice had ordered me to 'Be as Jesus' and to be constantly filled with a Christian (pronounced 'Chr-eye-steean') love for everybody I met. I voluntarily walked the children to school that morning, holding their little hands and feeling paternal, benevolent and loving. Larry's asking me, 'What's wrong, Daddy, why are you coming with us?' didn't faze me in the least. Back in my apartment study I re-read the Sermon on the Mount and most of the gospel of Mark, and when I said goodbye to Lil prior to her leaving on a shopping spree, I blessed her and showed her such tenderness that she assumed something was wrong. For a horrible instant I was about to confess my affair with Arlene and beg forgiveness, but instead I decided that that was another man – and another world. When I saw Lil again that evening she confessed that my love had helped her to spend three times more than she usually did.

I had a rendezvous scheduled with Arlene for late that very afternoon, but I knew then I would urge both her and myself to cease our sinning and pray for forgiveness. I tried to be especially compassionate with Frank Oster-flood and Linda Reichman, my morning patients, but it didn't seem to have much effect. I got a slight stir out of Mr Osterflood when I mentioned that perhaps raping little girls was a sin: he exploded that they deserved everything he did to them. When I read to him the Sermon on the

Mount he became more and more agitated until I reached a part about if the right eye offend thee pluck it out and if the hand offend thee . . . He lunged off the couch across my desk and had me by the throat before I'd even stopped reading. After Jake and Miss Reingold and Jake's patient for that hour had finally succeeded in parting us, Osterflood and I were both rather embarrassed and admitted very shyly that we had been discussing the Sermon on the Mount.

Linda Reichman seemed put off when, after she had stripped to the waist, I suggested that we pray together. When she began kissing my ear I talked to her about the necessity of spiritual love. When she got angry, I begged her forgiveness, but when she unzipped my fly I began reading from the Sermon on the Mount again.

'What the hell's the matter with you today?' she sneered. 'You're even worse than you were last time.'

'I'm trying to show you that there's a spiritual love far more enriching than the most perfect of physical experiences.'

'You really believe that crap?' she asked.

'I believe that all men are lost until they become filled with a great warm love for all men, a spiritual love, the love of Jesus.'

'You really believe that crap?'

'Yes.'

'I want my money back.'

I almost cried that day when I met Jake for lunch. I so wanted to help him, trapped by that relentless overcharged engine of his, zooming through life missing everything, and especially missing the great love that filled me. He was forking down great gobs of beef stew and lima beans and telling me about a patient of his who had committed suicide by mistake. I was searching for some way to break down the seemingly impenetrable wall of his armored self and finding none. As the meal progressed I became sadder and sadder. I felt tears forming in my eyes. I irritably stopped the sentimentality and searched again for some way to his heart.

'Some way to his heart,' was the very phrase I thought in that day. A certain vocabulary and style go with every personality and every religion; under the influence of being Jesus Christ I found I loved people, and the experience expressed itself in unfamiliar actions and in unfamiliar language.

'Jake,' I finally said. 'Do you ever feel great warmth and love toward people?'

He stopped with fork at mouth and gaped at me for a second.

'What's that?' he said.

'Do you ever, have you ever felt a great rush of warmth and love toward some person or toward all humanity?'

He stared a moment more, then said:

'No. Freud associated such feelings with pantheism and the stage of development of two-year-olds. I'd say the irrational flooding of love was regression.'

'And you've never felt it?'

'Nope. Why?'

'But what if such feelings are . . . wonderful? What if they seem better, more desirable than any other state? Would its being a regressive mode of feeling still make it undesirable?'

'Sure. Who's the patient? That Cannon kid you were telling me about?'

'What if I were to tell you that I feel such a surge of love and warmth for everyone?'

This stopped the steam-shovel machine.

'And especially love for you,' I added.

Jake blinked behind his glasses and looked – it's only

my interpretation of a facial expression I'd never seen on his face before – frightened.

'I'd say you were regressing,' he said nervously. 'You're blocked in some line of development and to escape responsibility and to find help you feel this great childish love for everyone.' He began eating again. 'It'll pass.'

'Do you think I'm joking about this feeling, Jake?'

He looked away, his eyes jumping from object to object around the room like trapped sparrows.

'Can't tell, Luke. You've been acting strangely lately. Might be a game, might be sincere. Maybe you ought to get back in analysis, talk it up with Tim there. I can't judge you here as a friend.'

'All right, Jake. But I want you to know that I love you and I don't think it has anything at all to do with object cathexis or the anal stage.'

He blinked at me nervously, not eating.

'It's a Christeean love, or rather, a Judaic–Christ-eean love, of course,' I added.

He was looking more and more terrified. I began to be afraid of him.

'I'm only referring to warm, passionate brotherly love, Jake, it's nothing to worry about.'

He smiled nervously, snuck in a quick squint and asked: 'Have these attacks very often, Luke?'

'Please don't worry about it. Tell me more about that patient. Have you finished your article about it?'

Jake was soon back on the main line, throttle wide open, his colleague, love-filled Lucius Rhinehart, successfully side-tracked at Podunk Junction, there to be stationed hopefully until it was possible to write an article about him.

'Sit down, my son,' I said to Eric Cannon when he entered my little green room at QSH that afternoon. I had been feeling very warm and Jesusy before buzzing for him to be brought in and, standing behind the desk, I looked at him now with love. He looked back at me as though he believed he could see into my soul, his large black eyes glimmering with apparent amusement. Despite his gray khakis and torn T-shirt he was serene and dignified, a lithe, long-haired Christ who looked as though he did gymnastics every day and had fucked every girl on the block.

He dragged a chair over near the window as he always did and flopped down with casual unconcern, his legs stretched out in front of him, a hole staring mutely at me from the bottom of his left sneaker.

Bowing my head, I said: 'Let us pray.'

He stopped open-mouthed in mid-yawn, his arms clasped behind his head, and stared. Then he drew in his legs, leaned forward and lowered his head.

'Dear God,' I said aloud. 'Help us this hour to serve Thy will, be in tune with Thy soul and breathe each breath to Thy glory. Amen.'

I sat down with my eyes still lowered, wondering where I went from here. In most of my early sessions with Eric, I had been my usual non-directive self and, much to my discomfiture, he became the first patient in recorded psychiatric history who, through his first three consecutive therapy sessions, was able to sit silent and thoroughly relaxed. In the fourth he talked nonstop the entire hour on the state of the ward and world. In subsequent sessions he had alternated between silence and soliloquy. In the previous three weeks I had tried only a couple of dice-dictated experiments and had assigned Eric to try feeling love for all figures of authority but he had met all my ploys with silence. When I raised my head now, he was looking at me alertly. Black eyes pinning me where I sat, he reached into his pocket, leaned forward and wordlessly offered me a Winston.

'Thank you, no,' I said.

'Just one Jesus to another,' he said with a mocking smile.

'No, thank you.'

'What's with the prayer bit?' he asked.

'I feel . . . religious today,' I answered, 'and I – '

'Good for you,' he said.

' – wanted you to share my feeling.'

'Who are *you* to be religious?' he asked with sudden coolness.

'I . . . I am . . . I am Jesus,' I answered.

For a moment his face held its cool alertness, then it broke into a contemptuous smile.

'You haven't got the will,' he said.

'What do you mean?'

'You don't suffer, you don't care enough, you don't have the fire to be a Christ actually living on the earth.'

'And you, my son?'

'And *I* do. I've had a fire burning in my gut every moment of my life to wake this world up, to lash the fucking bastards out of the temple, to bring a sword to their peace-plagued souls.'

'But what of love?'

'Love?' he barked at me, his body now straight and tense in the chair. 'Love . . .' he said more quietly. 'Yeah, love. I feel love for those who suffer, those on the rack of the machine, but not for the guys at the controls, not for the torturers, not for them.'

'Who are they?'

'You, buddy, and every guy in a position to change the machine or bust it or quit working on it who doesn't.'

'I'm part of the machine?'

'Every moment you play along with this farce of therapy

127

in this nurse-infested prison, you're driving your nail into the old cross.'

'But I want to help you, to give you health and happiness.'

'Careful, you'll make me puke.'

'And if I stopped working for the machine?'

'Then there'd be some hope for you. Then I might listen; then you would count.'

'But if I leave the system how will I ever see you again?'

'There are visiting hours. And I'm only going to be with you here for a little while.'

We sat in our respective chairs eyeing each other with alert curiosity.

'You aren't surprised that I began our session with a prayer or that I am Jesus?'

'You play games. I don't know why, but you do. It makes me hate you less than the others but know I should never trust you.'

'Do you think you're Christ?'

His eyes shifted away from mine to the sooty window.

'He who has ears to hear let him hear,' he said.

'I'm not sure you love enough,' I said. 'I feel that love is the key to it all, and you seem to have hate.'

He returned his gaze to me slowly.

'You might fight, Rhinehart. No games. You must know your friend and love him and know your enemy and attack.'

'That's hard,' I said.

'Just open your eyes. He who has eyes to see, let him see.'

'I'm always seeing good guys and bad guys yo-yoing up and down in the same person. I never see a target. I always want to forgive, to love.'

'The man behind the machine, Rhinehart, and the man who is part of the machine: they're not hard to see. The

128

lying and cheating and manipulating and killing: you've seen them. Just walk along the street and open your eyes and you won't lack for targets.'

'But do you ask us to kill them?'

'I ask you to fight them. There's a worldwide war on and everybody's drafted and you're either for the machine or you're against it, a part of it, or getting your balls raked by it every day. Life today is a war whether you want it to be or not, and so far, Rhinehart, you've been doing your part for the other side.'

'But thou shalt love thy enemies,' I said.

'Sure. And thou shalt hate evil,' he answered.

'Judge not, that ye be not judged.'

'He who sits on a fence, gets it up his ass,' he replied without a smile.

'I lack the fire: I like everybody,' I said sadly.

'You lack the fire.'

'What am I good for then? I wish to be a religious person.'

'A disciple, maybe,' he said.

'One of the twelve?'

'Most likely. You charge thirty bucks an hour?'

Sitting opposite Arturo Toscanini Jones a half-hour later I felt depressed and tired and unJesusy and didn't say much. Since as usual Jones was quiet too, we sat there pleasantly isolated in our private worlds until I rustled up enough energy to try to carry out my role.

'Mr Jones,' I finally said, looking at his tensed body and frowning face, 'although I agree that you're right not to trust any white man, try to assume for a moment that I, because perhaps of some neurosis of my own, feel an overwhelming warmth toward you and want deeply to help you in any way possible. What might I be able to do?'

129

'Get me out of here,' he said as if he'd been expecting the question.

I considered this. In the twenty or so sessions we'd talked I had found this to be his one all-consuming desire; like a caged animal he had no other.

'And after I've helped you be released what then might I do?'

'Get me out of here. Until I'm free I can't think about anything else. On the outside, well . . .'

'What would you do on the outside?'

He turned on me sharply.

'Goddam it, man, I said get me out of here, not more talk. You said you wanted to help and you keep on rapping.'

I considered this. It was clear that nothing I would do for Jones inside the hospital would be anything but the act of a white doctor. Unless I broke through that stereotype my love would never touch him. Once released he might well consider me a stupid Charlie that he had fucked good, but that seemed an irrelevant consideration. Inside the hospital there could only be hate. Outside . . .

I stood up and walked over to the sooty window and looked out at a group of patients playing a listless game of softball.

'I'll have you released right now. You can go home this afternoon, before supper. It will be slightly illegal and I may get into trouble, but if freedom is all I can give you then that's what I'll give.'

'You puttin' me on?'

'You'll be back in the city within an hour if I have to drive you there myself.'

'What's the catch? If I can go free today why couldn't I go free a month ago? I ain't changed none.' He sneered at his own grammar.

'Yes, I know. But I have.' I turned my back on him

130

again and stared out across the lawn and past the softball game to watch a little boy trying to fly a kite.

'I think this hospital is a prison and that the doctors are jailers,' I said, 'and the city is hell and that our society acts to kill the spirit of love which might exist between man and man. I'm lucky. I'm a jailer and not one of the jailed and thus I can help you. I will help you. But let me ask one favor of you.'

When I turned back to him he was leaning forward on the edge of the chair with concentrated animal tension. When I paused, he frowned and whispered out a 'How?'

That frown and whisper warned me that the two possible 'favors' I had in mind would both fail: 'Come and see me at my office' and 'be my friend.' A man didn't befriend his jailer for giving him freedom since the freedom was deserved, and the doctor–patient relation had failure built into it. I stood looking at him blankly.

'What do you want me to do?' he asked.

Outside I heard a boat's horn from the river groan twice, like warning snorts.

'Nothing,' I said. 'Nothing. I just remembered that I want to help *you*. Period. You don't have to do anything. You'll go free. Outside, what you do is what you do. You'll be free of this hospital and free of me.'

He stared suspiciously and I stared back, feeling serious and ham-actor noble. The urge to suggest verbally that I was being great for doing this was strong, but humble Jesus won out.

'Come on,' I said. 'Let's go and get your clothes and get out of here.'

As it turned out, it took more than an hour to get Arturo Toscanini Jones released and even then, as I had feared, it was illegal. I got him released from the ward in my custody, but such a release did not give him permission to leave the hospital. That took formal action of one of

131

the directors and was impossible for that afternoon. I'd talk to Dr Mann at lunch on Friday, or maybe phone.

I drove Jones to Manhattan and then uptown to his mother's home at 142nd Street. Neither of us said a single word during the entire drive and when I let him out he said only: 'Thanks for the ride.'

'That's okay,' I answered.

After a barely perceptible pause he slammed the door and strode away.

Strike up another scoreless innings for Jesus.

I was exhausted by the time I had gotten Arturo released from the hospital and my silence with him in the car was partly fatigue. Trying minute after minute to be someone not totally natural to the personality, as Jesus was for me, was hard work. Impossible work, as a matter of fact. During that whole day I noticed that after about forty minutes of *being* a loving Jesus my system would simply break down into apathy and indifference. If I continued the role past the forty-minute point it was purely mechanical rather than felt.

As I drove toward my rendezvous with Arlene my bleary mind tried to scrutinize my relations with her. Christianity frowns on adultery: this much I was able to come up with. Our relationship was a sin. Should Jesus simply avoid a rendezvous with His mistress? No. He would want to express His love for her. His agape. He would want to remind her of various relevant commandments.

Such was the intention of Jesus when he met Mrs Jacob Ecstein that afternoon at the corner of 125th Street and Lexington Avenue in Harlem and drove to an obscure section of the parking lot at La Guardia Airport overlooking the bay. The woman was cheerful and relaxed and spoke during most of the drive about *Portnoy's Com-*

plaint, a book which Jesus had not read. It was clear from her speaking, however, that the author of the novel had not discovered love, and that the effect upon Mrs Ecstein was to increase her cynical, guiltless, shameless devil-may-care immersion in her gin. It seemed to Jesus precisely the wrong mood for his beginning to discuss Judeo–Christian love.

'Arlene,' spoke Jesus, after He had parked, 'do you ever feel great warmth and love toward people?'

'Only for you, lover,' she replied.

'Have you never felt a great rush of warmth and love toward some person or toward all humanity?'

The woman cocked her head and thought.

'Occasionally.'

'To what do you attribute it?'

'Alcohol.'

The woman unzipped the fly of Jesus and reached a hand in and enclosed the Sacred Tool. It was, all accounts agree, filled only with agape.

'My daughter,' He said, 'are you not concerned with causing unhappiness to your husband or to Lillian?'

She stared at him.

'Of course not. I love this.'

'Are your husband's feelings of no concern to you?'

'Jake's feelings!' she shouted. 'Jake is completely well-adjusted. He doesn't have any feelings.'

'Not even love?'

'Perhaps once a week he has that.'

'But Lillian has feelings. God has feelings.'

'I know, and I think what you're doing to her is cruel.'

'That is true, and you and Dr Rhinehart must stop doing that which is so clearly sinful and which must hurt her.'

'We're not doing anything, it's *you* that makes her suffer.'

'Dr Rhinehart will be a better man.'

'Good. I hate to see her so upset with you.' She gave the Sacred Tool a little friendly squeeze and then lowered her head to His lap and sucked in the Spiritual Spaghetti.

'But Arlene!' He said. 'Dr Rhinehart's making love to you is fornication, is what might hurt her.'

The woman tempted Jesus further with her serpent's tongue, but producing no measurable effect, raised herself. Denied her sinful pleasure she looked peevish.

'What are you talking about? What's fornication, another of your perversions?'

'Physical intercourse with Dr Rhinehart is a sin.'

'Who's this Dr Rhinehart you keep talking about? What's the matter with you today?'

'What you have been doing is cruel and selfish and against the word of God. Your affair might have disastrous effects upon Lillian and the children.'

'How!?'

'If they found out.'

'She'd only divorce you.'

Jesus stared at the woman.

'We are speaking of human beings and of the Sacred Institution of Marriage,' He said.

'I don't know what you're talking about.'

Jesus became wrathful and thrust the woman's hand away and zipped up the Holy Fly.

'You are so buried in your sin you cannot see what you do.'

The woman was angry too.

'You've been enjoying yourself for three months and now all of a sudden you discover sin and that *I*'m a sinner.'

'Dr Rhinehart is a sinner too.'

The woman poked back at the Crotch.

'Not much of a one today,' she said.

134

Jesus stared out through the windshield of the car at a small cruiser plodding across the bay. Two gulls which had been following it swerved away and spiraled up about fifty feet and then spiraled down and over toward Him, wheeling out of sight past the car. A signal? A Sign?

Jesus realized humbly that of course he was being insane. By fucking Mrs Ecstein with great gusto for months in the body of Dr Rhinehart He had confused her. It was difficult for her to recognize him in the body of someone she had known playing the role of a sinner. Looking over at her, he saw her staring crossly out over the water, her hands clasping a half-finished almond bar in her lap. Her bare knees suddenly appeared to Him as those of a little child, her emotions those of a little girl. He remembered His injunction about children.

'I'm very very sorry, Arlene. I'm insane. I recognize this. I'm not always myself. I frequently lose myself. To cast you off by suddenly talking about sin and Lil and Jake must seem cruel hypocrisy.'

When she turned to face Him, He saw tears brimming at her eyes.

'I love your cock and you love my breasts and that's not sin.'

Jesus considered these words. They did seem reasonable.

'It is good,' He said. 'But there are greater goods.'

'I know that, but I like yours.'

They stared at each other: two alien spiritual worlds.

'I have to go now,' He said. 'I may return. My insanity is sending me away. My insanity says I will not be able to make love to you for a while.' Jesus started the car.

'Boy,' she said and took a healthy bite from the almond bar, 'you ought to be seeing a psychiatrist yourself *five* times a week if you ask me.'

Jesus drove them back to the city.

Chapter Sixteen

Ego, my friends, ego. The more I sought to destroy it through the dice the greater it grew. Each tumble of a die chipped off another splinter of the old self to feed the growing tissues of the dice man ego. I was killing past pride in myself as analyst, as article writer, as good-looking male, as loving husband, but every corpse was fed to the cannibalistic ego of that superhuman creature I felt I was becoming. How proud I am of being the Dice Man! Whose primary purpose is supposedly to kill all sense of pride in self. The only options I never permitted were those which might challenge his power and glory. All values might be shat upon except that. Take away that identity from me and I am a trembling dread-filled clod, alone in an empty universe. With determination and dice, I am God.

Once I wrote down as an option (one chance in six) that I could (for a month) disobey any of the dice decisions if I felt like it and if I shook a subsequent odd number. I was frightened by the possibility. Only the realization that the act of 'disobedience' would in fact be an act of obedience removed my panic. The dice neglected the option. Another time I *thought* of writing that from then on all dice decisions would be recommendations and not commands. In effect, I would be changing the role of dice from commander in-chief to advisory council. The threat of having 'free will' again paralyzed me. I never wrote the option.

The dice continually humbled me. They ordered me to get drunk one Saturday: an act which I had found to be inconsistent with my dignity. Being drunk meant an absence of self-control which was inconsistent also with the detached, experimental creature I was becoming as the Dice Man. However, I enjoyed it. The letting go was not very different from the insanities I had been committing while sober. I spent the evening with Lil and the Ecsteins and at midnight began making paper airplanes out of the manuscript pages of my proposed book on sadism and flying them out the window onto 72nd Street. My drunken pawing of Arlene was interpreted as drunken pawing. The incident marked another piece of evidence of the slow disintegration of Lucius Rhinehart.

I provided my friends with plenty of other pieces of evidence. I rarely ate lunch with my colleagues anymore since I usually was sent by the dice to other places whenever I had free time. When I did lunch with them the dice often had dictated some eccentric role or action which seemed to unsettle them. One day during a forty-eight-hour total fast (except for water) which the die had dealt me, I felt weak and decided not to let the die send me anyplace: I would share my fast with Tim, Jake and Renata.

They talked, as they had for several months, primarily to each other. Whenever they directed a question or comment to me they did it warily, like animal trainers feeding a wounded lion. This particular afternoon they were talking about the hospital's policy of releasing patients conditionally, and I, staring hysterically at Jake's sirloin steak, was drunk with hunger. Dr Mann was slobbering his scallops all over the table and his napkin, and Dr Felloni was delicately escorting each separate tiny piece of lamb (lamb!) to her mouth and I was insane. Jake as usual managed to talk and eat faster than both the others together.

'Got to keep 'em in,' he said. 'Harmful to us, the

hospital, society, everybody, if a patient is prematurely released. Read Bowerly.'

Silence. (Actually chewing [I heard every nibble], other restaurant voices, laughter, dishes clattering, sizzling [I heard every single bubble explosion] and a loud voice which said, 'Never again.')

'You're absolutely right, Jake,' I uttered unexpectedly. They were my first words of the afternoon.

'Remember that Negro released on probation who killed his parents? We were *idiots*. What if he'd only *wounded* them?'

'He's right, Tim,' I said.

Dr Mann didn't deign to interrupt his eating, but Jake shot me a second piercing squint.

'I'll bet,' he went on, 'that two-thirds of the patients released from QSH – and the other state hospitals – are released far too early, that is, when they're still a menace to themselves and society.'

'That's true,' I said.

'I know that the professional opinion in vogue is that hospitalization is at best a necessary evil, but it's a stupid vogue. If we've got anything to offer our patients, then our hospitals do too. There are three times as many doctor-hours for a patient as he gets in the best out-patient treatment. Read Hegalson, Potter and Busch, their revised edition.'

'And they don't miss appointments, either,' I added.

'That's right,' Jake went on, 'there's no home life to mess up their lives.'

'No wives or husbands or children or home-cooked meals.'

'Yeah.'

Dr Felloni interrupted: 'Isn't adjustment to the home environment what we're striving for though?'

'Adjustment to *some* environment,' Jake answered. 'I

138

try to get my Negro patients in group therapy to see the sickness of the white world so that they will end their *resentment* and find themselves satisfied with either their lives on the ward or their necessary ghetto existence.'

'And God knows,' I said, 'that the white world is sick. Look at the starving millions in East Germany.'

This slowed Jake down for a moment: he lived the rhythm of agreement but wasn't certain that my statement here was entirely satisfactory. With that brilliance which was his essence, he hedged: 'Our job is to shoot psychological penicillin into the whole social fabric, white and black, and we're doing it.'

'But with regard to Mrs Lansing,' Dr Felloni said, 'you do feel *she* should be released.'

'She's your baby, Renata, but remember, "When in doubt, don't let 'em out."'

Dr Mann sent up a belch as an apparent warning signal that he was about to speak. We all looked at him respectfully.

'Jake,' he said. 'You would have been at home as commander of a concentration camp.'

Silence.

Then I said: 'What a lousy thing to say. Jake wants to help his patients not exterminate them. And besides, in concentration camps the commander sometimes . . . didn't give them food.'

Silence. Dr Mann seemed to be chewing a cud; Dr Felloni was moving her head from side to side and up and down very slowly, like someone watching a tennis match consisting entirely of lobs. Jake, leaning forward intently and peering without fear into Dr Mann's bland face, said with the rapidity of a typewriter:

'I don't know what you mean by that, Tim. I'll stack my patient record against yours any day. My policy on

139

patient release is the same as the director's. I think you should apologize.'

'Quite right.' Dr Mann wiped his mouth with his napkin (or he may have been nibbling from it). 'Apologize. I'd be at home as commander too. Only one who wouldn't is Luke, he'd let everyone go – on a whim.' Dr Mann had not been enthusiastic about the release of Arturo Toscanini Jones.

'No, I wouldn't,' I said. 'If I were commander I'd increase food allotments two hundred percent and do experiments with the inmates which would advance psychiatry a hundred years past Freud in twelve months.'

'Are you talking about Jewish inmates?' Jake asked.

'Damn right. Jews make the best subjects for psychological experiments.' I paused about one and a half seconds, but as Jake started to speak, I went on. 'Because they're so intelligent, sensitive and flexible.'

That slowed Jake down. Somehow the racial stereotype I had created with my three adjectives didn't seem to leave him much to shoot at.

'What do you mean by flexible?' he asked.

'Not rigid – open-minded, capable of change.'

'What experiments would you perform, Luke?' Dr Mann asked, watching a chubby waiter quiver past with a platter of lobsters.

'I wouldn't touch the inmates physically. No brain operations, sterilizations, that stuff. All I'd do is this: Turn all the ascetics into hedonists; all the epicureans into flagellants; nymphomaniacs into nuns; homosexuals into heterosexuals, and vice versa. I'd train them all to eat non kosher food, give up their religion, change their professions, their styles of dress, grooming, walking and so on, and train them all to be unintelligent, insensitive and inflexible. I would prove that man *can* be changed.'

Dr Felloni looked a little startled; she was nodding

rather emphatically: 'We're going to do this at Queensborough State Hospital?'

'When I become director.' I answered.

'But I'm not certain it would be ethical,' she said.

'How would you do all this?' asked Dr Mann.

'Drole therapy.'

'Drole therapy?' Jake asked.

'Yes. Honker, Ronson and Gloop, *APB Journal*, August, 1958, pages sixteen to twenty-three, annotated bibliography. It's short for drama-role therapy.'

'Dessert menu, please, waiter,' said Dr Mann and seemed to lose interest.

'The same thing as Moreno?' Jake asked.

'No. Moreno has patients act out their fantasies in staged playlets. Drole therapy consists of forcing patients to *live* their suppressed latent impulses.'

'What's the *APB Journal*?' Jake asked.

'Jake, I agree with everything you say,' I said pleadingly. 'Don't challenge me. The whole thin tissue supporting our argument will tear and collapse the whole thing on us.'

'*I* wasn't urging experimentation on patients.'

'Then what do you do during a typical hour?'

'Cure 'em.'

Dr Mann began what might have been a long rumbling laugh but was infected by food swallowed the wrong way and ended as a fit of coughing.

'But, Jake,' I said, 'I thought it was our idea to gradually increase the facilities of and enrolment in mental hospitals one percent a year until the whole nation was being cured.'

Silence.

'You'd have to be first, Luke,' Jake said quietly.

'Let me start now, today. I need help. I need food.'

'You mean analysis?'

'Yes. We all know I need it badly.'

'Dr Mann was your analyst.'

'I've lost faith in him. He's got bad table manners. He wastes food.'

'You knew that before.'

'But I didn't know until now the importance of food.'

Silence. Then Dr Felloni:

'I'm glad you mentioned Tim's table manners, Luke, because for some time now . . .'

'How about it, Tim,' Jake said. 'Can I take on Luke?'

'Certainly, I only work with neurotics.'

That ambiguous remark (was I schizophrenic or mentally healthy?) essentially ended the conversation. A few minutes later I staggered away from the table engaged to begin analysis with Dr Jacob Ecstein on Friday in our mutual office.

Jake left the table like a man handed the Sonship of God on a silver platter; his greatest triumph was about to begin. And, by Fromm, he was right.

As for myself, when I finally ate again eighteen hours later, it killed my appetite for therapy, but, as it turned out, going back under analysis with Jake was a stroke of genius. Never question the Way of the Die. Even when you're starving to death.

Chapter Seventeen

Eventually, it had to happen; the dice decided that Dr Rhinehart should spread their plague – he was ordered to corrupt his innocent children into the dicelife.

He easily maneuvered his wife to a long three-day visit to her parents in Daytona Beach, employing the horrible premise that the nursemaid Mrs Roberts and he would take perfect care of the children. He then maneuvered Mrs Roberts to Radio City Music Hall.

Rubbing his hands together and grinning hysterically, Dr Rhinehart began to implement his hideous plan of drawing his innocent children into his web of sickness and depravity.

'My children,' he said to them from the living room couch in a fatherly tone of voice (Oh! the cloak which evil wears!) 'I have a special game for us to play today.'

Lawrence and little Evie clustered close to their father like innocent moths to a deadly flame. He took from his pocket and placed on the arm of the couch two dice: those awful seeds which had already borne such bitter fruit.

The children stared at the dice wide-eyed; they had never seen evil directly before, but the shimmering green light which the dice emitted sent through each of their hearts a deep convulsive shudder. Suppressing his fear, Lawrence said bravely:

'What's the game, Dad?'

'Me, too,' said Evie.

'It's called the dice man game.'

'What's that?' asked Lawrence. (Only seven years old, yet so soon to be aged in evil.)

143

'The dice man game goes like this: we write down six things we might do and then we shake a die to see which one we do.'

'Huh?'

'Or write down six persons you might be and then shake the dice and see which one you are.'

Lawrence and Evie stared at their father, stunned with the enormity of the perversion.

'Okay,' said Lawrence.

'Me, too,' said Evie.

'How do we decide what to write down?' asked Lawrence.

'Just tell me any strange thing which you think might be fun and I'll write it down.'

Lawrence thought, unaware of the downward spiral that this first step might mean.

'Go to the zoo,' he said.

'Go to the zoo,' said Dr Rhinehart and walked nonchalantly to his desk for paper and pencil to record this infamous game.

'Climb to the roof and throw paper,' Lawrence said. He and Evie had joined their father at the desk and watched as he wrote.

'Go beat up Jerry Brass,' Lawrence went on.

Dr Rhinehart nodded and wrote.

'That's number three,' he said.

'Play horsey with you.'

'Hooray,' said Evie.

'Number four.'

There was a silence.

'I can't think of anymore.'

'How about you, Evie?'

'Eat ice cream.'

'Yeah,' said Lawrence.

'That's number five. Just one more.'

'Go for a long hike in Harlem,' shouted Lawrence, and he ran back to the couch and got the dice. 'Can I throw?'

'You can throw. Just one, remember.'

He cast across the floor of his fate a single die: a four – horsey. Ah gods, in what nag's clothing comes the wolf.

They played, raucously, for twenty minutes and then Lawrence, already, Reader, I lament to say, hooked, asked to play dice man again. His father, smiling and gasping for breath, wobbled to the desk to write another page of the book of ruin. Lawrence added some new alternatives and left some old ones and the dice chose: 'Go beat up Jerry Brass.'

Lawrence stared at his father.

'What do we do now?' he asked.

'You go downstairs and ring the Brass's doorbell and ask to see Jerry and then you try to beat him up.'

Lawrence looked down at the floor, the enormity of his folly beginning to sink into his little heart.

'What if he's not home?'

'Then you try again later.'

'What'll I say when I beat him up?'

'Why don't you ask the dice?'

He looked up quickly at his father.

'What do you mean?'

'You've got to beat up Jerry, why not give the dice six choices of what you'll say?'

'That's great. What'll they be?'

'You're God,' his father said with that same horrible smile. 'You name them.'

'I'll tell him my father told me to.'

Dr Rhinehart couched, hesitated. 'That's . . . um . . . number one.'

'I'll tell him my mother told me to.'

'Right.'

'That I'm drunk.'

'Number three.'

'That . . . that I can't stand him.'

He was deep in excited concentration.

'That I'm practicing my boxing . . .' He laughed and hopped up and down.

'And that the *dice* told me to.'

'That's six and very good, Larry.'

'I throw, I throw.'

'That I'm practicing my boxing . . .' He laughed and the living room rung and yelled its command back to his father: 'Three!'

'Okay, Larry, you're drunk. Go get him.'

Reader, Lawrence went. Lawrence struck Jerry Brass. Struck him several times, announced he was drunk and escaped unpunished by the absent Brass parents or present Brass maid, but pursued already by the furies which will not leave unavenged such senseless evil. When he returned to his own apartment, Lawrence's first words were – I record them with shame:

'Where are the dice, Dad?'

Ah, my friends, that innocent afternoon with Larry provoked me into thought in a way my own dicelife until then never had. Larry took to following the dice with such ease and joy compared to the soul-searching gloom that I often went through before following a decision, that I had to wonder what happened to every human in the two decades between seven and twenty-seven to turn a kitten into a cow. Why did children seem to be so often spontaneous, joy-filled and concentrated while adults seemed controlled, anxiety-filled and diffused?

It was the Goddam sense of having a self: that sense of self which psychologists have been proclaiming we all must have. What if – at the time it seemed like an original thought – what if the development of a sense of self is normal and natural, but is neither inevitable nor *desirable*? What if it represents a psychological appendix: a useless, anachronistic pain in the side? – or, like the mastodon's huge tusks: a heavy, useless and ultimately self-destructive burden? What if the sense of being some-*one* represents an evolutionary error as disastrous to the further development of a more complex creature as was the shell for snails or turtles?

He he he. What if? indeed: men must attempt to eliminate the error and develop in themselves and their children liberation from the sense of self. Man must become comfortable in flowing from one role to another, one set of values to another, one life to another. Men must be free from boundaries, patterns and consistencies in order to be free to think, feel and create in new ways. Men have admired Prometheus and Mars too long; our God must become Proteus.

I became tremendously excited with my thoughts: 'Men must become comfortable in flowing from one role to another' – why aren't they? At the age of three or four, children were willing to be either good guys or bad guys, the Americans or the Commies, the students or the fuzz. As the culture molds them, however, each child comes to insist on playing only one set of roles: he must always be a good guy, or, for equally compulsive reasons, a bad guy or rebel. The capacity to play and feel both sets of roles is lost. He has begun to know who he is supposed to be.

The sense of a permanent self: ah, how psychologists and parents lust to lock their kids into some definable cage. Consistency, patterns, something we can label – that's what we want in our boy.

'Oh, our Johnny always does a beautiful bowel movement every morning after breakfast.'

'Billy just loves to read all the time . . .'

'Isn't Joan sweet? She always likes to let the other person win.'

'Sylvia's so pretty and so grown up; she just loves all the time to dress up.'

It seemed to me that a thousand oversimplifications a year betrayed the truths in the child's heart: he knew at one point that he didn't always feel like shitting after breakfast but it gave his Ma a thrill. Billy ached to be out splashing in mud puddles with the other boys, but . . . Joan wanted to chew the penis off her brother every time he won, but . . . And Sylvia daydreamed of a land in which she wouldn't have to worry about how she looked . . .

Patterns are prostitution to the patter of parents. Adults rule and they reward patterns. Patterns it is. And eventual misery.

What if we were to bring up our children differently? Reward them for varying their habits, tastes, roles? Reward them for being inconsistent? What then? We could discipline them to be reliably various, to be conscientiously inconsistent, determinedly habit-free – even of 'good' habits.

'What, my boy, haven't told a lie yet today? Well, go to your room and stay there until you can think one up and learn to do better.'

'Oh, my Johnny, he's so wonderful. Last year he got all "A"s on his report card and this year he's getting mostly "D"s and "F"s. We're so proud.'

'Our little Eileen still pees in her panties every now and then and she's almost twelve.' 'Oh, that's marvelous! Your daughter must be so *alive*.'

'Good boy, Roger, that was beautiful the way you walked off the field and went home to play ping-pong with the score tied and two out in the last of the eighth.

Every dad in the stands wished his kid had thought of that.'

'Donnie! Don't you dare brush your teeth again tonight! It's getting to be a regular *habit*.' 'I'm sorry, Mom.'

'Goddam son of mine. Hasn't goofed off in a week. If I don't find the lawn unmowed or the wastebaskets overflowing one of these days, I'm going to blow my top at him.'

'Larry, you ought to be ashamed of yourself. You haven't bullied a single one of the little kids on the block all summer.' 'I just don't feel like it, Mom.' 'Well, at least you could *try*.'

'What should I wear, Mother?' 'Oh I don't know, Sylvia. Why don't you try the cardigan which makes you look flat-chested and that ugly skirt your grandmother gave you which always twists. I've got a pair of nylons I've been saving for a special occasion: they've each got a run.' 'Sounds groovy.'

Teachers, too, would have to alter.

'Your drawings all tend to look like the thing you're drawing, young man. You seem unable to let yourself go.'

'This essay is too logical and well-organized. If you expect to develop as a writer you must learn to digress and be at times totally irrelevant.'

'Your son's work shows much improvement. His papers on history have become nicely erratic again, and his comportment totally unreliable (A–). His math remains a little compulsively accurate, but his spelling is a delight. I particularly enjoyed his spelling of "Stuntent" for "student".'

'We regret to inform you that your son behaves always like a man. He seems incapable of being a girl part of the time. He has been dating only girls and may need psychiatric treatment.' 'I'm afraid, George, that you're one of

149

our few ninth graders who hasn't acted like a kindergarten child this week. You'll have to stay after school and work on it.'

The child, we are informed, needs to see order and consistency in the world or he becomes insecure and afraid. But *what* order and consistency? The child doesn't have to have consistent consistency; it seemed to me he might grow equally well with consistent, dependable inconsistency. Life, in fact, is that way; if parents would only admit and praise inconsistency, children wouldn't be so frightened of their parents' hypocrisy or ignorance.

'Sometimes I'll spank you for spilling your milk and sometimes I won't give a damn.'

'Occasionally I like you when you rebel against me, son, and at other times I love to kick the shit out of you.'

'I'm usually pleased with your good grades in school, but sometimes I think you're an awful grind.'

Such is the way adults feel: such is the way children sense they feel. Why can't they acknowledge and praise their inconsistency? Because they think they have a 'self.'

Like the turtle's shell, the sense of self serves as a shield against stimulation and as a burden which limits mobility into possibly dangerous areas. The turtle rarely has to think about what's on the other side of his shell; whatever it is, it can't hurt him, can't even touch him. So, too, adults insist on the shell of a consistent self for themselves and their children and appreciate turtles for friends; they wish to be protected from being hurt or touched or confused or having to think. If a man can rely on consistency, he can afford not to *notice* people after the first few times. But I imagined a world in which each individual might be about to play the lover, the benefactor, the sponger, the attacker, the friend: and once known as one of those, the next day he might yet be anything.

150

Would we pay attention to this person? Would life be boring? Would life be livable?

I saw then clearly for the first time that the fear of failure keeps us huddled in the cave of self – a group of behavior patterns we have mastered and have no intention of risking failure by abandoning.

What if secretly before every agon or game the dice were thrown to determine whether the 'winner' or the 'loser' 'wins' the prize or the championship, with fifty-fifty being the odds for each? The loser of the game would thus end up half the time being congratulated for having been lucky enough to have lost, and thus won the prize. The man who won the game would be consoled for playing so well.

'But!!! The loser of the game would still feel bad, the winner still feel good.' But I remembered reading in a widely acclaimed book on children's games something which made Larry's affinity for diceliving make sense. I dug out the book and read confirmation of my thoughts with joy. Children, it said:

. . . rarely trouble to keep scores, little significance is attached to who wins or loses, they do not require the stimulus of prizes, it does not seem to worry them if the game is not finished. Indeed, children like games in which there is a sizeable element of luck, so that individual abilities cannot be directly compared. They like games which restart automatically, so that everybody is given a new chance.

It seemed to me that there were two quite different meanings of failure. The mind knows when it is blocked and when it has found a solution. A child trying to solve a maze knows when he fails and when he succeeds; no adult need tell him. A child building a house of blocks knows when the collapse of the house means failure (he wanted to build it higher) and when it means success (he

151

wanted it to fall). Success and failure mean simply the satisfaction and frustration of desire. It is real; it is important; the child doesn't have to be rewarded or punished by society in order to prefer success to failure.

The second meaning of failure is also simple: failure is failure to please an adult; success is pleasing an adult. Money, fame, winning a baseball game, looking pretty, having good clothes, car, house are all types of success which primarily revolve around pleasing the adult world. There is nothing intrinsic to the human soul in any of these fears of failure.

Becoming the dice man was difficult because it involved a continual risking of failure in the eyes of the adult world. As dice man I 'failed' (in the second sense) again and again. I was rejected by Lil, by the children, by my esteemed colleagues, by my patients, by strangers, by the image of society's values branded into me by thirty years of living. In the second sense of failure I was continually failing and suffering, but in the first sense I never failed. Every time I followed the dictates of the die I was successfully building a house or purposely knocking one down. My mazes were always being solved. I was continually opening myself to new problems and enjoying solving them.

From children to men we cage ourselves in patterns to avoid facing new problems and possible failure; after a while men become bored because there are no new problems. Such is life under the fear of failure.

Fail! Lose! Be bad! Play, risk, dare.

Thus, I exulted that evening of Larry's first diceday. I became determined to make Larry and Evie fearless, frameless, egoless humans. Larry would be the first egoless man since Lao-Tzu. I would let him play the role of father of the household and Evie the mother. I'd let them reverse roles. Sometimes they would play parents as they

152

perceive us to be and at other times as they think parents *should* be. We could all play television heroes and comic-strip characters. And Lil and I – every conscientious parent – would change his personality every other day or week.

'I am he who can play many games.' That is the essence of the happy child of four, and he never feels he loses. 'I am he who is x, y and z, and x, y and z only': that is the essence of the unhappy adult. I would try to extend in my children their childishness. In the immortal words of J. Edgar Hoover: 'Unless ye become as little children, ye shall not see God.'

Chapter Eighteen

Larry's first day as diceboy had been cut short by boredom with too much of the same thing. He liked the game; he was able to follow the commands of the dice even when they conflicted with his normal patterns, but after about three hours he simply wanted to play with his trucks and didn't want to risk this pleasure to the dice. Since I have often felt the same way (although not about trucks), I explained that the dice man game should only be played when he felt like it. I emphasized, however, that when he did play he must always follow the dice.

Unfortunately, my efforts during the succeeding two days to turn Larry into Lao-Tzu were confounded by his child's good sense; he gave the dice only extremely pleasant alternatives – ice cream, movies, zoos, horsey, trucks, bikes, money. He began to use the dice as a treasure chest. I finally told him that the dice man game always had to provide risk, that slightly bad choices had to be there too. Surprisingly he agreed. I invented for him that week a dice game which has since become one of our classics: Russian roulette. The initial version of the game for Larry was simple: out of every six alternatives one had to be decidedly unpleasant.

As a result, Larry had some interesting experiences over the next five or six days. (Evie returned to her dolls and to Mrs Roberts.) He took a long hike in Harlem (I told him to keep an eye open for a big muscular white man with candy named Osterflood) and he was arrested as a runaway. It took me forty minutes to convince the

26th Precinct that I had encouraged my seven-year-old son to take a hike in Harlem.

The dice sent him to sneak into the movie *I am Curious – Yellow*, a film involving a certain amount of naked sexual interplay, and he returned mildly curious and greatly bored. He crawled on all fours from our apartment down four flights of stairs and along Madison Avenue to Walgreen's and ordered an ice-cream sundae. Another time he had to throw away three of his toys, on the other hand the dice ordered him a new racing-car set. He twice had to let me beat him in chess and three times I had to let him beat me. He had a wonderful hour making ostentatiously stupid moves and thus making it difficult for me to lose.

The dice ordered him to play Daddy and me little Evie for one hour one day and he was soon bored: my little Evie was too weak and too stupid. But he enjoyed greatly playing Daddy to my Lil two days later. I didn't realize at the time that the seeds of group dice therapy and my Centers for Experiments in Totally Random Environments were being planted while Larry and I gambolled about as Daddy and Lil or Superman and a crook or Lassie and a dangerous hippopotamus.

The first and last crisis of this phase of Larry's dicelife occurred four days after Lil had returned from Florida. My contacts with Larry had decreased, and on his own he sometimes created such farfetched alternatives for the dice that when the dice chose them, he wasn't able to carry them out. For example, he told me just before the crisis that once he had given the die the option of his killing Evie (she had broken his racing-car set). When the die chose it, he said, he decided not to. I asked him why.

'She would have tattled on me and you wouldn't have fixed my car.'

'If she were dead how could she tattle on you?' I asked.

'Don't worry, she'd find a way.'

The crisis was simple: Larry's dice told him to steal three dollars from Lil's purse and he spent it on twenty-three comic books (a whim of the die which he told me he resented deeply, being quite fond of bubble gum, lollipops, dart guns and chocolate sundaes). Lil wondered where he got the money for all the comic books. He refused to tell her, insisting that she asked Daddy. She did.

'It's very simple, Lil,' I said and while she was putting on Evie's shoes for the fifth time within the hour I consulted the die: I was ordered (one chance in six) to tell the truth.

'I was playing a dice game with him and he lost and had to steal three dollars from your purse.'

She stared at me, a strand of blonde hair dangling on her forehead and her blue eyes momentarily blank with bewilderment.

'He *had* to steal three dollars from my purse?'

I was seated in my easy chair puffing on a pipe and with a copy of the *Times* spread across my lap.

'It's a stupid little game I invented while you were gone to help Larry learn self-discipline. Certain options are created by the player, some of them unpleasant, like stealing, and then the dice choose which one you have to do.'

'*Who* has to do?' She shooed Evie off to the kitchen and advanced to the edge of the couch, where she lit a cigarette. She'd had a good time in Daytona and we'd enjoyed a nice reunion, but she was beginning to look less tanned and more flushed.

'The player, or players.'

'I don't know what you're talking about.'

'It's simple,' I said (I love these two words: I always imagine Immanuel Kant pronouncing them before he set down the first sentence of *The Critique of Pure Reason*, or an American President before launching into an explanation of Vietnam War policy). 'To encourage Larry to branch out into new areas of his young – '

'Stealing!'

' – new areas of his young life, I invented a game whereby you make up things to do – '

'But stealing, Luke, I mean – '

'Which the dice then choose from among.'

'And stealing was one of the options.'

'It's all in the family,' I said.

She stared at me from near the edge of the couch, her arms folded across her chest, a cigarette between her fingers. She looked amazingly calm.

'Luke,' she began speaking slowly. 'I don't know what you think you're doing lately; I don't know whether you're sane or insane; I don't know if you're trying to destroy me or trying to destroy your children or trying to destroy yourself, but if you – if you – once more involve Larry in any of your sick games – I – I'll . . .'

Her amazingly calm face suddenly split like a broken mirror into dozens of cracks of tension, her eyes filled with tears and she twisted her face to the side and gasped a suppressed scream.

'Don't. Please don't,' she whispered, and she sat abruptly on the arm of the couch, her face still averted. 'Go tell him no more games. Never.'

I stood up, the *Times* fluttering to the floor.

'I'm sorry, Lil. I didn't realize – '

'Never – Larry – more games.'

'I'll tell him.'

I left the room and went to his bedroom and told him, and his career as diceboy, after only eight days, ended.

Until the Die resurrected it.

Chapter Nineteen

My childhood! My childhood! My God, I've now written over a hundred and fifty pages and you don't even know whether I was bottle fed or breast fed! You don't know when I was first weaned and how; when I first discovered that girls don't have any weeny, how much I brooded because girls don't have any weeny, when I first decided to enjoy the fact that girls don't have any weeny. You don't know who my great-grandparents were, my grandparents; you don't even know about my mother and father? My siblings! My milieu! My socio-economic background! My early traumas! My early joys! The signs and portents surrounding my birth! Dear friends, you don't know any of that 'David Copperfield kind of crap' (to quote Howard Hughes) which is the very essence of autobiography!

Relax, my friends, I don't intend to tell you.

Traditional autobiographers wish to help you understand how the adult was 'formed.' I suppose most human beings, like clay chamber pots, are 'formed' – and are used accordingly. But I? I am born anew at each green fall of the die, and by die-ing I eliminate my since. The past – paste, pus, piss – is all only illusory events created by a stone mask to justify an illusory stagnant present. Living flows, and the only possible justification of an autobiography is that it happened by chance to be written – like this one. Someday a higher creature will write the almost perfect and totally honest autobiography:

'I live.'

I will acknowledge, however, that I did, in fact, *have* a human mother. This much I admit.

158

Chapter Twenty

In November I received a telephone call from Dr Mann informing me that Eric Cannon had been acting up while I'd been away a week at a convention in Houston, that it had been necessary to increase his medication (tranquilizers) and would I please make a special trip over as soon as possible and see him. Eric might have to be transferred to another institution. In my temporary office on the Island I read through Head Nurse Herbie Flamm's report on Eric Cannon. It had a kind of novelistic power that Henry James sought for fifty years without finding:

It is necessary to report that Patient Eric Cannon is a trouble maker. There haven't been many patients in my lifetime that I would have to label that, but this is one. Cannon is a consciously evil troublemaker. He is disturbing the other patients. Although I have always kept this one of the quietest [sic] wards on the island, since he has been here it is noisy and a mess. Patients who haven't said a word in years now can't shut up. Patients that have stood always in the same corner now play pitch and catch with chairs. Many of the patients are now singing and laughing. This disturbs the patients who want peace and quiet to get better. Someone keeps destroying the television set. I think Mr Cannon is schizophrenic. Sometimes he wanders around the ward nice and quiet like he was in a dreamworld and other times he sneaks around like a snake, hissing at me and the patients like he was the boss of the ward and not me.

Unfortunately he has followers. Many patients are now refusing sedation. Some do not go to the machine shop for factory therapy. Two patients confined to wheelchairs have pretended to walk. Patients are showing disrespect for the hospital food. When one man was ill to his stomach, another patient began eating the vomit, claiming it tasted much better that way. We

159

do not have enough maximum-security rooms on the ward. Also patients who are refusing or not swallowing their sedation will not stop singing and laughing when we politely ask. Disrespect is everywhere. I have sometimes had the feeling on the ward that I do not exist. I mean to say no one pays attention anymore. My attendants are often tempted to treat the patients with physical force but I remind them of the Hippocratic Oath. Patients will not stay in their beds at night. Talking with each other is going on. Meetings, I think. They whisper. I do not know if there is a rule against this, but I recommend that a rule is made. Whispering is worse than singing.

We have sent several of his followers to ward W [the violent ward] but patient Cannon is tricky. He never does anything himself. I think he is spreading illegal drugs on the ward but none have been found. He never does anything and everything is happening.

I have this to report. It is serious. On September 10, at 2.30 P.M in the Main Room right in front of the destroyed and lifeless television set, a large group of patients began hugging each other. They had a circle with their arms around each other and they were humming or moaning and kept getting closer and humming and swaying or pulsating like a giant jellyfish or human heart and they were all men. They did this and attendant R. Smith attempted to break them up but their circle was very strong. I attempted to break their circle also as gently as I could but as I was so endeavoring the circle suddenly opened and two men physically clamped me with their arms and hands and I was drawn against my total will into the horrible circle. It was disgusting beyond my ability to say.

The patients showed no respect but continued their illegal hugging until four attendants from ward T plus R. Smith rescued me by breaking up the circle as gently as they could, unfortunately accidentally breaking my arm (the lower tibia minor, I believe).

This event is typical of the poor conditions which have developed on our ward since patient Cannon came. He was in the circle but since there were eight, Dr Vener said we couldn't send them all to ward W. Hugging is also not technically against the rules which again shows the need for more thinking.

The boy never talks to me. But I hear. Among the patients I have friends. They say he is against mental hospitals. You should know that. They say he is the ringleader of all the

160

trouble. That he is trying to make all the patients happy and not pay attention to us. They say he says that patients ought to take over the hospital. That he says even if he leaves them he will come back. These patients, my friends, say this.

Because of the facts what I have written I must respectfully recommend to you:

(1) that all sedation be given by needle to prevent patients from falsely swallowing their tranquilizers and remaining active and noisy during the day.

(2) that all illegal drugs should be strictly forbidden.

(3) that *strict rules* be developed and enforced regarding singing, laughing, whispering, and hugging.

(4) that a special iron mesh cage be developed to protect the television set and that its cord go directly from the set which is ten feet off the floor to the ceiling to protect the wire from those who would deny the television set to those who want to watch it. This is freedom of speech. The iron mesh must form about inch wide squares, thick enough to prevent flying objects from entering and smashing the screen but letting people still see the TV screen although with a waffle-griddle effect. The TV *must go on*.

(5) *Most important*. That patient Eric Cannon be transferred respectfully someplace else.

Head Nurse Flamm sent this report to myself, Dr Vener, Dr Mann, Chief Supervisor Hennings, State Mental Hospital Director Alfred Coles, Mayor John Lindsay and Governor Nelson Rockefeller.

I had seen Eric only three times since my Jesus session with him and he had been extremely tense each time and done very little talking, but when he walked into my office that afternoon he came as quietly as a lamb into a grassy meadow.

He moved to the window and stared out. He was wearing blue jeans, a rather soiled T-shirt, sneakers and a gray hospital shirt, unbuttoned. His hair was quite long, but his skin was paler than it had been in September. After about a minute he turned and lay down on the short couch to the left of the desk.

'Mr Flamm,' I said, 'reports that he believes that you are stirring up the patients to – improper behavior.'

To my surprise he answered right away.

'Yeah, improper. Bad. Lousy. That's me,' he said, staring at the green ceiling. 'It took me a long time to realize what the bastards are up to, to realize that the good-game is their most effective method of keeping their fucking system going. When I did, it made me rage against the way I'd been fooled. All my kindness and forgiveness and meekness just let the system step on everybody all the more comfortably. Love is groovy if it's for good guys but to love the fuzz, love the army, love Nixon, love the church, whoa man, that is one lost trip.'

While he was speaking I took out my pipe and began filling it with marijuana. When he finally paused I said:

'Dr Mann indicates that if Flamm continues to complain you'll have to be transferred to Ward W.'

'Oh, boohoohoo,' he said, not looking at me. 'It's all the same. It's a system, you see. A machine. You work hard to keep the machine going, you're a good guy; you goof off or try to stop the machine and you're a Commie or a loony. The machine may be blowing blacks under like weeds, or scattering ten-ton bombs over Vietnam like firecrackers or overthrowing reform governments in Latin America every other month, but the old machine *must be kept working*. Oh man, when I saw this I vomited for a week. Locked myself in my room for six months.'

He paused and we both listened to the birds singing away among the maple trees outside the building. I lit the pipe and took a deep toke. I exhaled, the smoke drifting idly in his direction.

'And all that time I began slowly to feel that something important was going to happen to me, that I was chosen for some special mission. I had only to fast and to wait. When I bopped my father in the face and was sent here I knew even more certainly that something was going to happen. *Knew* it.'

He stopped talking and sniffed twice. I took another drag on my pipe.

'Has anything happened yet?' I asked.

He watched me take another lungful and then settled back onto the couch. He reached into his hair and brought out a home made joint.

'Got a match?' he said.

'If you're going to smoke, share mine,' I said.

He leaned over to take the pipe, but it was out, so I handed him the matches too. He lit up and for the next three minutes we passed the pipe back and forth in silence. He was staring at the ceiling as if its green cracks contained, like the back of a turtle's shell, portents of the future. By the time the pipe went out a second time, I was pleasantly high. I felt happy, as if I were embarking on a new voyage that for the first time, even in my dice man life, represented real, rather than superficial change.

My eyes were focused on his face, which, under the influence of his high perhaps, was glowing. He smiled with a peacefulness well within my understanding. His hands were folded across his belly, and he lay like a dead man, but glowing, glowing. His voice when he spoke was slow, thick and gentle, as if it came from way off in the clouds.

'About three weeks ago I got up in the middle of the night when all the attendants were asleep to take a piss, but I didn't have to take a piss. I was drawn into the day room as if by a magnet and there I stared out through the window at the Manhattan skyline. Manhattan: the central cog of the machine, or maybe just the sewage system. I knelt and I prayed. Yeah, I prayed. To the Spirit which had lifted Christ above the mass of men to bring His Spirit to me, to give to me the light that could light the world. To let me become the way, the truth and the light. Yeah.'

He paused and I emptied the ashes out into an ashtray and began refilling the pipe.

'How long I prayed, I can't tell. Suddenly, *wham*! I was flooded by a light that made an acid trip seem like sniffing glue. I couldn't see. My body seemed to swell, my spirit swelled, I seemed to expand until I filled the whole universe. The world was me.'

He paused briefly, the sound of the Jefferson Airplane coming from someplace up the hall.

'I hadn't smoked a thing for three days. I wasn't loony. I filled the whole universe.'

He paused again.

'I was crying. I was weeping for joy. I was on my feet, I guess, and the whole world was all light and was all me and it was good. I stood with my arms outstretched to embrace everything and then I was conscious of this terrific mad grin I had on my face and the vision kind of faded and I shrunk back to me. But I felt that, I knew that I had been given a job . . . a role, a mission . . . yeah. This gray-green hellhouse couldn't be left standing. The gray factories, the gray offices, the gray buildings, the gray people . . . everything without light . . . has to go. I saw it. I see it. What I'd been waiting for had happened. The Spirit I'd been looking for, I . . . had . . . I know I'm not for all men. The mass of men will always see and live in the gray world. But a few will follow me, a few, and we'll change the world.'

I passed him the relit pipe when he'd finished talking and he took it and inhaled and passed it back to me. He didn't look at me.

'And you, what's your game?' he said. 'You're not smoking pot with me just because you feel like smoking pot.'

'No,' I said.

'Then why?'

'Just chance.'

He stared at the green ceiling until I passed him back the pipe. When he finally exhaled he said again as if from very far away: 'If you want to follow me you must give up everything.'

'I know.'

'Pot-smoking doctors who get stoned with mental patients don't stay doctors long.'

'I know.' I felt like giggling.

'Wives and brothers and fathers and mothers don't usually like my way.'

'So I gather.'

'Someday you will help me.'

We were both staring at the ceiling now, the hot bowl of the pipe resting unused in the palm of my hand.

'Yes,' I said.

'It's a marvelous game we'll play – the best,' he said.

'For some reason I feel I'm yours,' I said. 'Whatever you want me to do, I'll want to do.'

'Everything will happen.'

'Yes.'

'The blind bastards [his voice was quiet and serene and remote] will panic and kill, panic and kill, trying to control the uncontrollable, trying to kill what can only live.'

'We will panic and kill.'

'And I'll,' he interrupted himself with a chuckle, 'I'll try to save the whole fucking world. – '

'Yes.'

'I'm Divine, you know,' he said.

'Yes,' I said, believing it.

'I've come to wake the world to evil, to goose mankind to good.'

'We'll hate you – '

165

'To slash the mash-potato minds until their sin is seen.'
'We'll be blind – '
'Try to make the blind see, the lame walk, the dead live again.' He laughed.
'And we'll try to make the seeing blind, the walking lame, the living dead.' I smiled.
'I'll be the insane Savior of the world, and you'll kill me.'
'Whatever you want will be done.' I eased out a slow motion bubbling of mirth.
'I'll be . . .' He was chuckling too, in slow motion. 'I'll be . . . the Savior . . . of the world . . . and do nothing, and you . . .'ll kill . . . me.'
'And I – ' Goddam it, it was funny! How beautiful it was: '. . . I'll kill you.'
The room was a beautiful blur bouncing up and down on the bubbles of our laughter. Tears were in my eyes and I took off my glasses and put my face in my folded arms and laughed, my big body rumbling from cheeks to belly to knees, laughing, tears wetting my jacket, the soft cotton material caressing my wet face like bear's bristle, and crying with an ecstasy that I hadn't known before that moment, and looking up because I couldn't believe I was crying and Eric's face blurred, blurred bright but blurred and I looked for my glasses – such terror that I might never see again – and after groping for forty days I found them and put them on and looked at the blurred brightness and it was Eric's holy face flowing tears like mine and he wasn't laughing.

166

Chapter Twenty-one

[Being an edited tape from one of the early analytic sessions given by Dr Jacob Ecstein to Dr Lucius Rhinehart, neurotic. We are cutting into the tape about halfway through the analytic hour. The first voice is that of Dr Rhinehart.]

– I'm not sure why I entered into this affair but I think it may partially be aggression against the husband.

– How have your relations with Lillian been?

– Fine. Or rather, about as usual, which means up and down but essentially happy. I don't think it was or is aggression against Lil. At least I don't think it is.

– But against the husband.

– Yes. I won't use names or go into details because you know the people involved, but I find the husband too ambitious and conceited. I experience him as a rival.

– You don't need to hide the names. You know it would make no difference outside this office how I treated them.

– Well, maybe. I suppose you're right, but I don't think the names should be necessary if I can present everything else honestly.

– The details.

– Yes. Although I suppose you will know then immediately the people I'm talking about. But still, I'll omit the names.

– How did the affair start?

– I followed . . . a whim one night and went to her place, found her alone, and raped her.

– *Raped* her?

167

– Well, there was a good deal of cooperation. Actually she enjoyed it more than I did. But the original idea was mine.

– Mmm.

– We've been seeing each other off and on now for about half a year.

– Mmm.

– I go to her place when her husband's away, or occasionally we meet in a room I rent in a Puerto Rican neighborhood.

– Ahhh.

– Sexually it's been rewarding. The woman seems totally without inhibitions. I've tried just about everything my imagination can cook up and she seems to have more recipes than me.

– I see.

– The husband doesn't seem to suspect a thing.

– He doesn't suspect a thing.

– No. He seems completely wrapped up in his work. His wife says he pulls off a quick one about once every two weeks but with about as much passion or pleasure as when making an extended bowel movement.

– Mmmm.

– I once finished an orgasm in her while she was handing a towel in to her husband in the bathtub.

– You what?

– I was pumping away from behind while she leaned into the bathroom and talked to her husband and handed him a towel.

– Look here, Rhinehart, do you know what you're saying?

– I thought I did.

– How could you . . . How could you possibly . . .

– What's the matter?

– How could you possibly miss the significance of this affair?

– I don't know. It seems just . . .

– Free associate.

– What?

– I'll feed you words and you free associate.

– Oh, okay.

– Black.

– White.

– Moon.

– Sun.

– Father.

– Mother.

– Water.

– Ah . . . bathtub.

– Road.

– Roadway.

– Green.

– Yellow.

– Fucking from rear.

– Ar . . . ah . . . ah . . . artificial.

– Artificial?

– Artificial.

– How so?

– How should I know? I'm just free associating.

– Let's go on. Father.

– Figure.

– Lake.

– Tahoe.

– Thirst.

– Water.

– Love.

– Women.

– Mother.

– Women.

– Father.

– Women.

– White.

– Women.

– Black.

– Negresses.

– Well. That's enough. It was just as I expected.

– What do you mean?

– That was your father in the bathtub.

– It was?

– Obviously. Item number one: you associate father figure. You may consciously explain this as a result of the psychoanalytic phrase and it does refer to this, but the association also implies you associate a 'figure' – naturally a female figure – with father.

– Wow.

– Item number two. You associate 'fucking from rear' with artificial and you can blurt it out only after a significant delay. I challenge you to tell me what first flashed through your mind.

– Well . . .

– Go ahead.

– To be frank with you, I thought that the fucking was artificial, unnecessary, irrelevant. I was aiming to hurt someone . . . someone bigger.

– Precisely. Item number three: from the rear is obviously the position of sodomy, or male making love to male.

– But –

– Item number four: you associate lake with Tahoe. Tahoe, even if your conscious mind denies it, means in Cherokee 'Big Father Chief.' Lake obviously means water and you associated water with bathtub. Ergo: Big Father Chief was in the bathtub.

– Wow.

170

– Finally, although these are but trivial confirmations of what now is obvious to you, you associate with 'thirst', 'water.' You thirst not for women but for water, for bathtub, for your father. At the end, the free association seems to break down as you associate both your mother and father with women, but in fact it is further confirmation of the whole significance of your extramarital affair and of this free association your incestuous, homosexual love for your father.

– That's incredible. That's absolutely . . . wham . . . [Long pause] . . . But what . . . what does it all mean?

– How so? I've told you.

– I mean . . . what should I do about it?

– Ah so. Details. Your urge for this woman will probably evaporate now that you know the truth.

– My father died when I was two.

– Precisely. I need say no more.

– He was six foot and blond. The husband is five feet eight and dark.

– Displacement.

– My father never took baths, only showers, or so my mother tells me.

– Irrelevant.

– When a woman is handing a towel in to her husband and chatting with him, it's inconvenient to penetrate her from the front.

– Nonsense.

– I didn't know Tahoe meant Big Father Chief.

– Repression.

– I think I'm still going to enjoy making love to this woman.

– I challenge you to examine your fantasies when you do.

– I usually fantasize I'm doing it with my wife.

– The hour's up.

Chapter Twenty-two

Days pass, Reader. So do weeks. Since I have a poor memory and kept no journal during these now-to-be-recorded days, the precise sequence of events is no clearer in my mind than it is in these pages. The dice didn't order me to write my autobiography until almost three years after my discovery, and the historic value of everything I did was not apparent to me at the time.

On the other hand, my selective defective memory presumably is hitting only the high points. Perhaps it is giving to my random life a pattern which total recall would blur. Let us assume, then, that what I forget is on a priori grounds insignificant, and what I remember is, in the same way, of great moment. It may not seem that way to either of us, but it makes a convenient theory of autobiography. Also, if the transitions from chapter to chapter or scene to scene seem particularly illogical, attribute it to either my arbitrary memory or the random fall of a die: it makes the trip more psychedelic.

In the evolution of the totally random man the next event worth noting is that on January 2, 1969 at 1 A.M. I determined to begin the new year (I'm a slow starter) by letting the dice determine my long-term fate.

I wrote with unfirm hand and dazed eyes the first option, for snake-eyes or double sixes: I would leave my wife and children and begin a separate life. I trembled (which is hard for a man with so much meat on him) and felt proud. Sooner or later the dice would roll a two or a twelve and the last great test of the dice's ability to destroy the self would occur. If I left Lil there would be no turning back; it would be dice unto death.

But then I felt fatigued. The dice man seemed boring, unattractive, *other*. It seemed like too much work. Why not relax and enjoy everyday life, play around in minor ways with the dice as I had at the beginning, and forgo this senseless, theatrical challenge of killing the self? I had discovered an interesting tonic, more varied than alcohol, less dangerous than LSD, more challenging than stocks or sex. Why not accept it as tonic rather than try to make it a magic potion? I had but one life to lead, why sacrifice it to becoming locked in the cage of a rolling cube? For the first time in the six months since becoming the dice man, the thought of totally giving up the dice appealed to me.

I wrote as the option for a 6, 7 or 8 that I return to a normal diceless life for six months. I felt pleased.

But immediately thereafter, my friends, I felt frightened, depressed. The realization that I might be without the dice produced precisely the same heavy depression which the thought of being without Lil had produced. Erasing the 7 as a possibility for the option of giving up the dice, I felt a little better. I tore up the entire page and dropped it in the wastebasket: I would abandon the whole conception of long-range dice decisions. I heaved myself up out of my chair and walked slowly off to the bathroom where I brushed my teeth and washed my face. I stared at myself in the mirror.

Clark Kent stared back at me, clean-cut and mediocre. Removing my glasses helped, primarily because it blurred the image sufficiently so that my imagination was given leeway. The blurred face was at first eyeless and mouthless; a faceless nobody. By concentrating I conjured up two gray slits and a toothless mouth; a death's head. With my glasses back on it was just me again. Luke Rhinehart,

MD, the Clark Kent of New York psychoanalysis. But where was Superman? Indeed, that was what this water-closet identity crisis was all about. Where indeed was Superman if I went back to bed?

Back at my desk I rewrote the first two options; leaving Lil and giving up the dice. I then gave one chance in five to the option that I decide at the beginning of each of the next seven months (until the birthday of D-Day in mid-August) what each particular month was to be devoted to. I gave the same probability to the option that I try to write a novel for seven months. Slightly better odds went to the option that I spend three months touring Europe and the rest of the time traveling at the whim of the die. My last option was to turn my sex research with Dr Felloni over to the imagination of the dice.

The first bi-annual fate-dealing day had arrived – a momentous occasion. I blessed the dice in the name of Nietzsche, Freud, Jake Ecstein and Norman Vincent Peale and shook them in the bowl of my hands, rattling them hard against my palms. I gurgled with anticipation: the next half-year of my life, perhaps even more, trembled in my hands. The dice tumbled across the desk; there was a six and there was a . . . three. Nine – survival, anticli-max, inconclusion, even disappointment; the dice had ordered me to decide anew each month what my special fate was to be.

Chapter Twenty-three

National Habit-Breaking Month must have been dictated by the die in a fit of pique over my easy enjoyment of my dicelife; the month provided a hundred little blasts toward the breaking up of Lucius Rhinehart, MD Habit breaking had won out over (1) dedicated-psychiatrist month, (2) begin-writing-a-novel month, (3) vacation-in-Italy month, (4) be-kind-to-everybody month, and (5) help-Arturo-X month. The command was, to be precise, 'I will attempt at every moment of every day of this month to alter my habitual behavior patterns.'.

First of all it meant that when I rolled over to cuddle Lil at dawn I had to roll back again and stare at the wall. After staring a few minutes and then beginning to doze off, I realized that I never rose at dawn, so with effort and resentment, I got out of bed. Both feet were in my slippers and I was plodding toward the bathroom before I realized habit had me in his fist. I kicked off my slippers and plodded, then jogged into the living room. I still, however, felt like urinating. Triumphantly, I did so in a vase of artificial gladioli. (Three days later Dr Felloni remarked on how well they seemed to be doing.) A few minutes later I woke up in the same standing position, conscious that I still had a silly proud smile on my face. Careful examination of my conscience revealed that I did not make a habit of falling asleep on my feet after urinating in the living room so I let myself doze off again.

'What are you doing?' a voice said through my sleep.

'Huh?'

'Luke, what are you doing?'

'Oh.' I saw Lil standing nude with her arms folded across her chest looking at me.

'I'm thinking.'

'What about?'

'Dinosaurs.'

'Come back to bed.'

'All right.'

I started to follow her back to bed but remembered that following nude women into beds was habitual. When Lil had plopped in and pulled the blankets over her I crawled under the bed.

'Luke???'

I didn't answer.

The squeak of springs and the wandering low-cloud ceiling above me implied that Lil was leaning over first on one and then on the other side of the bed. The spread was lifted and her upside-down face peered into my sideways face. We looked at each other for thirty seconds. Without a word her face disappeared and the bed above me became still.

'I want you,' I said. 'I want to make love to you.' (The prosaicness of the prose was compensated for by the poetry of my position.)

When the silence continued I felt an admiration for Lil. Any normal, mediocre woman would have (a) sworn, (b) looked under the bed again, or (c) shouted at me. Only a woman of high intelligence and deep sensitivity would have remained silent.

'I'd love to have your prick inside me,' her voice suddenly said.

I was frightened: a contest of wills. I must not reply habitually.

'I want your left knee,' I said.

Silence.

'I want to come between your toes,' I went on.

176

'I want to feel your Adam's apple bob up and down,' she said.

Silence.

I began humming 'The Battle Hymn of the Republic.' I lifted the springs above me with all my might. She rolled off to one side. I changed my position to try to push her off. She rolled back into the middle. My arms were exhausted. Although whatever I did from under the bed was, a priori, a nonhabitual act, my back was aching. I got out from under, stood up and stretched.

'I don't like your games, Luke,' Lil said quietly.

'The Pittsburgh Pirates have won three games in a row but remain mired in third place.'

'Please come to bed and be yourself.'

'Which one?'

'Any one except this morning's version.'

Habit pulled me toward the bed, the dice pulled me back.

'I have to think about dinosaurs,' I said and, realizing I'd said it in my normal voice, I repeated it shouting. When I saw that I had used my habitual shout I started to emit a third version, but realized that three of anything approached habit and so half-shouted, half-mumbled, 'Breakfast with dinosaurs in bed,' and went into the kitchen.

Halfway there I tried to vary my walk and ended up crawling the last fifteen feet.

'What are you doing, Daddy?'

Larry stood sleepy-eyed but fascinated in the entrance to the kitchen. I didn't want to upset him. I had to watch my words carefully.

'I'm looking for mice.'

'Oh boy, can I look?'

'No, they're dangerous.'

'Mice?'

'These mice are man-eaters.'

'Oh Daddy . . . [Scornfully].'

'I'm teasing [An habitual phrase; I shook my head].'

'Go back to be – [Another!]'

'Look under your mother's bed, I think they may have gone under there.'

Not a great many seconds later Larry came back from our bedroom accompanied by a bathrobed Lil. I was on my knees at the stove about to heat a pot of water.

'Don't you involve the children in your games.'

Since I never lose my temper at Lil I lost it.

'Shut your mouth! You'll scare them all away.'

'Don't you say shut up to me!'

'One more word out of you and I'll ram a dinosaur down your throat.' I stood up and strode toward her, fists clenched.

They both looked terrified. I was impressed.

'Go back to bed, Larry,' Lil said, shielding him and backing away.

'Get down on your knees and pray for mercy, Lawrence, NOW!'

Larry ran for his bedroom, crying.

'Fie upon you!'

'Don't you dare hit me.'

'My God, you're insane,' Lil said.

I hit her, rather restrainedly, on the left shoulder.

She hit me, rather unrestrainedly, in the left eye.

I sat down on the kitchen floor.

'For breakfast is what?' I asked, at least reversing the syntax.

'Are you through?'

'I surrender everything.'

'Come back to bed.'

'Except my honor.'

'You can keep your honor in your underwear, but come back to bed and behave.'

I jogged back to bed ahead of Lil and lay as rigid as a board for forty minutes at which point Lil commanded me to get out of bed. Immediately and rigidly I obeyed. I stood like a robot beside the bed.

'Relax,' she commanded irritably from the dresser.

I collapsed to the floor, ending as painlessly as possible on my side and back. Lil came over and looked down at me for a moment and then kicked me in the thigh. 'Act normal,' she said.

I rose, did six squats arms extended and went to the kitchen. For breakfast I had a hot dog, two pieces of uncooked carrot, coffee with lemon and maple syrup, and toast cooked twice until it was blackened with peanut butter and radish. Lil was furious; primarily because both Larry and Evie wanted desperately to have for breakfast what I was having and ended up crying in frustration. Lil too.

I jogged down Fifth Avenue from my apartment to my office, attracting considerable attention since I was (1) jogging; (2) gasping like a fish drowning in air; and (3) dressed in a tuxedo over a red T-shirt with large white letters declaring The Big Red.

At the office Miss Reingold greeted me formally, neutrally and, I must admit, with secretarial aplomb. Her cold, ugly efficiency stimulated me to break new ground in our relationship.

'Mary Jane, baby,' I said. 'I've got a surprise this morning. I've decided to fire you.'

Her mouth neatly opened, revealing two precisely parallel rows of crooked teeth.

'As of tomorrow morning.'

'But – but Dr Rhinehart, I don't under – '

'It's simple, kneeknocker. I've been hornier in the last few weeks, want a receptionist who's a good lay.'

'Dr Rhinehart – '

'You're efficient, but you've got a flat ass. Hired a 38–24–37 who knows all about fellatio, post hoc propter id, soixante-neuf, gesticulation and proper filing procedures.'

She was backing slowly towards Dr Ecstein's office, eyes bulging, teeth gleaming like two parallel armies in disarray.

'She starts tomorrow morning,' I went on. 'Has her own contraceptive device, I understand. You'll get full pay through the end of the century. Goodbye and good luck.'

I had begun jogging in place about halfway through my tirade and at its conclusion I sprinted neatly into my office. Miss Reingold was last seen sprinting not so neatly into Jake's.

I assumed the traditional lotus position on my desk and wondered what Miss Reingold would do with my chaotic cruelties. After minimal investigation I concluded that she had been given something to fill her dull life. I pictured her years hence with two dozen nieces and nephews clustered around her chubby knees telling them about the wicked doctor who stuck pins in patients and raped others and, under the influence of LSD and imported Scotch, fired good, hard-working people and replaced them with raving nymphomaniacs.

Feeling superior in my imaginative faculties and uncomfortable in my yoga position I stretched both arms upward. A knock on the door.

'Yo!' I answered, arms still outstretched, my tuxedo straining grotesquely. Jake stuck his head in.

'Say, Luke, baby, Miss Reingold was telling me som – '

He saw me. Jake's habitual piercing squint couldn't quite negotiate the sight: he blinked twice.

'What's up, Luke?' he asked tentatively.

I laughed. 'Oh this,' I said, fingering the tuxedo. 'Late party last night. I'm trying to wake myself up before Osterflood comes. Hope I didn't upset Miss R.'

He hesitated, his chubby neck and round face still the only parts of him which had eased their way into the room.

'Well,' he said, 'yeah. She says you fired her.'

'Nonsense,' I replied. 'I was telling her a joke I heard at the party last night; it was a little raunchy perhaps, but nothing that would upset Mary Magdalen.'

'Yeah,' he said, his traditional squint gathering strength, his glasses like two flying saucers with slits concealing deadly ray guns. 'Righto,' he said. 'Sorry to bother you.'

His face vanished, the door eased shut. While meditating I was interrupted a few minutes later by the door opening and Jake's glasses reappearing.

'She wants me to make sure she's not fired.'

'Tell her to come to work tomorrow fully prepared.'

'Righto.'

When Osterflood strode in I was limping around the room trying to get the circulation back into my feet. He walked automatically to the couch but I stopped him.

'No, you don't, Mr O. Today you sit over there and I'll use the couch.'

I made myself comfortable while he lumbered uncertainly to the chair behind my desk.

'What's the matter. Dr Rhinehart, do you – '

'I feel elated today,' I began, noting in the corner of the ceiling an impressive cobweb. For how many years had my patients been staring at that? 'I feel I've made a major breakthrough on the road to the New Man.'

'What new man?'

'The Random Man. The unpredictable man. I feel today I am demonstrating that habits can be broken. That man *is* free.'

'I wish I could break the habit of raping little girls,' he said, trying to get the focus back on himself.

'There's hope, O., there's hope. Just do the opposite of everything you normally do. If you feel like raping them, shower them with candy and kindness and then leave. If you feel like beating a whore, have her beat you. If you feel like seeing me, go to a movie instead.'

'But that's not easy. I *like* hurting people.'

'True, but you may find you'll get a kick out of kindness, too. Today, for example, I found running to work much more meaningful than my usual cab ride. I also found my cruelty to Miss Reingold refreshing. I used to enjoy being nice to her.'

'I wondered why she was crying. What happened?'

'I accused her of bad breath and body odor.'

'Jesus.'

'Yes.'

'That was a horrible thing to do. I'd never do a thing like that.'

'I hope not. But the city health authorities had issued a formal complaint that the entire building was beginning to stink. I had no choice.'

In the ensuing silence I heard his chair squeak; he may have tipped back in it, but from where I lay I couldn't tell. I could see only part of two walls, bookcases, books, my cobweb and a single small portrait of Socrates draining the hemlock. My taste in soothing pictures for patients seemed dubious.

'I've been pretty cheerful lately too,' Osterflood said meditatively, and I realized I wanted to get the focus back on *my* problems.

'Of course, habit breaking can also be a chore,' I said. 'For example, I find it difficult to improvise new methods and places for urinating.'

'I think . . . I almost think you may have brought me toward a breakthrough,' Osterflood said, ignoring me.

'I'm particularly concerned with my next bowel movement,' I went on. 'There seem to be definite limits as to what society will stand for. All sorts of eccentricity and nonsensical horrors can be permitted – wars, murder, marriage, slums – but that bowel movements should be made anywhere except in the toilet seems to be pretty universally considered despicable.'

'You know that if . . . I felt that if I could just kick my little-girl addiction, just . . . lose interest, I'd be all right. The big ones don't mind, or can be bought.'

'Also locomotion. There are only a certain number of limited ways of moving from spot A to spot B. Tomorrow, for example, I won't feel free to jog to work. What can I do? Walk backward?' I looked over to Osterflood with a serious frown, but he was immersed in his own thoughts.

'But now . . . lately . . . I got to admit it . . . I seem to be losing my interest in little girls.'

'Walking backward's a solution, of course, but only a temporary one. After that and crawling and running backward and hopping on one foot, I'll feel confined, limited, repetitious, a robot.'

'And that's good, I know it is. I mean I *hate* little girls and now that I'm less interested in fucking them I feel that's . . . definitely an advance.' He looked down at me sincerely and I looked sincerely back.

'Conversations too are a problem,' I said. 'Our syntax is habitual, our diction, our coherence. I have a habit of logical thought which clearly must be broken. And vocabulary. Why do I accept the limits of our habitual words? I'm a clod! A clod!'

183

'But . . . but . . . lately . . . I'm afraid . . . I've sensed . . . I'm almost afraid to say it . . .'

'Umpwillis. Art fodder. Wishmonger. Gladsull. Parminkson. Jombie. Blit. Why not? Man has limited himself artificially to the past. I feel myself breaking free.'

'. . . that I'm, I feel I'm beginning to want, to be like . . . little boys.'

'A breakthrough. A definite breakthrough if I can continue to contradict my habitual patterns as I have this morning. And sex. Sexual patterns must be broken too.'

'I mean really *like* them,' he said emphatically. 'Not want to rape them or hurt them or anything like that, just bugger them and have them suck me off.'

'Possibly this experiment could get me into dangerous ground. I suppose since I've habitually not been interested in raping little girls that theoretically I ought to try it.'

'And boys . . . little boys are easier to get at. They're more trusting, less suspicious.'

'But really hurting someone frightens me. I suppose – No! It is a limitation. A limitation I must overcome. To be free from habitual inhibitions I will have to rape and kill.'

His chair squeaked, and I heard one of his feet hit the ground.

'No,' he said firmly. 'No, Dr Rhinehart. I'm trying to tell you, raping and killing aren't necessary anymore. Even hitting may be out.'

'Raping, or at least killing, is absolutely necessary to the Random Man. To shirk that would be to shirk a clear duty.'

'Boys, little boys, even teen-age boys, will do just as good, I'm *sure*. It's dangerous with little girls, Doc, I warn you.'

'Danger is necessary. The whole concept of the Random Man is the most dangerous and revolutionary

184

ever conceived by man. If total victory demands blood then blood it must be.'

'No, Dr Rhinehart, no. You must find another way to work it out. A less dangerous way. These are human beings you're talking about.'

'Only according to our habitual perceptive patterns. It may well be that little girls are actually fiends from another world sent to destroy us.'

He didn't reply but I heard the chair give one small squeak.

'It's quite clear,' I went on, 'that without little girls we wouldn't have women, and women – snorfu bock clisting rinnschauer.'

'No, no, Doc, you're tempting me. I know it, I see it now. Woman *are* human beings, they must be.'

'Call them what you will, they differ from us, Osterflood, and you can't deny it.'

'I know, I know, and boys don't. Boys are us. Boys are good. I think I could learn to love boys and not to have to worry so much about the police anymore.'

'Candy and kindness to girls, O., and a stiff prick to boys: you may be right. It would, for you, definitely be a habit breaker.'

'Yes, yes.'

Someone knocked on the door. The hour was up. As I dazedly rolled my feet onto the floor I felt Mr Osterflood pumping my hand vigorously: his eyes were blazing with joy.

'This has been the greatest therapeutic hour of my life. You're . . . you're . . . you're a *boy*, Dr Rhinehart, a genuine boy.'

'Thank you, O. I hope you're right.'

185

Chapter Twenty-four

Slowly and steadily, my friends, I was beginning to go insane. I found that my residual self was changing. When I chose to let the sleeping dice lie and be my 'natural self' I discovered that I liked absurd comments, anecdotes, actions. I climbed trees in Central Park, assumed the yoga position of meditation during a cocktail party and oozed esoteric, oracular remarks every two minutes which confused and bored even me. I shouted, 'I'm Batman,' at the top of my lungs at the end of a telephone conversation with Dr Mann – all not because the dice said so, but because I felt like it.

I would break into laughter for no reason at all, I would overreact to situations, becoming angry, fearful or compassionate far in excess of that normally demanded. I wasn't *consistent*. Sometimes I'd be gay, at others sad; sometimes I'd be articulate, serious, brilliant; at others, absurd, abstracted, dumb. Only my being in the process of analysis with Jake kept me free to walk the streets. As long as I did nothing violent, people could still feel relatively at ease: 'Poor Dr Rhinehart, but Dr Ecstein is helping him.'

Lil was becoming increasingly worried about me, but since the die always rejected the option that I tell her the truth, I kept making semi-rational excuses for my absurdities. She talked with Jake and Arlene and Dr Mann, and they all had perfectly rational and usually brilliant explanations of what was happening, but unfortunately no suggestions as to how to end it.

'In a year or two . . .' said Dr Mann benevolently to

Lil, who told me she almost started screaming. I assured her that I'd try harder to control my whims.

National Habit-Breaking Month certainly didn't help matters. How upset people become when confronting the breakdown of patterns, how upset or how joy-filled. My jogging into the office, my absurd speeches, my blasphemous efforts to seduce the sexless and incorruptible Miss Reingold, my drunkenness, my nonsensical behavior with my patients – all brought to those who witnessed them shock and dismay, but also, I began to notice, pleasure.

How we laugh and take joy in the irrational, the purposeless and the absurd. Our longing for these bursts out of us against all the restraints of morality and reason. Riots, revolutions, catastrophes: how they exhilarate us. How depressing it is to read the same news day after day. Oh God, if only something would happen: meaning, if only patterns would break down.

By the end of that month I was thinking if only Nixon would get drunk and say to someone, 'Fuck you, buddy.' If only William Buckley or Billy Graham would say, 'Some of my best friends are Communists'; if only a sportscaster would just once say, 'Sure is a boring game, folks.' But they don't. So each of us travels, to Fort Lauderdale, to Vietnam, to Morocco, or gets divorced, or has an affair, or tries a new job, a new neighborhood, 6a new drug, in a desperate effort to find something new. Patterns, patterns, oh, to break those chains. But we drag our old selves with us and they impose their solid oak frames on all our experience.

But in most ways National Habit-Breaking Month turned out to be impractical; I ended up at one point letting the dice decide when I would go to bed and for how long I would sleep. My sleeping a random number of hours at randomly selected times quickly made me irritable, washed out and occasionally high, specially when kicked by drugs or alcohol. When and whether I ate, washed, shaved, brushed my teeth were also dice-determined for a three-day period. As a result, I once or twice found myself using my portable electric razor in the middle of a midtown crunch of people (passers-by looking around for the camera crew), brushing my teeth in a night-club lavatory, taking baths and getting a rubdown at Vic Tanny's and eating my main meal at 4 A.M. at Nedick's.

Another time the Die ordered me to sensitize myself to every moment, to live each moment fully awake. It seemed a marvelously aesthetic thing to do. I pictured myself as Walter Pater John Ruskin Oscar Wilde all rolled into one. What I first became aware of during Aesthetic Sensitivity Day was that I had the sniffles. I may have had them for months, years even, and never noticed it. In January, thanks to this random command of the Die, I became conscious of a periodic intake of air through my nostrils running through some accumulated mucus which produced a sound normally denoted as a 'sniff.' Were it not for the dice I would have remained an insensitive clod.

I became aware of other previously unrealized sense experiences during that Sensitivity Week. Lying in bed with Lil in the early morning hours I would listen fascinated to the symphony of street noises from below, noises which previously I had named silence – meaning that Larry and Evie were not awake. Admittedly after about two days they became a quite monotonous and second-rate symphony, but for two mornings they – and I – lived again. Another day I went to the Museum of Modern Art and tried desperately to experience aesthetic bliss, decided after half an hour to shoot for simple pleasure and settled at the end of a footsore hour and a half for being content with a low level of pain. My visual sense

188

must have atrophied at some point and even the mighty dice couldn't resurrect it. The next day I was happy the dice killed off Walter Pater.

In general, during that month in clothes I wore what I never wore, in words I swore what I never swore, in sex I whored what I never whored.

Breaking sexual habits and values was the hardest of all. In rambling down the stairs to merge with Arlene I was not altering my sexual values: I was only fulfilling them. Adultery did break a habit of fidelity, but fidelity was the most trivial of my sexual habit-values. Mary, Mother of Jesus, once suggested that the nature of a person's sexuality defines his whole life, but she knew better than to assume that when one had defined an individual as heterosexual, homosexual, bisexual or asexual one was done. I at first didn't know better. I assumed in my typical mechanical way that breaking sexual habits meant changing favorite sexual positions, changing women, changing from women to men, from men to boys, changing to total abstention and so on. My polymorphous perverse tendencies were vaguely thrilled by this prospect and I began one night, returning from a party, by trying to penetrate my wife's anus at 2 A.M. in the apartment elevator. Lil, however, not so much indignant or inhibited as uninterested, insisted on getting out of the elevator and going to bed and going to sleep.

Since Arlene and I seemed to have made love in most of the normal conceivable ways, the only way to break habits there, I concluded, was to abstain, or even better, feel guilty about our affair.

When I turned for a new woman I realized that it was my duty according to the mandate to change my taste in women. Therefore my next conquest would have to be old, thin, gray-haired, wear glasses, have big feet and be fond of Doris Day–Rock Hudson movies. Although I'm sure many such women exist in New York, I soon realized that they were as difficult to locate and date as the equal number of women whose figures more or less matched that of Raquel Welch. I would have to lower my standards to old, thin and spiritual and let the other precise trivialities fall as they may.

The image of Miss Reingold leapt to my mind and I shuddered. If I were to break my sexual values I would have to seduce her. When consulted, the die said yes.

Seldom have I felt less respect for the die's judgment. Miss Reingold was undoubtedly the antithesis of all my sexual appetites, the Brigitte Bardot of my netherworld. She wasn't of course old; rather she had the remarkable ability to create at the age of thirty-six the impression she was sixty-three. The idea that she urinated was unthinkable, and I blush even to write about it here. In one thousand two hundred and six days with Ecstein and Rhinehart not once to our knowledge had she used the office bathroom. The only odor she gave off was the pervasive smell of baby powder. I didn't know whether she was flat-chested or not; one doesn't speculate on the measurements of one's mother or grandmother.

Her speech was more chaste than that of a Dickensian heroine; she would read back a report on the sexual activities of a superhuman nymphomaniac as if it were a long, bullish announcement of a corporation's phenomenal growth activities. At the end she would ask: 'Would you like me to change the sentence about Miss Werner's multiple intercourse into parallel structure?'

Nevertheless, not my will, O Die, but Thy will be done, and with morbid fascination I took her out to dinner one evening about three weeks through National Habit-Breaking Month and, as the evening progressed, began to sense, much to my horror, that I might succeed. I went to the men's room after dinner and consulted the die about several possible options, but all it told me to do was to smoke marijuana cigarettes; no cocaine before the tooth-pulling. Squirm as I might, I found myself later that evening sitting beside her on the couch discussing (I swear *I* didn't introduce the subject) nymphomaniacs. Although I'd begun to note as the hours wore by that she had a pretty smile (when she kept her mouth fully closed), her lowcut black dress on her white body reminded me somehow of a black drape hung on a vertical coffin.

'But do you think nymphomaniacs enjoy their lives?' I was saying with the spontaneous randomness and blissful indifference which pot smoking and Miss Reingold seemed to produce.

'Oh no,' she said quickly, nudging her spectacles up an eighth of an inch. 'They must be very unhappy.'

'Yes, perhaps, but I can't help wondering if the great pleasure they get from being loved by so many men doesn't compensate for their unhappiness.'

'Oh no. Dr Ecstein told me that according to Rogers, Rogers and Hillsman, eighty-two point five percent receive no pleasure from copulation.' She was sitting so stiffly on the couch that periodically my pot-polluted vision made me believe I was talking to a dressmaker's dummy.

'Yeah,' I said. 'But Rogers nor Rogers nor Hillsman have ever been nymphomaniacs. I doubt they've ever been women.' I smiled triumphantly. 'A theory I'm developing is that nymphomaniacs actually are joy-filled hedonists but lie to psychiatrists that they're frigid in order to seduce the psychiatrists.'

'Oh no,' she said. 'Who could ever seduce a psychiatrist?'

For a moment we blinked incredulously at each other, and then she went through a kaleidoscope of colors, ending with typing-paper white.

'You're right,' I said firmly. 'The woman is a patient and our code of ethics prevents our giving in to them, but . . .' I trailed off, losing the thread of my argument.

In her small voice, with her two hands wrestling with her handkerchief, she asked:

'But . . . ?'

'But?' I echoed.

'You said your code prevents you from ever giving in to them but . . .'

'Oh yeah. But it's hard. We're continually being excited but with no ethical way of satisfying ourselves.'

'Oh, Dr Rhinehart, you're *married*.'

'Married? Oh yes. That's true. I'd forgotten.' I looked at her, my face a tragic mask. 'But my wife practices yoga and consequently can only engage in sexual congress with a guru.'

She stared back at me.

'Are you certain?' she asked.

'I can't even do a modified headstand. I have come to doubt that I am a man.'

'Oh no, Dr Rhinehart.'

'To make matters worse, it has always depressed me that you never seem to be sexually attracted to me.'

Miss Reingold's face went through its psychedelic color show and again ended in typing-paper white. Then she said in the smallest audible voice I've ever heard:

'But I am.'

'You . . . you . . .'

'I am sexually attracted to you.'

'Oh.'

I paused, all the forces of the residual me mobilizing my body to run for the door; only religious discipline kept me on the couch.

'Miss Reingold!' I shouted impulsively. 'Will you make me a man?' I sat erect and leaned toward her.

She stared at me, removed her glasses from her face and placed them on the rug beside the couch.

'No, no,' she said softly, her eyes focusing vaguely on the couch between us. 'I can't.'

At first, for the only time in my life not dictated by the die, I was impotent. I had to sit on the bed beside her, nude, in a modified lotus position, not touching, and for seven or eight minutes meditate with all the powers of a yogi on Arlene's breasts, Linda Reichman's behind and Lil's innards, until, at last, with the powers properly concentrated, I assumed the cat's cradle position over Miss Reingold's assumed corpse position and lowered myself into *samadhi* (emptiness).

It is a frightening experience to make love to one's mother, especially one's mother as a corpse, and nowhere near what Freud imagined it. That I looked upon her as a mother image and yet succeeded in assuming the proper positions and fulfilling all the appropriate exercises is a tribute to my budding abilities as a yogi. It was a great step forward in the breaking of psychological barriers, and I trembled all the next day thinking about it. Surprisingly also, I've felt much closer to Miss Reingold ever since.

Chapter Twenty-five

But not *that* close.

Chapter Twenty-six

My friends, it's time for confession. Amusing as I or you may have found some of the events in my early dicelife, I must admit that being the dice man was sometimes hard work. Depressing, lonely and hard. The fact is, I didn't want to go bowling. Or to break up with Arlene for a month. Or play an outfielder for the Detroit Tigers. Or seduce Miss Reingold. Or have sexual intercourse in one sexual position when Lil wanted it in another. Fulfilling these missions of fate was a chore. Fulfilling many others was a chore. Sometimes when the dice sent me rolling randomly to a bowling alley or vetoed my playing Romeo, I felt like the slave you take me to be, yoked to an unsympathetic and unintelligent master, one whose whims were getting increasingly on my nerves. The resistance of my residual self to certain dice decisions never ceased and always dragged at my desire to become the Random Man. I was attempting to permit that one desire, the desire to kill my old self and to learn something new about the nature of man, to dominate the vast majority of the rest of my desires. It was an ascetic, religious struggle.

Sometimes, of course, the dice discovered and permitted the expression of some of my deepest (and previously unrealized) impulses, and as time passed this occurred more and more frequently. But at other times the dice discovered that I hadn't gone bowling for fourteen years because I didn't like to bowl, and I hadn't slept with a fat slob because I was correct in sensing I wouldn't enjoy it. I suppose some suppressed one-thousandth of me may

195

like bowling, clods, slobs and position twenty-three, but my level of perception wasn't able to record it.

And so you, my friends, when you've picked up a pencil and written a list of options and rolled the dice, you may be disappointed. You've gone through the motions a few times and then concluded that the dicelife is a fake and I a fraud.

One desire, my friends, one: to kill yourself. You must desire this. You must feel that a voyage of discovery is more important than all the little trips which the normal consumer-self wants to buy.

The dice save only the lost. The normal, integrated personality resists variety, change. But the split, compulsive, unhappy neurotic is given release from the prison of checks and balances. He becomes in a way an 'authoritarian personality,' but obeys not God, father, church, dictator or philosopher but his own creative imagination – and the dice. 'If the fool would but persist in his folly,' Yossarian once said, 'he would become the dice man.'

But it isn't easy; only saints and the insane ever try it. And only the latter make it.

Chapter Twenty-seven

For February the dice ordered me to experiment with the Felloni–Rhinehart sex investigation. Specifically: 'Do something new and valuable.' I squared up the cubes in their little box and spent several days trying to see what. I became depressed.

The limitations in experimenting with human beings were great. You could force them to answer anything, but force them to *do* nothing. With the other animals, of course, you could ask them nothing and make them *do* anything. You could castrate them, cut out half their brain, make them walk over hot coals to get their dinner or their mate, deprive them of food, water, sex or society for days or months, give them LSD in such massive dosages that they died of excess ecstasy, cut off their limbs one by one and study mobility and so on. Such experimentation tells us journals-ful about castrated mice, brainless rats, schizophrenic hamsters, lonely rabbits, ecstatic sloths and legless chimpanzees, but unfortunately nothing about man.

For ethical reason we aren't allowed to ask subjects to do anything which they or their society consider unethical. The problem to which I was devoting my life – how much a human being can be changed – could never be touched by scientists, since the bone ingredient of all men is their resistance to change; and it is unethical to insist that subjects do anything they don't want to do.

I decided to try to change some of the subjects of the Felloni–Rhinehart investigation. Since the research dealt with sexual behavior I would try to change sexual

197

attitudes, proclivities and actions. Unfortunately, I knew that it took two years of analysis to change a homosexual to heterosexual, and that then such change rarely occurred. Could I convert virgins to nymphomania? Masturbators to rakehood? Faithful wives to adulteresses? Seducers to ascetics? Very doubtful. But possible.

To change man, the audience by which he judges himself must be changed. A man is defined by his audience: by the people, institutions, authors, magazines, movie heroes, philosophers by whom he pictures himself being cheered and booed. Major psychological disturbances, 'identity crises,' are caused when an individual begins to change the audience for whom he plays: from parents to peers; from peers to the works of Albert Camus; from the Bible to Hug.. Hefner. The change from I-am-he-who-is-a-good-son to I-am-he-who-is-a-good-buddy constitutes a revolution. On the other hand, if the man's buddies approve fidelity one year and infidelity the next, and the man changes from faithful husband to rake, no revolution has occurred. The class rule remains intact; only the policy on a minor matter has been altered.

In first becoming the dice man, my audience was changed from my peers in psychiatry to Blake, Nietzsche, Lao-Tzu. My goal was to destroy all sense of an audience; to become without values, evaluators, without desires: to be inhuman, all-inclusive, God.

In moving the dice man into sexual research, however, what I aspired to was a piece of ass. Zeus wished to disguise himself as beast and fornicate with a beautiful woman. But my equal desire, as strong as lust, was to become the audience for our subjects. As audience I might be able to create an atmosphere of all-embracing permissiveness, one in which the virgin would feel free to express her latest lech; the queer to express his latent desire for cunt. The dice man had discovered that the experimenting man was permitted almost everything. Could I create an experimental situation for the subjects which would be equally permissive?

Such was my hope. Seduction is the art of making normal, desirable, good and rewarding what had previously seemed abnormal, undesirable, evil and unrewarding. Seduction was the art of changing another's audience and hence his personality. I refer, of course, to the classical seduction of the 'innocent' and not to the mutual masturbation of promiscuous adults.

Dr Felloni's dean-of-women dignity and my own rugged, professional look had convinced our subjects that we were the epitome of respectability. They had become more accustomed than the average person to discussing all sorts of outrageous sexuality with strange, noncondemning adults. All of this might ready them, so my thinking went, for any outrageous instructions we might give them.

'Now this afternoon, Mr F., in the next room is a shy but promiscuous young woman your own age. She has been paid to make love to you. Be a gentleman with her, but insist that she fuck good. At the conclusion of your experience fill out the questionnaire in this sealed envelope. Be as honest as possible with your answers; they will be completely anonymous.'

'Miss F., in the next room is a shy young man your own age named F. Like yourself he is a virgin. He has been told that you are a prostitute hired to teach him the art of love. For this experiment we wish to see how well you can play this role by interacting with him sexually to permit us to collect as much data as possible. If you overcome your inhibitions about nudity and intimate sexual contact with a man you will receive a bonus of one hundred dollars. If you permit him to have sexual intercourse you will receive a bonus of two hundred dollars. For other possible bonuses read pages five and six of the enclosed instruction sheet and questionnaire. You need not fear pregnancy, since the other subject has been medically certified as sterile.'

'Tomorrow afternoon, Mr J., you are to go to the address printed on this card. You will meet there a man who has been told you are a fellow homosexual. He will attempt to seduce you. You are to encourage him as much as possible, while noting your own feelings and reactions. If he achieves an orgasm you will receive a bonus of one hundred dollars for producing such significant data. If you also achieve orgasm you will receive an additional two-hundred-dollar bonus. We are interested in studying the social and sexual intercourse between normal men like yourself and homosexual men. Within the enclosed . . .'

Instructions like these came parading through my mind. I might have to hire prostitutes and homosexuals, but in some cases I might have subjects playing both roles. (Two heterosexual men banging away at each other collecting data.)

I began to believe that human beings are capable of anything. Our other-directed modern men are so accustomed to looking to the immediate social environment for approval or disapproval that, given the correct experimental leader, tone and situation, I should be able to get the subjects to alter their customary sexual roles.

It seemed a worthy project, worthy of the Marquis de Sade. Consciously, I wanted to confirm my theory of the malleability of man, but I seemed to be taking a rather fiendish non-rational delight in the prospect.

Chapter Twenty-eight

Hectic, hectic, hectic. The life of an experimenter is not easy. To set up mazes, find rats to run them, measure the results and to tabulate everything is hard. To set up sexual encounters, find people to run them, measure the results and *believe* everything is harder.

Nevertheless, in the next few weeks I completed the complicated task of setting up what was officially named the Rhinehart–Felloni Investigation of Amorality Tolerance, but which has become generally known among New York psychiatrists as 'Fuck Without Fear for Fun and Profit,' and in the New York *Daily News* as 'The Columbia Copulation Caper.' I had some trouble convincing Dr Felloni of the correctness of our joint venture, but I took her to lunch one day and just kept talking about 'test of the stability of behavioral patterns and attitudes under experimental conditions' and 'the Leiberwitz–Loom criteria for defining a homosexual,' and 'heterosexuality as defined operationally by the maintenance of an erection in the presence of a woman for five or more minutes' and, as my clincher, 'the complete quantification of all results.' She finally agreed and laid great professional stress on the necessity of anonymity for all subjects.

The first two weeks of the experiment were incredibly confusing. Too many of our hired personnel – prostitutes male and female – were failing to show up or, more usually, failing to follow instructions. Women hired to play hard-to-get would bring along a friend and give our subject an orgy. Another woman hired to exhaust a Don

Juan type sexually, fell asleep after fifteen minutes and couldn't be roused even by a gentle beating with a belt.

Many of our subjects, after seeming to agree to the experiment, disappeared. I was desperate for subjects, 'lab assistants' (our 'help' was so designated in our budget and foundation report) and data. I found myself tempted to hire my wife, Arlene, Miss Reingold even, to meet the various appointments. Dr Felloni reported that she was having the same problem with the group of subjects she was dealing with. The confusion was further compounded by our having to use the same two apartments for all our 'experimental sessions.'

I sent Arlene out to play the role of a lonely, prudish, love-sick housewife for a sexually hard-up and inhibited college student who had been instructed to play the role of a Henry Miller; she came back exhilarated. She announced that the evening had been a total success, although she admitted that nothing much had happened for the first two hours and that she may not have stuck completely to her assigned role when she walked into the living room nude after taking a shower. She volunteered to assist in any way she could if needed further for the experiment and even agreed not to tell Jake.

Finally I decided that the old coach himself had to get off the bench and into the game. Someone had to get in there who could plug up the holes when they needed to be plugged or burst up the middle of a score. A hush fell over the crowd when I trotted onto the field.

Miss T. was required by the instructions to: 'Spend the evening at the apartment of Mr O., age thirty-five. Man will have paid one hundred dollars to spend the evening with you. Mr O. is a lonely college professor whose wife died a year ago. He knows nothing about this experiment and believes a friend has provided him with a young,

202

inexperienced call girl. You are to try to give yourself to him as completely as possible. Examine closely your own attitudes and emotions and fill out the questions contained in the enclosed envelope.'

According to her answers on our attitude questionnaires, Miss T. was nineteen years old, had never had sexual intercourse, had 'necked heavily' with only two boys, had kissed 'less than ten' boys and had never had any conscious lesbian inclinations or experiences. She believed that premarital sexual intercourse was wrong because 'God punished it finitely,' it was 'psychologically unhealthy' and there was 'danger of pregnancy.' She affirmed that as a positive attribute it procreated the race. According to her she had never masturbated because 'God punished it finitely.' She was vaguely intolerant of all sexual deviations from the heterosexual norm, extremely conventional in most other attitudes and indicated no close relationships with anyone except her mother, to whom she seemed quite close. She reported that she was a believing Catholic and hoped to be a social work for emotionally disturbed children.

It seemed to me unlikely that Miss T. would even show up. Of the seven other subjects to whom I had given similar instructions (to meet each other or hired help), three had never appeared, and two of the desertees were quiet types like Miss T. The assigned time was 'around eight o'clock.' I, in a generous act of self-employment arrived at seven-thirty, and, after fixing myself a small drink, was settling down for a long wait when the bell rang. At the door I found a young woman who announced that she was 'Terry Tracy.' It was five of eight.

Terry Tracy looked up at me brightly like a teenager arriving for a baby-sitting assignment. She was short and pert, with warm brown eyes, soft brown hair and a nervous grace which reminded me of Natalie Wood. She was wearing a skirt and loose turtleneck sweater and carrying her homework crooked in her left arm (it turned out to be her sealed manila folder with the questionnaire.) I awkwardly invited her in, feeling like a decrepit and obscenely lecherous old man.

'Can I fix you a drink?' I asked. It occurred to me that this girl might have misunderstood the instructions.

'Yes, please,' she said and, walking into the middle of the room, looked around at the absolutely conventional modern couch, chairs, bureau, bookcase and rugs as if they had been imported from the moon.

'My name is Robert O'Connor. I'm a professor of history at Long Island University.'

'I'm Terry Tracy,' she said brightly, looking at me for all the world as though I were an interesting uncle about to beguile her with sea yarns.

I tried to meditate with pseudo-serenity upon my drink but felt ridiculous.

'Seen any good movies lately?' I asked.

'Oh no. I don't go to movies very much.'

'They're very expensive these days.'

'Oh yes. And a lot of them are . . . well . . . not very *worthwhile.*'

'That's true.'

She looked over at the fireplace. I looked at the fireplace. It had a little wood-burning grate that looked as though it hadn't been used since the apartment had been built ninety years ago.

'Would you like to have a fire?' I asked.

'Oh no. It's warm enough, thank you.'

I sipped at my drink and licked the sweat off part of the outside of the cold glass. It occurred to me that this might be the most sensuous thing I would do all evening.

'Come over and sit by me, why don't you.' A hippopotamus eating a daisy.

'I'm very comfortable here, thank you.' After looking nervously at the fireplace for a few moments she added, 'All right.'

Balancing her drink carefully like a child with her first cup of milk, she came over and seated herself about a foot from me on the couch. She modestly tugged down once on her miniskirt, which remained, however, a few feet above her knees. She seemed incredibly small. At six four I was used to looking down at people, but looking down at Terry Tracy to my left all I could see was her curly brown hair and her two seemingly nude legs.

'Hey,' I said.

She looked up with a smile, but a certain vagueness seemed to have crept into her eyes, as if her yarn-spinning uncle had just used the word *bordello*.

'May I kiss you?' I asked. At a hundred bucks a toss it didn't seem too much to ask.

Her eyes went vaguer and she said, 'Oh yes.'

I pulled her little body to me and leaned down to meet her lips. Without premeditation I found myself kissing only with my lips upon her lips. Her mouth was small, her lips dry. After a few seconds I straightened up.

'You're awfully pretty,' I said.

'Thank you.'

'Your lips are very nice.'

'Yours are too,' she said.

'Now you kiss me.'

She looked up and waited for me to lower my head, but I remained upright and even leaned back against the couch while still looking down at her, sexily.

After a moment's uncertainty, she placed her drink on the coffee table and got up on her knees. Putting her hands on my neck she slowly leaned toward me. My arms circled her, one hand closed hard around a buttock and I pressed my mouth and tongue against hers. For ten, fifteen, twenty, thirty seconds I kept my tongue in her mouth and moved my hands over her back, buttocks and thighs. Her body was small but firm, her little behind round and rubbery through the woollen skirt. Finally I pulled back and looked at her.

She smiled the smile of a straight-A student.

'That was awfully nice,' I said.

'Oh yes. It was good,' she replied.

'Put your tongue in my mouth,' I said, and as I slid sideways to a horizontal position on the couch, I pulled her over on top of me. She was remarkably light and her tongue came out of her small mouth in little tentative darts like a snake trying to frighten someone. I brought both my hands up under her skirt and panties and exploring between her legs, got lost. That is, of the two caves traditionally located in the underbrush, I was able to locate only one, and that, in the immortal words of Robert Frost, 'The one less traveled by.' Had she been sewn up? I discovered and caressed a slippery crack, but it led not to the warm-cushioned opening of a Lil or Arlene but to a dead end: a virgin with a vengeance.

She pulled up a few inches away from me.

'Please don't touch me there,' she said.

'I beg your pardon,' I said and delicately withdrew my hands and smoothed down her skirt.

She hesitated a moment and then brought her little mouth down warmly on mine, her hands framing my face. Her abdomen pressing down on my extended penis began to create climactic feelings so I broke our kiss and rolled us both into sitting positions again. She looked up at me brightly, as if pleased by having brought home a good report card. Of course it may have been the brightness of sexual excitement: certainly my gooey fingers didn't indicate scholarly interests. Looking at her a bit drunkenly I asked in a husky voice:

'Shall we go to the bedroom?'

'Oh no,' she said, 'I have to finish my drink.' Further straightening her skirt, she reached forward and took a healthier swig from her gin and tonic. I rediscovered my glass on the floor at my feet and finished it off.

'Are you a professor?' she asked.

'Yes, I am.'

'What of?'

'Of history.'

'Oh yes, you told me. That must be interesting. What history do you like best?'

'I'm a specialist in papal bulls of the Renaissance. Look, can't I get you another drink?'

'Oh really? I loved reading about Cesare Borgia and the Popes. I'd love another drink. Were the Popes really as bad as the books say?'

I walked liquorward a trifle aggressively but said over my shoulder: 'It all depends on what you mean by bad.'

'I mean have children and all.'

'Alexander I had several children as did Pope John IX, but before they became Popes.'

'The Church is much purer today.'

I poured her a huge gin, added a trickle of tonic, gave myself a bathtub-glassful of Scotch and marched back toward the couch.

'How much college have you finished?' I asked.

'This is my fourth semester at Hunter. I'm majoring in sociology, I think. Oh! – Er! – '

'What's the matter?' For a moment I thought I must have spilled her drink as I handed it to her, but it wasn't that. My fly wasn't open. But she looked frightened.

'Nothing,' she said and took a deep drink from her gin and tonic. 'But . . . how did you . . . I mean why did you think I went to college?'

207

'You seem intelligent,' I said. 'You couldn't know all about the Renaissance just from high school.'

She looked away from me at the grimy, unused fireplace and didn't seem to be as cheerful as she had been.

'Doesn't it seem . . . strange that a college girl should be . . . here?'

Ah. Her breach of role playing was bothering her.

'Certainly not,' I said firmly. 'According to my friend, almost all the call girls he knows are college students, many of them straight-A students. Tuition costs being what they are, what can a girl do?'

This line of reasoning seemed to take some time to absorb. She blushed and turned away at the phrase *call girl,* but finally said quietly:

'That's true.'

'Also,' I said, 'college girls learn how irrational all sexual inhibitions are. They learn how safe sexual intercourse can be and how profitable.'

'But – ' she said. 'But – of course some girls still fear that God – that sex – '

'You're right there, of course. But even many deeply religious college girls have also become call girls.'

She now looked up at me questioningly.

'They realize,' I went on, 'that God always examines the *reasons* we do anything. If a girl gives her body to a man to give him pleasure and to earn money so that she may educate herself and thus increase her ability to serve God she is actually performing a good act.'

She looked away nervously.

'But God says adultery is a sin,' she said.

'Ah, but the Hebrew word for adultery, *fornicatio*, actually means sexual intercourse had only for pleasure. The Commandment actually should be translated: "Though shalt not selfishly give yourself in adultery." Many of the girls at LIU in Bible History 162 have been quite surprised and pleased to realize the true nature of God's command.'

She was hunched over on the couch beside me drinking her gin with absentminded abandonment. She stared into her glass as if it might hold the ultimate answers.

'But God says that . . .' she started. 'Paul says that . . . the Church says that – '

'Only *selfish* pleasure. The Hebrew is absolutely explicit. In Second Corinthians, verse eight, the text reads: "She who lets a man know her for the glory of God is blessed, but woe unto her who in selfishness commits adultery. Verily the very earth will swallow her up." '

Again hesitation. Then:

'The glory of God?' she asked.

'Saint Thomas Aquinas interprets this as meaning any act which is intended to further the individual's ability to glorify God. He cites the case of Bathsheba's daughter who gave herself to the Aramite that she might convert him. He also cites the prostitute Magdalen of the New Testament who, according to tradition, continued to sell herself to men that she might better know them and testify to the Divinity of Christ.'

'Really?' she said sharply, as if at last Truth were being touched.

'In Dante's *Paradiso,* which you may have read, the religious prostitutes are placed in the third sphere of heaven, just below the saints, but above the nuns and virgins. In the words of Beatrice, his guide, "A fugitive and cloistered virtue can never reach as close to God as an active one. If the soul is pure the body cannot be soiled." '

'Oh, I read that. Was that Dante?'

'*Paradiso,* Canto Seventeen, I think. Milton paraphrased this verse in his famous essay on divorce.'

'It's funny . . .' she said and jiggled the remaining ice cubes in her glass before taking another swallow.

'The Church has naturally played down this tradition,' I said, taking a satisfied swallow from my own drink. 'It has felt that young girls might be seduced unnecessarily in their dream of converting men, and although such an act would not be sinful, it was decided to create the impression that all sex was evil. The masses, of course, have thus lived in ignorance of God's true purpose.'

At last she looked up at me and smiled sadly.

'I'm going to take more history,' she said.

I turned to her, and with my right hand brushed away her hair from her cheek.

'I'd love to have a student like you in one of my classes. I get so lonely for someone with whom I can talk about things.'

'Do you?'

'I feel spiritually lost, alone – since losing my wife. I've needed the warmth of a woman's mind and body, but until this evening all I've ever met were dull, pedantic women that weren't able to . . . unselfishly give themselves to me.'

'I like you very much,' she said tentatively.

'Ah Terry, Terry . . .'

I took her in my arms, spilling the last of her drink onto the floor and couch. I hugged her tenderly, my eyes, well above the level of her head, fixing idly on the manila folder on the bookcase. The radio was blaring, 'Why Don't We Do It in the Road?'

'Please, my darling,' I said, 'come with me now to the bedroom.'

She held herself still in my arms and didn't answer. The music stopped, and the radio announcer began running off at the mouth about the incredible power of Gleem toothpaste: he followed that without pausing for breath with kind words for Robert Hall's.

'You're so big,' she finally said.

'I have a great need for you.'

She remained still. I released my embrace and looked down at her. She looked up at me nervously and said: 'Kiss me first.' She reached her arms up around my neck, and as we kissed I slid heavily forward on top of her. We writhed together for more than a minute.

'Am I too heavy?' I asked.

'A little bit,' she said.

'Let's go to the bedroom.'

We disentangled and stood up. 'Where to?' she asked, as if we were about to begin a long hike.

'This way,' I said, and after we had negotiated the ten paces into the bedroom I added: 'That's the bathroom.' We looked at each other. 'You undress there. I'll undress here.'

'Thank you,' she said and walked into the bathroom, her shoulder just bumping the doorway as she entered. I undressed myself, dropping my clothes neatly in select piles between the bed and an old walnut dresser. Inside the kingsize double bed, I put my hand behind my head and watched the ceiling swirl like cosmic nebulae. Five minutes later the nebulae were still providing the only active entertainment.

'Terry?' I called neutrally.

'I can't,' she said from inside the bathroom.

'What?' I said loudly.

She came out fully dressed, her eyes red and the lipstick on her lower lip completely chewed away. Standing stiffly halfway between the bathroom door and the bed she said: 'It's been a mistake. I'm not who you think I am.'

'Then who are you?'

'I'm – I'm nobody.'

'Oh no, Terry, you're wonderful, whoever you are.'

'I'm – but I can't go to bed with you.'

'Ah Terry,' I said and started to get out of bed when I saw by her facial expression that she might run. Sitting up, I said: 'Well then, who are you?'

'I'm – I was sent here as part of a – an experiment of the Columbia Medical School.'

'No!' I said, flabbergasted.

'Yes, I'm really just a college girl, a pretty innocent college girl, I guess. I wanted to do the experiment the best I could, but I can't.'

'My God, Terry, that's incredible, that's wonderful. So was I.'

She looked at me blankly.

'So – were – you – what?'

'I was sent here as part of an investigation into the nature of human sexuality conducted by the Columbia Medical School. I'm Father Forbes of the Cathedral of St John the Divine.'

She stared at my bulky, nude torso.

'I see,' she said.

'The quirks of fate have sent together two innocents!' I raised my eyes to the ceiling briefly; it responded with a swirl.

'I've got to go,' she answered.

'My child, you can't go. Don't you see there is the hand of God in this? Have you ever given yourself to a man?'

'No, Father, and I must go.'

'My child, you must stay. By everything that is holy you must stay.' I rose with stately dignity from the bed and with a look of great fatherliness and agape, arms outstretched in welcome, I approached Miss T.

'No,' she said and held up one arm limply.

I never hesitated, but embraced her fully and fatherly,

stroking her hair with one hand and her back with the other.

'My sweet child, you are my salvation. Had I sinned with a prostitute I would be forever damned; the woman would have been acting selfishly and I would have been a cause of her sin. But sexual congress with a Catholic girl giving herself against her will, and thus unselfishly, is to liberate you from sin and me from corruption.'

She stood stiffly and unyielding in my loose embrace. Then she began crying.

'I don't believe you're a priest, I want to go home.' She huddled and sobbed against my upper belly.

'In nomine Pater incubus dolorarum; et filia spiritu grandus magnum est. Non solere sanctum raro punctilius insularum, noncuninglingus variorum delictim. Habere est cogitare.'

She looked up at me.

'But why are you here?'

'Manus Patri, manus Patri. For you, my child, that we may come together in a love spiritus delicti et corpus boner.'

'You're so strange,' she said.

'This is a sacred moment. Go, and come.'

When she came out of the bathroom a second time two minutes later she was modestly holding a towel against her belly, but exposing two cheerful, round little pink breasts.

I threw back the covers on her side and she hopped in, a ten-year-old child hopping into bed with her teddy bears.

Terry Tracy fulfilled her spiritual duties, my friends, with admirable warmth, poise, obedience and skill. Too much skill. When I had difficulty penetrating her at first, I encouraged her to baptize the uncircumcised child with the sacred water of her mouth and this she proceeded to do so devotedly that it was some several minutes before I recalled my central quest. By that time I was too spiritually primed to exert any pressure without the likelihood of my achieving immediate and complete divine grace. She sympathetically consoled me with her hands and then lowered her sacred mouth over the trembling child, bathing it: she spoke in tongues. I was groaning with total incoherence and indignity as one does during such emotional services when I felt the Holy Spirit ascending. I tried to withdraw the uncircumcised child from the holy temple and whispered 'Stop!' but the angel did not cease her ministrations. The nebulae, the child and I all exploded at once in a divine fusion of feeling: I plunged away in her mouth. After ten or fifteen seconds during which I was completely out of the mere world of mortal men, I returned from my spiritual journey.

Her mouth and hands were still warmly engulfing my penis and balls as if nothing had happened. I lay still for another half-minute and then putting a hand on Terry's hand I said:

'Terry.'

She raised her head from me for the first time in three or four minutes, but without even turning to me she swung her behind around much nearer me and said:

'Touch me. Oh please touch me.'

When I put my hands between her legs and began to stroke and poke, she pressed back fiercely. This time I slid a finger inside the appropriate and proper opening. Her mouth was trying to swallow a relatively relaxed and thoroughly baptized member. She rolled over and for the first time made a groan. Of sorts: it sounded distinctly like one of disappointment.

I was feeling depressed, guilty, angry and inadequate, but being the dice man playing the professor-priest-customer I merely rolled away from her and told her that it had been delicious.

She didn't say anything. We lay in silence for ten minutes. I was determined to ram home to victory as soon as I could rally my red army back into the peninsula, but for the time being all I could do was lie there and feel inadequate. I didn't even wonder what she was thinking.

'Can you try again?' she said.

We turned toward each other and fell into a passionate half-hate embrace, until she clawed at my shoulder to tell me I was squeezing too tight. After a few minutes of love play I lifted her up onto her hands and knees and invited myself to try to enter from the rear. We placed the dragon's head at the mouth of the cave and tried to encourage him to enter. It was like pushing a dog down the cellar stairs for a bath. We pressed again. A marvelous thing happened: my dragon suddenly sprung past the outside barrier and plunged in a full three-quarter inch. She screamed and fell forward. I began to apologize, but she got immediately back on her knees and was groping back between her legs: a steering committee. After a few more charges, the dragon had disappeared deep into the cave and seemed to be nuzzling contentedly at her stomach. My big hands manipulating her easily at the waist, I felt the present experience was well worth the wait. It was magnificent. The apartment doorbell rang.

For a moment both of us were so intent on the pleasure of my filling her insides that the noise didn't register. When it did, she raised her head like a deer smelling a rifle and said:

'What's that?'

Stupidly: 'The doorbell.'

She pulled herself down and away from me and rolled over. She was frightened.

'Who is it?'

Stupidly: 'I don't know.'

Then, regaining my superman self: 'It must be someone at the wrong apartment.'

'No. You'd better go see.'

Standing at the door was a short, thickset young man wearing glasses. He seemed stunned to see me.

'Is this – ' he glanced again at the door I was holding slightly ajar. 'Is this apartment 4-G?'

Not remembering, I leaned my naked torso out and around to look at what he had just looked at. It was 4-G.

'Yes, it is,' I said helpfully.

He stared at me.

'I thought – I was supposed – to meet someone here at nine o'clock.'

'Nine o'clock?' I was beginning to understand.

'I guess I'm a little late . . . Maybe – '

'Were you – were you supposed to meet a girl here who – '

'Yes,' he broke in. 'I was supposed to meet a girl here.' He smiled nervously and adjusted his blond-framed glasses. I noticed two pimples on his forehead.

'What's your name?' I asked, still holding the door ajar.

'Er – Ray Smith.'

'I see.' His real name as I remembered it was O'Reilly, and he was, according to his answers on the questionnaire, a smooth, uninhibited young man with women. He was to meet a prostitute, one I had personally hired and instructed to make him feel as inadequate as possible. He'd arrived ahead of schedule.

'Come in, Ray,' I said and swung open the door. 'My name is Ned Petersen. I'm here to make sure Terry – that's our girl's name – gives you her money's worth.'

He looked at me – I was naked – and at the absolutely

216

conventional furniture as if he were the first visitor to a Martian living room.

'Terry's already in bed. I was warming her up. You want to give her a ride now?'

'No. No. You go ahead. I'll read a book,' and he stared toward the bookcase.

'Don't be silly,' I said. 'She's here for you. I was just tuning her up, breaking her in.'

'But if you . . .' he looked at me conscientiously. There was egg or something near the shoulder of his sweater. Not too smooth.

'Tell you what,' I said. 'Let's both go in to her. It would be lonely for either of us alone out here.'

'No, no. You go ahead.'

'Won't do it. Absolutely refuse to leave you alone in the living room. Now come. Come on.'

I took him by the elbow and led him into the bedroom. The bed was empty.

'Terry?'

'Yes,' came a highly affected voice from the bathroom.

'A young student of mine is here. Young divinity student. Very lonely young man. Desperately needs companionship. Can he join us?'

What Ray Smith O'Reilly thought of that I didn't know. From the bathroom came silence.

'Who?' she finally asked.

I walked over close to the door.

'A very lonely young anchorite needs your attention. He has a deep need. He's almost crying. Can he join us in bed?'

'Oh yes,' she answered promptly.

Beside the bed where I had left him, Smith stood like an abandoned bulbless lamp. With great gentleness I helped him undress and guided him to the location of the bed. He pulled the covers up to his chin like an

217

eighty-year-old preparing for thirty below. Soon Terry, clutching the same towel at the same place, came modestly out of the bathroom. Smith stared at her as at another piece of Martian furniture.

'Terry Thrush, I'd like you to meet George Lovelace. George, this is Terry.'

'Oh, hi,' said Terry, with a bright smile.

'How do you do?' said George Ray Smith O'Reilly Lovelace.

'How would you like to fuck her, George?' I asked, my own penis lifting its head in more than idle curiosity.

'You first,' he blurted.

'Okay, me first, Terry. Give me your ass again.' Terry looked a little surprised, but quickly hopped into bed beside our young man, and stuck her little behind plumply into the air. Her face on a pillow, she turned, smiling brightly at George, whose head lay looking ceilingward on the other pillow a foot away. George looked sick.

I place my penis, prodded and poked, and, with all deliberate speed, it plunged deep into Terry's warm, wet interior. My God, that was good. Terry had helped aim me with her hands but now as I began easing myself in and out she moved herself on her elbows over to silent George and – undoubtedly smiling brightly to the last – moved her face over his and began giving him her sexy, snakelike kisses.

George lay as rigid as a dried straw, except for his central limb, which was as limp as a wet straw. I pulled Tiny Terry's thighs against me and more or less picked her bodily up and deposited her face on Georgie's belly. Discovering a poor, lonely, unloved cock, she did her duty.

The long and the short of it, Reader – and that is the usual sequence in these affairs – was that I made a splendid splash in Terry's interior and Terry did enough favorable groaning and straining to please everyone, presumably including herself. When she finally let go of old Sir George his limb was just as limp as before. However, as Terry rolled onto her back away from him I saw that the rest of him was at last limp too. Sir George too had seen the Holy Grail.

'Terry has a very nice mouth, don't you think, George?'

'Er, yes, she does,' he said.

'You're exceptionally beautiful in the interior, Terry,' I went on.

'Thank you,' she said. My two young friends were lying on their backs side by side while I had settled back on my knees near the foot of the bed. I was feeling very tired and depressed, and my mood was manifesting itself by my heavy-handed irony.

'Is your ass as warm and juicy as your cunt, Terry?'

'I don't know,' she said and she giggled.

'Live and learn, or in the immortal words of Leonardo da Vinci: "Anus delictoris ante uturusi sec." Tell me, George, do you feel now that someone loves you, that life does have a meaning after all?'

'I – beg pardon?'

'I was telling Miss Truss that you came here tonight very unhappy and lonely and unloved. Has she given you the spiritual nourishment which you needed?'

'A little bit, I guess.'

'Hear that, Terry, only a little bit. George must really be depressed. Don't you realize, George, that Terry kissed you and caressed you without your even *asking*? She gave herself unrequested and unselfishly for your pleasure and enlightenment. Now what do you say?'

His face contorted nervously, he looked at me. Finally he said: 'Thank you, I guess.'

'You're welcome,' said Terry. 'I like to help people.'

'Terry is unusually helpful, wouldn't you say, Ray?'

'Yes, she is.'

'Let's all have a drink. Scotch for you, Mr Lovelace?'

'Yes, thank you.'

As I plodded off nude to the liquor cabinet, I found myself for the first time wondering about the reliability of our questionnaires. Little Miss T., the inhibited Catholic virgin, had showed all the juiciness and technique of a forty-three-year-old nymphomaniac. And lover-boy O'Reilly . . . Well, back to the old data sheets.

After we'd finished our drinks, during which we had several sporadic conversations on *(a)* the weather (we need snow), *(b)* Renaissance history (Rabelais was actually a *serious* thinker), and *(c)* religion (it's frequently misunderstood), I said firmly to George: 'Your turn now, Lovelace.'

'Oh yes, thank you.'

Terry lay on her back to receive him, and after several youthful giggles, he seemed to enter the promised land. The doorbell rang.

For a moment I wondered if there weren't some electronic device deep in Miss Tracy's womb which triggered the apartment bell. It seemed unlikely, but . . .

I located a bathrobe this time, told the little ones to carry on without me and marched stoically to the door. There, as I leaned my slightly debauched face around the edge of the door, stood Dr Felloni. We exchanged stares in total disbelief for five full seconds. Then she blushed so fully that I can only describe it by saying that her head, which was of course nodding vigorously, had a climax. She turned and ran down the hall. The next day her secretary phoned to say that she was attending a conference in Zurich and would be away for two weeks.

Chapter Twenty-nine

My experience with Terry Tracy and the results of the Columbia Copulation Caper in general were a revelation to me. After Dr Felloni had left the apartment door that night and taken a taxi across the Atlantic to Zurich, I had returned to the bedroom to find Tracy and George moiling in the bed and as oblivious of my presence as they had apparently been of my absence. I stood there watching the sheet which covered George's behind rising and falling in regular rhythm and as the sheet shuddered I had something like a Religious Revelation. Other people also were capable of playing artificially imposed roles – and therefore dice-dictated roles. If Terry *had* in fact been even somewhat virginal, she was this evening demonstrating a remarkable ability to open herself to new experience. If she were in fact a nymphomaniac, she had earlier demonstrated a shyness and inhibition in marvelous contrast to her natural open-door policy. And George Lovelace seemed to be a good learner too; from clod to copulator in thirty minutes.

As I stood there I began to feel that I had only been playing at the dice man. It had been a *jeu d'esprit* of which I was proud but nothing more: a maladjusted man's way of *épater les bourgeois* without the bourgeoisie knowing about it. But had I innocently discovered gunpowder and then used it for firecrackers, when a larger man would have used it for explosives? Or a magnifying glass which I was using to create pleasant images but which might be used to see something new?

Shouldn't I try to turn other people into dice men? If Arlene enjoyed housewife-with-a-lech for a day and Terry call-girl-for-a-day, might not each enjoy other roles the dice might fling her way, as I had? Shouldn't I be using dice games as dice therapy for my friends and patients?

My dicelife had become almost a joke; at that instant it seemed a mission – a quest I might pursue to lift my fellow men to new heights. I had cast the dice as a bitter game I'd played against the world; now I would cast them to build New Selves, Random Men. Boredom would be wiped out with the vaccine of the dice, like a polio. I would create a New World, a better world, a Place of Joy and Variety and Spontaneity. I would become the Father of a new Race. Dicepeople.

'Could you please get us a towel?' Terry asked, most of her face and body hidden by the sheet and George's ample bulk.

Even this rude interruption did not destroy my elevation. During these glorious minutes I was taking myself totally seriously. I went to the bathroom and got them a towel and after a giggle or two they lay together silently, again oblivious of my presence. As the sheet lay limp and still over their silent forms I tiptoed to the spot where my trousers were deposited on the floor and extricated from the pocket my dice. 'Odd,' I would begin dice therapy, with George and Terry tonight; 'even,' I would not. Confidently I flipped a die onto the foot of the bed: a six. Hmmm. Like the good fairy who has left a dime under the pillow, I picked up my clothes and stole away into the night, the immortal words of Christ echoing in my ears: 'Physician, help yourself: thus you help your patients too. Let this be his best help that he may behold with his eyes the man who heals himself.' I was determined to rip from my body the undistinguished clothes of Dr Lucius Rhinehart and stand forth before my patients naked and revealed: The Dice Man.

Chapter Thirty

The first adult human being to be introduced into the dicelife by Dr Rhinehart was Arlene Ecstein, inconspicuous wife of Dr Jacob Ecstein, noted analyst and writer. Mrs Ecstein had been complaining for several years of various nervous ailments which she attributed to sexual frustration caused by the sporadic nature of her husband's attentions. Dr Ecstein, who didn't have *time*, finally decided in mid-January that she would enter analysis so that her problem might be treated in depth. With her husband's encouragement ('Give it to her, Luke, baby') she began analysis with Dr Rhinehart. The first few sessions had been penetrating and Mrs Ecstein found herself able to open up more frequently than before. Her husband noted that her nervous symptoms declined or disappeared and that her compulsive sexuality seemed relieved.

It was after a little over six weeks of this treatment (three times a week) that Dr Rhinehart, following his Religious Revelation during the Rhinehart–Felloni Study of Amorality Tolerance, determined to begin dice therapy. He began with the quiet dignity which so marked this whole stage of his life.

'Don't take off your bra, Arlene, I want to talk to you about something important.'

'Can't it wait?'

'No.' He took out two new silver dice, fresh from the factories of Taxco, Mexico, and placed them on his desk. He requested Mrs Ecstein to seat herself in front of the desk.

'What is it, Lukie?'

'Those are dice.'

'I see.'

'We are going to begin dice therapy.'

'Dice therapy?'

Dr Rhinehart explained with great clarity the practice and theory of casting dice to determine action. Mrs Ecstein listened with close attention although she squirmed frequently on her chair. When it was clear that he had finished, she remained silent awhile and then heaved a deep sigh.

'But I still don't see *why*,' she said. 'You say I might let the dice decide whether we fuck this morning or not. I think that's silly. I want to fuck. You want to fuck. Why bring the dice into it?'

'Because many small parts of you *don't* want to fuck. A small part of you wants to hit me, or wants to run back to Jake, or wants to talk to me about psychoanalysis. But these parts of you are never allowed to live. You suppress them because most of you just wants to fuck.'

'If they're small parts of me, let them stay small.'

Dr Rhinehart tipped back in his chair and sighed. He took out a pipe and began filling it. He took one of the silver dice and shook it in one hand and dropped it on his desk. He frowned.

'I'm going to tell you how a God was born: the birth of the Dice Man.'

Dr Rhinehart then narrated the story, slightly edited, of his discovery of the dice and his initial rape of Mrs Ecstein. He concluded:

'Had I not given a small part of myself a chance to be chosen by the die we wouldn't be sitting here right now.'

'You only gave it one chance in six?'

'Yes. The point is that I gave a minority self a chance to be heard.'

'Only one chance in six?'

'We can never be full human beings until we develop all important aspects of ourselves.'

'Only one-sixth of you wanted me?'

'Arlene, that was an historical accident. We're talking theory. Don't you see how yielding to the dice opens whole new areas of life?'

'I feel used.'

'If I seduced you out of cold-blooded lust you would feel pleased. Because I let chance intervene you feel used.'

'Don't you feel *any*thing strongly enough so that you don't want to use the dice?'

'Of course, but I try to overcome it.'

Dr Rhinehart and Mrs Ecstein looked at each other for a full minute, Dr Rhinehart smiling self-consciously and Mrs Ecstein looking awed. At last she pronounced judgment.

'You're insane,' she said.

'Absolutely. Look, I'll show you how it works. I write down two, say three options. A one or a two means we'll continue this conversation, a three or a four means we'll end the hour right now and each let the dice decide something else for us to do for the next forty minutes. A five and . . .'

'And a five or a six means we'll fuck.'

'All right, yes.'

Dr Rhinehart handed a die to Mrs Ecstein and after shaking it vigorously in both hands for a few seconds she asked, 'Shouldn't I be mumbling some mumbo-jumbo as I do this?'

'You may say simply: 'Not my will, Die, but Thy will be done.''

'Fuck us up good, Die,' she said and dropped it on the desk. It was a five.

'I don't feel like fucking anymore,' she said, but when she saw the frown on Dr Rhinehart's face she smiled and felt she was beginning to see the merits of a dicelife. But before she could begin to let the large part of herself go to work, Dr Rhinehart spoke.

'We may now toss the dice to determine *how* we will make love.'

She hesitated.

'What?' she said.

'There are innumerable ways to engage in sexual congress; parts of us are attracted to each of these ways. We must let the dice decide.'

'I see.'

'First of all, which of us shall be the sexual aggressor, I or you? If the dice say odd – '

'Wait a minute. I'm beginning to understand this game. I want to play too.'

'Go ahead.'

Mrs Ecstein picked up both dice and said:

'A one means we'll make love that funny way you seem to like.'

'Fine.'

'A two means I'll lie down and you use your hands, mouth, and Johnny Appleseed over every part of my body until I can't stand it and demand something else. A three – '

'Or rather we flip the die again.'

'A three . . . let's see: you play with my breasts for five minutes.'

'Go on.'

Mrs Ecstein hesitated and then a slow smile began to brighten her face.

'We must always let the dice decide, huh?' she asked.

'That's right.'

'But we control the options.'

'Very good.'

She was smiling happily as if she were a child who has just learned how to read.

'If the die is a four or a five or a six it means we have to try to make a baby.'

'Ahh,' said Dr Rhinehart.

'I've removed that rubber sort of plug Jake had a doctor put in me and I think I've just ovulated. I read a book and it's told me the two best positions to make a baby.'

'I see. Arlene. I – '

'Shall I toss?'

'Just a minute.'

'What for?'

'I – I'm thinking.'

'Hand me the die.'

'I believe that you have loaded the odds a bit,' said Dr Rhinehart with his accustomed professional coolness. 'Let's say if it's a six we'll try one sexual position after another as determined from a list of six we will give it. Two minutes on each. Let the orgasms come where they may.'

'But the four and five still mean we make a baby?'

'Yes.'

'Okay. Do I flip?'

'All right.'

Mrs Ecstein dropped the die. It read four.

'Ahh,' said Dr Rhinehart.

'Yippee,' said Mrs Ecstein.

'Precisely what are these two medically recommended fucks?' Dr Rhinehart asked a trifle irritably.

'I'll show you. And whoever has the most orgasms wins.'

'Wins what?'

'I don't know. Wins a free pair of dice.'

'I see.'

'Why didn't we begin this therapy a long time ago?' Mrs Ecstein asked. She was rapidly undressing.

'You understand,' the doctor said, slowly preparing himself for the operation, 'that after we have made love once, we must consult the die again.'

'Sure, sure, come here,' said Mrs Ecstein and she was soon hard at work with Dr Rhinehart in concentrated dice therapy. At 11 A.M. Dr Rhinehart buzzed his secretary to announce that because he was probing particularly deeply that morning and because his work might bear long-range fruit, it would be necessary to cancel the hour with Mr Jenkins so that he and Mrs Ecstein might continue.

At noon, Mrs Ecstein, glowing, left the doctor's office. The history of dice therapy had begun.

Chapter Thirty-one

Professor Orville Boggles of Yale tried it; Arlene Ecstein found it productive; Terry Tracy rediscovered God through it; patient Joseph Spezio of QSH thought it was a plot to drive him insane: dice therapy slowly but surely, and unbeknownst to my wife and colleagues, grew; but the Great Columbia Copulation Caper climaxed and was spent. Two Barnard College girls who had been instructed separately to enter into lesbian relations with each other complained to their dean of women, who promptly began investigating. Although I assured her that Dr Felloni and I were bona fide professionals, members of the American Medical Association, registered Republicans and in only moderate opposition to the war in Vietnam, she still found the experiment to be 'suspiciously outrageous' and I ended it.

Actually all our scheduled appointments had already been completed. Less than sixty percent had taken place as set up, and two graduate students and I were busy for weeks afterward trying to collect the manila folders with the completed questionnaires and trying to interview our lab assistants; but the experiment was finished. When I published an article on our work in the fall (Dr Felloni declined to be associated with the article or the experiment), it created a mild stir and was one of the pieces of evidence used by my enemies to have me exiled from the AMA.

Although most of our subjects seem to have derived pleasure from their participation in the study, a few were traumatized. About ten days after my own *pas de trois* my office received a request that I treat one of Dr Felloni's subjects in our joint experiment. This Miss Vigliota maintained that she had become neurotic because of her participation in our experiment and she was requesting therapy. The appointment was set up and the next day I was seated in my office at the scheduled hour elaborating in writing upon new dice exercises I had been creating. My office door opened and closed, a small girl entered, and when I looked at her, she staggered forward and collapsed on the couch.

It was Terry 'Tracy' Vigliota. It took me twenty minutes to assure her that I was really Dr Rhinehart, a psychiatrist, and that my participation with her in the experiment had been a perfectly natural extension of my data-gathering role. When she had become calm, she told me why she had come requesting therapy. She sat on the edge of the couch with her short legs dangling many inches from the floor. Dressed in a conservative grayish suit with short skirt, she seemed, as she discussed her problems, more slight, nervous and intense than she had less than two weeks before. I noticed as she talked and in subsequent sessions that she found it difficult to look at me and always entered or left the office with her soft brown eyes on the floor, as if absorbed in thought.

Terry had apparently undergone an identity crisis as a result of her unusual evening with me and George. Her conversation with the professor of history and with Father Forbes had given her new insights into her Catholic faith, but her sexual experience had not been related, she began to think, to the 'greater glory of God.' She found herself increasingly indifferent to the glory of God and increasingly interested in men. But lust and sex were evil, or so her whole previous life had told her. But Father Forbes had indicated that the Church enjoyed sex. But Father Forbes had turned out to be a psychiatrist, a scientist, a doctor; but they also enjoyed sex. She had felt fulfilled in

230

relieving the loneliness of George X, but after Father Forbes had left it seems George permitted her to relieve his loneliness one more time and then began berating her as a whore and a slut. She found as a result of all this that she could no longer believe in anything. All of her desires and beliefs had been shattered by the emotions of her experimental evening: nothing new was taking its place. All seemed unreliable and meaningless.

Although anxious to begin dice therapy with her, I had to let her pour out her troubles uninterrupted over the first two analytic hours. In the third session – she was still sitting, her legs dangling, staring at the floor – she finally ran out of misery and began repeating that most human of refrains: 'I don't know what to do.'

'You keep coming back to the same basic feeling,' I said. 'That all of your desires and beliefs are illusory and meaningless.'

'Yes. I asked for therapy because I can't stand the feeling of emptiness. After that evening I didn't know who I was. When I got you as my therapist last week I thought I must be going insane. Even my emptiness seemed empty.'

She smiled a sad, soft Natalie Wood smile, her eyes downcast.

'What if you're right?' I said.

'Pardon?'

'What if your feeling that all desires are unreliable and all beliefs illusions is *right*, is the mature, valid vision of reality, and the rest of men are living under illusions which your experience has permitted you to shed?'

'Of course, that's what I think,' she said.

'Then why not act upon your belief?'

The smile left her face and she frowned, still not looking at me.

'What do you mean?'

231

'Treat all of your desires as if they had equal value and each of your beliefs as if it were as much an illusion as the next.'

'How?'

'Stop trying to create a pattern, a personality; just do whatever you feel like.'

'But I don't feel like doing anything; that's the trouble.'

'That's because you're letting one desire, the desire to believe strongly and *be* a clearly defined person, inhibit the rest of your various desires.'

'Maybe, but I don't see how I can change it.'

'Become a dice person.'

She lifted her head and looked up into my eyes slowly and without emotion.

'What?'

'Become a dice person,' I repeated.

'What do you mean?'

'I,' I leaned forward with appropriate gravity, 'am the Dice Man.'

She smiled slightly and looked away and to the side.

'I don't know what you're talking about.'

'You believe that each of your desires is as arbitrary, meaningless and trivial as the next?'

'Yes.'

'In some sense it makes absolutely no difference what you do or don't do?'

'That's exactly it.'

'Then why not let the flip of dice – chance – decide what you do?'

She looked up again.

'Is that why you keep changing roles and acting so strangely?'

'Partly.'

'You let . . . chance . . . a pair of dice decide your life?'

'Within limits, yes.'

'How do you do it?'

For the first time her eyes brightened. Legs dangling, she listened intently as I explained briefly my option-creating, dice-deciding life.

'My God,' she said when I had finished. She stared some more. 'That's wonderful.' She paused. 'First you were a professor of history, then Father Forbes, then a lover, a pander, a psychiatrist, and now you're – the dice man.'

My face was aglow with triumph.

'Actually,' I said, 'I work for "Candid Camera."'

Terry paled: it took two minutes for me to reassure her that I'd been joking. When she'd recovered, or seemed to have recovered, she smiled her soft smile, looked up at me, grinned and then began giggling. She giggled for about two more minutes and stopped. She took a handkerchief from a pocket in her suit jacket and wiped away the tears. Biting at her lower lip but trying to look me in the eye, she said quietly:

'I think I might like to try to be a – dice woman.'

'It will be good for you,' I said.

'It can't be any worse.'

'That's the spirit.'

As a matter of fact Terry and I got nowhere at first. She was too apathetic and skeptical to obey dice decisions except in the most perfunctory way. Her apathy led her to create unimaginative options, or, when I pressed her to be more daring, to disobey the die.

It was almost two weeks later that we finally had a session which led to her breakthrough into belief in the dicelife. She was the one who got to the core of the problem:

233

'I . . . I'm having trouble . . . believing. I have to have
. . . faith, but I don't . . .' She trailed off.

'I know,' I said slowly. 'The dicelife is related to having
faith, to religion, to genuine religion.'

There was a silence.

'Yes, Father,' she said, and gave me a rare smile.

I smiled back at her and continued:

'A healthy skepticism is an essential ingredient of
genuine religion.'

'Yes, Father,' she said, still smiling.

I leaned back in my chair.

'Maybe I ought to preach to you.' I flipped a die onto
the desk between us. It said yes to the lecture. I frowned.

'I'm listening,' she said as I continued my pause.

'This may sound Father Forbesish, but who am I to
question the will of the Die?' I stared at her and we both
looked solemn. 'Christ's message is clear: you must lose
yourself to save yourself. You must give up personal,
worldly desires, become poor in spirit. By surrendering
your personal will to the whim of the die you are
practicing precisely that self-abnegation prescribed in the
scriptures.'

She looked at me blankly as if listening but not
understanding.

'Do you see,' I went on, 'that the only selfless action is
one not dictated by the self?'

She frowned.

'I can see that following the dice might be selfless, but I
thought the Church wanted us to overcome sinfulness on
our own.'

I tipped forward and stretched forth an arm to take one
of Terry's little hands in my own. I felt – and naturally
looked – totally sincere in what I was saying.

'Listen carefully, Terry. What I'm about to say contains
the wisdom of the world's great religions. If a man

234

overcomes what he calls sinfulness by his own willpower, he *increases* his egopride, which, according to even the Bible, is the very foundation stone of sin. Only when sin is overcome by some external forces does the man realize his own insignificance; only then is pride eliminated. As long as you strive as an individual self for the good, you will either have failure – and an accompanying guilt – or pride, which is simply the basic form of evil. Guilt or pride: those are the gifts of self. The only salvation lies in having faith.'

'But faith in what?' she asked.

'Faith in God,' I answered.

She looked puzzled.

'But what happened to the dice?' she asked.

'Look. I'm going to read a passage to you from a sacred book. Listen carefully.' I reached into my desk and brought out some notes I'd been making lately in connection with my evolving dice theory and, after browsing a half-minute to find what I was looking for, I began reading.

'"Verily it is not a blasphemy when I teach: Over all things stand the heaven Accident, the heaven Innocence, the heaven Prankishness, the heaven Chance. And Chance is the most ancient Divinity of the world, and behold, I come to deliver all things from their bondage under Purpose and to restore on the throne to reign over all things the heaven Chance. The mind is in bondage to Purpose and Will, but I shall free it to Divine Accident and Prankishness when I teach that in all, one thing is impossible: reason. A little wisdom is possible indeed, just enough to confuse things nicely, but this blessed certainty I have found in every atom, molecule, substance, plant, creature or star: they would rather *dance* on the feet of Chance.

'"Oh heaven over me pure and high! Now that I have

learned that there is no purposeful eternal spider and no spider web of reason, you have become for me a dance floor for divine accidents; you have become a divine table for divine dice and diceplayers. But my listeners blush? Do I speak the unspeakable? Do I blaspheme, wishing to bless you?"'

I ended my reading and after checking to see if there might be more related material I looked up.

'I didn't recognize it,' Terry said.

'It's Zarathustra. But did you understand it?'

'I don't know. I liked it. I liked something about it very much. But I don't – I don't see why I should have faith in the dice. I guess that's the trouble.'

'Not a sparrow falls to the ground that God does not see.'

'I know.'

'Can a single die fall to the table unseen by God?'

'No, I guess not.'

'Do you remember the great ending to the Book of Job? God speaks from the whirlwind and asks Job how he can presume to question the ways of God. For three long, beautiful chapters God indicts man's abysmal ignorance and impotence. He says things like:

"Where were you when I laid the foundation of the earth? . . ."

"Or who shut in the sea with doors, when it burst forth from the womb?"

And "have you commanded the morning since your days began?"

"Have the gates of death been revealed to you?"

On and on God rubs it in to poor Job, but stylishly – in the most beautiful poetry in the world – and Job realizes that he has been wrong in complaining and questioning. His last words to the Lord are:

"I know that thou canst do all things, and that no purpose of
   thine can be thwarted . . .
Therefore I despise myself, and repent in dust and ashes."'

I paused, and Terry and I looked silently at each other
for several moments.

'God can do all things,' I went on. 'No purpose of His
can ever be thwarted. Never.'

'Yes,' she replied.

'We must despise ourselves and lose ourselves if we are
to be saved.'

'Yes.'

'God sees the tiniest sparrow fall.'

'Yes.'

'The tiniest die tumble upon the table.'

'Yes.'

'You will always know what options you have given to
the Die.'

'Yes.'

'Terry, the reason you must have faith in the Die is
simple.'

'Yes.'

'The Die is God.'

'The Die is God,' she said.

Chapter Thirty-two

I was sitting at a board meeting of Queensborough State Hospital one Wednesday evening that spring, when the idea of Centers for Experiments in Total Random Environments came to me. Fifteen old men, all doctors, PhDs and millionaires, were seated around a huge, rectangular table discussing plumbing expansion, salary scales, medication charts and rights-of-way, while the patients in the square mile around us settled ever more comfortably into their various defined stupors. In the middle of doing a doodle of a multi-armed, multi-legged, multi-headed Shiva, whammo! It hit me; a Dice Center, an institution to convert people into random men. I suddenly saw a short-term total environment of such overwhelming impact that the principles and practices of the dicelife would be infused after a few weeks to the same degree that they had in me after many, many months. I saw a society of dicepeople. I saw a new world.

Old man Cobblestone, our tall, dignified chairman, was speaking with great deliberation about the intricacies of Queensborough law regarding rights of appropriation; six pipes, three cigars and five cigarettes were giving the green-walled room a milky, underwater effect; a young doctor (forty-six) beside me had been wiggling his foot in the same motion for forty minutes without pause. Pens lay dormant by paper except for mine: the sole doodler. Yawns were smothered into coughs or hidden behind pipes. Cobblestone gave way to Dr Wink on the inefficiency of bureaucratic systems in dealing with plumbing problems and suddenly, leaping at me from the seven arms, six legs and three heads of Shiva, was the idea of the Dice Center.

I took my green die from my vest pocket and gave it a fifty-fifty chance that I would create such an institute. It said 'yes.' I stifled a scream. Whatever sound emerged slowed but did not stop the wiggling foot beside me. Four heads turned minutely toward me then back respectfully to Dr Wink. I was ablaze with my idea. I cast the die a second time on the doodle pad.

'Gentlemen!' I said loudly and I shoved back my chair and stood. I towered over Dr Wink, who stood just opposite me staring at me openmouthed. The others all turned to me respectfully. Foot-wiggler wiggled on.

'Gentlemen.' I said again, groping for the right words. 'Another sewer will only permit us to handle the shit better; it won't solve anything.'

'That's true,' a voice said encouragingly and several heads nodded.

'If we are to fulfill our duties as trustees we must have a vision of an institution which will change our patients and send them into the world as free men.' I was speaking slowly and pompously and I earned two nods and a yawn.

'As Ezra Pound wrote in a late poem, a mental hospital is a total institution: it engulfs each patient with a consistency of rule, habit and attitude which effectively isolates him from the more unpredictable problems of life in the outside world. A patient can adjust successfully to hospital life because he can count on its limiting its horrors to certain predictable patterns. The outside world holds no such hope for him. He is thus often able to adjust to hospital life and yet be frightened footless by the thought of having to leave. We have effectively prepared our patients to live adequately in the mental hospital and no place else.'

239

'Is this to the point?' old Cobblestone asked from his seat at the head of the table.

'Oh it is, sir. It is,' I said a bit more quickly. Then with dignity: 'I have a dream. A vision: we want to prepare our patients to fulfill themselves happily in all environments, to free the individual from the need to lock himself away from challenge and change. We – '

'This . . . but, Dr Rhinehart,' Dr Wink stammered uncertainly.

'We want to create a world of adult children without fear. We want the multiplicity built into each one of us by our anarchic and contradictory society to break free. We want people to greet each other on the street and not know who is who and *not care*. We want freedom from individual identity. Freedom from security and stability and coherence. We want a community of creators, a monastery for joy-filled madmen.'

'What are you talking about?' old man Cobblestone said firmly. He was standing.

'For Christ's sake, Luke, sit down,' Dr Mann said. Heads turned to each other and then back to me.

'Oh we've been fools! Fools!' I slammed my fist down on the table. 'A million years we've believed that the choice lies only between control and discipline on the one hand and letting go on the other: we don't realize that both are equally methods of sustaining consistent habit, attitude and personality. The Goddam personality!' I grit my teeth and shuddered. 'We need disciplined anarchy, controlled letting go. Queen for a day, Russian roulette, veto, eeny-meeny-miney-moe: a new way of life, a new world, a community of dice men.' I made my appeal directly to old Cobblestone, and he didn't even blink.

'What are you talking about?' he asked again more gently.

'I'm talking about converting QSH into a Center in

240

which patients will be systematically taught to play games with life, to act out all of their fantasies, to be dishonest and enjoy it, to lie and pretend and feel hate and rage and love and compassion as determined by the whim of the dice. I'm talking about creating an institution where the doctors periodically pretend to be patients, for days, for weeks, where the patients pretend to be doctors and give therapy sessions, where the attendants and nurses play the roles of patients and visitors and doctors and TV repairmen, where the whole fucking institution is one great stage upon which all walk free.'

'I rule you are out of order, Dr Rhinehart. Please sit down.' Dr Cobblestone stood erect at the end of the table and his face was neutral as he spoke these words. As the heads all swung back to me there was a total silence. When I spoke it was almost to myself.

'The great Goddam machine society has made us all into hamsters. We don't see the worlds within us waiting to be born. Actors only able to play one role: whoever heard of such nonsense. We must create random men, dicepeople. The world needs dicepeople. The world shall *have* dicepeople.'

Someone had a firm grip on one of my arms and was pulling at me to come away from the table. About half the other doctors seemed to be standing now and jabbering to each other. I resisted the tug and raised my right arm with clenched fist and boomed out to old Cobblestone:

'One more thing!'

A fearful silence followed. All stared at me. I lowered my clenched fist and released the green die onto the doodle pad in front of me: a five.

'All right,' I said. 'I'll leave.' I picked up the die, replaced it in my vest pocket and left. I learned later that an entirely new sewage disposal system was rejected by unanimous vote and a system of temporary stop-gap repairs initiated to the satisfaction of no one.

Chapter Thirty-three

As the normal, healthy, neurotic reader knows, one of the chief delights of life is daydreaming. After careful study of my own fantasies and those of hundreds of dicestudents met in dice therapy, I have noted that our dreams at any moment act as a block or a boost to our playing different roles. Moreover, I have discovered that about every four years from childhood until death the average man changes the goals of his daydreams and that these changes evolve in a remarkably predictable pattern. Since all the dreams are in a way related to power, I am modestly suggesting that the phenomenon be called the Rhinehart Power Pattern for Men.

Daydreams begin sometime in the child's first decade, usually around the age of eight or nine. At this age the boy inevitably projects himself in terms of raw power. Frequently he is faster than a speeding bullet, more powerful than a locomotive and can leap buildings at a single bound. He becomes the Genghis Khan of the fourth grade, the Attila the Hun of the local shopping center, the General George Patton of Cub Scout Local 216. His parents are being tortured to death in a horribly creative way: for example, over some tremendous fire at the end of sharpened spears they are being fried as marshmallows. Sometimes the child arrives in time to save his parents; sometimes, in fact most times, he arrives just too late and, after demolishing the villains, concentrates his imagination on himself marching in the middle of a giant state funeral procession bathed in tears. The procession is attacked by the enemy and he leaps with his sword . . .

By the age of thirteen the scene has usually shifted to Yankee Stadium, where the boy, playing for the hopeless Yankees, with the bases loaded, two outs and his team trailing by three runs in the last half of the ninth inning in the seventh game of the World Series, manages to stroke a 495-foot drive off the highest part of the fence in right center field and, with a fantastic flash around the bases and an impossible headfirst slide, just touches home plate with the extended uncut fingernail of his left pinky. In December, late in the fourth quarter and his team trailing by five points he runs back an intercepted pass 109 yards, carrying fourteen men over the goal line on his back, eleven opposition players, one incompetent referee and two fans who are already trying to congratulate him. In the spring, with two seconds left to win the game he sinks a one-handed jump shot from the foul line, his own foul line.

In the world of sports, girls are absent, but by the age of sixteen or seventeen the stroke of a baseball has been replaced by other strokes, and the only ones intercepting passes are female. The boy has become a man, and the man is commander-in-chief of a harem. Here things go on beyond the wildest imagination of anyone – except that of the boy doing the dreaming. A woman, panting help-lessly, flings her nude body onto the hero, who, puffing nonchalantly on a Corsican cigarette and tastefully sipping a glass of rare New York State wine, and steering his Aston-Martin at 165 miles per hour down a rarely used road in the Alps, manages to give the girl the most exciting love experience of her life. If a male at the age of seventeen is sometimes once again Attila the Hun it is in order to round up the conquered Roman women and, twirling his sword and his mustache, choose fifteen or sixteen to spend the night with him. If he once again scores the winning touchdown, it is in order to walk dramatically into the senior prom, limping badly and trailing blood along the floor behind him like a leaky oil truck, and watch the women melt into gooey syrup at the sight of him.

But by the age of twenty-one our male is either engaged, married or sated; the world he wants to rule is a new world – he has become Horatio Alger. With grim determination and uncanny acuity he invests fifty-six dollars in the stock market and after buying and selling with cool nonchalance over a period of six months, finally sells out, pocketing a cool $4,862,927.33. When the board of General Motors is panicked by the threat of disarmament he calmly presents his invention of an inexpensive jet sportscar built in the shape of a Polaris missile and getting fifty miles per gallon of jet fuel. In three weeks he is on the covers of *Time, Fortune* and *Success*!

But in the next few years he is earning a modest salary as second clerk at Pierce, Perkins and Poof and is upset at the injustice and hypocrisy that exist in the world: a world in which some men are athletic stars, James Bonds and millionaires and he is not; he is morally appalled. In his dreams he recreates the world, righting all wrongs, eliminating suffering, redistributing wealth, redistributing women, ending all wars. He becomes a reincarnation of Gautama Buddha, Jesus Christ and Hugh Hefner. Evil governments topple, corrupt churches collapse, laws are revised, and Truth, written in Xeroxed tablets of stone by our hero, is presented to the world. Everyone is happy.

Except our hero, whose income continues to be modest. At the age of twenty-five he has reached the first apex of the Rhinehart Power Pattern for Men: the dream of reforming the world. By the age of twenty-eight or -nine regression has begun. His wife is reminding him that the world is still unreformed and that other men are earning . . . et cetera. He returns to his dreams of success. Only

244

now they are more modest, more limited. Now he rules only Pierce, Perkins and Poof and not General Motors. Now his coup on the stock market is only a thousand dollars, not four million. Middle age, like rigor mortis, has set in.

The regression continues: in three or four years he reassumes his position as managing director of a harem, but it isn't what it used to be. It is populated with secretaries, receptionists and, on particularly good days, a famous movie star. Jane Fonda, while protest picketing at Pierce, Perkins and Poof, takes on glance at him and drags him off to a commune where – but it doesn't seem quite real, so he returns to the conquering of the little telephone operator Maggie Blemish.

At the age of thirty-seven he suddenly resigns from Pierce, Perkins and Poof to join the New York Football Giants. The prospect of running 109 yards or dragging fourteen men on his back no longer seems as jolly as it did at the age of thirteen, so he joins the Giants as head coach. Although his team has finished dead last for six consecutive seasons and still has the same incompetent men, our male introduces a new spread formation with three running quarterbacks separated by thirty yards and a center who can hike the ball to any one of them, and the Giants, running new quadruple reverses off fake-draw quick kicks, all season, win fourteen straight. He takes over as head coach of the New York Hockey Rangers at midseason and, thanks to a revolutionary introduction of six men into the forward line – but the pattern is familiar.

At the age of forty-one it is complete; the male, resigning his six head-coach-ships, once again dreams of conquering the world. The accumulated bitterness of the years asserts itself, he becomes as fast as a speeding bullet, as powerful as a locomotive and can leap buildings with three powerful strides. He becomes a General Curtis

LeMay and bombs China back into the Stone Age. He becomes a Spiro Agnew and puts the blacks and hippies and liberals firmly in their places. His wife and children are being tortured to death in some horribly creative way: over a fire at the end of sharpened sticks they are being roasted as marshmallows. Sometimes he arrives in time to save his children, sometimes even his wife. But most times he arrives just too late. The giant state funeral procession in which, in tears, he is marching is attacked by the enemy, and leaping back into action with his tactical nuclear weapons . . .

The Rhinehart Power Pattern for Men should now be clear. In Dice Therapy we can predict with great precision the roles which a male student will most want to play by examining his age and relating it to our pattern. There exist variations, of course, some men mature late, and others, a few, are precocious. Eric Cannon, for example, at only nineteen, was saving the world, and I, at the age of only thirty-five, am again, as at age eight, in the process of destroying it . . .

Chapter Thirty-four

I had only one session with Eric Cannon to try to introduce him to dice therapy, because he and his father had reached some kind of agreement whereby Eric was to be released three days later. He was naturally keyed up about leaving and didn't listen carefully as I began a Socratic dialogue to get him into dice therapy. Unfortunately, the Socratic method entails a second person at least willing to grunt periodically and since Eric remained absolutely mute I gave up and told him in a twenty-minute lecture what a dicelife was all about. He became quite alert. When I'd finished he shook his head from side to side slowly.

'How do you stay loose, Doc?' he asked. 'How do you keep yourself on *that* side of the desk?'

'What do you mean?'

'How come they don't lock you up?'

I smiled.

'I am a professional man,' I answered.

'A professional loony. Giving psychotherapy.' He shook his head again. 'Poor Dad. He thought I was being cured.'

'The concept of the dicelife doesn't fascinate you?'

'Of course it does. You've turned yourself into a sort of computer like our air force use in Vietnam. Only instead of trying to kill the maximum number of the enemy, you program yourself to drop your bombs at random.'

'You miss the point. Since there is no real enemy, all of life's wars are games, and the dicelife permits a variety of

247

war games instead of the continual sluggish trench warfare of the typical life.'

"There is no enemy,"' he quoted quietly, looking at the floor in front of him. "'There is no enemy." If there's one thing that makes me want to puke more than anything else it's people who think there is no enemy. Your dicelife is a hundred times as sick as my father even. He's blind, so he's got an excuse, but *you!* "No *enemy*!" And Eric writhed in his chair, his face distorted with tension. He twisted his muscular body upward until he was standing, his neck still rolling tensely, his eyes on the ceiling. Clenching his fists he finally held himself reasonably quiet.

'You big fool,' he said. 'This world is a madhouse with killers loose, torturers, sick depraved sadists running churches, corporations, countries. It could be different, could be better, and you sit on your lump of fat and toss dice.'

I didn't say anything since I was not in the mood for a wrestling match and was, as I listened, for some reason feeling guilty.

'You *know* this hospital is a farce, but tragic suffering – a tragic farce. You *know* there are nuts running this place – nuts! – not even counting *you*! – that makes most inmates look like Ozzie and Marriat and David and Ricky. You *know* what American racism is. You *know* what the war in Vietnam is. And you toss dice! You toss dice!!'

He banged both fists down on the desk before me two, three, four times, his long hair falling forward at each blow like a black mantilla. Then he stopped.

'I'm leaving, Doc,' he said to me calmly. 'I'm going out into the world and try to make it better. You can stay here and drop your random bombs.'

'Just a minute, Eric.' I stood up. 'Before you go – '

'I'm leaving. Thanks for the pot, thanks for the silences,

thanks even for the games, but don't say another word about tossing your fucking dice, or I'll kill you.'

'Eric . . . I'm . . . You're . . .'

He left.

Chapter Thirty-five

Dr Rhinehart should have known when Mr Mann summoned him to his office at QSH that there was trouble. And seeing old Cobblestone erect and solemn as he entered made Dr Rhinehart certain there was trouble. Dr Cobblestone is tall and thin and gray-haired, and Dr Mann is short and plump and balding, but their facial expressions were identical: stern, firm, severe. Being called to a director's office at QSH reminded Rhinehart of being summoned to the principal's office at age eight for winning money off sixth graders at craps. His problems hadn't changed much.

'What's this about dice, young man?' Dr Cobblestone asked sharply, leaning forward in his chair and banging once noisily on the floor the cane he held upright between his legs. He was the senior director of the hospital.

'Dice?' asked Dr Rhinehart, a puzzled expression on his face. He was wearing blue jeans, a white T-shirt and sneakers, a dice decision which had made Dr Mann pale when he had entered the office. Dr Cobblestone had not seemed to notice.

'I think we ought to take things in the order you suggested earlier,' Dr Mann said to his co-director.

'Ah yes. Yes, indeed.' Dr Cobblestone banged his cane again as if it were some accepted signal for the restarting of a game. 'What's this we've heard about your using prostitutes and homosexuals in your sex research?'

Dr Rhinehart didn't answer immediately but looked intently from one stern face to another. He said quietly:

'The research will be detailed in our report. Is there anything wrong?'

'Dr Felloni says she has withdrawn entirely from the project,' said Dr Mann.

'Ahh. She's back from Zurich?'

'She states she withdrew because subjects were being asked to commit immoral acts,' said Dr Cobblestone.

'The subject of the experiment was sexual change.'

'Were the subjects asked to commit immoral acts?' Dr Cobblestone continued.

'The instructions made it clear that they didn't have to do anything they didn't want to.'

'Dr Felloni reports that the project encouraged young people to fornicate,' said Dr Mann neutrally.

'She should know. She helped me draw up the instructions.'

'*Does* the project encourage young people to fornicate?' asked Dr Cobblestone.

'And old people t – Look, I think perhaps you ought to ask to have a copy of my research report when it's finished.'

The two stern faces had not relaxed, and Dr Cobblestone went on:

'One of your subjects claims that he was raped.'

'That's true,' replied Dr Rhinehart. 'But our investigation indicated that he either fantasized or prevaricated the rape to suppress his active unconscious participation in the act of which he complains.'

'What's that?' said Dr Cobblestone, irritably cupping an ear at Dr Rhinehart.

'He enjoyed being laid and is lying about the rape.'

'Oh. Thank you.'

'You realize, Luke,' said Dr Mann, 'that in letting you use some of our patients here at QSH for your research that we are legally and morally responsible for what occurs in that research.'

'I understand.'

'Certain attendants and nurses have reported that a large number of patients were volunteering for your sex research project and have claimed that prostitutes were being supplied to the patients.'

'You can read my report when it's done.'

Dr Cobblestone banged his cane a third time.

'A report has reached us that you yourself participated in . . . as . . . as . . . in this experiment.'

'Naturally.'

'Naturally?' asked Dr Mann.

'I participated in the experiment.'

'But our report stated that . . .' Dr Cobblestone's face grew red with his exasperation at not finding the right words. '. . . that you interacted with the subjects . . . sexually.'

'Ahh,' said Dr Rhinehart.

'Well?' asked Dr Mann.

'Some neurotic young person I presume is the author of this slander?' said Dr Rhinehart.

'Yes, yes,' said Dr Cobblestone quickly.

'Projecting his latent desires onto the dreaded authority figure?' Dr Rhinehart went on.

'Precisely,' said Dr Cobblestone, relaxing just a bit.

'Tragic. Is someone trying to help him?'

'Yes,' replied Dr Cobblestone. 'Yes. Dr Vener has . . . How did you know it was a young man?'

'George Lovelace Ray O'Reilly. Projection, compensation, displacement, anal cathexis.'

'Ah, yes.'

'Is there anything else?' said Dr Rhinehart, making motions of rising to leave.

'I'm afraid there is, Luke,' said Dr Mann.

252

'I see.'

Dr Cobblestone gripped his cane carefully in both hands and, aiming, banged it a fourth time on the floor between his legs.

'What's this about dice, young man?' he asked.

'Dice?'

'One of your patients has complained that you're making him play some strange game with dice.'

'The new one, Mr Spezio?'

'Yes.'

'We have patients working with clay, cloth, paper, wood, leather, beads, cardboard, lathes, wire . . . I saw no reason not to let a few select patients begin playing with dice.'

'I see,' said Dr Cobblestone.

'Why?' asked Dr Mann blandly.

'You can read my report when it's done.'

No one spoke for a while.

'Anything else?' Dr Rhinehart asked at last.

The two older men glanced uneasily at each other and Dr Cobblestone cleared his throat.

'You general behavior lately, Luke,' said Dr Mann.

'Ahhh.'

'Your impolite and . . . unusual behavior in our last board meeting,' said Dr Cobblestone.

'Yes.'

'Your erratic, socially upsetting eccentricities,' said Dr Mann.

'Your interruption of Dr Wink,' added Dr Cobblestone.

'We've received complaints from a few nurses here at QSH, several board members naturally, from Mr Spezio, and . . .'

'And?' suggested Dr Rhinehart.

'And I myself am not blind.'

'Ahh.'

'Batman over the telephone is not my idea of a joke.'

There was a silence.

'Your behavior has been undignified and unprofessional,' said Dr Cobblestone.

Silence.

'You can read my report when it's done,' said Dr Rhinehart finally.

Silence.

'Your report?' asked Dr Cobblestone.

'I'm writing an article on the variety of human response to socially eccentric behavior.'

'Yes, yes, I see,' said Dr Cobblestone.

'My hypothesis is – '

'No more, Luke,' said Dr Mann.

'Pardon?'

'No more. You've just about convinced everyone but Jake that you're splitting apart. He alone has faith – '

'My hypothesis is – '

'No more. Your friends have protected you all they're going to. Either back into the old Luke Rhinehart or you're finished as a psychiatrist.'

Dr Cobblestone arose solemnly.

'And if you wish to bring up your idea for some sort of new center to help our patients you must have it placed on the agenda *before* our meeting.'

'I understand,' said Dr Rhinehart, also standing.

'No, more, Luke,' said Dr Mann.

Dr Rhinehart understood.

Chapter Thirty-six

I should have known when Lil sat me down on the armchair opposite her without even touching her champagne that there was trouble. As part of a one-in-six die decision I had been courting her anew with all the unselfish and romantic love I could imagine, and we'd been having a marvelous week. I'd climaxed four days of traditional courting (two plays, a concert, an evening of love on hashish) by suggesting that we end Love Lil Week by taking a three-day skiing holiday at a Canadian ski resort. I had bought her flowers at the airport and champagne for our first night. It had begun snowing thickly after we arrived and although the next day we both skied like untrained walruses, we soon made an art out of tumbling. The snow fell lightly and wetly in the afternoon and we removed our skis and made snowballs and wrestled and rolled and munched the snow more or less like a couple of aged dogs reliving their puppyhood, I a Saint Bernard and she a collie.

She was pretty and bright-eyed and girlishly athletic, and I was handsome and affectionate and boyishly uncoordinated, and we enjoyed playing together again. We danced before a roaring fire and drank more champagne and played brilliant bridge against a couple from Boston and made sweet love under a foot-high mountain of blankets and slept the sleep of the just.

We did the same the next day and the next, and on our last evening, a little high on champagne and marijuana, we spent half an hour holding hands in front of the fire and another ten minutes sitting on our bed with the lights off staring out our window at the moonlight lighting in pale blue the slopes of snow which stretched away from the hotel. I'd opened another bottle of champagne and felt warm and complete and serene. The touch of Lil's hand seemed holy. But then Lil asked me to sit opposite her in the armchair and shook her head when I tried to hand her a glass of champagne, and I knew there was trouble.

After turning on the bedside lamp, I looked up at her and was surprised to see tears in her eyes. She reached forward and took one of my hands and drew it to her face. Her lips touched my fingers delicately and she looked into my eyes. She smiled, slightly, lovingly, but with a tear running down one side of her face.

'Luke,' she said, and she paused for several seconds looking into my eyes. 'What have you been acting so strangely for so long now?'

'Ah Lil,' I began, 'I'd like to tell you . . .' and I stopped.

'I know you aren't really unbalanced,' she went on. 'It's some . . . *theory* you're working on, isn't it?'

The warmth I'd been feeling froze, the lover solidified to stone. Sitting mute, hand being held, was a wary dice man.

'Please tell me,' she said.

She was wetting her lips and squeezing my hand.

'Luke, we're together again. I feel so whole, so full of love for you, yet . . . I know that tomorrow, the next day, you may change again. Everything that has made these last few days so sweet will disappear. And I don't know why. And I *won't* know why.'

Maybe Lil could become the Dice Woman. It sounded like the name of a villainess on the Batman show but it offered me at the moment the only rationalization I could find for betraying the secret of my life and permitting me

256

to hold Lil's happiness and love. I wavered. The band downstairs was playing a waltz. It wasn't too modern a ski resort.

'I – ' I started. The dice man still fought.

'Tell me,' she said.

'I've been experimenting, Lil,' I began for a third time, 'with practicing eccentric behavior, unusual roles, attitudes, emotions – in order to discover the variety of human nature.' I paused: wide-eyed she waited for what I was going to say. Narrow-eyed, so did I. I reached to my side and turned off the light again. Our faces, separated by only three feet, were still quite visible in the moonlight.

'I didn't want to tell you until . . . I had learned whether the experiment had value: you might have rejected me, fought the experiment, ended our love.'

'Oh no, I wouldn't.'

'I knew a moment would come when I could tell you everything. Last week I decided to end the experiment for a while so we could be together again.'

Her grip on my hand was frightening.

'I would have gone along,' she said. 'I would have, sweetheart. Those asses think you're losing your mind. I would have laughed at them if I knew. [Pause] Why? You should have told me.'

'I know that now. I knew that as soon as I freed myself from the experiment: I should have done it all with you.'

'But . . .' Still staring, her eyes glittering in the moonlight, she seemed nervous, uncertain, curious. 'What were the kind . . . kinds of experiments?'

I was so pale and stonelike in the moonlight I imagine I looked like an abandoned statue.

'Oh, going to places I'd never seen before, pretending to be someone different from myself to see people's reactions. Experimenting with food, fasting, drugs, even getting drunk that time was a conscious experiment.'

257

'Really?' And she smiled, tears wetting her cheeks and chin, like a child in the rain.

'It proved that when I'm drunk I act like other people that are drunk.'

'Oh Luke, why didn't you tell me?'

'The mad scientist in me insisted that if I revealed to you that I was experimenting, your reaction would be experimentally useless and a wealth of evidence would be missing.'

'And . . . and the experiment is . . . over?'

'No,' I answered. 'No, Lil, it isn't. But now we'll begin . . . experimenting together, and the loneliness we've both felt will end.'

'But . . .'

'What is it, honey?'

'Will our life like the last few days end too?'

A roar of laughter came from the assembled guests downstairs. 'Sounds like they're having a good time,' I said.

'Will this end?' she asked again softly.

'Of course it will, honey,' I said, trying to dare look at her. 'It would end whether I returned to experimenting or not, you know that. The good things we've felt these last few days have come because they follow such hell. One doesn't have to be a scientist to know that bliss doesn't last.'

She came forward heavily into my arms, sobbing.

'I want it to last. I want it to last,' she said.

I stroked her, kissed her, mumbled sweet nothings, felt numbly that I was handling the situation horribly, felt terrible. A part of me imagined drawing Lil into even more radical dice deals than I could manage alone; perhaps I'd even change her. Another part of me felt utterly abandoned by everyone.

She down-shifted from sobs to sniffles, then left me to

258

trot to the bathroom. When she returned to her same spot on the bed with her face and hair tidied up, I was surprised to see that she was looking at me coldly.

'Have you kept a written record of these experiments?' she asked.

'Of some. And I've written brief essays of analysis of various hypotheses I've been testing.'

'Have you experimented with me?'

'Of course I have, honey. Since it's *me* I experiment with, and me lives with you, you've been affected by many of the experiments.'

'I mean have you directly experimented . . . tried to get me to do things?'

'I . . . no, no, I haven't.'

'Have you experimented with sex? With other women?'

Bingo!

I hesitated.

My male friends, attention. There are some questions which demand any answer *except* hesitation. 'Do you love me?' for example, is not a question; it is intended as a stimulus in the stimulus-response sequence 'Do-you-love-me?-Oh-my-precious-yes.' 'Did you sleep with her?' demands a yes-or-no answer immediately: hedging implies guilt. 'Have you experimented with other women?' demanded an immediate answer of 'Yes, of course, honey, and it's made me closer to you than ever.' This would bring tears, slaps, revilings, withdrawal and eventually, curiosity and reconciliation. Hesitation on the other hand . . .

Hesitation brought Lil leaping to her feet.

'You Goddam bastard,' she said. 'Don't touch me.'

'You don't even know what the experiments were.'

'I know your mind. I know . . . oh my God . . . I know . . . Arlene! You and Arlene!' She was rigid and trembling.

'Honey, honey, honey, you're blowing up about nothing. My experiments didn't include infidelity – '

'I'll bet they didn't. I'm no fool. I'm no fool,' she shouted and, sobbing, crumpled onto the couch.

'Oh. I'm such a fool,' she moaned, 'such a fool.'

I went over and tried to comfort her. She ignored me. After another minute's crying she got up and went into the bathroom. When I followed about two minutes later the door was hooked closed.

Now remember, my friends, I was still supposed to be playing the lover. For seven days I had *been* the lover, at one with the role; now I was only artificially trying to go through the proper motions and emotions. The love was dead, but the lover was commanded to live on.

I knocked and called and finally received a 'Go away'; unoriginal but, I fear, sincere. My impulse was to do just that, but my mind warned me that real lovers never leave their beloved in such cases except to blow out their brains or to get drunk. Considering the alternatives I threw my shoulder against the door twice and broke in.

Lil was sitting on the edge of the tub with a pair of scissors in her hand; she looked up at me dully when I stumbled in. A quick scrutiny indicated she had not slashed anything.

'What are you doing?' I asked.

'I thought I'd mend your pants, if you don't mind.' Beside her, prosaically enough, was, in fact, some thread and the pants I'd ripped down the backside on the slopes that afternoon.

'Mend my pants?'

'You have your experiments and I have . . . [she almost started crying again] my art projects. Pants and . . . I'm being pathetic and maudlin.'

She placed the pants on the rim of the tub and turned on the water in the sink and began scrubbing her face.

When she'd finished, she brushed her teeth. I stood in the doorway, trying to marshal my creative faculties to tell a tall tale.

'Lil, an hour ago we had something which we can and will have again. But you've got to know all about my experiments or – '

She looked up at me foaming at the mouth, toothbrush in hand.

'I'll listen to it all, Luke, to every scientific word but not now. Just not now.'

'You may not want to listen, but I *must* tell you. This hour is too important, our love is too – '

'Crap!'

'Important to let a night go by with this rock between us.'

'I'm going to bed,' she said as she left the bathroom and began to undress.

'Then *go*, but listen.'

She threw off her clothes onto her dresser, got into a nightgown and went to bed. She pulled the covers up so that only the top of her head was showing and turned her back to me. I began lumbering back and forth at the foot of the bed. I was trying to prepare a speech. I wanted to document my series of harmless, faithful-husband experiments but was floundering in the sea of harmful, faithless-husband facts. I didn't know what to do.

I knew door-slamming only postponed the ultimate confrontation and further soothing necessitated my saying something, an act I wished to avoid for a decade or two. Moreover, modest spiritual caresses would leave her free to continue thinking, and thinking, when you are guilty of something (and what man dare cast the first stone), is dangerous and must be stopped. Such soothing would also encourage her to consider the guiltless and abused party, a truth best left unconsidered.

I paced like a starving rat back and forth at the foot of the bed, staring at the food I wanted (Lil) and at the electric grid which would make the eating painful (Lil). Irritably I threw back the covers. Her nightgown was twisted tightly around and pulled almost to the knees. My blood, seeing that delicious, plump, helpless rear, sent representatives racing with the news to the capillaries of my penis.

I retrieved the scissors from the floor and with stealth and delicacy snipped the heavier material at the neck of her nightgown and with a swift yank tore it from top to bottom. Lil twisted upwards screaming and clawing.

The further details, while perhaps of anthropological value, would read something like the dry documentation of some invasion of a Japanese Pacific island during the Second World War: circling movements; advance of right thigh to position 'V'; repulse of fingernail attack on left flank; main artillery piece to attack position; main artillery piece forced to withdraw when caught in classic pincers movement by two enemy ranks, etc.

Forced carnal knowledge, whatever else it may be, is good physical exercise and represents meaningful variation on normal marital relations. As pleasure, however, it has its limitations. For myself, I was so distracted that night by scratches, bites and screams, and by wondering whether one could be arrested for violating one's wife (was pinching a felony or a misdemeanor?), that I must warn male readers that although desirable as tactic, as pleasure one might better employ a quiet night alone with pornography.

The next morning my ears, neck, shoulders and back looked as if I'd spent the night wrestling with thirty-three kittens in a briar patch crisscrossed with barbed wire during a hailstorm. I was bloody and Lil was unbowed. But though she was cold and distant, she listened to my long, scientific report during the bus ride and plane flight back to New York and although she seemed unimpressed with my claims of innocence with Arlene, a part of her believed the rest. I told her nothing about my use of the dice, keeping it all a matter of some vague, temporary psychological testing having to do with responses to eccentric patterns. How much of her believed me isn't clear, but her majority self announced unequivocally that if I did not cease my experiments – whatever they might be – and cease them forthwith, she and the children would leave me forever.

'No, more, Luke,' she said as I left for work the first day back in Manhattan. 'No more. From now on you're normal, eccentric, boring Dr Rhinehart, or I'm done.'

'Yes, dear,' I said (the die had fallen a two), and left.

Chapter Thirty-seven

Dr Rhinehart should have known when Mrs Ecstein summoned him to her living room couch that Wednesday that there was trouble. They hadn't met in her apartment since she had begun therapy with him. After letting him in she seated herself sedately on the couch, folded her hands and looked at the floor. Her mannish gray suit, her glasses and her hair tied back severely in a bun, made her look strikingly like a door-to-door purveyor of Baptist religious tracts.

'I'm going to have a baby,' she said quietly.

Dr Rhinehart sat down at the opposite end of the couch, leaned back and mechanically crossed his legs. He looked blankly at the wall opposite him, on which hung an ancient lithograph of Queen Victoria.

'I'm happy for you, Arlene,' he said.

'This is now the second straight month I've missed my period.'

'I'm happy.'

'I asked the Die what I should name it and gave it thirty-six options and the Die named it Edgar.'

'Edgar.'

'Edgar Ecstein.'

They sat there quietly not looking at each other.

'I gave ten chances to Lucius but the dice chose Edgar.'

'Ahh.'

Silence.

'What if it's a girl?' Dr Rhinehart asked after a while.

'Edgarina.'

'Ahh.'

'Edgarina Ecstein.'

Silence.

'Are you happy about it, Arlene?'

'Yes.'

Silence.

'It hasn't been decided yet who the father is,' Mrs Ecstein said.

'You don't know who the father is?' asked Dr Rhinehart, sitting up.

'Oh *I* know,' she said and turned smiling to Dr Rhinehart. 'But I haven't let the dice decide who I should *say* is the father.'

'I see.'

'I thought I'd give you two chances out of three of being the father.'

'Ahhh.'

'Jake, of course, will get one chance in six.'

'Unhuh.'

'And I thought I'd let "someone you don't know" have one chance in six.'

Silence.

'The dice will decide then who you tell Jake is the father?'

'Yes.'

'What about abortion? You're only in the second month, did you let the dice consider abortion?'

'Oh, of course,' she said again smiling. 'I gave abortion one chance in two hundred and sixteen.'

'Ahhh.'

'The dice said no.'

'Mm.'

Silence.

'So in seven months you're going to have a baby.'

'Yes, I am. Isn't it wonderful?'

'I'm happy for you,' said Dr Rhinehart.

'And after I find out who the father is I'll have to let the dice decide whether I should leave Jake to be true to the father.'

'Uhh.'

'And then let the dice decide whether I'm to have more children.'

'Um.'

'But before that they'll have to tell me whether I should tell Lil I'm having a baby.'

'Ahh.'

'And whether I should tell Lil who the father is.'

'Uh.'

'It's all so wonderfully exciting.'

Silence.

Dr Rhinehart took from his suit-jacket pocket a die and after rubbing it between his hands dropped it on the couch between himself and Mrs Ecstein. It was a two.

Dr Rhinehart sighed.

'I'm happy for you, Arlene,' he said and collapsed slowly back in a heap against the couch, his blank eyes swiveling automatically to the blank wall opposite, on which hung only the ancient lithograph of Queen Victoria. Smiling.

Chapter Thirty-eight

Unfortunately for normal old Luke Rhinehart and his friends and admirers, the dice kept rolling and rolling, June turned out to be National Role-Playing Month and a bit too much. I was ordered to consult the die regularly about varying the person I was from hour to hour, or day to day or week to week. I was expected to expand my role playing, perhaps even to test the limits of the malleability of the human soul.

Could there exist a Totally Random Man? Could a single human so develop his capabilities that he might vary his soul from hour to hour at whim? Might a man be an infinitely multiple personality? or rather, like the universe according to some theorists, a steadily expanding multiple personality, one only to be contracted at death? and then, even then, who knows?

At dawn of the second day I gave the die six optional persons, one of whom I would try to be during the whole day. I was trying to create only simple, non socially upsetting options. The six were: Molly Bloom, Sigmund Freud, Henry Miller, Jake Ecstein, a child of seven and the old pre-dice man Dr Lucius Rhinehart.

The die first chose Freud, but by the end of the day I had come to feel that being Sigmund Freud must have been something of a bore. I was aware of many unconscious sources of motivation where I usually overlooked them, but having seen them I didn't feel I had gained too much. I tried to examine my unconscious resistances to being Freud and uncovered the sort of thing Jake was good at in analysis: rivalry with the Father, fear of

267

unconscious aggression being revealed: but I didn't find my insights convincing, or rather I didn't find them relevant. I might have an 'oral personality' but this knowledge didn't help me change myself as much as did a single flip of the die.

On the other hand, when I read of a man who killed himself by slashing his wrists I immediately noted the sexual symbolism of the cutting of the limbs. I began thinking of other modes of suicide: throwing oneself into the sea; putting a pistol in one's mouth and pulling the trigger; crawling into an oven and turning on the gas; throwing oneself under a train – All seemed to have obvious sexual symbolism and be necessarily connected with the psychosexual development of the patient. I created the excellent aphorism: Tell me the manner in which a patient commits suicide and I'll tell you how he can be cured.

The next day I scratched Freud from my list, replaced him with a 'slightly psychotic, aggressively anti-Establishment hippie' and cast a die: it chose Jake Ecstein.

Jake I could do very well. He was a real part of me and his superficial mannerisms and speech patterns I could easily imitate. I wrote half an article for the *Journal of Abnormal Psychology* analyzing the dice man concept from an orthodox Jakeian point of view and felt marvelous. During my analytic hour with Jake I entered so completely into his way of thinking that at the end he announced that we had covered more ground in this one session than in our previous two and a half months together. In a later article he wrote about my analysis, 'The Case of the Six-Sided Man' – (Jake's reputation will be eternal on the basis of his titles alone), he discussed this analytical hour in detail and attributes its success to the accidental discovery of a rarely read article by Ferenczi which he stumbled upon the night before lying open to a key page under his bathroom sink and which gave him the key 'which began to unlock the door to the six-sided cube.' He was ecstatic.

The dice rolled on and rolled me from role to roll to role in a schizophrenic kaleidoscope of dramatic play. Life became like a series of bit parts in a bad movie, with no script, no director, and with actresses and actors who didn't know their lines or their roles. I did most of my role playing away from people who knew me, for reasons which are obvious.

I can remember only vaguely what I did and said in those days; images are clearer than dialogues: I as Oboko the Zen master sitting mostly mute and smiling while a young graduate student tries to question me about psychoanalysis and the meaning of life: I as a child of seven riding a bicycle through Central Park, staring at the ducks in the pond, sitting crosslegged to watch an old Negro fishing, buying bubblegum and ballooning out a big one, racing another cyclist on my bike and crashing and scratching my knee and crying, much to the bewilderment of the passers-by: 240-pound crybabies being a rarity.

Despite all my efforts to limit my expanding personalities to strangers and to maintain a certain amount of normality around my friends and colleagues, I always gave the Die at least an outside chance to undo me, and the Die, being God, couldn't long resist.

Chapter Thirty-nine

Once upon a time Dr Rhinehart dreamed he was a bumblebee, a bumblebee buzzing and flitting around, happy with himself and doing as he pleased. He didn't believe he was Dr Rhinehart. Suddenly he felt that he had awakened, and he was old Luke Rhinehart lying in bed beside the beautiful woman Lil. But he didn't know if he was Dr Rhinehart who had dreamed he was playing the role of a bumblebee, or a bumblebee dreaming he was Dr Rhinehart. He didn't know, and his head was buzzing. After several minutes he shrugged: 'Perhaps I'm actually Hubert Humphrey dreaming I'm a bumblebee dreaming of being Dr Rhinehart.'

He paused for several more seconds and then rolled over and snuggled up to his wife.

'In any case,' he said to himself, 'in this dream of being Dr Rhinehart I'm glad I'm in bed with a woman and not a bumblebee.'

Chapter Forty

Dr Abraham Krum, the German-American researcher, had in just five years astounded the psychiatric world with three complex sets of experiments, each of which proved something unique. He began by being the first man in world history able experimentally to induce psychosis in chickens, a creature previously considered of too low intelligence to achieve psychosis. Secondly, he had managed to isolate the chemical agent (moratycemate) which caused or was associated with the psychosis, thus being the first man to prove conclusively that chemical change could be isolated as a crucial variable in the psychosis of chickens. Thirdly, he discovered an antidote (amoratycemate) which completely cured ninety-three percent of the chickens of their psychosis in just three days of treatment, thus becoming the first man in world history to cure a psychosis exclusively by chemical means.

There was considerable speculation about the Nobel Prize. His current work on schizophrenia in pigeons was followed like stock market reports by large numbers of people in the psychiatric world. The drug amoratycemate was being experimentally administered to psychotic patients at several mental hospitals in Germany and the United States with interesting results. (Side effects involving blood clots and colitis had not yet been conclusively confirmed, nor had they been eliminated.)

Dr Krum was to be the guest of honor at a party given by Dr Mann for his friends and certain luminaries of the New York psychiatric world. It was to be a major occasion, with the president of PANY (Dr Joseph

Weinburger), the director of the New York State Department of Mental Hygiene and two or three other extremely big deals whom I can never remember. The dice, imps of the perverse, ordered that I vary my person every ten minutes or so throughout the evening among six roles: a gentle Jesus, an honest dice man, an uninhibited sex maniac, a mute moron, a bullshit artist and a Leftist agitator.

I had created the options under the influence of marijuana, which I had smoked for half an hour as the result of an option created under the influence of alcohol, which I had drunk because the dice – ad infinitum. My dicelife was getting out of control and the party for Dr Krum was the climax.

Dr Mann's apartment manages to resemble both a funeral home and a museum. His servant, Mr Thornton, a cadaver, opened the door that evening with all the warmth of a mechanical skeleton, removed Lil's coat, ignored her plunging neckline, said, 'Good evening, Dr Rhinehart,' as if Dr Mann had just died, and led us down the hall – filled with portraits of famous psychiatrists – and into the living room.

Whenever I entered the room I was always surprised to find living people there. Jake was against a wall of bookcases in one corner talking with Miss Reingold (there to take notes for Jake), Professor Boggles (there because my dice had said to invite him and his dice had said to accept) and a couple of other men, presumably world-famous psychiatrists. On an immense oriental couch in front of a Victorian fireplace sat Arlene, Dr Felloni (who nodded her head rapidly at my appearance) and an elderly woman, presumably somebody's mother. Arlene was dressed as briefly as Lil and with a slightly more spectacular effect: her two luscious breasts made it look as if lovely white balloons had been stuffed into her dress from above but threatened to float out at any moment. In easy chairs opposite the couch were an elderly, retired big deal I vaguely knew, a chubby woman, presumably somebody's wife, and a small man with a tiny pointed beard, slump-shouldered yet intense: the Dr Krum I knew from photographs.

Dr Mann greeted us wineglass in hand, his face slightly flushed with glory, worry and booze and led us toward the women and Dr Krum. I shook the tiny die in a specially built watchcase in my pocket, eased it out and glanced at the result to discover which of the six roles I was now to play for ten minutes or so.

'Dr Krum, I'd like you to meet a former student and colleague of mine, Dr Lucius Rhinehart,' said Dr Mann. 'Luke, this is Dr Krum.'

'Dr Rhinehart, a pleasure, a pleasure. Your work I have not read but Dr Mann says highly of you.' Dr Krum shook hands with short emphatic stabs and bared his teeth in an exaggerated grimace as he looked confidently up into my face, looming nearly a foot above him.

'Dr Krum, I'm speechless. I never hoped to meet a man who'd done such work in my own lifetime. I'm deeply, deeply honored.'

'It's nothing, nothing. In a few years, *then* I will show you – My dear, delighted, delighted.' He bowed slightly to Lil and clicked his heels as he shook her hand with two quick pumps. He looked up at her and then at me with a pleased, flushed face.

'Such lovely ladies this evening, lovely ladies. I regret verking with chickens.' He laughed.

'Dr Krum, your loss is the world's gain.' As I said this, Lil glanced briefly at me, raised her eyes ceilingward and turned to talk to Jake, who had edged to the outskirts of our group. Arlene was sunk into the couch smiling up at me and I smiled broadly back at her.

'You're terrific, Arlene, you really are. You look sexier every time I see you.' She flushed prettily.

'Who are you tonight?' she asked nonchalantly, sitting up a bit straighter and inflating her balloons.

'Just terrific, Arlene, you really are. I don't understand, Dr Krum, these women, why they try to distract us when we want to talk about your work.'

Dr Krum, an elderly has-been named Latterly and I were all looking with dazed grins at Arlene until I turned to Dr Krum and said: 'Your ability to isolate variables amazes me.'

'My verk, my verk.' He turned to me, shrugged his shoulders and stroked his tiny beard. 'I'm verking now with pigeons.'

'The whole world knows,' I said.

'Knows what?' asked Jake, joining us with a Scotch for me and some purple something for Dr Krum.

'Dr Krum, I trust you know my colleague, Dr Ecstein.'

'Of course, of course, the accidental breakthrough. Ve met.'

'Jake is probably the finest theoretical analyst practicing in the United States today.'

'Yeah,' said Jake without expression. 'What were you talking about?'

'Dr Krum has moved to pigeons and the whole world knows.'

'Oh yeah. How's it going, Krum?'

'Good, good. We haven't induced schizophrenia complete yet, but the pigeons are nervous.' He laughed again, a quick ratatat-tat heh-heh-heh.

'Have you tried injecting 'em with that chicken stuff – that psychotic stuff – you discovered?' Jake asked.

'Oh no. No. It has no effect on pigeons.'

'What methods of inducing schizophrenia in your sub-

274

jects have you tried after the failure of your cubical maze?' I asked.

'Presently ve teach homing pigeons to find home. Then ve move pigeon long vay avay and move the home. Pigeon gets very vorried.'

'What problems have you encountered?' I asked.

'Ve lose pigeons.'

Jake laughed, but when I glanced at him he cut it short and squinted nervously at me. Dr Krum stroked his beard, focused his eyes intently on my knees and went on.

'Ve lose pigeons. It is nothing. Ve have many pigeons, but chickens could not fly. Pigeons are smart but ve may have to remove their vings,' he frowned.

Dr Mann joined us, glass in hand, Jake asked a question and I removed my watchcase and glanced at the single die for a second role.

The tall, gaunt Mr Thornton arrived, dispensing tiny hors d'oeuvres, crackers with minute pearl-like deposits on them like fish eggs waiting to be fertilized. Each of my three colleagues mechanically took one, Jake downing his in a swallow, Dr Mann briefly holding his under his nose and then chewing it for the next ten minutes and Dr Krum taking an intense experimental bite, like a chicken pecking at seed.

'Dr Rhinehart?' Mr Thornton asked, holding the silver tray and its obscene deposits up toward my chest where I could see it.

'Unununununun,' I vibrated noisily, my lower lip hanging sloppily and my eyes attempting an animal vacancy. With my huge right paw I swept up and clutched six or seven crackers, almost upsetting the tray, and stuffed them into my mouth, pieces falling in a splendid dry waterfall down my shirt front to the floor.

A flicker of human surprise crossed for a millisecond the erased face of Mr Thornton as he looked into my vacant gaze and watched me chew ineptly, a bit of moist semi-chewed cracker dangling briefly from my lip before falling forever to the deep brown rug below.

'Unununun,' I vibrated again.

'Thank you, sir,' said Mr Thornton and turned to the ladies.

Dr Krum was emphatically stabbing the air in front of Dr Mann's stomach as if performing some magic rite before making an incision.

'Proof! Proof! They do not know the meaning of the verd. They raise money with bribes, they are bankers, barbarians, businessmen, beasts, they – '

'Shit, who cares?' interrupted Jake. 'If they want to get rich and famous, let 'em. We're doing the real work.' He squinted at me; or was it a wink?

'That is true. That is true. Scientists like us and businessmen like them have nutting in common.'

'Un unun,' I said, looking at Dr Krum, my mouth half-open like a fish gasping wide-eyed on the deck of a ship. Dr Krum looked up at me seriously and respectfully and then stroked his beard three, four times.

'There are two classes of men: the creators and the – how you say – drudges. Is possible to tell immejetly creators. Immejetly, drudges.'

'Unununununun.'

'I do not know your verk, Dr Rhinehart, but from the moment you speak to me, I know, I know.'

'Unnh.'

'Dr Rhinehart has the brains all right,' Dr Mann said. 'But he's got a writing block. He prefers to play games. He expects every article to surpass Freud.'

'He ought, he ought. Is good to surpass Freud.'

'Luke's got a book in the works about sadism,' said Jake, 'which may make Stekel and Reich read like Grandma Moses.'

276

It was a wink.

They all three looked up expectantly at me. I continued to stare vacant-eyed, mouth agape, at Dr Krum. There was a silence.

'Yes, yes. Is interesting, sadism,' Dr Krum said, and his face twitched.

'Unnnnnnnh,' I vibrated, but steadier.

Jake and Dr Krum looked at me hopefully while Dr Mann took a graceful sip of his wine.

'You have been verking lung on sadism?'

I stared back at him.

Dr Mann suddenly excused himself and went to greet three more arrivals at the party, and Arlene took Jake's arm and whispered something in his ear. He turned reluctantly to talk to her. Dr Krum was still looking at me. I was only half-conscious of the conversation; I was focused on the crumb in his beard.

'Unununun,' I said. It was a little like a faulty transformer.

'Vunderful – I thought myself of experimenting with sadism in chickens, but is rare. Is rare.'

Dr Mann returned with two other people, a man and a woman, and introduced them to us. One was Fred Boyd, a young psychologist from Harvard I knew and liked, and the other was his date, a plump, pleasant blonde with a cream-smooth complexion – a Miss Welish. She reached out her hand when she was introduced to me, and when I failed to grasp it, she blushed. Looked at her I said: 'Unununununun.' She blushed again.

'Hi, Luke, how's it going?' asked Fred Boyd. I turned to him blankly.

'How did Herder do with his grant application to Stonewall?' Dr Mann asked Fred.

'Not so good,' Fred answered. 'They wrote that their funds are tied up this year and – '

277

'Is that *the* Dr Krum?' a voice asked at my elbow.

I looked down at Miss Welish and then over at Dr Krum. The crumb was still in his beard, although better hidden now.

'Blnnh,' I asked.

'Fred thinks so too,' Miss Welish said and she turned us aside from the other conversation. 'He says one reason he admires you is that you don't stand for any nonsense.'

Impulsively I lifted one great paw and dangled it loosely over her shoulder. She was wearing a silver, high-necked dress and the shimmering scales were rough against my wrist.

'I beg your pardon,' she said, and when she backed away my paw slid down over a breast and swung briefly like a pendulum at my side.

She blushed and glanced quickly at the three men talking nearby.

'Fred says that Dr Krum is very good at what he does, but that what he does isn't really important. What do you think?'

'Unn,' I said loudly and stamped one giant foot.

'Oh me too. I don't like animal experimenters myself. I've been doing social work in Staten Island now for two years and there's so much to be done with *people*.'

She looked now over at the couch where Dr Felloni, the elderly lady and the thin old big deal were talking: Miss Welish seemed to be relaxing in my company.

'Even here, in this very room, there are people whose lives are unfulfilled, people who need help.'

I was silent, but a bit of drool escaped from my lower lip and began its pilgrimage down my shirt front.

'Unless we can learn to relate to each other,' Miss Welish went on, 'to be *aware* of each other, all the chicken cures in the world won't help.'

I was staring at Arlene's balloons undulating in the light

278

of the chandelier. A small orgasm of saliva spilled again from my lower lip.

'What fascinates me about you psychiatrists is the way you hold yourselves in, remain detached. Don't you ever *feel* the suffering you have to deal with?' Miss Welish turned toward me again and grimaced at the sight of my tie and shirt front.

I began groping clumsily in my pocket for my watchcase with the die.

'Don't you *feel* the suffering?' Miss Welish repeated.

Pulling out the watchcase I let my head twitch three times sideways and grunted a single, 'Un.'

'Oh, God, you men are so *hard*.'

I slowly raised my lower jaw; it ached from its drooped position. Running my tongue over my dry upper lip, I used my handkerchief to wipe the saliva from my chest and turned my eyes full on Miss Welish.

'What time *is* it?' she asked.

'Time for us to stop playing word games and get down to business,' I said.

'I think so too. I can't stand cocktail-party chatter,' she looked pleased that we were at last going to be above it all.

'What's underneath that lovely dress?'

'You like it? Fred bought it for me at Ohrbach's. Don't you like the way it – glimmers?' She gave the upper part of her body a little shake: her dress shimmered and her chubby arms vibrated.

'You're built, baby – Look, what's your first name?'

'Joya. It's corny, but I like it.'

'Joya. It's a beautiful name. You're beautiful. Your skin is incredibly smooth and creamy. I'd love to run my tongue over it.' I reached my hand up and caressed her cheek and then the back of her neck. She reddened again.

'I was born with it, I guess. My mother has a lovely complexion and Dad too. In fact, Dad – '

'Are your thighs and your belly and your breasts that same creamy white color?'

'Well . . . I guess they are. Except when I get a tan.'

'I'd love to be able to run my hands over your whole body.'

'It's nice. When I put suntan lotion on, it feels so smooth.'

I lowered my lids a little and tried to look sexy.

'You've stopped drooling,' she said.

'Look, Joya, this cocktail-party chatter is giving me a headache. Can't we go someplace for a few minutes where we can be alone?' I edged her away toward a hallway which I knew led to Dr Mann's office.

'Oh talk talk talk. It gets so sickening after a while.'

'Let me show you Dr Mann's office. He has some fascinating illustrated books on primitive sexual practices.'

'No pictures of chickens?' and she laughed happily at herself, and I laughed too. Dr Felloni nodded her head at us as we passed the couch, and Jake squinted over an Important Person's shoulder as we passed behind the Krum group and Arlene jiggled her breasts slightly and smiled and we were down the hall and into Dr Mann's office. I heard a shrill squeak when we entered and saw then that Dr Boggles and Miss Reingold were seated on the floor with a pair of green dice between them, and Boggles, with two-thirds of his clothes removed, was just reaching triumphantly to remove Miss Reingold's (smiling triumphantly) blouse.

As we backed out, Miss Welish said: 'Oh that's disgusting. In Dr Mann's study! That's disgusting.'

'You're right, Joya, let's go to the bathroom.'

'The bathroom?'

'It's down this way.'

'What are you talking about?'

'A place to talk privately.'

'Oh.' She had stopped in the middle of the hall now and her hands were both clenching her drink.

'No,' she said. 'I want to get back to the party.'

'Joya, all I want to do is use your beautiful body. It won't take long.'

'What will we talk about?'

'What? We'll talk about Harry Stack Sullivan's theory of post-operative malaise. Come on.'

As she still remained immobile I realized I was being entirely too middle-class for the uninhibited sex maniac the Die certainly had in mind and, when Miss Welish began talking of going back to the living room again, I strode forward, knocked her drink to the floor and tried to kiss her powerfully on the mouth.

The explosion of pain in my balls was so intense that for a moment I thought I had been shot. I was blinded with pain and staggered back against the wall with a thud. With the fierce willpower of a saint I forced my eyes open and saw the shimmering silvery back of Miss Welish returning toward the living room – Thank God! – leaving me alone with my disaster.

I assumed I wouldn't be able to move from my folded-up position for a month and wondered vaguely if Mr Thornton would dust me regularly. The question also came to my mind how an 'uninhibited sex maniac' would react to a major kick in the balls. The answer seemed unequivocal: maniac, gentle Jesus, psychotic hippie, mute moron, Jake Ecstein, Hugh Hefner, Lao-Tzu, Norman Vincent Peale, Billy Graham – all would react as I, simple, bespectacled Luke Rhinehart, was acting. Although both my hands were at the scene of the accident, they weren't touching anything; they seemed to be there to do something if anything could ever be done –

say next month. Yet, I couldn't force my hands back to a different position. Dr Krum and Arlene Ecstein were coming down the hall. I tried to straighten up and almost screamed. They stared down at the broken fragments of glass and then stopped in front of me.

'Nasty stomach-ache,' I said. 'Severe abdominal cramps. May need an anesthetic.'

'Vell, vell. Tummy-ache, you say?'

'Lower tummy, abdomen, help.' I was whispering.

'Luke, what game are you playing now?' Arlene said and looked down at me (I was folded down a full foot and a half from my normal height) with a bemused smile.

'You're – you're terrific, baby,' I gasped. 'Take off – that dress.' I collapsed slowly sideways to the floor, the pain in my elbow being an almost blissful distraction from the other.

I heard Fred Boyd's voice from farther up the hall asking, 'What happened?' and then heard him almost directly over me, laughing.

'I think he's been shot,' Dr Krum said. 'Is serious.'

'Oh, he'll survive,' Fred said, and I felt his hands on one of my arms and then Arlene's on the other, and Fred lifted one arm around his shoulder and dragged me into a bedroom. They threw me on to the bed.

The pain was, in fact, subsiding, and after the three had left, I was able to move a bit, my eyes mostly, but it was progress. Then I remembered it was time for a fresh consultation of the Die and, shuddering at the possibility of a second round of uninhibited sex maniac, I painfully drew the fake watch case out of my pocket and looked: a three: the honest diceman.

I lay back on the bed for a while and stared at the ceiling. I heard voices passing by out in the hall and then only the blurred distant buzz from the living room. The door opened and Lil came in.

'What happened?' she asked sharply. She was immaculately beautiful in her black, lowcut cocktail dress, but her eyes and mouth were set and cold. I looked up at her and felt a hollowness inside me: what a time and place for this.

'Dr Krum said you were sick. You disappear with Blondie and then turn up sick. What happened?'

I struggled to a sitting position and dragged my legs off the bed to the floor. I looked up at her.

'It's a long story, Lil.'

'You made a pass at Blondie.'

'Longer than that, much longer.'

'I hate you.'

'Yes. It's inevitable,' I said. 'I'm the Dice Man.'

'Had you met her before? I thought Fred told me he'd just met her himself.'

'I'd never met her before. She was thrown into my path and the dice said take her.'

'The *dice*? What're you talking about?'

'I am the Dice Man.' Hunched over and disheveled, I'm afraid it wasn't too impressive a moment. We stared at each other, separated by only six feet in the little bedroom off the hallway of Dr Mann's museum mausoleum. Lil shook her head as if trying to clear it.

'What, if I may ask, is the dice man?'

Dr Krum and Arlene again appeared, Dr Krum carrying a black bag similar to those carried by general practitioners in the early nineteenth century.

'You are better?' he said.

'Yes. Thank you. I will rise again.'

'Good, good. I have an anesthetic. You vant?'

'No. It won't be necessary. Thanks.'

'What is the dice man, Luke?' Lil repeated. She hadn't moved since entering the room. I saw Arlene start and felt her eyes upon me as I turned back to Lil.

283

'The Dice Man,' I said slowly, 'is an experiment in changing the personality, in destroying the personality.'

'Is interesting,' Dr Krum said.

'Go on,' Lil said.

'To destroy the single dominant personality one must be capable of developing many personalities; one must become multiple.'

'You're stalling,' Lil said. 'What is the dice man?'

'The Dice Man,' I said, and I shifted my gaze to Arlene, who, wide-eyed and alert, watched me as if I were an entralling movie, 'is a creature whose actions are decided from day to day by the roll of dice, the dice choosing from among options created by the man.'

There was a silence which lasted perhaps five seconds.

'Is interesting,' Dr Krum said. 'But difficult with chickens.'

Another silence followed and I turned my eyes back to Lil who, straight, dignified and beautiful, raised now a hand to her forehead and rubbed softly just below the hairline. Her expression was one of shock.

'I – I never meant a thing to you,' she said quietly.

'But you did. I have to fight my attachment to you time and time again.'

'Come on, Dr Krum, let's get out of here,' Arlene said.

Lil turned her head and looked away out the darkened window, oblivious of Arlene and Dr Krum.

'You could do the things you did, to me, to Larry, to Evie, because the dice . . .?' she finally said.

This time I didn't reply. Dr Krum looked perplexed from me to Lil to me, shaking his head.

'You could use me, lie to me, betray me, mock me, whore me and remain . . . happy?'

'For something greater than either of us,' I said.

Arlene had pulled Dr Krum away and they disappeared out the door.

284

Lil looked down at the wedding ring on her left hand, felt its texture between her fingers, her face soft, wistful.

'Everything . . .' she shook her head slowly, dreamily. 'Everything between us for a year, no. No. For all, for all our lives, becomes ashes.'

'Yes,' I said.

'Because . . . because you want to play your maniac, your adulterer, your hippie, your dice man.'

'Yes.'

'And what, what if I told you now,' Lil went on, 'that for a year I've been having an affair with – I know it sounds silly – but an affair with the garage attendant downstairs?'

'Lil, that's wonderful.'

Pain flashed across her face.

'What if I told you that tonight before coming here, in tucking the children in goodnight, in following a theory of mine to show detachment, I had . . . I had strangled Larry and Evie?'

There we were opposite each other, an old married couple chatting about the doings of the day.

'If it were done for a . . . a useful theory it would be . . .'

Greater love hath no man than this: that he lay down his children's lives for his theory.

'You would, of course, kill them if the dice told you to,' Lil said.

'I don't think I'd ever give that particular option into the hands of the dice.'

'Only adultery, theft, fraud and treason.'

'I might give Larry and Evie into the hands of the Die, but myself too.'

She was rocking now on her heels, her hands clenched in front of her, still immaculately beautiful.

'I guess I should be thankful,' she said. 'The mystery is

over. But . . . but it's not easy to have the death of the man you loved most in the world told to you by . . . by his corpse.'

'Interesting point,' I said.

Lil's head jerked back at my reply and her eyes widened slowly until, suddenly, she threw herself on me with a convulsive shriek, pulling my hair and then beating me with her fists. I hunched over to protect myself, but I felt so hollow inside that Lil's blows were like a gentle rain falling on an empty barrel. It occurred to me that it was long past time to consult the Die again. I wasn't interested. I didn't feel interested in anything. The blows stopped and Lil, crying loudly, ran toward the door. Arlene was standing there, looking terrified, and caught Lil in her arms. They disappeared, and I was alone.

Chapter Forty-one

As I sit here writing of that distant night, the tragedies and comedies bloom like flowers around me still, and I continue on from day to day or year to year to play a role, and certainly, sooner or later, I'll abandon that of dice man too. A role, a role. Star billing one day, walk-on the next. Vaudeville standup comic Shakespearian fool. Alceste in the morning, Gary Cooper and a hippie during the day, Jesus at night. I no longer remember precisely when I stopped acting: when the fallen die began to click to life roles where there was no residual me fighting them and no dice man me feeling proud, only lives being lived. I do remember that alone in that room that night after Lil left I felt a full joyous uninhibited grief. I was in pain, I suffered, I was there.

And you, Friend, sprawled on your bed or sitting in your chair, you giggle perhaps as I slobber as Caliban, smile at my sufferings as an honest man, or sigh when I ponderously play the fool, philosophizing my madness, lecturing you on the metaphor of life as play. But I *am* the honest man – with all his senseless suffering for those who will feel; I *am* the fool. I've been Raskolnikov climbing the stairs, Julien Sorel hearing the clock strike ten, Molly Bloom writhing beneath the rhythmic push of Blazes Boylan's prick. Agonies are one of my changes of garments – fortunately not worn as often as my motley – of the fool.

And you, Reader, good friend and fellow fool my reader, you, yes you, my sweet cipher, are the Dice Man. Having read this far, you are doomed to carry with you burned forever in your soul the self I've here portrayed: the Dice Man. You are multiple and one of you is me. I have created in you a flea which will forever make you itch. Ah, Reader, you never should have let me be born. Other selves bite now and then no doubt. But the Dice Man flea demands to be scratched at every moment: he is insatiable. You will never know an itchless moment again – unless, of course, you become the flea.

Chapter Forty-two

On the edge of the bed, alone, the party outside seeming to settle into precisely the businesslike buzz it manifested before, Dr Rhinehart sat hunched over, numbed. There was no retreat now. He was the Dice Man or he was no one. His body knew, although he could not yet be aware consciously, that Luke Rhinehart was now an impossible existence. Numbed, he disobeyed the Die by not consulting the watch for almost ten minutes. Then, having no place else to go, no one else to be, he took out the watch with the die and looked.

Slowly he straightened himself up and, standing, bowed his head in a brief prayer. Then he smoothed down his clothing and his hair and moved toward the party. He wanted first to see his wife, to abase himself before her. He walked down the hall to the living room and from the doorway squinted through the random clusters of faces, looking for her. Those talking and drinking paid him no special attention, but Mrs Ecstein came up behind him and said that his wife was in Dr Mann's office.

He followed her down the hall and over the broken glass to the office. He found Dr Mann and Dr Ecstein standing awkwardly on either side of his wife, who sat, childlike, on the edge of Dr Mann's consulting couch.

The sight of her, hunched over and small, her face pale but streaked with smeared eye shadow, her hair in disarray, an ugly man's sweater draped clumsily over her shoulders, knocked Dr Rhinehart without conscious intention to his knees, with his chest and head too lowering forward until he groveled at his wife's feet.

The room was silent that they could all hear quite distinctly from the center of the house the ratatattat of Dr Krum's laughter.

'Forgive me, Lil, I am mad,' Dr Rhinehart said.

No one spoke.

Dr Rhinehart raised his head and chest from the floor to look at his wife and he said: 'For what I have done there is no forgiveness in this world; but I am repentant. I . . . I have been purified . . . by the hell that I am causing. I . . .' His eyes suddenly brightened with eagerness. 'I feel only love for you and for all here. The world can be a blessed place if we but love one another.'

'Luke, baby, what are you . . .?' Dr Ecstein said, and he took a step forward as if to raise Dr Rhinehart up but stopped.

'Beautiful, beautiful Jake, I'm talking about love.' Dr Rhinehart shook his head slowly as if confused, and a childlike smile appeared on his face. 'I've been all mixed up, all wrong; love, loving, loveliness is all there is.' He turned and stretched out his arms to his wife. 'Lil, my darling, you must realize that Heaven is here, is now, with me.'

His wife returned his gaze for a moment and then slowly raised her eyes to Dr Mann beside her. A look of immense relief began to appear on her face.

'He *is* insane, isn't he?' she asked.

'I don't know,' Dr Mann said. 'Now, of course, but he keeps changing so. It may be only temporary.'

'You fools, we've all been insane,' Dr Rhinehart said. 'I but look at each of you and love. God is shining forth from each of you like fluorescent lights. Open your eyes and see.'

He was erect now on his knees, his fists clenched and his face strangely exalted.

'Better give him a shot of sodium amytal, Tim,' Dr Ecstein said to Dr Mann in a whisper.

'I've only got pills here in the house,' Dr Mann whispered back.

'Careless,' Dr Ecstein said.

'But why why why,' Dr Rhinehart began forcefully, 'do you want to quiet God? I am among you spraying love and you do not hear, do not see, do not let it refresh you.' He arose. 'I must beg forgiveness of that poor innocent girl and show her my new love.' And he abruptly strode from the room.

Down the hall and over the broken glass again and into the living room. Miss Welish was with Dr Boyd beside the bookcase in one corner. When he went to them, Dr Boyd came protectively between Dr Rhinehart and the girl.

'What now, Luke?' he said.

'I am deeply sorry for the insane attack I made on you, Miss Welish. I sincerely regret it. Only now do I see the true meaning of love.'

Miss Welish, round-eyed, peeked around her escort's shoulder.

'Oh come off it, Luke,' Dr Boyd said.

'You are beautiful; you are both beautiful, and I deeply regret having marred this wonderful evening.'

'I hope I didn't hurt you,' Miss Welish said.

'My pain was the initial source of my seeing the light. I can't thank you enough.'

'Any time,' Dr Boyd said. 'Come on, Joya, let's leave.'

'But I have to . . .' The voice of Miss Welish was lost behind the retreating figure of Dr Boyd.

'You are better, true?' Dr Krum said suddenly from below and beside Dr Rhinehart as the two others moved away. The thin, elderly former Big Deal was with him, and so was a fiftyish Important Person puffing on a pipe.

As they began talking, Dr Weinburger, president of PANY, and the chubby middle-aged woman joined them.

'I am whole at last,' Dr Rhinehart replied.

'What was this about the dice man, hey? Vas interesting.'

'The Dice Man is a deeply sick concept, totally lacking in love.'

'Seemed a bit schizophrenic the way Dr Krum described it,' said Dr Weinburger.

'But the idea of destroying the personality: is interesting,' Dr Krum went on.

'Only if it shatters the shell which hides our love,' Dr Rhinehart replied.

'Love?' Dr Weinburger inquired.

'Our love.'

'Vat has love to do vith anything?' asked Dr Krum.

'Love has something to do with everything. If I do not love I am dead.'

'How true,' the woman said.

'My whole recent life has been thrown away in a cold, mechanical dicelife. I see that now as clearly as your beautiful, handsome faces.'

'Luke, I'd like you to come outdoors with me for a few minutes now,' Dr Ecstein's voice said at Dr Rhinehart's side.

'I will, Jake, but I must explain something first to Dr Krum.' He turned to the little man beside him with a warm, pleading expression.

'You must stop your work with pigeons and work only with man. You can never approach what is essential to man's health and happiness through torturing chickens and pigeons. Schizophrenia is a failure to love, a failure to see loveliness. It will never be cured by a drug.'

'Oh, Dr Rhinehart, you are being sentimental like poet,' Dr Krum said.

'A single line of Shelley tells us more of man than all your chicken pigeon droppings ever can.'

'People haf been spouting love two thousand years. Nothing. With chemicals we change the world.'

'Thou shalt not kill,' Dr Rhinehart said.

'Ve do not kill, only make psychotics.'

'You do not love your chickens.'

'Is impossible. No one who works with chickens can ever luf them.'

'A spiritual man loves all with a spiritual love that is never selfish, possessive or physical.'

'Oh, for Christ's sake, Luke – ' Dr Ecstein said.

'Precisely,' said Dr Rhinehart. 'Excuse me a moment.' With the eminent physicians looking on, Dr Rhinehart consulted his watchcase. He groaned.

'Is late?' Dr Krum asked.

Dr Rhinehart's eyes swiveled over the room like artillery radar seeking its target.

'I didn't know Dr Rhinehart was an existentialist humanist,' the woman said.

'He's a nut,' Dr Ecstein said, 'even if he is my patient.'

'Meetcha outside in five minutes, Jake. So long fellas,' Dr Rhinehart said and strode off toward the entrance hall, but after passing a cluster of people behind the couch he veered to his right and went down the same hallway again.

As he crunched over the broken glass he saw Miss Welish and Mrs Ecstein emerging from the room opposite the one he had been carried to. They stopped at the end of the hall and looked at him warily.

'Lil's been given a pill and is resting,' Mrs Ecstein said. 'I don't think you should disturb her.'

'My God, Arlene, your boobs make my mouth water. Let's go into the john.'

Mrs Ecstein stared at him for a moment. She looked sideways at Miss Welish and then back to the doctor. Then, still staring at her mentor, she shook her tiny purse up and down three times, opened it a crack, and peeked in. Closing the purse, she said: 'I love your big prick, Luke. Let's go.'

Miss Welish looked in awe from one to the other.

'You too, baby,' Dr Rhinehart said to her.

'Come along, Joya,' Mrs Ecstein said. 'It'll be fun.' She touched Miss Welish lightly on the breasts and went into the bathroom to her left. Miss Welish watched Mrs Ecstein leave and then found herself face to face with Dr Rhinehart again.

'Most beautiful body in the world, baby, except your knee. Let's go.'

She stared at him.

'But here?' she said.

'Here and now, baby, that's all there is.'

He moved around her to the bathroom, held the door open and waited. With a swift backward glance up the empty hallway she walked toward the bathroom.

'You people are really amazing,' she said. 'Are all psychiatrists' parties like this?'

'Only Dr Mann's,' Dr Rhinehart said and followed her in.

Chapter Forty-three

[Being excerpts from Dr Ecstein's case history entitled, 'The Case of the Six-Sided Man'.]

After R had erratically broken off his conversation with the three psychiatrists, he left the party area. The three discussed the situation briefly and then were joined by Dr M. After further discussion it was decided that R ought to be taken immediately to a private clinic. M telephoned the Clinic and asked for an ambulance. M and Dr E then went along with Dr B to locate R.

He was not outside, nor was he in M's office, but it was soon ascertained that he had locked himself in the bathroom. At first the doctors were concerned for R's life, but were reassured by the sound of other voices from the room. He called to those inside, but received no answer. B banged loudly on the door until E warned him it might be dangerous to excite R. For two minutes M tried to talk rationally with the patient but E, B and M heard only grunts in reply. B wanted to break the door down and enter, but M and E urged caution considering R's bulk and strength. An ambulance with attendants would soon arrive. Then female screams were heard from within the bathroom, and it was ascertained that the women with R were in all likelihood A and JW, female acquaintances of E and B.

The door was broken down. It was disclosed that R had been in the process of raping the two females. The clothes of both were in extreme disarray and R's genitals were exposed and tumescent. He stood in the center of the room slobbering lasciviously and grunting. He seemed to have regressed to the bestial state. He could answer none of our questions and resisted our efforts to separate him from the females only in the most clumsy and ineffectual way. He had become docile.

The two females seemed in a state of shock and could not explain their delay in calling for help. Whether it was the threat of R's great strength or some inexplicable hypnotic power occasionally exerted by the mentally imbalanced has never been determined. B had a different theory. Eventually, both females emerged from shock and burst into tears.

'It was horrible,' said A.

'The things he tried to make us do,' said JW.

R only slobbered and grunted. The doctors had to dress him themselves, since he seemed incapable of it himself. K and M both advanced the hypothesis that the patient had subsided into a catatonic state. E, however, even at this early date, was able to postulate that R's breakdowns were random and sporadic and that a spontaneous remission of symptoms should be expected.

Such was the case. Ten minutes later as all sat quietly and in great fatigue waiting for an ambulance, R began talking again. He apologized sincerely and realistically for his behavior, praised the doctors for the gentle and intelligent way they had handled a difficult situation, reassured them that he was now at last completely himself again, and after twenty minutes or so had most of those present laughing at the whole situation, when abruptly, just as the ambulance arrived, he threw himself on the only woman left in the room, Dr F, and seemed to be attempting coitus. The attendants and doctor arrived, he was pulled off, an injection was administered and the patient was taken to – Clinic . . .

Thus, the following day, June 16, E, as his psychiatrist, was able to visit him. It soon became apparent that R was

296

under the illusion that he was a young hippie of extremely sarcastic bent. Although he related to E, it was in a negative, aggressive way. The patient, although in complete contact with reality and often extremely observant, *was not himself*, and thus was still insane.

On June 17 it was reported by the clinic that the patient spent his time in total silence, staring into space and occasionally grunting. He had to be spoon-fed and was unable to control his excretory functions. It seemed that a permanent catatonic state might have been reached.

But R's recuperative powers continued to amaze. On the next day it was reported that he was talking again, relating well to the staff and physicians and requesting reading material, mostly of a religious nature. This last fact naturally worried E, but on June 19, 20 and 21 no new change was reported, so on June 22 E visited R again at the clinic.

Chapter Forty-four

While I bounced nicely from role to role in the Kolb Clinic, the rest of the world continued, I regret to say, to exist. Dr Mann informed me that the executive committee of PANY had decided to consider the motion of Dr Peerman for my expulsion from the organization at its monthly meeting on June 30. He believed that although he himself was urging the committee to permit me to quietly resign, it was almost certain that they would vote to expel me and to write to the AMA suggesting that organization do the same.

Arlene wrote me that the dice had told her that I was the father of the baby-to-be and that she had told Lil and Jake and most of the rest of the world the truth, or most of it, and thus Jake knew of our affair and of the dicelife. She said she couldn't come to therapy for a while.

Lil came to visit me just once to congratulate me on my future fatherhood and to announce that she had initiated divorce proceedings by taking out the necessary separation papers and that her lawyer would be visiting me shortly. (He did, but I was in the state of catatonia at the time.) She stated that separation and divorce were clearly best for both of us especially since I would undoubtedly be spending much of the rest of my life in mental institutions.

Dr Vener of QSH told me that my former patient Eric Cannon had, after two months of leading a growing herd of hippies in Brooklyn and in the East Village, been recommitted to the hospital by his father and was asking to see me. He also noted that Arturo Toscanini Jones had also been recommitted – on a technicality unearthed by diligent police – and was not asking to see me.

In fact, the only good news I was getting from the rest of the world was from my patients in dice therapy. All took my being locked up perfectly in their stride, continued to develop their dicelife on their own and waited patiently and confidently for my return to them. Terry Tracy visited me twice at the clinic and spent two and a half hours trying to convert me to the Ultimate Truth of the Religion of the Die. I was deeply moved.

Professor Boggles wrote me a long letter about a mystical experience he had had in Central Park after following the Die and writing a particularly nonsensical article on Theodore Dreiser and the Lyrical Impulse. Two of my new patients visited me regularly during my second week at the clinic and had me continue therapy with them there.

Arlene, too, seemed to grow in dice stature during this crisis period. Her letter explaining what was happening on the home front made me quite proud of her and prepared me for my interviews with Jake. She told me that Jake had taken her confession of infidelity quite calmly but had bawled her out for keeping it all to herself. It seems it was her ethical duty to provide him with as much information as possible about herself and everyone she knew since he could not fulfill his therapeutic duties without honesty and information. She had therefore gone on to tell him about her own and my dicelife and our dice games together. He had taken extensive notes and asked a lot of questions but was very calm. He had ordered her to limit her dicelife to the socially conventional until he had an opportunity to study the situation. She had then suggested that it might be of help to him if he experimented with some of the dice games with her in order to understand her problems and my problems better. He agreed, and they had had the best night together that they had had since high school days. Jake said he found it interesting. Arlene wrote that she could come visit me as soon as the Die said it was okay.

When Jake visited me on June 22 in the early evening I apologized to him immediately for any of my actions in the past which might have hurt him. It so fell that I was in the first day of The Old Pre-D-Day Luke Rhinehart Week – a role I found very hard to play. I told him that by all conventional standards what I had done in seducing his wife was unforgivable, but that I hoped he understood my philosophical aims in following the dice.

'Yeah, Luke,' he said, sitting down in a chair opposite my bed and in front of a lovely barred window overlooking a wall. 'But you're a strange one, got to admit. Tough nut to crack, so to speak.' He took out a small note pad and a pen. 'Like to know more about this dice man life of yours.'

'You're sure, Jake,' I said, 'that there's no, well, no resentment over any of the ways which I may have betrayed you, lied to you or humiliated you?'

'Can't humiliate me, Luke; a man's mind should be above emotion.' He was looking down at his pad and writing. 'Tell me about this dice man stuff.'

I was sitting up in my bed and I leaned back comfortably into the four pillows I had had piled behind me and prepared to tell Jake what I had learned.

'It's really amazing, Jake. It's shown me emotions in myself I never knew existed.' I paused. 'I think I've stumbled onto something important, something psychotherapy has been looking for for centuries. Arlene told you I've got a small group of students in dice therapy. There are other doctors trying it as well. It's . . . well,

300

maybe I'd better give you the whole background theory and history . . .'

'You want I should cheer?'

With much dignity, praise and detail, I summarized in about half an hour the Dice Man in theory and practice. I thought a lot of what I had to say was quite funny, but Jake never smiled, except professionally: to give me confidence to go on.

Finally I concluded: 'And thus my eccentricities, inconsistencies, absurdities, and breakdowns of the last year have all been the logical consequences of a highly original but highly rational approach to life, liberty and the pursuit of happiness.'

There was a silence.

'I realize that in developing dice theory I have done things which have caused suffering to others as well as myself, but in so far as all was necessary to bring me to my present spiritual state, it may be justified.'

Again there was a silence until at last Jake raised his head.

'Well?' I asked. With my arms folded on my chest I awaited with incredible tension Jake's evaluation of my theory and my life.

'So?' he said.

'So?' I replied.   'But why not? I . . . aren't I developing a facet of man too long impressed in the jail of personality?'

'You've just described to me in great detail the classic symptoms of schizophrenia: multiple selves, detachment, elation-depression: you want I should cheer?'

'But the schizophrenic becomes split and multiple against his will; he longs for unity. I have consciously created schizophrenia.'

'You show a total inability to relate to anyone personally.'

301

'But if the dice tell me to I can.'

'If it can be turned on and off it's not normal human relatedness.' He was looking at me calmly and without expression, whereas I was getting excited.

'But how do you know that normal, uncontrollable human relatedness is more desirable than my switch-button variety?'

He didn't answer. After a while he said: 'Did the dice tell you to tell me?'

'They told Arlene.'

'Did they tell you both to throw some lies in too?'

'No, that was our personal contribution.'

'The dice are wrecking your career.'

'I suppose so.'

'They've ruined your marriage.'

'Naturally.'

'They make it impossible for me or anyone else to rely on anything you say or do from now on.'

'True.'

'They mean that anything you begin may be abandoned right at the point of fruition by a whim of a die.'

'Yes.'

'Including the investigations of the dice man.'

'Ah, Jake, you understand perfectly.'

'I think I do.'

'Why don't you try it too?' I asked warmly.

'It's possible.'

'We could become the Dynamic Dice Duo, dealing dreams and destruction to the pattern-plagued world of modern man.'

'Yes, that's interesting.'

'You're about the only one I know intelligent enough to understand what the Dice Man is really all about.'

'I suppose I am.'

'Well?'

'Have to think it over, Luke. It's a big step.'

'Sure, I understand.'

'It's got to be Oedipal; that damn father of yours.'

'Wha – what?'

'That time when you were three and your mother – '

'Jake! What are you talking about?' I asked loudly and with irritation. 'I've just unfolded the most imaginative new life system in the history of man and you start talking old Freudian mythology.'

'Huh? Oh, I'm sorry,' he said, smiling his professional smile. 'Go ahead.'

But I laughed, bitterly I'm afraid.

'No, never mind. I'm tired of talking today,' I said.

Jake leaned forward and stared at me intently.

'I'll cure you,' he said. 'I'll tie you back into the old Luke or my name isn't Jake Ecstein. Don't you worry.'

I sighed and felt sad.

'Yeah,' I said dully. 'I won't worry.'

Chapter Forty-five

The pre-D-Day Luke Rhinehart created by the dice for the week of June 22 appeared so conventional, so rational, so ambitious and so interested in psychology that Doctors Ecstein and Mann decided to take a chance and permit me to defend myself at the meeting of the executive committee of PANY on June 30. Jake, while not yet convinced of the soundness of my theory, was increasingly enjoying certain dice exercises to which Arlene was introducing him and wished to be generous. Dr Mann, not having been informed of the radical nature of my dicelife, was vaguely hopeful that the rational, conventional, ambitious man he talked to during the week of June 22 would still exist on the 30th. The executive committee had agreed to my presence because they could find nothing in their bylaws which forbade it.

The charges against me were simple – my theories and practice of dice therapy were incompetent, ridiculous, unethical and of no 'lasting medical value.' Consequently, I should be expelled from PANY and a letter should be sent to the president of the AMA urging that I be forbidden to practice medicine anywhere in the United States or Canada (the southern part of the hemisphere being considered beyond salvation). I looked forward to the meeting as a welcome break from the confinement of the Kolb Clinic.

Then occurred one of those unfortunate accidents which flaw even the most well-ordered dicelife: I absent-mindedly gave the dice a foolish option and the Die chose it. When considering what to do about the PANY indict-

304

ment – to which my residual self was indifferent – the old Luke Rhinehart I was being that week created as an option that if the committee voted to expel me I would cease dice therapy and diceliving for one year. I gaily toppled a die onto my hospital bed and lost my gaiety: the Die chose that option.

In so far as anything is certain in this Die-dictated universe, it was certain that the executive committee would find me guilty. Not one of the five members of the committee was likely to be sympathetic. Dr Weinburger, the chairman, was an ambitious, successful, conventional genius who hated everything that took time away from his glory-producing activities at his Institute for the Study of Hypochondria in the Dying. He had never heard of me before his brief brush with me at the Krum party and it was clear he would hope never to hear of me again.

Old Dr Cobblestone was a fair, rational, open-minded and just man who would thus naturally vote against me. Although Dr Mann had been trying to get the fellow members of the committee to agree to force me to resign quietly from PANY, after he failed in this effort he would naturally vote to condemn everything he detested. Namely me.

The fourth member of the committee was Dr Peerman, who had initiated the proceedings against me when two of his brightest young psychiatrist interns – Joe Fineman and Fuigi Arishi – had suddenly deserted him and begun practicing dice therapy under my random tutelage. He was a slight, pale, middle-aged man with a high-pitched voice, whose fame rested securely on his widely acclaimed research demonstrating that teenagers who smoked maru-juana were more likely to try LSD than teenagers who did not. His vote in my favor seemed doubtful.

Finally there was Dr Moon, an ancient body in the

heavens of New York psychoanalysis, a personal friend of Freud, the creator, in the early 1920s, of the widely discussed theory of the natural, irreversible depravity of children and a member of the executive committee of PANY since its origin in 1923. Although he was seventy-seven years old and one of the leading subjects in Dr Weinburger's Institute for the Study of Hypochondria in the Dying, he still tried to take vigorous part in the proceedings. Unfortunately, his behavior was some-times so erratic that from what I had heard it seemed he might be a secret diceperson, although his colleagues attributed his 'slight eccentricities' to 'incipient senility.' Although he was reputed to be the most reactionary member in all of PANY, his was the only vote that – because of his unreliability – didn't seem certain to go against me.

Having considered the likely attitudes of my judges, I gave the Die a one-in-thirty-six chance that I kill myself. Unfortunately, it spurned the offer.

But the fact remained that if the committee expelled me the Die had ordered me to abandon the dicelife for one year, and this thought depressed me beyond all my previous experience. It so terrified me that for the three days before the scheduled meeting I worked every hour to prepare what seemed to me a reasonable case for my dice theory and therapy. I took notes, wrote articles, practiced speeches and considered what roles would best permit me somehow to sway Doctors Cobblestone and Mann to vote against my expulsion. Then my only hope would lie in some accident permitting the erratic old Dr Moon to also be on my side.

Such dedicated work was possible since I was still in The Old Luke Rhinehart Week, but on June 29 it would end and the Die would have to choose a new role or roles for the last two days. Would the Die choose that I switch

306

roles rapidly as at the Krum party? Would it permit me to be my most rational and articulate? Would it tell me to blow the whole thing?

I wouldn't know until the die was cast.

Chapter Forty-six

On June 28, 1969, at approximately 2.30 in the afternoon in the New York Public Library at 42nd Street, where Jake had permitted me to go with a bodyguard attendant, I discovered the laughing men in the sky.

I was sitting a trifle despondent at an isolated table alongside row upon row of stacks doing research on my defense. To my right was a small table with two men and a teen-age boy. There was no one at my table except an old woman opposite me with bushy eyebrows and hairy arms reading behind a pile of books. My attendant was standing in the corner near the window reading a comic. I had been sitting there for perhaps forty minutes, running my big fingers over the uneven grained surface of the table and daydreaming about what some of my options might be for my mode of defense and finding that my mind seemed drawn to such cheerful ones as strangling Dr Peerman, sitting wordlessly throughout the proceedings but maintaining a continually low giggle, or peeing ostentatiously on any papers they might bring. With an effort I decided that I must force my mind back to its defense and I asked again, almost in an audible whisper: 'What, then, can I do to save myself?' As I was repeating this question to myself and doodling with a wooden pencil in one of the cracks in the table, there came above the street noises the sound of bubbling human laughter.

The sound made me smile; then I realized its unlikelihood in the New York Public Library. I looked around. The old lady opposite me was looking with knitted bush brows at one of her pile of books; the three males at the other table seemed neither amused nor offended; my attendant was scowling as if stuck with some tough words. Yet the bubbling laughter continued, even growing louder.

Then, surprise: the laughter must be my hallucination.

I sat back in my chair and tried briefly to block it out, but the laughter continued to flow. When I looked up, I saw very far away and high up a fat man shaking with laughter and pointing a finger at me. He seemed to think that my effort to find the right defense was the play of a silly fool. He also found amusing my effort to smile at the realization that I was a fool. He thought my seeing his laughter at my smiling at his laughing was also funny. When I finally frowned, he laughed even harder. 'Enough,' I said loudly, but began to laugh myself.

The old woman with the bushy brows stared at me coldly. The two men at the other table turned their heads. My attendant turned a page at last. The fat man above shook again with laughter, and I laughed harder, my big belly bumping against the table; I was almost out of control. The people stared, even the attendant. At last I stopped.

So did the fat man, although he still smiled, and I felt very close to him. I thought again of the spectacular, nonsensical options that I'd been considering and decided I'd throw them out. The fat man began laughing again. I looked up startled, smiled socially at him and decided that I would instead *use* all three non-rational options. He laughed harder. With a flush I realized that I would have to abandon the dicelife completely, but the fat man laughed on and was joined by three, four other fat men all pointing at me and laughing joyously.

My mind was filled suddenly with the vision of thousands of fat men sitting up there in that fourth dimension watching the antics of human aspiration and purpose, and laughing – not a single one sober or compassionate or pitying. Our plan, hopes, expectations, and promises, and the realities of the future which they could also see: only a source of laughter. The men (they were both men and women actually, but all fat) often crowded together to look at one particular human whose life seemed to evoke special ironies or humor.

When I realized that neither abandoning the dicelife nor retaining it would end the eternal amusement of the fat people in the sky I felt like a man on some television show who is asked to guess what's behind the green wall. No matter what he guesses, the audience, which can see what is behind the wall while he can't, laughs. All my writhings in the present to find a future which will please me evoke only laughter in the audience in the sky. 'The best laid plans of mice and men gang aft astray,' said Napoleon with a chuckle on his return from Moscow.

I was laughing again with my fat men, and the woman opposite me and my attendant with a finger to his lips were both hissing violent 'shhhhshes.'

'Look!' I said with a huge smile, and pointed off toward the ceiling and the fourth dimension. 'It's all there,' I went on between chuckles. 'The answer – up there.'

The old woman glanced sternly up at the ceiling, adjusted her glasses twice and then looked back at me. She looked embarrassed and a little guilty.

'I . . . I don't see it, I'm afraid,' she said.

I laughed. I looked up at my fat man and he laughed at my laughing. I laughed at him.

'That's all right,' I said to the old lady. 'Don't worry about it. You'll be all right.'

The two men from the next table were firing 'shhhs,' and my attendant was standing nervously beside me, but I raised my hand to silence them. Smiling warmly I said:

310

'The great thing about the answer . . .' and I began again, big belly bubbling and joyous, 'The great thing is that it doesn't do us any good at all.'

Laughing, I thumbed my nose at the laughing men in the sky – who laughed – and began walking through the library, trailed by my attendant and leaving behind me like a big boat a wake of 'shhhhhs' as I passed.

'It's all right,' I said loudly to everyone. 'Knowing the answer doesn't matter. You don't have to know.'

Interestingly enough, no one approached me as I walked on through the central reading room of the New York Public Library, my belly booming out its Answer to the stack upon stack of answers and the row upon row of seekers. Only at the exit did I find someone who responded to me. An ancient portly library guard with flushed face and huge Santa Claus pot came up to me as I was about to leave and, smiling as if his face would burst, said in a louder voice than mine:

'Gotta tone down the laughing during hours,' and then we both roared out into new laughter louder than ever until I turned and left.

Chapter Forty-seven

The Die is my shepherd; I shall not want;
He maketh me to lie down in green pastures, I lie;
He leadeth me beside the still waters, I swim.
He destroyeth my soul:
He leadeth me in the paths of righteousness
For randomness sake.
Yea, though I walk through the valley of the shadow of death,
I will fear no evil: for Chance is with me;
Thy two sacred cubes they comfort me.
Thou preparest a table before me
In the presence of mine enemies:
Thou anointest my head with oil;
My cup runneth over.
Surely goodness and mercy and evil and cruelty shall follow
    me
All the days of my life:
And I will dwell in the house of Chance forever.

— from *The Book of the Die*

Chapter Forty-eight

The meeting of the executive committee of the Psychoanalysts' Association of New York took place early on the afternoon of June 30 1969, in a large seminar room at Dr Weinburger's Institute for the Study of Hypochondria in the Dying. Dr Weinburger, a bushy-haired, thickset man in his late forties, sat impatiently behind a long table with Doctors Peerman and Cobblestone on one side of him and Old Dr Moon and Dr Mann on the other. All the gentlemen looked serious and intent except for Dr Moon, who was sleeping quietly between Chairman Weinburger and Dr Mann, occasionally sliding slowly sideways to rest against the shoulder of the one, and then, like a pendulum that badly needs oiling, after a hesitation, sliding slowly back across the arc to rest against the shoulder of the other.

The table at which the five sat was so long that they looked more like fugitives huddled together for mutual protection rather than judges. Dr Rhinehart and Dr Ecstein, who was present as friend and personal physician, sat on stiff wooden chairs in the middle of the room opposite them. Dr Ecstein was slumped and squinting, but Dr Rhinehart was erect and alert, looking extremely professional in a perfectly tailored gray suit and tie and shoes shined to such a luster that Dr Ecstein wondered whether he hadn't cheated by using black Day-glo.

'Yes, sir,' Dr Rhinehart said before anyone else had said a word.

'One moment, Dr Rhinehart,' Dr Weinburger said sharply. He looked down at the papers in front of him.

313

'Does Dr Rhinehart know the charges being brought against him?'

'Yes,' said Doctors Mann and Ecstein at the same time.

'What's all this about dice, young man?' Dr Cobblestone asked. His cane lay on the table in front of him as if it were a piece of evidence relevant to the proceedings.

'A new therapy I'm developing, sir,' Dr Rhinehart replied promptly.

'I understand that,' he said. 'What we mean is that you should explain.'

'Well, sir, in dice therapy we encourage our patients to reach decisions by casting dice. The purpose is to destroy the personality. We wish to create in its place a multiple personality: an individual inconsistent, unreliable and progressively schizoid.'

Dr Rhinehart spoke in a clear, firm and reasonable voice, but for some reason his answer was greeted by a silence, broken only by Dr Moon's harsh, uneven breathing. Dr Cobblestone's stern lower jaw became sterner.

'Go on,' said Dr Weinburger.

'My theory is that we all have minority impulses which are stifled by the normal personality and rarely break free into action. The desire to hit one's wife is forbidden by the concept of dignity, femininity and covetousness of unbroken crockery. The desire to be religious is stopped by the knowledge that one "is" an atheist. Your desire, sir, to shout "stop this nonsense!" is stopped by your sense of yourself as a fair and rational man.

'The minority impulses are the Negroes of the personality. They have not enjoyed freedom since the personality was founded; they have become the invisible men. We refuse to recognize that a minority impulse is a potential full man, and that until he is granted the same opportunity for development as the major conventional selves, the

314

personality in which he lives will be divided, subject to tensions which lead to periodic explosions and riots.'

'Negroes must be kept in their place,' said Dr Moon suddenly, his round, wrinkled face suddenly coming alive with the appearance of two fierce red eyes in its ravaged landscape. He was leaning forward intensely, his mouth, after he had finished his short sentence, dangling open.

'Go on,' said Dr Weinburger.

Dr Rhinehart nodded gravely to Dr Moon and resumed.

'Every personality is the sum total of accumulated suppressions of minorities. Were a man to develop a consistent pattern of impulse control he would have no definable personality: he would be unpredictable and anarchic, one might even say, *free*.'

'He would be insane,' came Dr Peerman's high-pitched voice from his end of the table. His thin, pale face was expressionless.

'Let us hear the man out,' said Dr Cobblestone.

'Go on,' said Dr Weinburger.

'In stable, unified, consistent societies the narrow personality had value; men could fulfill themselves with only one self. Not so today. In a multivalent society, the multiple personality is the only one which can fulfill. Each of us has a hundred suppressed potential selves which never let us forget that no matter how mightily we step along the narrow single path of our personality, our deepest desire is to be multiple: to play many roles.

'If you will permit me, gentlemen, I would like to quote to you what a dicepatient of mine said in a recent therapy session which I taped.' Dr Rhinehart reached into his briefcase beside his chair and drew out some sheets of paper. After leafing through them, he looked up and continued: 'What Professor O. B. says here seems to me to dramatize the crux of the problem for all men. I quote:

315

'"I feel I ought to write a great novel, write numerous letters, be friendly with more of the interesting people in my community, give more parties, dedicate more time to my intellectual pursuits, play with my children, make love to my wife, go hiking more often, go to the Congo, be a radical trying to revolutionize society, write fairy tales, buy a bigger boat, do more sailing, sunning and swimming, write a book on the American picaresque novel, educate my children at home, be a better teacher at the University, be a faithful friend, be more generous with my money, economize more, live a fuller life in the world outside me, live like Thoreau and not be taken in by material values, play more tennis, practice yoga, meditate, do those damn RCAF exercises every day, help my wife with the housework, make money in real estate, and . . . and so on.

"And do all these things seriously, playfully, dramatically, stoically, joyfully, serenely, morally, indifferently – do them like D. H. Lawrence, Paul Newman, Socrates, Charlie Brown, Superman, and Pogo.

"But it's ridiculous. When I do any *one* of these things, play any one of these roles, the *other selves are not satisfied*. You've got to help me satisfy one self in such a way that the others will feel that they are somehow being considered too. Make them shut up. You've got to help me pull myself together and stop spilling all over the goddam universe without actually doing *any*thing."'

Dr Rhinehart looked up and smiled. 'Our Western psychologies try to solve O. B.'s problem by urging him to form some single integrated personality, to suppress his natural multiplicity and build a single dominant self to control the others. This totalitarian solution means that a large standing army of energy must be maintained to crush the efforts of the minority selves to take power. The normal personality exists in a state of continual insurrection.'

'Some of this makes sense,' added Dr Ecstein helpfully.

'In dice theory we attempt to overthrow the totalitarian personality and – '

'The masses need a strong leader,' interrupted Dr Moon.

The silence which followed was broken only by his uneven breathing.

'Go on,' said Dr Weinburger.

'All I've got to say for now,' replied Dr Moon, closing the shutters on the red furnaces of his eyes and beginning to swing in a slow arc toward the shoulder of Dr Mann.

'Go on, Dr Rhinehart,' said Dr Weinburger, his face expressionless but his hands crumpling up the papers in front of him like octopi demolishing squid.

Dr Rhinehart glanced at his wristwatch and went on.

'Thank you. In our metaphor – which has that same admirable degree of scientific precision and rigor as Freud's famous parable of the superego, the ego, and the id – in our metaphor, the anarchic chance-led person is governed in fact by a benevolent despot: the Die. In the early stages of therapy only a few selves are able to offer themselves as options to the Die. But as the student progresses, more and more selves, desires, value and roles are raised into the possibility of existence; the human being grows, expands, becomes more flexible, more various. The ability of major selves to overthrow the Die declines, disappears. The personality is destroyed. The man is free. He – '

'I see no need to let Dr Rhinehart go on,' said Dr Weinburger, suddenly standing up. 'Although, as Dr Ecstein has so helpfully observed, some of it makes sense, the idea that the destruction of the personality is the way to mental health may be rejected on a priori grounds. I need only remind you gentlemen of the first sentence of Dr Mann's brilliant textbook on abnormal psychology: "If a person has a strong sense of his identity, of the permanency of things and of an integral self-hood, he will be secure."' He smiled over at Dr Mann. 'I therefore move . . .'

'Precisely,' said Dr Rhinehart. 'Or rather, precisely,

sir. It is always rejected on a priori grounds and not on empirical grounds. We have never experimented with the possibility of a strong man being able to demolish his personality and become more various, happy and creative than he was before. The first sentence of our textbook will read: "If a person can attain a strong confidence in his inconsistency and unreliability, a strong yea-saying sense of the impermanency of things and of an unintegrated, nonpatterned chaos of selves, he will be fully at home in a multivalent society – he will be joyous . . ."'

'We have plenty of empirical evidence regarding the destruction of the personality,' said Dr Cobblestone quietly. 'Our mental hospitals are overflowing with people who have a sense of an unintegrated, nonpatterned chaos of selves.'

'Yes, we do,' replied Dr Rhinehart calmly. 'But why are they there?'

There was no answer to this question, and Dr Rhinehart, after waiting while Dr Weinburger sat down again, continued: 'Your therapies tried to give them a sense of an integral self and failed. Isn't it just possible that the desire *not* to be unified, *not* to be single, *not* to have one personality may be the natural and basic human desire in our multivalent societies?'

Again there was a silence, except for Dr Moon's expiring breaths and an irritable throat-clearing by Dr Weinburger.

'Whenever I look at the Western psychotherapies of the last hundred years,' Dr Rhinehart went on, 'it seems to me incredible that no one acknowledges the almost total failure of these therapies to cure human unhappiness. As Dr Raymond Felt has observed: "The ratio of spontaneous remission of symptoms and the rate of supposed 'cures' by the psychotherapies of the various schools has remained essentially the same throughout the twentieth century."

'Why have our efforts to cure neurosis been so uniformly unsuccessful? Why does civilization expand unhappiness faster than we can develop new theories about how it occurs and what we ought to do about it? Our mistake is becoming obvious. We have carried over from the simple, unified, stable societies of the past an image of the ideal norm for man which is totally *wrong* for our complex, chaotic, unstable and multi-valued urban civilizations of today. We assume that "honesty" and "frankness" are of primary importance in healthy human relations, and the lie and the act are, in the anachronistic ethics of our time, considered evil.'

'Ah, but Dr Rhinehart, you can't – ' said Dr Cobblestone.

'No, sir. I regret to say I'm serious. Every society is based upon lies. Our society of today is based on conflicting lies. The man who lived in a simple, stable, single-lie society absorbed the single-lie system into a unified self and spouted it for the rest of his life, uncontradicted by his friends and neighbors, and unaware that ninety-eight percent of his beliefs were illusions, his values artificial and arbitrary and most of his desires comically ill-aimed.

'The man in our multi-lie society absorbs a chaos of conflicting lies and is reminded daily by his friends and neighbors that his beliefs are not universally held, that his values are personal and arbitrary and his desires often ill-aimed. We must realize that to ask this man to be honest and true to himself, when his contradictory selves have multiple contradictory answers to most questions, is a safe and economical method of driving him insane.

'On the other hand, to free him from his unending conflict we must urge him to let go, to act, to pretend, to

319

lie. We must give him the means to develop these abilities. He must become a diceperson.'

'See! See!' Dr Peerman interrupted. 'He just confessed to advocating a therapy which encourages lying. Did you hear him?'

'I believe we have been listening to Dr Rhinehart, thank you, Dr Peerman,' said Dr Weinburger, again mangling the papers in front of him. 'Dr Rhinehart, you may go on.'

Dr Rhinehart glanced at his watch and continued.

'When all men lie by their very being in a multi-lie society, only the sick try to be honest, and only the very sick ask for honesty in others. Psychologists, of course, urge the patient to be authentic and honest. Such methods – '

'If our methods are so bad,' asked Dr Weinburger harshly, 'then why do any of our patients improve at all?'

'Because we've encouraged them to play new roles,' Dr Rhinehart answered promptly. 'Primarily the role of "being honest", but also the roles of feeling guilty, having sinned, being oppressed, discovering insights, being sexually liberated and so on. Of course, the patient and therapist are under the illusion that they are getting at *true* desires, when in fact they are only releasing and developing new and different selves.'

'Good point, Luke,' said Dr Ecstein.

'The limitations placed on this new role playing are catastrophic. The patient is being pressed to get at his "true" feelings and thus to be single and unitary. In discovering unlived roles in his search for a "true self" he may experience brief periods of liberation, but as soon as he is urged to enthrone some new self as the true one, he will again feel locked up and divided. Dice therapy alone acknowledges what we all know and choose to forget: man is multiple.'

'Sure, man is multiple,' Dr Weinburger said, banging his fist abruptly on the table. 'But the whole point of civilization is to keep the rapist, the killer, the liar and the cheat locked up, suppressed. You seem to be saying we should unlock the cage and let all our minority murderers roam free.' Dr Weinburger gave an irritable shrug of his left shoulder, sending the inert body of Dr Moon on its slow journey through its orbit to come to rest against the softer but no less irritable shoulder of Dr Mann.

'That's right, Luke,' said Dr Mann, looking coldly across the table at Dr Rhinehart. 'Just because we have a fool within us is no reason to feel he ought to be expressed.'

Dr Rhinehart glanced at his watch, sighed, took out a die, dropped it from his right hand into the palm of his left and looked at it.

'Fuck it,' he said.

'Beg pardon?' asked Dr Cobblestone.

'The idea of freeing the rapist, the murderer and the fool seems nutty,' continued Dr Rhinehart, 'to the jailer called the normal, rational personality. So does the idea of freeing the pacifist seem nutty to the jailer personality of a murderer. But the normal personality is today a study in frustration, boredom and despair. Dice therapy is the only theory which offers to blow up the whole works.'

'But the social consequences – ' began Dr Cobblestone.

'The social consequences of a nation of dicepeople are, by definition, unpredictable. The social consequences of a nation of normal personalities are obvious: misery, conflict, violence, war and a universal joylessness.'

'But I still don't see what you've got against honesty,' Dr Cobblestone said.

'Honesty and frankness?' Dr Rhinehart said. 'Jesus! They're the worst possible things in normal human relations. "Do you really love me?": this absurd question, so

321

typical of our diseased minds, should always be answered, "My God, NO!" or "More than mere reality is my love; it is imaginary." The more someone tries to be honest and authentic, the more he's going to be blocked and inhibited. The question "How do you *really* feel about me?" ought always to be answered with a belt in the teeth. But if someone were asked: "Tell me fantastically and imaginatively how you feel about me," he'd be free from that neurotic demand for unity and truth. He could express any of his conflicting selves – one at a time of course. He'd be able to play each role to the hilt. He'd be at one with his schizophrenia.'

Dr Rhinehart stood up.

'Mind if I pace about a bit?' he asked.

'Go ahead,' said Dr Weinburger. Dr Rhinehart began striding back and forth in front of the long table, for a while his pace just matching the shorter roll of Dr Moon between the shoulders of his two colleagues.

'Now, about how all this works in practice,' he began again. 'It's tough starting dice therapy with a patient. His resistance to chance is as great today as was his resistance to Freud's sexual mythology seventy years ago. When we ask a typical miserable American to let the dice make a decision he goes along only if he thinks it's a temporary game. When he sees I seriously expect him to make important decisions by *chance*, he inevitably pees in his pants.

'Figuratively speaking. In most cases this *initial resistance* – pants-peeing, we call it – is overcome and the therapy begins.

'We have to begin in the most trivial ways. The psychotic has no areas free to be spontaneous and original. The neurotic has few, normal, "healthy" persons like yourselves have only a small handful. All other areas are controlled by the dictatorship of personality. It's the job

322

of dice therapy, like the job of revolution in the world as a whole, to enlarge free territory.

'We work first in areas where there's not much threat to the normal personality. Once a patient's got the ground rules and got into the spirit of playfulness, we expand the dice decisions into other areas.'

'Exactly what do your patients do with the dice?' Dr Cobblestone asked.

'Well, first we let the dice make decisions for the patient where he's in conflict. "Two roads diverged within a wood, and I, I took the one directed by the Die, and that has made all the difference." So Little Red Riding Hood wrote, and so we must all do. The patients groove to this use of the dice right away.

'We also show them how to use the dice as a veto. Every time they do something we ask them to shake a die and if it comes up a six-they can't do it; have to ask the die to choose something else for them. Veto's a great method but hard. Most of us go through our lives from one thing to the next mechanically, without thought. We study, write, eat, flirt, fornicate, fuck as the result of habitual patterns. "Pop" comes a dice veto: it wakes us up. In theory, we're working toward the purely random man, one without habit or pattern, eating from zero to six or seven times a day, sleeping haphazardly, responding sexually randomly to men, women, dogs, elephants, trees, watermelons, snails and so on. In practice, of course, we don't shoot so high.

'Instead we let the patient judge at first how he uses the dice. Of course, sooner or later he sticks himself in some small slot of diceliving where he's willing to let the dice play. Unless he's pushed he'll stay clogged up there forever.'

'How do you overcome the patient's reluctance to

expand his use of the dice?' Dr Cobblestone asked. He seemed interested.

Dr Rhinehart stopped in front of him and smiled. 'To overcome this secondary resistance – constipation we call it – we use mostly the method of *scare*. We tell the patient to cast the dice concerning his biggest problem: "Give the dice the option of your getting into bed with your mother and feeling her up." "Let the dice decide whether you say: 'Up yours, Dad.'" "Cast a die to see whether you're going to destroy your diaries."'

'What happens?'

'The patient generally craps or faints,' said Dr Rhinehart, beginning to pace again while scowling at the floor. 'But when he revives we suggest something a little less threatening but still outside his previous diceliving area. In utter gratefulness he goes along.' Dr Rhinehart's face brightened, and he smiled at each of the doctors as he passed them in his pacing.

'Then he's on his way. Within a month we hope he'll have achieved either ecstatic liberation, abandonment of dice therapy, or a psychosis. The psychotic break is caused by his need to avoid admitting that he *can* act, and he *can* change, that he can do something about his problems. He can't face the fact that he's free, and not the helpless, pitiable object he's under the illusion he is.

'He feels *liberated* when he realizes that his horrible problems can be solved, but are not *his* to worry about any longer: they've been shifted to the square shoulders of the dice. He becomes ecstatic. He experiences the transfer of control from an illusory self to the dice as a conversion or as salvation. It's something like newly born Christians giving up their souls to Christ or God, or the Zen student or Taoist surrendering to the Tao. In all these cases the ego-control game is abandoned and the student surrenders to a force which is experienced as being outside himself.

'Let me quote to you what one of our dicestudents has written about his experience.' Dr Rhinehart returned to his chair, extracted some papers from his briefcase and began to read from one.

It was great. It was a real religious feeling, a spiritual thing. Suddenly I was free of all my hangups about raping little girls and buggering boys. I gave up the struggle and put the whole mess into the hands of the dice. When they ordered rape, I raped. When they ordered abstention, I abstained. No problem. When they say fly to Peru, I fly to Peru. It's like being in the middle of a movie I've never seen before. It's tremendously interesting and I'm the star. In the last couple of months I haven't even bothered to give the dice any little-girl or little-boy options. I don't know, everything else is so fascinating I just don't seem to have the old get-up-and-go anymore.

Dr Rhinehart placed the paper back on his chair and resumed his pacing.

'Of course, it takes a while for our students to reach this level of freedom. At first they often cast the dice and think: "Now I must have the willpower to do it." That's bad. The illusion that an ego controls or has "willpower" must be abandoned. The student's got to see his relation to the dice first as that of a baby in a rubber raft on a flooded river: each motion of the river is pleasant; he doesn't need to know where he's going or when, if ever, he'll arrive. Motion is all. And then he's got to reach the point where he and the Die are each playing with one another. It's not that the person has gained equality with the Die, it's that the human vessel is now so infused with the Spirit of the Die that it's become in effect a Sacred Vehicle, a Second Cube. The student has become Die.'

Dr Rhinehart stopped pacing for the moment and looked intently at his listeners. He had become increasingly excited by what he was saying and five doctors behind the table had begun staring at him with increasing awe, except for Dr Moon, who was still settled in openmouthed sleep against Dr Mann.

'Actually, I may be going too fast for you,' Dr Rhinehart began again. 'Maybe I should tell you about some of our dice exercises. Emotional roulette, for example. The student lists six possible emotions, lets a dice choose one and then expresses that emotion as dramatically as he can for at least two minutes. It's probably the most useful of the dice exercises, letting the student express all kinds of long-suppressed emotions which he usually doesn't even know he has. Roger Meters reports that a dicestudent of his found after ten minutes of a dice-dictated love for a specific person that he remained in love: in fact, the student has since married her.'

Dr Rhinehart paused in his pacing to smile benevolently at Dr Weinburger.

'Let's see, in the Horatio Alger–Huck Finn game,' he went on, 'a die determines at regular intervals whether the student is to work hard, achieve and be fantastically productive or to goof off and laze around and do nothing. It's good in this exercise to have the intervals very short: the absurdity of hard work is nicely alternated with the absurdity of *trying* to laze around and do nothing.'

'Dr Rhinehart,' interrupted Dr Weinburger, squeezing the crumpled papers in his fist. 'It would – '

'Wait! Wait! Russian roulette. We've got two versions. In one the student creates from three to six unpleasant options and casts a die to see which if any he has to do. In the second, he creates one extremely challenging option – say, quitting a job, insulting a mother or husband, robbing a bank, murder – and gives it a long-shot chance of being chosen.

'This second form of Russian roulette is one of our best

326

dice exercises. Dr Rhineholt Budweir cured what seemed to be a hopeless case of death anxiety by every morning taking out a revolver loaded with one live cartridge, spinning the cylinder, placing the barrel at his temple and casting two dice. If they came up snake eyes, he pulled the trigger. The odds each morning were thus two hundred and sixteen to one against his death.

'From the moment he discovered the dice exercise Dr Budweir's death anxiety disappeared: he felt a lightness such as he hadn't experienced since his earliest childhood. His sudden death last week at the age of twenty-nine is a tragic loss.'

As he looked from one doctor to another, Dr Rhinehart's eyes glittered behind his glasses. He continued.

'Then there's Exercise K – named in honor of the eminent German-American researcher, Dr Abraham Krum.' Dr Rhinehart smiled at Dr Mann. 'The student lists six optional roles or selves he might adopt for periods varying from a few minutes to a week or more. Exercise K is the key to a successful dicelife. The student who practices this daily for an hour or two, or each week for a whole day, is on his way to becoming a full-blooded diceperson.

'Families and friends assume, of course, that the student is on the road to insanity and that his therapist is already there, but ignoring doubt and ridicule is a necessary part of becoming a diceperson. Dr Fumm tells me that a student of his expanded Exercise K hour by hour until he had gone from an hour a day to twenty-three hours a day, varying who he was every day of the week – except Sunday, which he reserved for rest. At first his friends and family were hysterical with fear and rage, but once he'd explained to them what he was doing they began to adjust. At the end of a few months his wife and children would simply ask him at breakfast each morning

327

who he was and make the necessary accommodations. Since among his many roles he was Saint Simeon Stylites, Greta Garbo, a three-year-old child and Jack the Ripper, the members of his family deserve a lot of credit for their psychological maturity. May they rest in peace.' Dr Rhinehart stopped pacing and looked, solemn and sincere, directly at Dr Mann.

Dr Mann stared back blankly; then his face flushed. Scowling at the floor briefly, Dr Rhinehart resumed his pacing.

'As you can see,' he said, 'like all potent medications dice therapy has certain not-so-hot side effects.

'For example, the student usually gets the idea that the dice ought to determine whether he stays in therapy or not. Since he gives the option a lot of chances, the dice sooner or later order him to leave therapy. Sometimes they tell him to return. And then leave again. Sometimes they tell him to pay his therapy bill, sometimes not. It must be admitted that dicestudents are, as patients, a little unreliable. You'll be happy to know, however, that the more unreliable a student becomes, the closer he probably is to total cure.

'A second side effect is that a student does zany things, thus attracting attention to both himself and, inevitably, his psychotherapist.

'Another thing is that during *tertiary resistance* the student is likely to try to kill the psychotherapist.'

Dr Rhinehart paused in his pacing in front of Dr Peerman and, looking benevolently into Dr Peerman's averted eyes, said:

'This should normally be avoided.'

He resumed his pacing.

'A fourth side effect is that the student insists that the therapist also make decisions by the die. If the therapist is honest in his options he's likely to have to do something

328

inconsistent with medical ethics. It must be admitted that the more medical ethics that the therapist tramples on, the more progress the student makes.'

Dr Rhinehart stopped his pacing at the far end of the room, glanced at his wristwatch and then marched back along the table, looking solemnly into the faces of each of his judges as he passed.

'Prognosis,' he went on. 'You probably want to know about prognosis.

'Students who enter dice therapy are usually normal, everyday, miserable Americans. About one out of five can't get past pants-peeing and drops out of therapy within two weeks. Another fifth succumb within two months to one of the periodic onsets of constipation. We're less certain of this fraction since it's possible that some of those who disappear from therapy within those first months have actually liberated themselves and no longer need the therapist to continue their diceliving.

'Of the thirty-three students who have worked with the dice for more than two months, six are now in mental institutions with little hope of ever being released.'

'Good God,' exclaimed Dr Cobblestone, retrieving his cane from the top of the table as if preparing to defend himself.

'You'll be glad to know, however, that one of these six, although he's been catatonic for six weeks, may, in fact, be totally cured on May 13 of next year. His last recorded dice decision six weeks ago resulted in his being ordered to go into a catatonic state and remain there for one year.'

Dr Rhinehart stopped in front of Dr Cobblestone and smiled warmly at the bleak-faced old director.

'It is my personal prediction that after that year is gone the student will undergo a "spontaneous remission" of all his symptoms and thus be released a few decades thereafter.'

329

The doctors behind the table were now staring open-mouthed at Dr Rhinehart.

'The other five inmates seem to be victims of the psychotic break, which is an obvious danger if the student is pushed too rapidly into sensitive areas of his life. In the majority of these cases, however, the therapist believes that the personality of the student improved considerably after the psychotic break.'

Dr Rhinehart glanced again briefly at his watch. He hurried on.

'Of the remaining twenty-seven patients who have stayed in dice therapy for more than two months, sixteen are still oscillating between bliss and breakdown; nine seem to have achieved a stable level of high joy, and two are dead, having both died in the line of duty. So to speak.'

Dr Rhinehart stopped in the center of the room, his back to Dr Ecstein, and faced his five judges, a soft, serene smile on his face.

'Such results are not all that could be hoped for,' he said, and after another pause, 'but it should be noted that we have not with our method produced any well-adjusted miserable humans. All thirty-one of our surviving dice-students are completely maladjusted to the insane society. There is thus hope.' Dr Rhinehart was beaming.

'I see no reason to let him go on,' said Dr Mann quietly, shrugging his right shoulder in an effort to dislodge Dr Moon.

'I think perhaps you're right,' said Dr Weinburger, neatening the crumpled papers in front of him.

'Dice therapy and money,' Dr Rhinehart said, and began his intent pacing again. 'Since Freud's pioneer work, not much has been done with the problem of money. As you gentlemen know, Freud associated money with excrement and argued shrewdly that "Tightness" was

330

an effort to withhold excrement, to maintain, in his immortal phrase, "an Immaculate Anus."'

'Dr Rhinehart,' interrupted Dr Weinburger, 'if you don't mind, I think – '

'Two more minutes,' said Dr Rhinehart, glancing at his watch. 'Freud postulated that a neurotic will find outflow of money, excrement, time or energy a loss, a sullying of the soul, or, more precisely, the anus. Obviously any such effort to withhold is doomed to failure. As Erich Fromm has so acutely observed: "It is the tragedy inherent in the fate of man that he shit."' Dr Rhinehart's eyes gleamed in his solemn face. 'I forget the reference.

'Obviously the old therapies couldn't solve this dilemma. Whereas conventional psychoanalysis sees the desire for an Immaculate Anus as neurotic and counter-productive, we maintain that the desire, like all desires, is good, and causes trouble only when followed too consistently. The individual must come to embrace, in effect, both the Immaculate Anus and the excreted lumps of turd.'

He was standing in front of Dr Cobblestone and leaned on the table in front of him with both immaculately tailored arms. 'We look not for moderation in the excretory functions, but a joyful variety: a random alteration, as it were, of constipation and diarrhea, with, I suppose, sporadic bursts of regularity.'

'Dr Rhinehart, please – ' said Dr Cobblestone.

'Figuratively speaking, of course. In curing a man of compulsive worry about money we begin by giving him simple dice exercises which require him to spend or not spend small amounts of money at the whim of a die and which make him let the Die determine how the money is spent. Slowly but surely we increase the stakes.'

'That's all,' said Dr Weinburger, standing and

confronting Dr Rhinehart, who moved over and stopped opposite him. 'You've had your say; we've heard enough.'

Dr Rhinehart glanced at his watch and then pulled a die from his pocket and glanced at it.

'You'll never get him to stop,' said Dr Mann quietly.

'I guess I'm done,' said Dr Rhinehart, and he walked back and resumed his seat. Dr Ecstein was staring at the floor.

Dr Weinburger again made motions of trying to neaten up the pile of crumpled papers in front of him and cleared his throat noisily.

'Well, gentlemen,' he said, 'I suppose while Dr Rhinehart is still here I ought to ask if any of you have any questions for him before we proceed to the vote.' He looked nervously first to his right where Dr Peerman was grinning sickly and Dr Cobblestone was staring sternly at the head of his cane between his legs. Neither responded. Dr Weinburger then looked nervously to his left where Dr Moon, his breath coming in even harsher and more uneven gasps than earlier, was beginning a slow arc from Dr Mann toward the chairman.

Dr Mann said very quietly:

'The man is no longer human.'

'I beg your pardon?' said Dr Weinburger.

'The man is no longer human.'

'Oh. Yes.' Dr Weinburger stood up. 'Then if there are no further questions, I must ask Dr Rhinehart to leave the room so that we may proceed to a vote on the issue before us.'

'I'm inhuman, you say?' said Dr Rhinehart quietly, remaining in his chair next to Dr Ecstein. 'Big deal, I'm inhuman. But with the human pattern such as it is these days can the word *inhuman* constitute an insult? Considered in the light of normal, everyday, garden-variety human cruelty in the marketplace, the ghetto, the family, in war, your *inhuman* refers to the abnormality of my actions, not their level of moral depravity.'

'Dr Rhinehart,' Dr Weinburger interrupted, still standing, 'would you please – '

'Come on, I've only been talking nonsense an hour, give me a chance.'

He stared wordlessly at Dr Weinburger until the chairman slowly lowered himself into his chair.

'The suffering our dice-dictated actions causes is clearly nothing as compared man for man to that caused by rational, civilized man. Dicepeople are amateurs at evil. What seems to disturb you guys is that others are sometimes manipulated not by an ego-motivated me but by a dice-motivated me. It's the seeming gratuity of the occasional suffering we cause that shocks. You prefer purposeful, consistent, solidly structured suffering. The idea that we create love because the dice order us to, that we express love, that we feel love, all because of accident, shatters the fabric of your illusions about the nature of man.'

When Dr Weinburger began to rise in his chair again Dr Rhinehart simply raised his huge right arm and continued calmly:

'But what is this nature of man you're so gung-ho to defend? Look at yourselves. Whatever happened to the real inventor in you? to the lover? or the adventurer? or the saint? or the woman? You killed them. Look at yourselves and ask: "Is this image the Image of God in which man was created?"' Dr Rhinehart looked from Peerman to Cobblestone to Weinburger to Moon to Mann. 'Blasphemy. God creates, experiments, rides the wind. He doesn't wallow in the accumulated feces of His past.'

Dr Rhinehart put two sheets of paper back into his briefcase and stood up.

'I'm going now, and you can vote. But remember, you are all potentially chameleons of the spirit, and thus of all the illusions that rob men of their divinity this is the cruelest; to call the rocklike burdensome shell of "character" and "individuality" man's *greatest* development. It's like praising a boat for its anchor.'

Dr Rhinehart walked away alone to the door.

'A genuine fool,' he said. 'A few genuine fools. A few a generation, a few per nation. Until the discovery of the Die it was too much to ask.' With a final smile at Dr Ecstein, he left the room.

Chapter Forty-nine

[Being a Special Die-Dictated Dramatization of the Judicial Deliberations of the Executive Committee of PANY as Recreated from the Tape Recording and Testimony of Dr Jacob Ecstein.]

For several moments the five members of the committee sat in silence, broken only by the harsh, uneven breathing of the sleeping Dr Moon. Doctors Weinburger, Cobblestone and Mann, were all staring at the door which had closed behind Dr Rhinehart. Dr Peerman broke the silence:

'I believe we should conclude our business.'

'Ah. Ah. Ah, yes,' said Dr Weinburger. 'The vote. We must have the vote.' But he remained staring at the door. 'Thank God, he's insane,' he added.

'The vote,' repeated Dr Peerman in his shrill voice.

'Yes, of course. We are now voting on Dr Peerman's motion that our committee expel Dr Rhinehart for the reasons listed and request that the AMA consider taking action against him as well. Dr Peerman?'

'I cast my vote in favor of my motion,' he said solemnly to the chairman.

'Dr Cobblestone?'

The old doctor was fingering nervously the cane held erect between his legs and staring blankly at the empty chair of Dr Rhinehart.

'I vote aye,' he said neutrally.

'Two votes to condemn,' announced Dr Weinburger. 'Dr Mann?'

Dr Mann shrugged his right shoulder violently and jarred Dr Moon into a more or less vertical position, Moon's eyes flaming open briefly and erratically.

'I still think we ought to have asked Dr Rhinehart quietly to resign,' said Dr Mann. 'I make a pro forma vote of no.'

'I understand, Tim,' said Dr Weinburger sympathetically. 'And you, Dr Moon?'

Dr Moon's body was balanced erect, and his eyelids slowly rose, revealing the red coals of his dying eyes. His face looked as if it had suffered all the miseries of every human that had ever lived.

'Dr Moon, do you vote yes to the motion to expel this man we've been listening to, or do you vote no in order to permit him to continue?'

Dr Moon's fierce red eyes seemed the only things alive in his wrinkled, ravaged face, but they were staring at nothing, or at the past or at everything. His mouth was open; he drooled.

'Dr Moon?' repeated Dr Weinburger a third time.

Slowly, so slowly that it must have taken thirty or forty seconds for him to complete the motion, Dr Moon raised his two arms up over his head, feebly closed the palms of his hands into a half-fist, and then, mouth still open, dropped them with a crash onto the table in front of him.

'NO!' he thundered.

There was a shocked silence, broken only by the explosive gasps of Dr Moon's now totally sporadic breathing.

'Would you care to explain your vote?' Dr Weinburger asked gently after a while.

Dr Moon's body was beginning to slump and slide toward Dr Mann's shoulder again and his fierce, all-seeing eyes were now only half-open.

'My vote's obvious,' he said weakly. 'Get on with it.'

Dr Weinburger stood up with a dignified smile on his face.

'The vote on the motion to expel Dr Rhinehart being tied at two to two, the chairman is obliged to cast his vote to break the tie.' He paused briefly and poked formally at the crumpled papers in front of him. 'I vote yes. Consequently, by a vote of three to two, Dr Rhinehart is expelled from PANY. A letter will be sent to – '

'Point of order,' came Dr Moon's weak voice, his eyes now open just a slit, as if permitting people only the tiniest of glances into his red inferno.

'Beg pardon?' said the surprised chairman.

''Cording to our bylaws . . . man presenting charges 'gainst colleague can't . . . vote . . . on motion to accept . . . charges.'

'I'm afraid I don't understan – '

'Created bylaw m'self in thirty-one,' continued Dr Moon with a gasp. He seemed to be trying to push himself away from Dr Mann's shoulder but lacked the strength. 'Peerman brought charges. Peerman can't vote.'

No one spoke. There was only the hoarse explosive rattle of Dr Moon's occasional breath.

Dr Mann finally said in a very quiet voice:

'In that case the vote is two to two.'

'Vote's two to one for acquittal,' said Dr Moon and, after a desperate, hollow, rattling intake of air, he finished:

'Chairman of committee can't vote except to break ties.'

'Dr Moon, sir,' said Dr Weinburger weakly, bracing himself against the table to keep himself from fainting: 'Could you please consider changing your vote or at least explaining it?'

The red coals of Dr Moon's dying eyes blazed forth one

last time from the face which looked as if it had suffered all the miseries of every human that had ever lived.

'M'vote's obvious,' he said.

Dr Weinburger began recrumpling the papers which he had finished neatening in front of him.

'Dr Moon, sir,' he said again weakly. 'Would you consider changing your vote in order to . . . simplify . . . to simplify . . . Dr Moon! Dr Moon!'

But the silence in the room was total.

Was total.

Chapter Fifty

Dr Moon's death in the line of duty was greeted with mixed reviews in the psychiatric world of New York as was my momentary escape from the fate I so obviously deserved. I quietly resigned from PANY, but Dr Weinburger wrote a personal letter to the president of the AMA; my removal from the elite sections of civilization continued its slow, rational, bureaucratic course.

They probably would have kept me locked up in Kolb Clinic forever, but Jake Ecstein was my psychiatrist and unlike most other ambitious, successful doctors, Jake listened only to Jake. Thus, when I seemed perfectly normal (it was back to Normalcy Month) he ordered them to let me out. It seemed an unreasonable thing to do, even to me.

Chapter Fifty-one

'Luke, you're a quack,' Fred Boyd said to me, smiling and looking out our kitchen windows toward the old barn and poison ivy fields.

'Mmmm,' I said, as Lil moved past our table back outdoors to get the groceries.

'A Phi Beta Kappa quack, a brilliant quack, but a quack,' he said.

'Thanks, Fred. You're kind.'

'The trouble is,' he said, dunking a somewhat stale doughnut into his lukewarm coffee, 'that some of it makes sense. That confuses the issue. Why can't you just be a complete fool or charlatan?'

'Huh. Never thought of that. I'll have to let the Die consider it.'

Lil and Miss Welish came in from the yard with the two children clamoring after them, clawing at the bags of groceries Lil carried in her arms. When Lil took out a box of cookies and distributed three each to the two children, they wandered back outdoors, arguing halfheartedly about who had the largest.

Miss Welish, dressed in white tennis shirts and blouse, bounced girlishly and a bit chubbily across the floor to hustle up some fresh coffee and deliver the fresh pastry we'd been promised. Fred watched her, sighed, yawned and tipped way back in his chair, his hands clasped behind his head.

'And where's it all going to end, I wonder?' he said.

'What?' I said.

'Your dice therapy business.'

340

'The Die only knows.'

'Seriously. What do you think you'll achieve?'

'Try it yourself,' I said.

'I have. You know I have. And it's fun; I admit it. But my God, if I took it seriously I'd have to change completely.'

'Precisely.'

'But I like the way I am.'

'So do I, but I'm getting bored with you,' I said. 'It's variety and unpredictability we like in our friends. Those capable of the unexpected we cherish; they capture us because we're intrigued by how they "work." After a while we learn how they work, and our boredom resumes. You've got to change, Fred.'

'No, he hasn't,' said Lil, bringing us lemonade, a Sara Lee Coffee Cake and a bottle of vitamins and sitting at the end of the table. 'I liked Luke the way he was before, and I want Fred to stay just the way he is.'

'It's just not so, Lil. You were *bored* and unhappy with me before I became the Dice Man. Now you're *entertained* and unhappy. That's progress.'

Lil shook her head.

'If it weren't for Fred, I don't think I'd have survived, but he's made me see your behavior for what it is: the sick rebellion of an elephantine child.'

'Fred!'

'Now wait a minute, Lil,' he said. 'That isn't quite what I think at all.'

'All right,' Lil said. 'The sick rebellion of an elephantine Phi Beta Kappa child quack.'

'That's better,' he said, and we laughed.

Miss Welsh brought us coffee and sat down with her cup in the chair in front of the window. She smiled at our thank yous and took a big bite out of a sugared bun.

'Actually,' Lil said, 'now that you've let me know what

you're up to and I no longer give a damn about you, I find it interesting. You should have told me about your dicelife before.'

'The dice didn't tell me to.'

'Don't you ever do anything all by yourself?' Miss Welish asked.

'Not if I can help it.'

'Luke is the only man I've ever known,' Fred said, 'who consults his God every time before going to the john.'

'I think Dr Rhinehart is a true scientist,' Miss Welish said. We all looked at her. She flushed.

'He doesn't let personal considerations enter into anything he does,' she went on. She flushed again.

'So I've noticed,' said Lil. There was a somewhat embarrassed silence. Lil had questioned me extensively on my return from the clinic about what had occurred in Dr Mann's bathroom that night, and I had told her the truth, which was extensive. She had replied extensively, and I had begun an extensive period of sleeping alone in my study. Presumably Fred had questioned Miss Welish extensively also, but her replies didn't seem to have deflected his aim. Since the Krum party, Fred had slowly but surely, with all that scholarly discipline and thoroughness for which Harvard men are renowned, worked his way into Miss Welish's not inconsiderable pants; he seemed undisturbed about whether other scholars had worked on the subject previously or not.

'The only problem I can see with all this,' Fred said, 'is that you've got a poor sense of limits, Luke. To a degree, diceliving has value, extraordinary value. I've experienced it. I've talked to Orv Boggles and that Tracy girl and a couple of other students of yours and I know. But good God, Luke, the trouble you've caused by not taking it easy, not using common sense.'

'Understatement of the century,' said Lil.

342

'I may overdo it occasionally, but in good cause. A good cause. "The road of excess leads to the palace of wisdom" – so said Calvin Coolidge, and I believe him.'

'But no more Krum parties, okay?' Fred asked with a smile.

'I promise never to play six roles at a party ever again.'

'But he's got to keep experimenting,' Miss Welish said.

'I promise to be only a moderate quack,' I said. 'All day.'

'Well, is it tennis, a swim at the ocean, the club, or a sail?' Fred said and got up from the table.

'We need two more options,' Lil added.

'I throw,' said Miss Welish, and she got up to go to the cupboard and get out our family dice. Eventually we all gathered around the kitchen table as Miss Welish flipped the die onto the soiled tablecloth: tennis. We cast again to see whose car we would take and once more to see who played whom and we were off.

It was the first weekend of August, and we were vacationing in our old farmhouse out in the poison ivy fields of eastern Long Island, and things were going quite well. Lil, after questioning me all month about dice theory and therapy, had become more and more interested and less antagonistic. I had brought Professor Boggles home for dinner one night and he had given a fine testimonial to the gifts of the Die.

Our separation and divorce was in temporary abeyance. Lil was putting up with me on the condition that I behave myself with rational irrationality.

Fred Boyd had been a frequent visitor since my release from the clinic in mid-July, and we'd enjoyed half a dozen discussions of dice theory and practice. He tended to quote Jung or Reich or R. D. Laing to show that my ideas weren't all that original, but in doing so he seemed also to be implying that they might be credible. He began experimenting with dice play himself. He even hinted that it might have helped in his scholarly penetration into Miss Welish.

Lil had granted me my conjugal rights again near the end of July and, although she had refused bitterly at first to try any of my dice bed games, she had in the last week surrendered somewhat. We had had two interesting sessions together, Lil especially enjoying one half-hour of the sinner-saint game in which the dice had twice made me a saint and she a sinner.

When we played chess she often tossed a die to determine which of two moves she would make, and she always let a die choose which movie we would see. She even let Larry play with the dice again as long as she had veto power over the options.

But the real breakthrough in our relations had come when we had played a game of emotional roulette together one afternoon when the children were at the beach. We had simplified the standard game by using only three emotions as options – love, hate and pity – but had complicated it by having both of us randomized at the same time. We had each cast a die to determine what would be our first individual three-minute emotion. Lil got hatred, I got love.

I pleaded and she reviled me; I tried to embrace her and she kicked me hard in the left thigh (thank God!); I got down on my knees and she spit on me. The three-minute sand egg-timer finally ran out and we cast again. I got pity and she got hatred again.

'Poor Lil,' I said to her as soon as I saw my dice command, and if I hadn't ducked I think her fist would have gone through my head and come out the other side. The bitterness of months and years, which had earlier been expressed only in restrained sarcasm, came flooding out in physical action and verbal massacre. She was crying

344

and screaming, gritting her teeth and flailing at me with her fists, and even before the timer had run out she collapsed on the edge of the bed in tears.

'Onward,' I said when the time was up and cast a die and got hate. She lethargically cast and got love.

'You lifeless clump of cunt,' I hissed out at the little bitch. 'You scarecrow zombie, you weepy tomb. I'd rather caress Miss Reingold's left elbow than have to touch your corpse.'

At first I saw anger flare in her eyes and then, like a flashbulb going off in her head, her eyes lit up, and she looked tender and compassionate.

' – boobs like bee-bees, ass so flat and bony you can use it to iron with – '

'Luke, Luke, Luke,' she repeated gently.

'LooLooLoo yourself, bitch. You have no more courage than a squashed ant. A mouse. I married a mouse.'

Anger flared again across her face.

'Look at her – can't even follow a dice command for thirty seconds without losing control . . .'

Bewilderment. I paced in intense anger in front of her.

'To think, I might have been fucking a *woman* all these years: a big-boobed bundle of orgasms like Arlene – '

'Luke – ' she said.

' – or a honey-cunted tiger like Terry – '

'My poor, poor Luke – '

'I get a beady-eyed red-rimmed, tail-dragging mouse.'

She was smiling and shaking her head and her eyes, though red-rimmed, were clear and bright.

' – me puke to think of it.' I was towering over her, fists clenched, sneering and hissing and gasping for breath. It felt so good, but she was looking up at me soft-eyed and defenseless and unhurt. It made me rail harder and harder until I was shamelessly repeating myself.

'Luke, I love you – ' she said when I paused.

'Pity, stupid. You're supposed to feel pity. Can't even play a game right – '

'My Luke – '

'Brainless, chestless, assless clump of – '

'My poor sweet sick hero.'

'I'm *not sweet*! You bitch. I'll stick a dustmop up your – '

'Time,' she said. 'It's time.'

'I don't give a fuck. I'd like to chop off your mousy head and peddle your cunt to lepers. I'd like – '

'The three minutes is up, Luke,' she said quietly.

'Oh,' I said, towering over her and slobbering.

'Oh. Sorry about that,' I added.

'It's enough for now,' she said. 'And thanks.'

She then proceeded to bury her face in my belly and we went on to a fine fierce diceless fuck, such as is usually associated with the highly charged emotions of the beginnings or ending of an affair. She'd been compassionate or loving ever since. Mostly.

That morning when the Die chose tennis we drove afterward to a beach on the day and swam and played keep away with Larry and Evie and sunned and swam and back at the farmhouse had nice stiff gin drinks and talked some more, eating soup and cheeseburgers and smoking pot and while Lil made brownies Miss Welish played her guitar and Fred and I sang a duet about Harvard and Cornell and we smoked more pot and retired to our rooms, Lil and I making a slow, languorous giggly love and she cried, and Fred wandered in naked and asked if he could join us in an orgy and after casting the Die I had to say no and he said fuck the Die and I cast again which said that he could fuck the *Die* but not us and Miss Welish came in, Lil not casting the Die but saying no, and we all sat around discussing poetry and promiscuity and pot and pornography and the pill and possible positions and penises and pudenda and potency and permissiveness and playing and pricks.

Much later I made another long, languorous, giggly love to Lil who was all honeyed up from all the talk and before we fell asleep she said to me dreamily, 'Now the dice man has a home' and I said, 'mmmm' and we slept.

Chapter Fifty-two

'I want you to help me to escape,' Eric said quietly, holding the tuna-fish-salad sandwich in his hands lightly, as if were delicate. We were in the Ward W cafeteria crowded in amongst other patients and their visitors. I was dressed casually in an old black suit and a black turtleneck shirt, he was in stiff gray mental-hospital fatigues.

'Why?' I asked, leaning toward him so I could hear better over the surrounding din of voices.

'I've got to get out; I'm not doing anything here anymore.' He was looking past my shoulder at the chaos of men in line behind my back.

'But why me? You know you can't trust me,' I said.

'I can't trust you, *they* can't trust you, no one can trust you.'

'Thanks.'

'But you're the only untrustworthy one on *their* side who knows enough to help us.'

'I'm honored.' I smiled, leaning back in my chair and self-consciously taking a sip from the straw leading into my paper carton of chocolate milk. I missed the beginning of his next sentence.

'. . . will leave. I know that. Somehow it will come to pass.'

'What?' I said leaning forward again.

'I want you to help me to escape.'

'Oh, that,' I said. 'When?'

'Tonight.'

'Ahhhh,' I said, like a doctor being given an especially interesting set of symptoms.

'Tonight at 8 P.M.'

'Not eight fifteen?'

'You will charter a bus to take a group of patients to see *Hair* in Manhattan. The bus will arrive at 7.45 P.M. You will come in and lead us out.'

'Why do you want to see *Hair*?'

His dark eyes darted at me briefly, then back to chaos beyond my shoulder.

'We're not going to see *Hair*. We're escaping,' he went on quietly. 'You'll let us all off on the other side of the bridge.'

'But no one can leave the hospital like that without a written order signed by Dr Mann or one of the other directors of the hospital.'

'You will forge the order. If a doctor gives it to the nurse in charge no one will suspect a forgery.'

'After you're free, what happens to me?'

He looked across at me calmly and with utter conviction said:

'That is not important. You are a vehicle.'

'I am a vehicle,' I said.

We looked at each other.

'A bus, to be exact,' I added.

'You are a vehicle, you will be saved.'

'That's a relief to know.'

We stared at each other.

'Why should I do this?' I finally asked. The noise around us was terrific and we had unconsciously brought our heads closer and closer to each other until they were separated now by only six inches. For the first time a hint of a smile crossed his lips.

'Because the Die will tell you to,' he answered softly.

'Ahhh,' I said, like a doctor who has finally found the

349

symptom which makes the whole syndrome come together. 'The Die will tell me to – '

'You will consult It now,' he said.

'I will consult It now.'

I reached into my suit-coat pocket and pulled out two green dice.

'As I may have already explained to you, *I* control the options and their probability.'

'It makes no difference,' Eric said.

'But *I* don't think much of the option to lead you in such an escape.'

'It makes no difference,' he said, his slight smile returning.

'How many am I supposed to take to *Hair* with you?'

'Thirty-seven,' he said quietly.

I believe my mouth fell open.

'I, Dr Lucius M. Rhinehart, am going to lead thirty-seven patients in the largest and most sensational mental-hospital escape in American history tonight at eight?'

'Thirty-eight,' he said.

'Ah, thirty-eight,' I said. We probed into each other's eyes at six-inch range, and he seemed utterly without the slightest doubt about the outcome of events.

'Sorry,' I said, feeling angry. 'This is the best I can do.' I thought for several seconds and then went on: 'I'm going to cast one die. If it's a two or a six I'll try to help you and thirty-seven others escape somehow from this hospital sometime tonight.' He didn't reply. 'All right?'

'Go ahead and shake a six,' he said quietly.

I stared back at him for a moment and then cupped my hands, shook the die hard against my palms and flipped it onto the table between my empty milk carton and two lumps of tuna salad and the salt. It was a two.

'Ha!' I said instinctively.

'Bring us some money too,' he said, leaning back

slightly but without expression. 'About a hundred bucks should do.'

He pushed back his chair and stood up and looked down at me with a bright smile.

'God works in a mysterious way,' he said.

I looked back at him and for the first time realized that I too wanted not *my* will but the Die's will to be done.

'Yes,' I said. 'The vehicles of God come in many shapes and sizes.'

'See you tonight,' he said and edged his way out of the cafeteria.

Actually I wouldn't mind seeing *Hair* again, I thought, and then, smiling in dazed awe at the day I had before me, I set to work planning the Great Mental Hospital Escape.

Chapter Fifty-three

'You're cured,' Jake said. 'If I do say so myself.'

'I'm not sure, Jake,' I said. We were in his office that afternoon and he was trying to tell me that this would be our last analytic session together.

'Your interest in dice therapy has given you a rational base upon which to work with the dice. Before, you were using the dice to escape your responsibilities. Now they have become your responsibility.'

'That's very acute, I must admit. But how do we know the Die won't flip me off in some new direction?'

'Because you've got a purpose now. A goal. You control the options, right?'

'True.'

'You think dice therapy's hot stuff, right?'

'Sometimes.'

'You aren't going to risk the advance of dice therapy for another roll in the hay with some dumb broad. You're not. You know now what you want?'

'A smart broad?'

'The advance of dice therapy. The advance of dice therapy. It gives your life precisely that foundation which it's been lacking since you rejected your father in the form of Freud and Dr Mann and began this random rebellion.'

'But a good dice therapist must lead a random life.'

'But he's got to meet the patient regularly. He's got to show up.'

'Mmmmm.'

'He's got to listen. He's got to teach.'

'Hmmm.'

'Moreover, you've got Lil trying dice therapy, your kids. Your new self is being accepted. You don't have to play the fool anymore.'

'I see.'

'*I* even accept the new Luke. Arlene has introduced me to several valid positions of dice therapy. I spoke to Boggles. Dice therapy makes sense.'

'It does?'

'Of course it does.'

'But it will tend to break down the sense of a stable self so necessary for a human to feel secure.'

'Only superficially. Actually, it builds a dicestudent's – Jesus, I'm using your terms already – a patient's strength by forcing him into continual conflict with others.'

'Builds ego strength?'

'Sure. You're not afraid of anything now, are you?'

'Well, I don't know.'

'You've made an ass of yourself so many times that you can't be hurt.'

'Ahh, very acute.'

'That's ego strength.'

'Without any ego.'

'Semantics, but it's what we're after. I can't be hurt because I analyze everything. A scientist examines his wound, his wounder and his healer with equal neutrality.'

'And the dicestudent obeys the dice decision, good and bad, with equal passion.'

'Right,' he said.

'But what kind of a society will it be if people begin consulting the Die to make their decisions?'

'No problem. People are only as eccentric as their options and most of the people who will go through dice therapy are going to develop just like you; that's what makes your case so important. They're all going to go through a period of chaotic rebellion and then move into a lifetime of moderate, rational use of the dice consistent with some overall purpose.'

'That's very nice, Jake,' I said and leaned back on the couch from the alert sitting position I had been in.

'I'm depressed,' I added.

'Moderate, rational use of the dice is rational and moderate and every man should try it.'

'But the dicelife should be unpredictable and irrational and immoderate. If it isn't, it isn't dicelife.'

'Nonsense. You're following the dice these days, right?'

'Yes.'

'You're seeing your patients, living with your wife, seeing me regularly, paying your bills, talking to your friends, obeying the laws: you're leading a healthy, normal life. You're cured.'

'A healthy, normal life – '

'And you're not bored anymore.'

'A healthy, normal life unbored – '

'Right. You're cured.'

'It's hard to believe.'

'You were a tough nut to crack.'

'I don't feel any different than I did three months ago.'

'Dice therapy, purpose, regularity, moderation, sense of limits: you're cured.'

'So this is the end of my booster analysis?'

'It's all over but the shouting.'

'How much do I owe you?'

'Miss R'll have the bill for you when you leave.'

'Well, thank you, Jake.'

'Luke, baby, I'm finishing up "The Case of the Six-Sided Man" this afternoon and after poker tonight. I thank *you*.'

'It's a good article?'

'Tougher the case, better the article. By the way I've

asked old Arnie Weissman to try to get you invited to speak at this fall's annual AAPP convention – on Dice Therapy. Pretty good, huh?'

'Well, thank you, Jake.'

'Thought I'd present "The Case of the Six-Sided Man" on the same day.'

'The dynamic duo,' I said.

'I thought of titling the article "The Case of the Mad Scientist," but settled on "The Six-Sided Man." What do you think?'

'The "Case of the Six-Sided Man." It's beautiful.'

Jake came around from behind his neat desk and put his arm way up on my shoulder and grinned up into my face.

'You're a genius, Luke, and so am I, but moderation.'

'So long,' I said, shaking his hand.

'See you tonight for poker,' he said as I was leaving.

'Oh that's right. I'd forgotten. I may be a bit late. But I'll see you.'

As I was softly closing the door behind me, he caught my eye one last time and grinned.

'You're cured,' he said.

'I doubt it, Jake, but you never can tell. Die be with you.'

'You too, baby.'

Chapter Fifty-four

[*From* The New York Times, *Wednesday, August 13, 1969, late edition.*]

In the largest mass escape in the history of New York State Mental Institutions, thirty-three patients of Queensborough State Hospital of Queens escaped last night during a performance of *Hair* at the Blovill Theater in mid-town Manhattan.

By 2 A.M. this morning ten of these had been recaptured by city police and hospital officials, but twenty-three remained at large.

At the Blovill Theater the patients sat through the first act of the hit musical *Hair*, but as the second act was beginning they made their escape. Most of the patients began to snake-dance their way onto the stage to the music of the first number of Act II 'Where Do I Go?', mingled with the cast, and then fled backstage and hence to the street. The Blovill audience apparently assumed the performance of the patients was part of the show.

Hospital officials claim that someone apparently forged the signature of Hospital Director Timothy J. Mann, MD, on documents ordering staff members to make arrangements to transport thirty-eight patients from the admissions ward to see the musical by chartered bus.

Dr Lucius M. Rhinehart, whom the forged documents had ordered to organize and guide the expedition, stated that he and his attendants had concentrated on holding the three or four potentially dangerous patients and could not make an effort to pursue the majority when they fled backstage. In all, five patients were restrained within the theater.

'The excursion was ill-timed and ill-planned – ridiculous in fact and I knew it,' he said. 'But I failed on four separate occasions to get in touch with Dr Mann to question him about the request, and, failing, had no choice but to carry it out.'

Police indicated that the size of the mass escape, the character of some of the patients involved, and the complicated series of forgeries needed to fool responsible staff members indicate a plot of major proportions.

Among those who escaped were Arturo Toscanini Jones, a Black Party member who recently made news when he spat in Mayor Lindsay's face during one of the mayor's walking tours of Harlem, and hippie figure Eric Cannon, whose followers recently caused a disturbance at the Cathedral of St John the Divine during the Easter Mass.

A complete list of the names of those who have escaped was being withheld pending communication by hospital officials with the relatives of those who fled.

The patients who escaped were dressed for the most part in khakis and T-shirts and informal footwear such as sneakers, sandals, and slippers. A few patients, it was reliably reported, had been wearing pajama tops or bathrobes.

Police warned that some of the patients might be dangerous if cornered and urged citizens to approach all known escapees with caution. They noted that among them were two of Mr Jones's Black Party followers.

A full investigation of the breakout was under way.

Officials of the Blovill Theater and Hair Productions, Inc., denied that they had managed the mass escape as a publicity stunt.

How simple it all seems now reading about it again in the *Times*. Forge documents, charter bus, drive to theater, flee during performance.

Do you have any idea how many documents have to be forged to get *one single patient* released for *one single hour* from a mental hospital? From the time I left Eric at 11.30 A.M. that morning until my analytic hour with Jake at 3 P.M. I was continually typing documents, forging Dr Mann's signature and rushing away to have the orders delivered to the appropriate staff. I got so I could sign Dr Mann's signature faster and more accurately than he. As it was, I still had signed eighty-six fewer documents than were legally required for such an excursion.

Would you be suspicious if someone called up in

muffled voice with a hint of a Negro accent and requested a forty-five-seat bus to take thirty-eight mental patients to a Broadway musical on six hours' notice that very evening? Have you ever tried to lead thirty-eight mental patients off a ward when half of them don't know where they're going or don't want to go, aren't dressed for it or want to watch the Mets' night game on TV? Since I didn't know which thirty-eight of the forty-three patients on the ward my sponsor wanted to lead to freedom, I had to choose at random thirty-eight names – which naturally did not correspond with those Mr Cannon had in mind. Do you think that the head nurse or Dr Lucius M. Rhinehart would permit any substitution for the names on this list?

'Look here, Rhinehart, two of my best men are not on this list,' Arturo whispered desperately into my ear at seven fifty-three that night.

'They'll have to see *Hair* another night,' I said.

'But I want these men,' he went on fiercely.

'These are the thirty-eight names on the list. These are the thirty-eight patients whom I will escort to *Hair*.'

He dragged me farther off into the corner.

'But Cannon said only that the dice said – '

'The dice said only that I would try to help Mr Cannon and thirty-seven other mental patients escape. It mentioned no names. If *you* want to take some initiative, I assure you *I* don't know Smith from Peterson from Klug, but I myself am taking only people who call themselves Smith, Peterson and Klug.'

He rushed away.

Five minutes later Head Nurse Herbie Flamm waddled up:

'Say, Dr Rhinehart, I don't see Heckelburg on this list but I just saw him leave with that last group with your attendants.'

'Heckelburg?' I said. 'Perhaps not. I'll check.' I walked away.

Flamm caught me again just as I was leaving.

'Sorry to bother you again, Doc, but four of the guys on your list are still here and four guys who aren't on your list have just left.'

'Are you positive, Mr Flamm, that you now have five patients left on the ward?'

'Yes, sir.'

'And that only thirty-eight have left?'

'Yes, sir.'

'Are you sure my name is Rhinehart?'

He stared up at me and began caressing his big belly nervously.

'Yes, sir. I think so, sir.'

'You *think* my name is Rhinehart?'

'Yes, sir.'

'Who is that patient – over there?' I asked, pointing to one I'd never seen before and hoped was a new admission.

'Er . . . ah . . . him?'

'Yes, he,' I said coldly towering over him.

'I'll have to check with the attendant, Higgens. He – '

'We're going to be late for the opening curtain, Mr Flamm. I'm afraid I can't rely on your fuzzy memory for names to delay us any longer. Goodbye.'

'Goo – goodbye, Doc – '

'Rhinehart. Remember it.'

Have you ever walked down Broadway in the middle of a line of thirty-eight men dressed variously in khakis, sneakers, sandals, Bermuda shorts, hospital fatigues, torn T-shirts, African capes, bathrobes, bedroom slippers, pajama tops and sweat suits and led by an utterly serene eighteen-year-old boy wearing a white hospital robe and whistling 'The Battle Hymn of the Republic'? Have you ever then walked beside the beatific boy to lead such a line into a Broadway theater? And looked natural? And relaxed? When half the seats were in the front row? (The summer doldrums made it possible for me to get seats at the last minute – 4.30 P.M. that afternoon – but twenty of them cost $8.50 apiece.)

Have you then tried to seat thirty-eight odd people when half the seats were scattered like buckshot over a five-hundred seat theater? When three of your patients were walking zombies, four manic-depressives and six alert homosexuals? Have you then tried to maintain a sense of dignity, firmness and authority when one of these unfortunates keeps coming up to you and whispering hysterically about when are they all supposed to escape?

'Rhinehart!' Arturo X hissed at me in anguish. 'What the hell are we doing here at *Hair*?'

'My orders were to bring you to *Hair*. This I have done. The die specifically rejected the option that I release you on Lexington Avenue. I hope you enjoy yourself.'

'There're four pigs standing at the back. I saw them when we came in. Is this some sort of trap?'

'I know nothing about the police. There are other ways out of a theater. I hope you enjoy yourself. Be happy.'

'The Goddam houselights are dimming. What the hell are we supposed to do?'

'Listen to the music. I have brought you to *Hair*. Enjoy yourself. Dance. Be happy.'

Through it all Eric Cannon retained the serenity of a golfer with a two-inch putt and never once approached me – except for two seconds just after the end of the first act ('Groovy show, Dr Rhinehart, glad we came'). But Arturo X squirmed in his seat every second that he wasn't lunging up the aisle to speak to one of his followers or to me.

'Look, Rhinehart,' he hissed at me near the end of the

intermission. 'What will you do if we all get up and dance and go onto the stage?'

'I have brought you to *Hair*. I want you to enjoy yourselves. Be happy. Dance. Sing.'

He stared into my eyes like an oculist searching for signs of retinal decomposition and then barked out a short laugh.

'Jesus . . .' he said.

'Have a good time, son,' I said as he left.

'Dr Rhinehart, I think the patients are whispering among themselves,' one of my big attendants said about three minutes later.

'A dirty joke no doubt,' I said.

'That Arturo Jones has been going around to everyone whispering.'

'I told him to remind everyone to catch the bus back to the island with us.'

'What if someone tries to make a break for it?'

'Apprehend him gently but firmly.'

'What if they all make a break for it?'

'Apprehend those with the most acute socially debilitating illnesses – the zombies and killers in brief – and leave the rest to the police.' I smiled at him serenely. 'But no violence. We must not give our hospital attendants a bad name. We must not upset the audience.'

'Okay, Doctor.'

I seated myself between the most clearly homicidal patients, and when the men in our row began to rise to join the dance to the stage, I wrapped one of my huge arms around the throat of each of them and squeezed until they seemed strangely sleepy. I then watched the interesting opening to Act II where thirty or so oddly dressed members of the cast who had apparently been posing as members of the audience around me began to dance down the aisles and up onto the stage frolicking with each other in a friendly roughhouse way. The onstage part of the cast pretended slight confusion but continued to sing on as the new weirdies mixed with the Act I weirdies and sang and danced and frolicked, all singing the opening number 'Where Do I Go?' until most of the newcomers had gone.

The police questioned me for about half an hour at the theater, and I phoned the hospital and told the appropriate staff members there of the slight difficulties we had encountered and I phoned Dr Mann at my apartment and informed him that thirty-three patients had escaped from *Hair*. My phone call had pulled him away from a hand in which he was holding a full house, aces over jacks, and he was as upset as I've ever heard him.

'My God, my God, Luke, thirty-three patients. What have you done? What have you done?'

'But your letter said – '

'What letter? NO, no, no, Luke, you *know* I would never write any letter about thirty-three – oh! – you *know* it! How could you do it?'

'I tried to see you, to phone you.'

'But you didn't seem upset. I had no idea. Thirty-three patients!'

'We held onto five.'

'Oh Luke, my God, the papers, Dr Esterbrook, the Senate Committee on Mental Hygiene, my God, my God.'

'They're just people,' I said.

'Why didn't someone call me during the day, a note, a messenger, something? Why was everyone so stupid? To take thirty-three patients off the ward – '

'Thirty-eight.'

'To a Broadway musical – '

'Where should we have taken them? Your letter said – '

'Don't *say* that! Don't *mention* any letter by me!'

'But I was just – '

'To *Hair!*' and he choked. 'The newspapers, Esterbrook, Luke, Luke, what have you done?'

'It'll be all right, Tim. Mental patients are always recaptured.'

'But no one ever *reads* about that. They get loose – that's news.'

'People will be impressed with our permissive, progressive policies. As you said in your let – '

'Don't *say* that! We must never let a patient out of the hospital again. Never.'

'Relax, Tim, relax, I've got to talk some more to the police and the reporters and – '

'Don't say a word! I'm coming down. Say you've got laryngitis. Don't talk.'

'I've got to go now, Tim. You hurry on down.'

'Don't say – '

I hung up.

I talked to police and the reporters and minor hospital officials and then Dr Mann in person for another hour and a half, not getting back to the poker party at my apartment until close to midnight.

Lil, I'm happy to report, was winning substantially, with Miss Welish and Fred Boyd the primary losers and Jake and Arlene breaking even. They were all rather interested in what had happened to so upset Dr Mann, but I played it down, called it a minor Happening, a tempest in a teapot, implied that some subversive underground group had conspired a series of forgeries, and insisted I was sick of the subject and wanted to play poker.

I was tremendously keyed up and could barely sit still in my chair, but they kindly dealt me in, and by ignoring their further questions I was finally left to concentrate on my abominably bad luck with the cards. I lost badly to Fred Boyd on the first hand and even worse to Arlene on the second. By the end of seven hands without a winner I was thoroughly depressed and everyone else (except Miss Welish, who was sleepy and bored) was quite gay. The phone had rung just once and I had told the police that I didn't *know* how I had been cut off during my attempted phone call to Dr Mann that afternoon, but that it obviously wasn't me since I was talking on the phone at the time. I told them that I talked to Arturo Jones at *Hair* because he was an acute drama critic and that I had single-handedly held on to two of the most dangerous patients and that I'd appreciate a little *respect* since I felt badly enough about losing as it was.

I lost two more hands of poker and got gloomier and the party broke up with Fred telling about how he was using dice therapy with two of his patients and Jake telling me about a sentence he'd written in his article, and they were gone and Lil, laughing happily, went off to bed. I, despite several of her most obscene kisses, remained behind slumped in the easy chair brooding about my fate.

Chapter Fifty-five

The events which occurred between 1.30 A.M. and 3.30 A.M. that morning, being of some historical note, must be recorded objectively. Dr Rhinehart had realized for several weeks that the early morning hours of August 13 were, in effect, the first anniversary of his relationship with the Die. He had planned to do as he had at the beginning of 1969; create a list of longer-range options from which the Die would choose to direct his life.

He found, however, that he was too distraught over the possible consequences of his activities of the previous day to concentrate on options running much longer than a few minutes. A year before, he had been bored and restless; now he was overexcited and restless. He lunged back and forth across the living room, gritting his teeth, clenching his fists, stroking them against his tensed belly, gulping in huge lungfuls of air, trying to determine whether the police would be able to build a convincing case against him. His only hope, as he saw it, was that when one or more of Mr Cannon's or Mr Jones's recaptured followers began alleging that he (Dr Rhinehart) had aided and abetted their escape, their allegations would be taken as the statements of mentally imbalanced persons, creatures legally unfit to give reliable testimony. Dr Rhinehart spent close to twenty minutes concocting his defense – mostly a lengthy indictment of the secret black and hippie conspiracy to frame all white doctors named Rhinehart.

At last, however, in exasperation at his nervousness, Dr Rhinehart returned to reality and cast a die to determine whether he would brood about his problems with the police and Dr Mann for zero, five, ten or thirty minutes or one day, or until the problems were resolved, and the die ordered ten more minutes. When the time had elapsed, he breathed an immense sigh and smiled. 'Now. Where are we?' he thought.

He then recalled that it was his anniversary, and with that inhuman casualness for which future generations of healthy normal people were to condemn him and for which future generations of dicepeople have admired him, he dictated that should he flip a one, a three or a five he would go downstairs and try to engage in sexual congress with Mrs Ecstein. The die fell three and he arose, informed his wife that he was going for a walk and left the apartment. Since this episode is of little importance, we report it in Dr Rhinehart's own words:

I clumped down the stairs, past the rusty railing and cast-off advertising circular and rang the doorbell. It was 2.20 A.M., a little late this year, and certainly no time for a little *tête-à-tête*. Arlene came bleary-eyed clutching Jake's old bathrobe – to her throat.

'Oh,' she said.

'I've come to engage in sexual congress, Arlene.'

'Come in,' she said.

'The dice told me to do it again.'

'But Jake's here,' she said, blinking her eyes absently and letting the robe fall slightly open.

'He's working in his study at the end of the hall.'

'I'm sorry, but you know how the Die is,' I said.

'I promised not to hide anything from him anymore.'

'But did you consult the Die about that?'

'Oh, you're right.'

She turned and went down the hall a short way and then into her bedroom. I joined her at her vanity table, where successive flips of a die determined that she was to tell Jake everything and that she was to permit sexual congress with me, but only in Kama Sutra positions eighteen and twenty-six, which, she said, were particularly suited for women in their fifth month of pregnancy.

I then followed her up the hall and watched over her shoulder as she stood in the slightly open doorway of Jake's study looking in at her husband hard at work at his desk.

'Jake?' she said tentatively.

'What's up?' he barked back, not looking up.

'Luke's here,' she said.

'Oh. Come on in, Luke baby, I'm just about finished.'

'We're sorry to bother you, Jakie,' Arlene said, 'but the Die said Luke had to – '

'I've got a ring-dinger last chapter, Luke, if I do say so myself,' Jake said, smiling, and scratching furiously with his pen across some errant phrase.

' – engage in sexual congress,' I heard Arlene finish.

'What's that?' Jake said and looked up again.

'What?'

'It's our anniversary,' I added.

He scratched his throat and grimaced and looked a little annoyed.

'Oh that,' he finally said. 'Jesus, Moses, Freud. I don't know what the world's coming to.' He stared at us both a long time, squinting horribly. Then he reached to his side, rolled a die across his desk and frowned again. 'Yeah, well, take it easy with my bathrobe.'

'We will,' Arlene said, wheeling around with a beaming smile, and she bounced past me back up the hall to her room.

Dr Rhinehart returned to his own apartment approximately thirty-eight minutes after leaving it and again felt depressed. The exhilaration he had felt a year ago upon returning from a superficially similar undertaking was absent. He cast himself into the easy chair in his living room in a tired, anxious, apathetic state such as he had not previously experienced in his dicelife. When he became aware again of his merely human anxiety, he grunted an extremely loud 'Ahhggh,' and surged out of the chair to get paper, pencil and dice.

As he returned from his study to the living room, however, he was met by his wife, who had been awakened by his loud grunt and stood in the bedroom doorway to inquire sleepily if everything was all right.

367

'Everything is confused and unreliable,' Dr Rhinehart said irritably. 'If I could only count definitely upon either the stupidity or the intelligence of the police – '

'Come to bed, Lukie,' his wife said and lifted her slender arms up around his neck and leaned sleepily against him. The bed warmed body that Dr Rhinehart's hands found themselves enclosing was unconfused and reliable, and with a different sounding 'Ahhhh' he lowered his head and embraced his wife.

'But I have miles to go before I sleep,' he said softly when he had broken their kiss.

'Come to bed,' Mrs Rhinehart said. 'The police will never touch you when you're in your wife's bed.'

'Had I but world enough and time – '

'There's plenty of time – come,' and she began to drag her husband into their bedroom. 'I've even dreamed of a new option,' she said.

But Dr Rhinehart had stopped a few feet inside the door, and, slump-shouldered and bedraggled, he said: 'But I have miles to go before I sleep.'

Mrs Rhinehart, still holding one of his large hands in hers, turned dreamily and smiled and yawned.

'I'll be waiting, sweetheart,' she said, and with an unintended swinging of the more desirable parts of her anatomy, she moved to her bed and climbed in.

'Goodnight, Lil,' Dr Rhinehart said.

'Mmmm,' she said. 'Check the kids 'fore you come.'

Dr Rhinehart, still holding in his left hand the paper, pen and two dice, walked quickly to the children's bedroom and tiptoed in to look at Larry and Evie. They were sound asleep, Larry with his mouth open like a child drunk and Evie with her face so buried by the sheet that he could only make out the top of her head.

'Have good dreams,' he said and silently left the room and returned to the living room.

He placed the paper, pencil and dice on the floor in front of the easy chair and then, with a sudden lunge, took four strides toward his bedroom and stopped. Sighing, he returned to kneel on the rug beside the tools of his trade. To relax himself and prepare for what he had to do, he performed a series of random dice exercises; four random physical exercises, two one-minute spurts of the sinner-saint game, and one three-minute period of emotional roulette – the Die choosing self-pity, an emotion he found himself expressing with enthusiasm. Then he placed the two green dice on the easy chair in front of him and, kneeling on the rug, intoned a prayer:

> Great Godblob Die, I worship thee;
> Awaken me this morn
> With thy green gaze,
> Quicken my dead life
> With thy plastic breath,
> Spill into the arid spaces of my soul
> Thy green vinegar.
>
> A hundred hungry birds scatter my seed,
> You roll them into cubes and plant me.
>
> The people I fear are
> Puppets poking puppets,
> Playthings costumed by my mind.
> When you fall, O Die,
> The strings collapse and
> I walk free.
>
> I am thy grateful urn, O Die,
> Fill me.

Dr Rhinehart felt a serene joy such as always came to him when he surrendered his will to the Die: the peace which passeth understanding. He wrote upon the white, blank paper the options for his life for the next year.

If the dice total two, three or twelve: he would leave his wife and children forever. He recorded this option with dread. He'd given it once chance in nine.

He gave one chance in five (dice total of four or five) that he would completely abandon the use of his dice for at least three months. He desired this option as a dying man the wonder drug to end his ills and feared it as a healthy man does a threat to his balls.

Dice total six (one chance in seven): he would begin revolutionary activity against the injustice of the established order. He didn't know what he had in mind by the option, but it gave him pleasure to think of thwarting the police, who were making him so uncomfortable. He began daydreaming about joining forces with Arturo or Eric until a police siren on the street outside his apartment building so frightened him that he thought of erasing the option (the mere writing of it might be a crime) and then decided to go quickly on to the others.

Dice total of seven (one chance in six): he would devote the entire next year to the development of dice theory and therapy. Recording this brought such pleasant excitement that he considered giving it the totals of eight and nine as well, but fought back such human weakness and went on.

Dice total of eight (one chance in seven): he would write an autobiographical account of his adventures.

Dice total nine, ten or eleven (one chance in four): he would leave the profession of psychiatry, including dice therapy, for one year, letting the dice choose a new profession. He recorded this with pride; he would not be the prisoner of his fascination for his beloved dice therapy.

Examining his six options, Dr Rhinehart was pleased; they showed imagination and daring. Each of them represented both threat and treat, both the danger of disaster and the possibility of new power.

He placed the paper by his side and the two green dice in front of him on the floor.

'Tuck me in, Dad,' a voice said from the other end of the room. It was his son Larry, practically asleep on his feet.

Dr Rhinehart arose irritably, marched to the swaying boy, lifted him up into his arms and carried him back to his bed. Larry was asleep as soon as his father had pulled the sheet up to his neck again, and Dr Rhinehart rushed back to his position on his knees in the living room.

The dice in position before him, he knelt silently for two minutes and prayed. He then picked up the two dice and began shaking them gaily in the bowl of his hands.

> Tremble in my hands, O Die,
> As I so shake in yours.

And holding the dice above his head he intoned aloud:

> 'Great bleak Blocks of God, descend, quiver, create.
> Into your hands I commit my soul.'

The dice fell: a one and a two – three. He was to leave his wife and children forever.

Chapter Fifty-six

How about that?

Chapter Fifty-seven

The heavens declare the glory of Chance;
And the firmament showeth his handiwork.
Day unto day uttereth accident,
And night unto night showeth whim.
There is no speech nor language
Where their voice is not heard.
Their line is gone out through all the earth,
And their deeds to the end of the world.
In them hath Chance set a tabernacle for the sun,
Whose going forth is from the end of the heaven,
And his circuit unto the ends of it:
And there is nothing hid from the heat thereof.
The law of Chance is perfect, converting the soul:
The testimony of Chance is sure, making wise the simple.
The statutes of Chance are right, rejoicing the heart:
The commandment of Chance is pure, enlightening the eyes.
The fear of Chance is clean, enduring forever:
The judgments of Chance are true and righteous altogether.

– from *The Book of the Die*

Chapter Fifty-eight

Freedom, Reader, is an awful thing: so Jean-Paul Sartre, Erich Fromm, Albert Camus and dictators throughout the world continually tell us. I spent many days that August thinking about what I would do with my life, oscillating hour to hour from joy to gloom, madness to boredom.

I was lonely. There was no one to whom I could go and say: 'Aren't I wonderful; I left Lil and my job in order to toss dice and become a totally random man. If you're lucky the dice may let me finish this conversation.'

I had not given a last kiss to Lil and the children. I hadn't left a note. I had gathered up a few personal notebooks, a checkbook, two or three books (chosen by a die at random), several pairs of green dice and left the apartment. I returned two minutes later and left the only message in the world I felt Lil might understand and believe: on the floor in front of the easy chair I had placed two dice, their upturned faces showing a two and a one.

I had thought at first that nothing should be *impossible* to the Dice Man at any given moment. It was an elevating aspiration. I might not be more powerful than a locomotive, faster than a speeding bullet, or able to leap tall buildings at a single bound, but in terms of being free at any given moment to do whatever the dice or the spontaneous 'I' might dictate, I would be, compared to all known past human beings, a superman.

But I was lonely. Superman at least had a regular job and Lois Lane. But being a real superbeing, one capable of marvels and miracles compared to the mechanical and repetitious acrobatics of Superman and Batman, was lonely, I'm sorry, fans, but that's how I felt.

I had gone to a dingy hotel in the East Village that made the geriatrics ward at QSH seem like a plush retirement villa. I sweated and sulked and wandered out to play a few dice roles and dice games and sometimes I enjoyed myself thoroughly, but those nights alone in that hotel room were not among the high points of my life.

The problem of boredom which the Die had so successfully solved seemed, now that I was approaching the totally free state, to be reappearing. My own family and friends had been boring enough, but I began to feel that the average humans I was encountering in the streets and bars and hotels of Fun City were far worse. The dice had introduced me already to such variety that I was beginning to find, like Solomon, that it was difficult to find anything new under the sun.

As a wealthy southern aristocrat I had seduced a young, reasonably presentable typist and kept her two nights ('Y'all shore do have a nice boahdy') before the dice reincarnated me as a Bowery bum. I stored all my cash and some new clothes I had bought in a locker, stopped shaving and for two days and nights panhandled and got drunk on the lower East Side. I didn't get much sleep and felt lonelier than ever, my only friends being an occasional stray derelict who would hang around until he was sure I was really broke. I got so hungry that I finally straightened up my clothes as best I could and stole a box of crackers and two cans of tuna fish from a small supermarket. A young clerk looked very suspicious but after I'd finished my 'browsing' I asked him if they sold amoratycemate and that shut him up while I left.

As a life-insurance salesman looking for a fresh lay, I failed to get anywhere and spent another lonely night.

The dice permitted me to phone the police three times:

375

once to say in a thick Negro accent that the Black Panthers had sprung Arturo Jones from the hospital; once as Dr Rhinehart to inform that I had left my wife but if they wanted to question me about anything I'd make myself available; and once as an anonymous hippie informer, telling them that Eric Cannon had been permitted to escape by an act of God.

I spent two days playing with a thousand dollars in a Wall Street brokerage house, letting the Die buy and sell or hold at its discretion and I only lost two hundred dollars but I was still bored.

About nine o'clock one hot August evening, sitting crowded and lonely at one end of a packed Village bar and having crumpled up in the course of the previous two days at least four separate lists of options, I had to face the fact that now that I was free to be absolutely anything, I was rapidly becoming interested in absolutely *nothing*: a somewhat distressing development. It was such an original experience, however, that I began to laugh happily to myself, my big belly shaking like an old engine warming up. I would obviously have to give the dice a brief vacation and see what happened. I would grow for a few weeks organically instead of randomly.

Having thus decisively decided not to decide, I felt vaguely better, even with a tart, rather evil-tasting beer awash in my tummy and unfinished in my glass. I wanted rest. I'd left Lil: a great triumph (I felt tired). Let me drift in peace.

Trying to feel serenity I left the noisy bar and, after a half-hour's organic wandering, entered another just like it. The beer tasted the same too. I thought of telephoning Jake and pretending to be Erich Fromm calling from Mexico City. I dismissed it as a symptom of loneliness. I thought of yelling, 'Drinks on me!' but my organic frugality vetoed the impulse. I daydreamed about buying a yacht and circling the globe.

'Well, if it isn't old coitus-interruptus himself.'

The voice, sharp and feminine, was followed by the fact, soft and feminine, and the recognition, hard and masculine, of the half-smiling face of Linda Reichman.

'Er, hello, Linda,' I said, not too suavely. I found myself instinctively trying to remember what role I was supposed to be playing.

'What brings you here?' she asked.

'Oh. I . . . don't know. I sort of drifted here.'

She edged between my neighbor and me and placed her drink on the bar. Her eyes were heavily made up, her hair a more deeply bleached blonde than I remembered it, her body – no need to speculate about her measurements; her breasts swayed bralessly against a tight-fitting multicolored T-shirt. She looked very sexy in a debauched sort of way and she eyed me with curiosity.

'Drifted? The Great Psychiatrist drifted? I had the impression that you never even picked your nose without writing a treatise proving its value.'

'That was the old days. I've changed, Linda.'

'Ever managed an orgasm?'

I laughed and she smiled.

'How about yourself?' I asked. 'What've you been doing?'

'Disintegrating,' she said and gracefully swallowed the last of her drink. 'You ought to try it, it's fun.'

'I think I'd like to.'

A man appeared next to her, a small frail man with glasses who looked like a graduate student in organic chemistry, and after glancing once at me, he said to Linda: 'Come on. Let's go.'

Linda slowly turned her eyes to the man and, with a look that made all previous looks I'd seen on her face

377

seem like idolatrous admiration, announced: 'I'm staying awhile.'

Organic chemistry blinked at her, looked at my impressive bulk nervously and took her by the elbow.

'Come on,' he said.

She lifted the dregs of her drink carefully off the bar past my face and poured it slowly down organic chemistry's back inside his shirt, ice cubes and all.

'Go change your shirt first,' she said.

He never batted an eye. With a barely perceptible shrug of the shoulders he merged back into the surrounding mob.

'You think you'd like to disintegrate, huh?' she said to me and then signaled to a bartender for another drink.

'Yes, but it seems an awfully hard thing to do. I've been trying it for over a year now and it takes tremendous effort.'

'A year! You don't look it. You look like a middle-class insurance salesman who comes once every four months to the Village for a fresh lay.'

'You're wrong. I've been trying to disintegrate myself. But tell me, how do *you* go about it?'

'Me? Same as always. I haven't changed since you last saw me. Get my kicks the same ways. I spent three months in Venezuela – even lived with a man for almost a month, twenty-four days to be precise – but nothing's new.'

'Then you're failing,' I said.

'What d'you mean?'

'I mean if you're really trying to disintegrate you're not succeeding. You're not changing. You're staying the *same*.'

She wrinkled her clear, still youthful brow and took a big gulp from her fresh drink.

'It was just a word. Disintegration doesn't mean anything. I'm just living my life.'

'Would you like a new kick, one you've never had before and really disintegrate the old self?'

She laughed abruptly. 'I've had enough of your brand of kicks.'

'I've developed new brands.'

'Sex bores me. I've made love with every possible number and configuration of men, women and children, had penises and other appropriatcly shaped objects up every orifice in every possible combination and sex is a bore.'

'I'm not necessarily talking about sex.'

'Then maybe I'm interested.'

'It will mean a partnership with me for a while.'

'What kind of partnership?'

'It will mean giving up your freedom entirely into my hands for – well – a month, let's say.'

She looked at me intently, thinking.

'I become your slave for one month?' she asked.

'Yes.'

A middle-aged woman with dyed black hair, sharp dark eyes and no makeup knifed out of the moiling sea behind us, glided up beside Linda and whispered in her ear. Linda, watching me, listened.

'No, Tony,' she said. 'No. I've changed my plans. I may not be able to make it.'

Another whisper.

'No. Definitely no. Goodbye.'

The raven-haired shark fell back into the sea.

'I do whatever you want for one month?'

'Yes and no. You follow a special way of life which I've developed. It gives you a new kind of freedom, but if you're going to get the kicks, you must follow the system unconditionally.'

She smiled a little bitterly: 'I'm not sure I really need any more kicks.'

'You'll learn more about yourself and life in one month than you have in all your previous twenty-five years.'

'Twenty-eight,' she said indifferently. She placed her half-empty drink on the bar and started to move away restlessly but returned. She stared at the ring of sweat her glass had made on the counter and then looked up at me coldly.

'Where does old coitus-interruptus suddenly get all the time?' she asked. 'The famous half-lay method not getting good results?'

'I've retired,' I said.

'You've *retired*!'

'I've left my wife, my job and my friends and I am on vacation for life.'

She eyed me with new respect: as one citizen of hell to another.

'Jesus, you don't do things in fractions,' she said. But then a cold sneer returned: 'But I become your slave for a month? Huh. I know a lot of people who would pay plenty for that privilege. What do I get in return?'

'In return?' I said, momentarily impressed with the logic of recompense. 'I will do whatever you want for one month following your service to me.'

'*After* I've been *your* slave, big deal. What guarantee do I have?'

'None. Except that when you experience your new life with me and my madness, you'll realize that my form of slavery is desirable.'

'Why don't you be my slave first?'

'Because you wouldn't be an intelligent and imaginative master. I've been practicing this game on myself for years. I'll teach you first and then submit.'

'Maybe,' Linda said to me. 'But first I bat. For the next

twenty-four hours you be my slave. You obey all I say except what might physically harm you or unnecessarily destroy your professional image. The same will be true when I obey you. How's that?'

'All right,' I said.

We looked at each other speculatively.

'How do we seal this agreement?' she asked.

'Total slavery is a new path and we both want to travel new paths – that's what disintegration is all about. I'm satisfied you have the desire and will live up to the agreement.'

'Okay. Have we begun?'

I glanced at my watch. 'We have begun. I obey you until tomorrow evening at nine forty-five. For the sake of anonymity my name is Charlie, Herbie (Flamm).'

'Your name is what I choose.'

'Yes, all right.'

'Follow me.'

Leaving the bar, we hailed a taxi and she took me to an apartment – hers I supposed – on the West Side in the twenties. There, after she had had me fix her a drink, she pulled her knees up under her on the couch and stared up at me with a look of cold analysis.

'Stand on your head.'

With an effort I awkwardly tried to balance myself on my head. Despite my recent efforts at yoga and yoga meditation I collapsed, tried and collapsed. About the fifth time down she said: 'All right, stand up.'

She lit a cigarette, her hand trembling – perhaps from all she had drunk.

'Take off your clothes,' she said.

I took them off.

'Masturbate,' she said quietly.

'It seems like a waste,' I said.

'When I want you to say something I'll say so.'

The command was easier said than done. Like most other red-blooded healthy American youth I had masturbated my way through high school and part of college and after graduating to more frequent social and sexual intercourse with women, had more or less abandoned the habit. I had been pleased to learn when I studied psychology that my mind was not deteriorating after all, but a residual layer of guilt somewhere remained. After all, can we picture Jesus beating his meat? Or Albert Schweitzer? Undoubtedly Linda believed in the intrinsic indignity of masturbation or she wouldn't have assigned it to me. For some reason I didn't find it easy to create images of fantasies of pleasure which would raise the old cannon into firing position. I stood there immobile, trying to think sexy thoughts.

'I said play with yourself.'

Linda must have been under the impression that masturbation was primarily a case of self-caresses. In the immortal words of General MacArthur: 'Nothing could be further from the truth.' Nevertheless, I began fondling myself. It was difficult to maintain a sense of dignity and I therefore stared hard at the floor at Linda's feet.

'Look at me while you're doing it,' she said.

I looked at her. Her cold, tense, bitter face immediately stirred me: I imagined myself sexually revenging myself on her in the month ahead. My cannon bobbed upward, my mind concentrated hard for several minutes on my imaginary encounter, and with careful manual manipulation of the firing mechanism, I blasted off onto the floor. I tried hard to maintain a neutral, dignified expression throughout.

'Lick it up,' she said.

A great weariness flowed through me; I'm sure my face sagged. But I slowly got down on my knees and began licking at the tiny pools of semen.

382

'Look at me,' she said.

Somewhat awkwardly I tried to look at her and accomplish her command at the same time. I noted that the floor between the rugs was shiny and that someone had abandoned a male slipper under an easy chair. I didn't feel too supermanish.

'All right, get up.'

I stood up, still looking at her neutrally, or so I hoped.

'You ought to be ashamed of yourself, Doctor,' she said with a smile.

I became ashamed of myself and my head and shoulders sagged.

'Are these the sort of things you plan to do with me?' she asked.

'No.' I hesitated. 'I imagine men have treated you sadistically before.'

'So I'm not doing too well, huh?'

'Oh no, I think you are. I think you've chosen well, beyond what I'd expected. You've given me a new experience, one I won't forget.'

She stared at me, puffing sporadically on a cigarette; she'd finished her drink.

'What if I were to phone a friend of mine, a queer, and order you to perform sexually with him. Could you do it?'

'Your command is my wish,' I said.

'Does the thought interest or frighten you?'

I introspected obediently.

'It bores and depresses me.'

'Good.'

She had me fix her another drink and went to a telephone and dialed two numbers, asking at both for Jed and hanging up each time disappointed.

'Lie down on the floor, on your face, while I think.'

As I presented myself I began to look back with

383

pleasure at being just old Luke. After a while she said: 'All right, let's go to bed.'

I followed her into a bedroom, neutrally removed her clothes piece by piece at her command and followed her into a narrow double bed. We both lay quietly not touching for a few minutes. I was conscientiously trying not to do a thing unless she commanded me. I felt her hand run down my chest across my belly and come to rest a few inches from my pubic hair. She turned to me and nibbled at my ear, licked my neck, kissed me slowly, wetly, languorously on the mouth and throat. And neck. And chest. And belly. And et cetera. Her maneuvers had a predictable effect despite my recent shameful behavior. She noted the effect, rolled over to the other side of the bed and said nothing else. She tossed and turned a long time and then I guess I must have fallen asleep.

Sometime later I was dreaming that I was going to take a bath and as I sank into the tub I paused to feel the delicious warmth on my balls and penis and awoke to realize that Linda had warmed and stiffened my cock with her mouth. When I touched her hair and groped for her body, she gave one last farewell lick and nibble and came up over me and spread herself and placed me inside her and put her lips to mine and began to churn.

The state of semi-sleep is sometimes like that of being lightly stoned and I let Linda do all the work, which consisted mainly of making waves of wanton wiggles with her hips and her insides, and streams of wanton licks and nibbles on my chest, shoulders and neck, and when she said, 'Pump,' I pumped, clasping in my hands her perfect buttocks like two hot firm grapefruit, and she groaned and became tense and grinding, tense and grinding, grinding and then relaxed.

She lay on me and I dozed off and then was awakened to feel her moving again, I stiff within her, her mouth on my throat and her insides caressing me like waves of hot eels wrapped around me and she moved but I dozed off again to awaken to her hard mouth enclosing my prick in her hands caressing and pinching and generally laying waste the lower erogenous zones and when I touched her hair she groaned and rolled over and took me on top of her and ground away at me and told me to move but not to come so I pumped and swirled and tried to think about Willy May's batting average statistics for the 1950s and after a while her body went limp and she nudged me to roll off her and I did and I dozed off and slept and awakened again already inside her, and she again on top of me moving easily and gently and it must have been near dawn because now I was more awake and began to move too but she said no and tongued and bit my ears, and neck and moved three directions at once down below and when she said okay I dug my fingers into her crack around her buttocks and tried to ram her right over my head and she made a lot of nice noises and I emptied a lake inside her lake and we both moved on awhile and then fell apart into another sleep.

I awoke on my stomach with a knee touching her body someplace; it was well into the morning and I felt hungry. Linda was staring wide-awake at the ceiling.

'I command you,' she said slowly, 'to give me any commands you wish, I will obey them until I cease to feel like it and order you to do something.'

'I'm to be your temporary master?'

'That's right. And I want you to give me orders that you really *want* me to do.'

'Look at me,' I said.

She looked over at me.

'What we're doing is very important. The commands . . .'

'I don't want lectures.'

'I command you to listen to me.'

'You can order me to do a lot of other things, but no lectures. Not in these twenty-four hours.'

'I see,' I said. I paused. 'Return my kiss tenderly, with affection but without lust.'

She sat up beside me, looked coldly into my eyes for a moment and then, softening, brought her lips gently to mine.

I lay back onto the pillow and said: 'Kiss my face with the tenderness you'd feel . . . if my face were the white rose.'

A brief tautness crossed her face before, eyes closed, she framed my face with her hands and lowered her lips to begin gently kissing it.

'Thank you, Linda, that was beautiful. You are beautiful.'

She didn't open her eyes or interrupt her delicate kissing but after a while I said: 'Lie back now on the bed and close your eyes.'

She obeyed. Her face looked more relaxed than I had ever seen it.

'Pretend that I am a prince who loves you with a spiritual devotion beyond anything known outside of the most overdone fairy tale. You are worshipped by him. Your beauty exceeds that of any creature that God has ever created. And you are a perfect perfect person, without spiritual or physical flaw. And the prince, your husband, comes to you now on your wedding night to express at last the pure, religious, sacred, holy passion he has for you. Receive his love with joy.'

I had spoken slowly and hypnotically and began with what I hoped was appropriate delicacy and religiosity to caress her body and touch it with the most spiritual kisses. Spiritual kisses, for the average reader's information, are

386

relatively dry, gentle and poorly aimed: that is, they approach central target zones but always manage to just miss. I was proceeding with increasing devotion and pleasure when her body suddenly disappeared: she had leapt out of bed.

'Stop touching me,' she yelled.

I felt embarrassed and undignified as I had the night before.

'Are you taking away my power already?' I said.

'Yes, yes!' She was trembling.

I remained on my hands and knees looking up at her.

'Get dressed,' she said. 'Get out.'

'But Linda – '

'The deal is over. Off. Get out.'

'Our deal was – '

'Out!' she shouted.

'Okay,' I said, getting down off the bed. 'I'll leave. But at nine forty-five tonight I'll be back. The deal is on.'

'No. No no no. It's off. You're insane. I don't know what you want, but no, never, it's off.'

I slowly dressed and, receiving no new command from a sitting, face-averted Linda, I left.

I remained outside the apartment building, trailed her downtown when she left about an hour later, remained outside an apartment in the Village until five thirty in the afternoon and then followed her to a restaurant, where she ate. She didn't seem to be aware that I was following her or even that I might be following. Organic chemistry picked her up after supper and starting with him, she wandered from bar to bar, picking up friends, losing them, gaining others, drinking heavily and generally doing nothing interesting. At nine forty-five on the dot I moved in. Linda was seated at a table with three men I'd never seen before; she looked drowsy and drunk. One of the men had his hand way up under her skirt. I came to the table, looked hypnotically into her eyes and said: 'It's a quarter to ten now, Linda. Come with me.'

Her blurred eyes cleared briefly, she coughed and wobbled to her feet.

'Hey, where you going, baby?' one of the men asked. Another took hold of her arm.

'Linda is following me,' I said and took a step nearer the guy who had taken her arm and loomed over him and stared down with what I tried to make seem suppressed fury. He released her.

I glared once briefly at each of the other two men and turned and left. With what must have been considerably less dignity than Peter or Matthew following Jesus, Linda followed.

Chapter Fifty-nine

[Being a questioning of Dr Lucius Rhinehart by Inspector Nathaniel Putt of the New York City police regarding the unfortunate escape of thirty-three mental patients from a performance of Hair. *Six of the patients are still at large.]*

'Mr Rhinehart, I – '

'It's *Dr* Rhinehart,' interrupted Dr Mann irritably.

'Oh, excuse me,' said Inspector Putt, ceasing his pacing briefly to stare back at Dr Mann seated beside Dr Rhinehart on a low, ancient couch in the inspector's office. 'Dr Rhinehart, first, I must inform you that you are entitled to have a lawyer present to rep – '

'Lawyers make me nervous.'

' – resent you. I see. All right. Let's proceed. Did you or did you not meet with Eric Cannon in the cafeteria of QSH between the hours of ten thirty and eleven fifteen on August 12?'

'I did.'

'You *did*?'

'I did.'

'I see. For what purpose?'

'He invited me to see him. Since he was a distinguished former patient of mine, I went.'

'What did you talk about?'

'We talked about his desire to see the musical *Hair*. He informed me that many of the patients wanted to see *Hair*.'

'Anything else?'

'I shook the dice and determined that I would do

everything in my power to take Eric and thirty-seven others to see *Hair*.'

'But, Luke,' interrupted Dr Mann. 'You must have realized the incred – '

'Steady, Dr Mann,' said Inspector Putt. 'I'll handle this.' He came and stood directly in front of Dr Rhinehart, his tall, slender body leaning forward, his sharp gray eyes falling coldly on his suspect. 'After you decided to help Cannon and others to leave the hospital, what did you do?'

'I forged Dr Mann's signature on letters to me and to several others and proceeded to effect the temporary release of the patients.'

'You admit this?'

'Of course I admit this. The patients wanted to see *Hair*.'

'But, but – ' said Dr Mann.

'Steady, sir,' interrupted the inspector. 'If I understand your position now correctly, Dr Rhinehart, you are now confessing that you did, in fact, forge Dr Mann's signature, and on your own initiative obtain the release to go to Manhattan of thirty-seven mental patients.'

'Thirty-eight. Absolutely. To see *Hair*.'

'Why did you lie to us before?'

'The Die told me to.'

'The . . .' The inspector stopped and stared at Dr Rhinehart. 'The die . . . yes. Please describe your motivation in taking the patients to *Hair*.'

'The Die told me to.'

'And why did you cover up your trail by forging Dr Mann's signature and pretending to try to see Dr Mann?'

'The Die told me to.'

'Your subsequent lying was – '

'The Die told me to.'

'And now you say – '

'The Die told me to.'

There was a very long silence, during which the inspector stared neutrally at the wall above Dr Rhinehart's head.

'Dr Mann, sir, perhaps you could explain to me precisely what Dr Rhinehart means.'

'He means,' said Dr Mann in a small, tired voice, 'that the dice told him to.'

'A cast of the dice?'

'The dice.'

'Told him to?'

'Told him to.'

'And thus,' said Dr Rhinehart, 'I had no intention of permitting any patients to escape. I plead guilty to forging Dr Mann's signature on trivial letters which, as I understand it, is a misdemeanor, and to showing poor judgment in the handling of mental patients, which, since it is universally practiced by everyone else associated with mental hospitals, is nowhere considered a crime of any sort.'

Inspector Putt looked down on Dr Rhinehart with a cold smile.

'How do we know that you did not agree to help Cannon and Jones and their followers escape?'

'You have my statements and, when you get close enough to talk to him again, you will have Mr Cannon's statements, which, however, will be inadmissible as evidence no matter what he says.'

'Thanks a lot,' the inspector said ironically.

'Does it not occur to you, Inspector, that in telling you that I forged Dr Mann's signature, I may be lying because the Die has told me to?'

'What – '

'That in fact my original statements of innocence may be the true ones?'

'What? What are you suggesting?'

'Simply that yesterday when I heard that you wished to question me again, I created three options for the Die to choose from: that I tell you I had nothing to do with the order to go to *Hair*; that I tell you that I initiated the excursion and forged the orders and thirdly, that I tell you I conspired with Eric Cannon to help him escape. The Die chose the second. But which is the truth seems to me to be still an open question.'

'But, but – '

'Steady, Inspector,' said Dr Mann.

'But – What are you saying?'

'The Die told me to tell you that the Die told me to take the patients on an excursion to *Hair*.'

'But is that story the truth?' asked Inspector Putt, his face somewhat flushed.

Dr Rhinehart shook a die onto the little coffee table in front of him. He examined the result.

'Yes,' he announced.

The inspector's face became redder.

'But how do I know that what you have just said – '

'Precisely,' said Dr Rhinehart.

The inspector moved in a daze back behind his desk and sat down.

'Luke, you're relieved of all your duties at QSH as of today,' said Dr Mann.

'Thank you, Tim.'

'I suppose you're still on our board of management for the simple reason that I don't have the authority to fire you from that, but in our October meeting – '

'You could forge Dr Cobblestone's signature, Tim.'

There was a silence.

'Are there any more questions, Inspector?' Dr Rhinehart asked.

'Do you wish to initiate criminal proceedings against

Dr Rhinehart for forgery, sir?' the inspector asked Dr Mann.

Dr Mann turned and looked a long time into the black, sincere eyes of Dr Rhinehart, who returned his gaze steadily.

'No, Inspector, I'm afraid I can't. For the good of the hospital, for the good of everyone, I wish you'd keep this whole conversation confidential. The public thinks the escape was a conspiracy of hippies and blacks. For all we know, as Dr Rhinehart so kindly points out, it still may *be* a conspiracy of hippies and blacks. They also wouldn't understand why all Dr Rhinehart has done only constitutes a misdemeanor.'

'It confuses me, sir.'

'Precisely. There are some things we must protect the common man from knowing as long as we can.'

'I think you're right.'

'May I go now, fellows?' asked Dr Rhinehart.

Chapter Sixty

The Die is our refuge and strength,
A very present help in trouble.
Therefore will not we fear, though the earth be removed,
And though the mountains be carried into the midst of the
   sea;
Though the waters thereof roar and be troubled,
Though the mountains shake with the swelling thereof,
I had rather be a doorkeeper in the house of my Die
Than to dwell in the tents of consistency.
For the Lord Chance is a sun and a shield:
Chance will give grace and glory and folly and shame:
Nothing will be withheld from them that walk randomly.
O Lord of Chance, My Die, blessed is the man that trusteth
   in thee.

— from *The Book of the Die*

Chapter Sixty-one

'Your free will has made a mess of things,' I told Linda after explaining at length my dice theory. 'Give the Die a try.'

'You sound like a TV commercial,' she said.

Nevertheless, Linda and I began living a dicelife together, the first full dice-couple in history. She knew she'd reached a dead end with her 'real' self and enjoyed trying to express a variety of others. Her sexual and social promiscuity was a good preparation for the dicelife; it disinhibited her in an area which often blocks the whole life system. On the other hand, she had repressed the whole spiritual side of herself: she was as ashamed of having to pray in front of me as would be most other people of having to perform soixante-neuf at the communion rail. But she could do it (and probably the other too). She prayed.

I was tender and warm with her and – when the Die so chose – I treated her like a cheap slut, using her body to satisfy the most perverse desires whim could create and Whim choose. I insisted that her reactions to my tenderness and to my sadism be determined by the Die – whether she responded to my tender love with a bitchy self or with a sweet, giving self, or whether she was a bitter, cynical whore, half-enjoying being abased by me sexually, or a flower deeply crushed by cruelty.

She followed the Die's commands with the intense fanaticism of the new convert to any religion. Together we prayed, wrote poems and prayers, discussed dice therapy and practiced our randoming lives. Although she wanted to give up her sexual promiscuity, I insisted that it was a part of her and must be given a chance to be expressed. One night the Die commanded her to go out and pick up a man and bring him back to the apartment and she did and the Die ordered me to join them and the two of us worked with her diligently for two hours. I shook the Die next morning to see how I was to treat her and it said 'in a surly fashion,' but the Die told her 'not to worry about last night' and to 'love me' no matter how I acted, and she did.

In the fall the Die set us the assignment of infiltrating the numerous encounter groups in New York City. We were trying to introduce some of their group members into diceliving. We varied who we were from one encounter or sensitivity group to the next, sometimes acting as a couple, sometimes as strangers.

I remember one time in particular: a weekend marathon we attended at the Fire Island Sensitivity Training Headquarters of Encounter Resources Society in late October, 1969.

As with most psychotherapies, FISTH provided mental first aid by the prospective rich (the therapists) for the already rich (the patients), and the dozen people at this marathon were representative Americans: a magazine editor, a fashion designer, two corporation executives, a tax lawyer, three well-to-do housewives, one stockbroker, a freelance writer, a minor TV personality and a mad psychiatrist – seven men and five women, plus I should add, two young hippies present tuition-free, as an extra added attraction for the two-hundred-dollar weekend paying clients. I was one of the two corporation executives and Lil a well-to-do housewife (divorced). The leaders were Scott (small, compact, athletic) and Marya (tall, lithe, ethereal), both of whom were fully qualified psychotherapists. Our main meeting place was the huge living room of a huge Victorian house on the ocean outside Quoquam, Fire Island.

Friday evening and all day Saturday we did a few loosening-up exercises to get to know each other better: we played pitch and catch for a while with the hippie girl; we had a tug of war; we stared into each other's eyes like used-car salesmen; we symbolically gangbanged the woman who had the first crying jag: shouted shitheads and cocksuckers at each other for an invigorating half-hour; played musical chairs with half the group being sitters and the other half being chairs; played 'get the guest' with the minor TV personality, by taking turns seeing who could be the most obnoxious to her; played blind man's buff with everybody blind – except for Marya, who stood by whispering hoarsely, 'Really FEEL him, Joan, put your HANDS on him.'

By Saturday evening we were exhausted, but felt very close to one another and very liberated for doing publicly with strangers what previously we had only done privately with friends: namely, feeling each other up and calling each other shitheads and cocksuckers. The more bizarre games reminded me pleasantly of life on a dull day in a Dice Center, but every time I'd begin to relax and enjoy some pattern-breaking event, one of our leaders would start getting us to talk honestly about our feelings and it would begin to rain clichés.

So by close to midnight we were all lying in various informal states of decomposition against the walls of the bare living room watching the spontaneous light-show the firelight was making on our faces from the blazing logs, while Marya tried to get the other corporation executive, a balding little man named Henry Hopper, to open up about his *true* feelings. I'd just called him a 'liberal fink,' Linda had called him a 'virile looking hunk of man,' and the hippie girl had called him a 'capitalist pig.' For some reason Hopper was maintaining that he was confused in his feelings. Two or three of the group were trying to help Marya, assuming that we were beginning another round of 'get the guest,' but many of the others looked tired and a bit bored. Nonetheless, Marya, a slender, bright-eyed fanatic on the subject of honesty, pressed onward in a soft husky voice that reminded me of a bad actress doing a bedroom scene.

'Just tell us, Hank,' she said. 'Let it come out.'

'Frankly, I don't feel like saying anything right now.' He was nervously breaking open peanut shells and eating peanuts.

'You're chicken, Hank,' a big, beefy tax lawyer contributed.

'I'm not chicken,' Mr Hopper said in a quiet voice. 'I'm just scared shitless.' Linda and I and Mr Hopper were the only ones who laughed.

'Humor is a defense mechanism, Hank,' leader Marya said. '*Why* are you scared?' she asked, her blue eyes blazing sincerely.

'I guess I'm afraid the group won't like me as much if I tell them I think we're wasting our time.'

'Right,' said Marya, smiling with encouragement.

Mr Hopper just looked at the floor and arranged the peanut shells on the rug in front of him.

'You're not sharing with us, Hank,' Marya said after a while. She smiled. 'You don't trust us.'

Mr Hopper just stared at the floor, the firelight reflecting brightly off his balding head.

After another few minutes of unsuccessful sniping, co-leader Scott suggested we try some trust exercises with Hank: namely, play pitch and catch with him to help him come to trust us. So we formed a circle and tossed him around among ourselves until he had a blissful smile on his face, and then Marya had him lowered to the floor, where she knelt by him and, smiling with half-closed eyes, suggested in a soft voice that he tell us the truth about everything. Before he could begin, though, Linda interrupted.

'Lie,' she said.

'Beg pardon,' he said, still smiling dreamily from the flowing caresses of being manipulated by a roomful of people.

'Tell lies,' Linda said. 'It's much easier.' She was seated against the wall opposite the fire with her feet tucked under her.

'Why, Linda, what are you saying?' Marya asked.

'I'm suggesting Hank really let go and just lie to us. Tell us whatever he feels like saying with no inhibiting effort to get at some illusion we call truth.'

'Why are you afraid of truth, Linda?' Marya asked, smiling. Her smile had begun to remind me of Dr Felloni's nod.

'I'm not afraid of truth,' Linda answered with a slow drawl, half-imitating Marya's. 'I just find it far less fun and far less liberating than lies.'

'You're sick,' contributed the burly tax lawyer.

'Oh, I don't know,' I said from my corner of the room. 'Huck Finn was the greatest liar in American literature and he seemed to have a lot of fun and be pretty liberated.'

The sudden appearance of two challengers to the god-head of honesty was unprecedented.

'Let's get back to Mr Hopper,' said co-leader Scott pleasantly. 'Tell us now, Hank, why were you so scared before?'

Mr Hopper answered promptly: 'I was scared because you wanted truth, and both the answers I felt like making seemed to me to be half-lies. I was confused.'

'Confusion is only a symptom of repression,' Marya said, smiling. 'You *know* there are unpleasant aspects to your true feelings which you're ashamed of. But if you'd just share them with us, they'd no longer bug you.'

'Lie about them,' Linda said, stretching her lovely legs into the middle of the room. 'Exaggerate. Fantasize. Make up some junk that you think will entertain us.'

'Why do you want the spotlight?' Marya, smiling and tense, asked Linda.

'I enjoy lying,' Linda answered. 'And if I can' talk, I can't lie.'

'Ah come on,' said the magazine editor. 'What's so much fun about lying?'

'What's so much fun about pretending to be honest?' she replied.

'We're not aware that we're pretending, Linda,' Scott said.

'Maybe that's why you're all tense,' Linda countered.

Since Linda was more relaxed at this point than either Marya or Scott, it was one-upmanship *parfait*, and several people smiled.

'Lies are a way of covering up,' Marya said.

'Being honest and truthful the way we do here is like cheap striptease, a lot of motion to reveal that there are boobs and pricks and asses in the world, something we all knew in the first place.'

'Aren't boobs and pricks beautiful, Linda?' asked Marya in her softest and most sincere voice.

'Sometimes yes, sometimes no. Depends on which illusion I feel like supporting.'

'Our genitalia are always beautiful,' Marya said.

'You obviously haven't looked lately,' Linda answered, yawning.

'I doubt you've ever really faced your sexual shame and guilt,' Marya said.

'I have and they bore me,' replied Linda, smothering another yawn.

'Boredom is – '

'Are your breasts and cunt beautiful?' Linda asked Marya abruptly.

'Yes, and so are yours.'

'Then show us your beautiful genitalia.'

No one was particularly bored now. Marya sat with her back to the fire and a fixed smile on her face, staring vaguely at Linda. Scott cleared his throat noisily and leaned forward to the rescue.

'This isn't a beauty contest, Linda,' he said. 'You're obviously trying – '

'Marya has a beautiful cunt. She's not ashamed of it. We're not supposed to be ashamed of it. Let's see it.'

'I don't think this is an appropriate occasion,' Marya said. She wasn't smiling.

'A thing of beauty is a joy forever,' Linda replied. 'Don't deny us.'

'I partly feel that my role as leader – '

'*Partly!*' Linda said, waking up. '*Partly?* You mean in fact that feelings and truth can be broken into parts?' Linda began taking off her blouse.

'I don't wish to cause embarrassment to anyone here,' Marya said. 'Our purpose is to get at real attitudes, real feelings, to . . . ah . . . ah, to explore . . . ah . . .'

But no one was paying much attention, since Linda, with serene concentration, had now removed her bra and her skirt and her panties and was sitting nude, legs apart, with her back to the wall. When she finished she had to smother another yawn. The firelight made a decidedly splendid effect on her white skin. For a while there was silence.

'Are you embarrassed, Linda?' Marya asked quietly, her face again frozen in a smile.

Linda sat silently with her back to the wall, looking at the rug between her legs. Tears began to form in her eyes. She suddenly drew up her knees, put her face into her hands and sobbed.

'Oh yes, yes,' she said. 'I'm ashamed! I'm ashamed!' She was crying.

No one spoke or moved.

'You needn't feel that way,' Marya said, getting on her knees and beginning to crawl toward Linda.

'My body is ugly ugly ugly,' Linda sobbed. 'I can't stand it.'

'I don't think it's ugly,' said Mr Hopper, pushing his peanuts away from him off to the side.

'It's not ugly, Linda,' Marya said, putting a hand on her shoulder.

'It is. It is. I'm a slut.'

'Don't be silly. You can't really feel that.'

'I can't?' Linda asked, raising her head with a startled expression.

'Your body is beautiful,' Marya added.

'Yeah, I agree,' said Linda, abruptly sitting back and stretching out her legs again. 'Good round teats, good firm ass, juicy cunt. Nothing to complain about. Anyone want a feel?'

Everyone was caught leaning forward sympathetically with his mouth open and eyes bulging and nothing to say.

'If it's beautiful, touch it, Marya,' Linda added.

'I'll volunteer,' Mr Hopper said.

'Not yet, Hant,' Linda said, smiling affectionately at him. 'Marya's got a thing about beautiful genitalia.'

We all looked at Marya, who hesitated, and, then, with tight-lipped determination, put her hands delicately on Linda's shoulders, then her breasts. Her face relaxed a bit and she slid her hands down to the tummy and across the pubic hair and onto the thighs.

'You're lovely, Linda,' she said, sitting back on her heels and smiling a relaxed, almost triumphant smile.

'Would you like to suck me off?' Linda asked.

'No . . . no thank you,' Marya answered, flushing.

'Your love of beauty and all.'

'Is it my turn?' asked Mr Hopper.

'What are you trying to prove?' Scott snapped out at Linda.

Linda looked over at him and patted Marya on her bare knee.

'Nothing,' she said to Scott. 'I just feel like acting the way I'm acting.'

'You admit you're just acting?' he asked.

'Of course,' she answered. Then she sat up and directed her sincere blue eyes at Mr Hopper. 'I'm afraid a part of you is embarrassed by all this, right, Hank?'

'Yes,' he said, and he smiled nervously.

'But part of you is enjoying it.'

He laughed.

'Part of you thinks I'm a nervy bitch.'

He hesitated and then nodded.

'And part of you thinks I'm the most honest one here.'

'You're damn right,' he answered abruptly.

'Which one is the real you?'

He frowned and seemed to be concentrating on self-analysis.

'I guess the *real* me is the one – '

'Oh shit, Hank. You're not being honest.'

'I'm not? I didn't even tell you which one – '

'But is one any more real than the next?'

'You sophist whore!' I blurted out.

'What's with you, Big Daddy?' Linda asked.

'You're a sick sophist hypocritical Communist nihilist slut.'

'You're a big handsome brainless nobody.'

'Just because you're pretty, you seduce poor Hopper into liking you. But the *real* Hopper knows you for what you are: a cheap, neurotic two-bit sophist anti-American divorcée.'

'Now just a minute – ' Scott interrupted, leaning toward me.

'But I know her type, Scott,' I went on. 'Stagestruck since she first grew pubic hair, subverting her way into good men's pants with cheap, five-and-dime-store sophist sex techniques, and ruining the lives of one hundred percent American men. We all know her: nothing but a diseased anarchist hippie uptight sophist bitch.'

Linda's mouth twisted grotesquely, tears formed again in her eyes and she finally burst into tears, rolling onto her stomach and flexing her buttock muscles impressively in grief. She sobbed and sobbed.

'Oh I know, I know,' she said finally between gasps. 'I am a slut, I *am*. You've seen the *real* me. Take my body and do what you will.'

'Jesus, the dame is nuts,' said the burly tax lawyer.

'Should we comfort her,' asked Mr Hopper.

'Stop pretending!' snapped Scott. 'We know you don't *really* feel guilty.'

But Linda, still crying, was getting back into her clothes. When dressed again, she curled up in a corner in the foetal position. The room was very quiet.

'I know that type,' I said confidently. 'A hot, slimy, ball-breaking one-time sophist feminist lay, but nervous as a vibrator.'

'But which is the real Linda?' Mr Hopper said dreamily to no one in particular.

'Who cares?' I sneered.

'Who cares?' echoed Linda, sitting up again and yawning. Then she leaned toward Mr Hopper.

404

'What are your true feelings now, Hank?' she asked him.

For a moment the question caught him off guard; then he smiled.

'Happy confusion,' he said loudly.

'And how do *you* feel now, Linda?' asked Marya, but the question was met by six or seven groans from group members seated around the room.

Linda flipped a pair of green dice out onto the middle of the rug and, after looking mischievously at each of us in turn, asked quietly:

'Anyone want to play some games?'

Linda was marvelous. What people needed in these groups was someone to let himself go so completely that inhibitions were knocked away. Linda could strip, simulate all kinds of love, could rage, cry, could argue convincingly, all in such rapid succession that she soon made everyone experience existence inside the group as a game; nothing seemed to matter. After we'd gotten most of the members of an encounter group to splinter off the original leader and meet only with us (as happened on Fire Island that weekend), they came to see that with us truth and honesty were irrelevant; we approved good acting and bad, role playing and out-of-role playing, baddie roles and goodie roles, truth and lies.

When one individual would try to pretend to be his 'real' self and call the others back to 'reality,' we would try to encourage our diceplayers to ignore him and go right on playing their dice-dictated roles. When someone else, as the result of playing out some role dammed up inside him for years, broke down and cried, the group would at first rally round the bawler to reassure him, as they'd gotten used to doing in traditional encounter groups. We tried to show them that this was the worst thing they could do; the crier should be ignored or be responded to solely within the roles that were already being played.

We wanted them to come to realize that neither 'immorality' nor 'emotional breakdowns' earn either condemnation or pity except when the Die so dictates. We wanted them to come to see that in group diceplay they are free of the usual games, rules and behavior patterns. Everything is fake. Nothing is real. No one – least of all us, the leaders – is reliable. When a person becomes reassured that he lives in a totally valueless, unreal, unstable, inconsistent world, he becomes free to be fully all of his selves – as the dice dictate. In those cases when the other group members respond conventionally to someone's breakdown, our work is undone: the sufferer feels frightened and ashamed. He believes that the 'real world' and its conventional attitudes exist even in group diceplay.

And it's his illusions about what constitutes the real world which are inhibiting him. His 'reality,' his 'reason,' his 'society': these are what must be destroyed.

All that fall Linda and I did our very best.

In addition to our work with various groups, Linda went to work on H.J. Wipple, a philanthropist whom I'd gotten interested in building a Dice Center for us in Southern California, and construction soon speeded up considerably. Work even began in renovating a boys' camp in the Catskills for a second Center. The world was getting ready for dicepeople.

Chapter Sixty-two

Naturally Dr Rhinehart felt a little guilty about leaving his wife and children without the slightest hint of when he'd return, but he consulted the Die, which advised him to forget about it. Then four months after he'd left home, a random Whim chose one of his random whims and ordered him to return to his apartment and try to seduce his wife.

Mrs Rhinehart greeted him at two o'clock in the afternoon in a stylish new pants suit he'd never seen before and a cocktail in her hand.

'I've got a visitor now, Luke,' she said quietly. 'If you want to see me come back about four.'

It was not precisely the greeting Dr Rhinehart had expected after four months of mysterious disappearance, and while he was rallying his mental faculties for a suitable riposte he discovered the door had gently been closed in his face.

Two hours later he tried again.

'Oh, it's you,' said Mrs Rhinehart as she might have greeted a plumber just back with a fresh tool. 'Come on in.'

'Thank you,' said Dr Rhinehart with dignity.

His wife walked ahead of him into the living room and offered him a seat, herself leaning against a new desk covered with papers and books. Dr Rhinehart stood dramatically in the middle of the room and looked intently at his wife.

'Where you been?' she asked, with a tone of bored interest discouragingly close to what she might have used asking her son Larry the same question after he'd been out of the house for twenty minutes.

'The dice told me to leave you, Lil, and . . . well, I left.'

'Yes. I figured as much. What are you doing these days?'

Speechless for a few seconds, Dr Rhinehart nevertheless managed to look intently at his wife.

'I'm doing a lot of work these days with group dice therapy.'

'How nice,' Mrs Rhinehart said. She moved away from the desk over in front of a new painting Dr Rhinehart had never seen before and glanced at some mail which was lying on a table beneath the painting. Then she turned back to him.

'Part of me has missed you, Luke.' She smiled warmly at him. 'And part of me hasn't.'

'Yeah, me too.'

'Part of me was mad mad mad,' she went on, frowning. 'And part of me,' she smiled again, 'was glad glad glad.'

'Really?'

'Yes. Fred Boyd helped me let go of the mad mad mad business and that's just left me with . . . the other.'

'How'd Fred do it?'

'After I'd cried and complained and raged for an hour or so two days after you'd left, he said to me: "You ought to consider suicide, Lil."' Lil paused to smile at the memory. 'That sort of caught my attention so to speak, and he went on to say: "Shake the dice also to see whether you should try to kill Luke."'

'Good friend, old Fred,' Dr Rhinehart interjected, and began pacing nervously back and forth in front of his wife.

'Another option he suggested was that I divorce you and try to marry him.'

'One of my *real* pals.'

408

'Or also, that I not divorce you but begin sleeping with him.'

'Greater love hath no man than this: that he lay down his best friend's wife – '

'He then gave me a sincere impassioned lecture on how I had let my compulsive tie to you limit me in every way, let it starve all the creative and imaginative selves that would otherwise live.'

'My own theories turned against me.'

'So I shook a Die and Fred and I have been enjoying each other ever since.'

Dr Rhinehart stopped his pacing and stared.

'Exactly what does that mean?' he asked.

'I'm trying to state the matter delicately so you won't be upset.'

'Thanks a lot. Are you serious?'

'I consulted the Die and It told me to be serious with you.'

'You and Fred are now . . . lovers?'

'That's what the novels call it.'

Dr Rhinehart looked at the floor for a while (the realization that it was a new rug registered dimly on his consciousness), then back up at his wife.

'How about that?' he said.

'It's pretty good, as a matter of fact,' Lil replied. 'Just the other night – '

'Er no, Lil, the details really aren't necessary. I'm . . . hmmm. I'm . . . well, what else is new?'

'I'm enrolled this fall at Columbia Law School.'

'You're *what*?'

'I gave the dice a choice of several of my lifelong daydreams and they chose that I become a lawyer. Don't you want me to broaden myself?'

'But *law* school!' Dr Rhinehart said.

'Oh Luke, for all your supposed liberation you've still got an image of me as a helpless beautiful female.'

'But you know I can't stand lawyers.'

'True, but have you ever slept with one?'

Dr Rhinehart shook his head dazedly.

'You're supposed to be heartbroken, distraught, anxiety filled, helpless, desperate, incompet – '

'Oh stuff that shit,' Mrs Rhinehart said.

'Did Fred teach you such language?'

'Don't be a child.'

'True,' Dr Rhinehart said, suddenly collapsing in a heap on the couch – it, he was glad to note, remained the same as from his old life. 'I'm proud of you, Lil.'

'You can stuff that too.'

'You're showing real independence.'

'Don't bother, Luke,' Mrs Rhinehart said. 'If I needed your praise I wouldn't *be* independent.'

'Are you wearing a bra?'

'If you have to ask, it's not worth asking.'

'The Die told me to re-seduce you, but I can't see even where to begin.' He looked up at her as she leaned against against her new desk. She was smoking and her elbows stuck out sharply and she didn't look too mousy. 'I'm not in the mood for a knee in the groin.'

Mrs Rhinehart dropped a die onto the desk beside her and after looking at it said quietly to her husband:

'Out you go, Luke.'

'Where am I going?'

'Just out.'

'But I haven't seduced you yet.'

'You've tried and failed. Now you're leaving.'

'I haven't seen my children. How is my diceboy Larry?'

'Your diceboy Larry is fine. I told him when he came home from school this afternoon that you might be

410

dropping by, but he had an important touch-football game and had to rush away.'

'Is he practicing the dicelife, like a good boy?'

'Not very much. He says his teachers won't recognize dice decisions as a legitimate excuse for not doing homework. Now out, Luke, you've got to go.'

Dr Rhinehart looked away out the window and sighed. Then he dropped a die on the couch beside him and looked at it.

'I refuse to leave,' he said.

Mrs Rhinehart walked out of the room and returned with a pistol.

'The die told me to make you leave. Since you deserted me, legally you have no right to be in this room without my permission.'

'Ahh, but my die told me to try to stay.'

Mrs Rhinehart consulted a die on the desk beside her.

'I'm counting to five and if you're not out of here I'm going to fire.'

'Don't be silly, Lil,' Dr Rhinehart replied, smiling. 'I'm not – '

'Two, three . . .'

'Doing anything which merits such extreme measures. It seems to me – '

BAM!! The noise from the gun shook the whole room.

Dr Rhinehart snapped up from the couch without undue delay and began moving toward the door.

'A hole on the couch is – ' he began, trying to smile, but Mrs Rhinehart had consulted the Die again and was counting to five and, having only a limited desire to hear her reach the end of the recitation, Dr Rhinehart sprinted with all deliberate speed to the door and left.

Chapter Sixty-three

It must be admitted that the thought of penetrating the hairy anus of a man or of being so penetrated held all the allure of giving or receiving an enema on the dais before the American Association of Practicing Psychiatrists. The thought of caressing, kissing and mouthing a male penis somehow dimly reminded me of being forced at the age of six or seven to eat baked macaroni.

On the other hand, the occasional fantasy of being a woman writhing beneath some dim male was exciting – until the dim male grew a beard (shaven or not), a hairy chest, hairy buttocks and an ugly vein-bulging penis. Then I lost interest. Being a female could, in an occasional fantasy, be exciting. Being a male having 'intercourse' with any precisely seen male seemed disgusting.

All of this I knew long before that November day in my habit-breaking life that the Die definitely asked me to shoulder the burden of going out into the world and being had. I went to the Lower East Side, where Linda told me I could find several gay bars, one of whose names in particular I remembered: Gordo's.

At about 10.30 P.M. I entered Gordo's, a perfectly harmless-looking bar, and was shocked to see men and women sitting together drinking. Moreover, there were only seven or eight people in the place. No one even looked at me. I ordered a beer and began doing research in my memory to see if I had in fact repressed or misheard the true name of the gay bar. Gordon's? Sordo's? Sodom's? Gorki's? Mordo's? Gorgon's? Gorgon's! What a perfect name for a gay place! I went to a pay phone and searched for Gorgon in the Manhattan directory. I drew a blank. Surprised and dejected, I sat in the booth and brooded out at the ineptly normal bar. Four young men moved suddenly past the glass door of my booth toward the front of the bar. Where had they come from?

I left the booth and wandered toward the back, where I saw some stairs leading to the upper floors; from above I heard music. I wandered up, met the steely gaze of some ex-Cleveland Brown defensive tackle who was sitting at the head of the stairs and moved past him into a small anteroom. From behind large double doors came the music. I opened them and walked in.

Three feet from me rocked two young men engaged in a passionate, deep-throated kiss. I felt as if I had been half-slammed, half-caressed in the belly with a slippery bagful of wet cunts.

I moved past them into a melee of dancing boys and men and made my way to a vacant table. It was about two inches by three and held the remains of three beer bottles, eleven cigarettes and a lipstick. After staring noncommittally and unseeingly into the chaos of noise, smoke and males for a minute or two, a young man asked me if I wanted a drink and I ordered a beer. Glancing around, I saw that at the two dozen tables only a few people were now sitting, all men except for one middle-aged couple immediately to my right. The man had a sickly smile on his face and the woman looked cool and amused. When I looked over, she stared at me as she might at an inmate in a mental hospital, her husband simply appeared nervous; I winked at him.

My eyes couldn't seem to focus on any single person or couple but only on the torsos of males dancing. Finally, I raised my eyes and looked at the two men dancing nearest to me. The man, or rather the tallest of the two men, was in his late twenties, rather ruggedly homely, with a crooked nose and bushy eyebrows. The other person was shorter, younger and very good-looking in a young Peter Fonda sort of way. They were dancing rather disinterestedly and looking past each other at other couples. As I was watching, the younger man suddenly turned his eyes on me, lowered his lashes and raised one shoulder and gave me a sensual feminine sexual parting of moist lips. It was a sexual shock. It was one of the most lecherous and exciting looks I had ever received.

Ping! Did this mean that all my life I had secretly been a latent homosexual? Did my sexual response to a female come-on in a male body imply healthy heterosexuality, debased perversion or healthy bisexuality?

It was time to take stock. Was it the intention of the Die that I be active or passive: Zeus to Ganymede or Hart Crane to a sailor? Was I to be Socrates entering into the old dialogue with one of his boys, or Genet supine and spread before the onslaught of some six-foot walking erection? The Die had been ambiguous, but it seemed more appropriate and habit breaking to be passive and feminine than aggressive and masculine. But where would I find a Zeus to my six-foot-four Ganymede? Where was the Great Cock that could split me in two? It would be much easier to find someone who saw in me the Awful Erection of his dreams. But ease was irrelevant. I needed to be a woman, to play the role of a woman. Even if I loomed over my husband like Mount Everest over a stunted shrub I must learn to spread myself supine before him. My femininity must be given freedom. The dice man could never be complete until he was a woman.

'Can I buy you a drink?' the man asked, standing above me like Everest above a stunted shrub. It was the ex-Cleveland Brown defensive tackle, and he looked down at me with world-weary knowingness. And a smile.

Chapter Sixty-four

You must never question the wisdom of the Die. His ways are inscrutable. He leads you by the hand into an abyss and, lo, it is a fertile plain. You stagger beneath the burden he places upon you and, behold, you soar. The Die never deviates from the Tao, nor do you.

The desire to manipulate your surrender to the Die so that you may gain from it is futile. Such surrender never frees you from the pains of the ego. You must give up all your struggling, all your purposes, values and goals, and then, only then, when you have given up the belief that you can use the Die to gain some ego end, will you discover liberation from your burdens and your life flow free.

There is no compromise: you must surrender everything.

– from *The Book of the Die*

Chapter Sixty-five

'I'm a virgin,' I said in a thin, delicate voice. 'Please be gentle.'

Chapter Sixty-six

There are two paths: you use the Die, or you let the Die use you.

    – from *The Book of the Die*

Chapter Sixty-seven

'Christ,' I said heavily, 'am I going to be sore.'

Chapter Sixty-eight

Dear Dr Rhinehart,

I admire your work so much. My husband and I do our dice exercises every morning after breakfast and again before bedtime and we feel years younger. When are you going to have your own TV show? Before we began playing with emotional roulette and Exercise K we almost never spoke to each other, but now we're always shouting or laughing even when we're not playing dice games. Could you please give us some advice as to how we might better bring up our daughter Ginny to serve the Die?

She's a willful girl and doesn't say her prayers to It regular and is almost always the same sweet shy girl and frankly we're worried. We've tried to get her to do the dice exercises with us in the morning or by herself, but nothing seems to work. My husband beats her every now and then when the Die says to but it doesn't help much either. The only dicedoctor in these parts left for Antarctica three months ago so we have no one to turn to but you.

Yours by Chance,
Mrs A.J. Kempton,
(Missouri)

Dear Dr Rhinehart

I discovered my sixteen-year-old daughter on our living room couch with the postman this afternoon, and she referred me to you. What the hell is this all about?

Sincerely Yours,
John Rush

Chapter Sixty-nine

The birth of the first dicebaby in the world was I suppose, an event of some historical importance. It was just after Christmas in 1969 that I got a phone call from Arlene announcing that she and Jake were rushing off to the hospital to have our dicebaby. They knew where I could be reached, since I'd stopped off two days before to give them each a Christmas present: Arlene a set of the *Encyclopedia Brittanica* and Jake a rakish bathing suit (Not my will, O Die, but Thy will be done).

When I arrived, Arlene was still in labor, and her private room was something of a messy jumble from two huge opened suitcases, filled, as far as I could see, entirely with baby clothes. I noticed at least thirty diapers with two green dice branded on each, and many of the pajamas, shirts, pants and tiny baby socks seemed to be similarly monogramed. I found this to be in bad taste and told Arlene so while she was in the middle of a labor pain, but when she stopped groaning (she claimed it was mostly pleasurable), she assured me the Die had picked a one-in-three shot and ordered the monograms.

The three of us chatted about our hopes for the baby, with Arlene doing most of the talking. She told us that she had given 215 chances in 216 that she practice natural childbirth and breast-feed the child and that much to her delight the Die had chosen that she should do both. But most of her talk was about when the child should be potty trained and when it should be dicetrained.

'We've got to start early,' Arlene kept saying. 'I don't

want our baby corrupted by society the way I was for thirty-five years.'

'Still, Arlene,' I said, 'for the first two or three years I think the child can develop randomly without using the dice.'

'No, Luke, it wouldn't be fair to him,' she replied. 'It would be like keeping candy away from him.'

'But a child tends to express all his minority impulses – at least until he gets to school. They may batten down the hatches there.'

'Perhaps, Lukie,' she said, 'but he'll see me casting dice to see which breast he gets or whether we go for a walk or whether he naps, and he'll feel left out. What I'd like to do is . . .'

But she went into such a long labor pain and it came so soon after the previous one that Jake buzzed for the nurse and they wheeled her off to the delivery room. Jake and I trailed after her down the hall.

'I don't know, Luke,' Jake said after a while, squinting up at me hopefully. 'I think this dice business may be getting out of hand.'

'I think so too,' I said.

'The dice may be good for us uptight adults, but I'm not sure about two-year-olds.'

'I agree.'

'She could confuse the poor kid before he developed any patterns to break.'

'Right.'

'It's possible the kid might grow up to be something of a weirdie.'

'True. Or worse yet, he might end up rebelling against diceliving and opt for permanent conformity to the dominant social norm.'

'Hey, that's a possibility. You think he might?'

'Sure,' I said. 'Boys always rebel against their mothers.'

Jake paused in his pacing and I stopped beside him and looked down; he was staring at the floor.

'I suppose a little dicethrowing won't hurt him,' he said slowly.

'And in any case, who cares?'

Jake looked sharply up at me.

'Aren't you concerned about your baby?' he asked.

'Now, remember, Jake, it's *our* baby, not mine. Just because the dice told Arlene to tell you that I'm the father doesn't mean necessarily that I am.'

'Hey, that's right.'

'You may actually be the father but the dice told Arlene to lie.'

'That's a good point, Luke.'

'Or she may have been sleeping with dozens of guys that month and not know *who* the actual father is.'

He looked down at the floor again.

'Thanks for the reassurance,' he said.

'So let's just call it our baby.'

'Let's just call it hers.'

Chapter Seventy

Dear Dr Rhinehart,

I have been a fan of yours ever since I read that interview in *Playboy*. I have been trying to practice the dicelife now for almost a year but have run into several problems which I hoped you might be able to help me with. First, I was wondering if it were really necessary or important to follow the Die no matter what it says. I mean sometimes it vetoes something I really want to do or chooses the most absurd of the options I've created for it. I've found that disobeying the Die in such cases makes me feel real good, as if I were getting something for free. I find the Die most helpful in doing the things I want to do, mostly making girls. It's a big help there, since I never feel guilty when I try something that doesn't work since the Die told me to do it. And I don't feel guilty when it does work since if the girl gets knocked up, it was the Die that did it. But why do you keep saying one should always follow the Die? And why bother to expand the areas it makes decisions in? I've got a good thing going and find a lot of your stuff distracts me from my end if you know what I mean.

Also I must warn you that when my girl took up using the dice and we tried some of those dice sex exercises some real problems developed. The sex exercises were fine, but my girl keeps telling me the Die won't let her see me anymore for a while. Sometimes she makes a date and then breaks it, blaming the Die. Aren't there some sort of rules I can impose on her? Do you have a code of dice ethics for girls I could show her?

Also another girl I introduced to the dicelife began insisting that I ought to include as an option that I marry her. I only give it one chance in thirty-six, but she insists I cast the dice about it every time I go out with her. What is the probability of my losing if I date her ten more times? Twenty? Please include a table or graph if possible.

You've got some good ideas, but I hope you do more thinking

about how special rules might be developed for girl dicepeople.
I'm getting worried.

Sincerely,
George Doog

Chapter Seventy-one

'It's a girl,' Jake said, smiling dazedly.

'I know, Jake. Congratulations.'

'Edgarina,' he went on. 'Edgarina Ecstein.' He looked up at me. 'Who named her that?'

'Don't ask silly questions. The baby's healthy, Arlene's healthy, I'm healthy: that's what counts.'

'You're right,' he said. 'But do daughters rebel against their mothers too?'

'Here she comes,' I said.

Two nurses wheeled Arlene down the hall and past us into her room and, after she'd settled back into bed, they brought the baby in for her to hold. Jake and I watched benevolently. The baby squirmed a bit and hissed but didn't say much.

'How'd it go, Arlene?' I asked.

'It was a snap,' she said, cuddling the child against her swollen breasts and smiling ecstatically. She stared at her infant and smiled and smiled.

'Doesn't she look just like Eleanor Roosevelt as a baby?' she said.

Jake and I looked; I think we both concluded it might be true.

'Edgarina has dignity,' I said.

'She's born for greatness,' Arlene said, kissing the top of the baby's head. 'Die willing.'

'Or nothingness,' I said. 'You don't want to force any patterns on her, Arlene.'

'Except for making her cast the dice about everything she does, I plan to let her be entirely free.'

'Oh Jesusjesus,' said Jake.

'Cheer up, Jake,' I said, putting my arm around him. 'Don't you realize that as a scientist you're getting in on the ground floor of something which is of immense scientific importance?'

'Maybe,' he said.

'No matter how Edgarina turns out under Arlene's regime, it's scientifically significant. Genius or psychotic, something new has been demonstrated.'

Jake perked up a bit.

'I suppose you're right,' he said.

'This may be your greatest case study since "The Case of the Six-Sided Man."'

Jake looked up at me, beaming.

'Maybe I ought to do some more experimenting with the dicelife,' he said.

'You'll need a title, of course,' I went on.

'You certainly should,' Arlene snapped at Jake. 'Any father of Edgarina Ecstein had better be a full-fledged diceperson or I'll disown and discredit him.'

Jake sighed.

'That won't be necessary, honey,' he said.

'"A Case of Random Rearing,"' I suggested. 'Or perhaps, "Dieper Training."'

Jake shook his head slowly and then squinted aggressively up at me.

'Don't bother trying, Luke. It's beyond your depth. The title has already been made: "The Case of the Child of Whim."' He sighed. 'The book may take a little longer.'

Chapter Seventy-two

The sun dazzled down and warmed and softened my mountain of flesh. I writhed myself deeper into the hot sand, feeling the rays above like long-range caresses on my skin. Linda lay beside me, bikinied and beautiful, her lovely breasts breathing skyward against the strip of cloth that was theoretically a bikini top like two fruit growing and shrinking in a speeded-up biological film of the growing process. She had been reading Stendhal's *The Charterhouse of Parma* and we had been talking about group dice therapy, but for the last fifteen minutes we had both lain silently, enjoying the solitude of the vast expanse of the Bahamas beach and the love-making of the hot touch of the sun. It was February in New York, but summer here.

'What do you really *want*, Luke?' Linda suddenly asked. From the smudge at the corner of my half-closed eyes I gathered she had sat up or raised herself on an elbow.

'Want?' I said, thinking. The rhythmic thud of the surf thirty yards away made me long for a swim, but we'd only been out of the water for fifteen minutes and were only just now dry.

'Everything, I guess,' I finally said. 'To be everybody and do everything.'

She tossed her hair back away from her face with one hand and said:

'That's modest of you.'

'Probably.'

A sea gull careered into my reduced field of vision and then out again.

'You've been sort of quiet today. Just another dice decision?'

'I've just been sleepy all the time.'

'My ass. Is it a dice decision?'

'What difference does it make?'

She was definitely sitting up, her legs spread, leaning back on her upright arms.

'I sometimes wonder what *you* want, not the dice – '

'Who's me?'

'That's what I want to know.'

I sat up, blinking my eyes and looking toward the ocean past the rise of sand in front of me. Without my glasses it was only tan blur and blue blur.

'But don't you see,' I said. 'To know "me" that way is to limit me, cement me into something stonelike and predictable.'

'Diceshit! I just want to know a you that's soft and predictable. How am I supposed to enjoy being with you if I feel you can go "poof" any minute from some random fall of a die?'

I sighed and lowered myself back onto my elbows.

'Were I a healthy, normal neurotic human lover, my love might evaporate any moment in just as haphazard a fashion.'

'But then I could see it coming; I could run out on you first.' She smiled.

I sat abruptly up.

'Everything may evaporate at any instant. Everything!' I said with surprising vehemence. 'You, me, the most rocklike personality since Calvin Coolidge: death, destruction, despair may strike. To live your life assuming otherwise is insanity.'

'But Luke,' she said putting a warm hand on my

428

shoulder. 'Life's going to go on more or less the same and ourselves too. If – '

'Never!'

She didn't speak. She slid her hand gently from my shoulder to the back of my neck and it played there with my hair. After a few moments I said quietly: 'I love you, Linda. The "I" that loves you will always love you. Nothing is more certain than that.'

'But how long will this "I" last?'

'Forever,' I said.

Her hand became motionless.

'Forever?' she said in a very low voice.

'Forever. Maybe even longer.' I turned onto my side and took her hand and kissed the palm. I looked into her eyes with a playful smile.

Staring seriously back at me, she said:

'But that "I" which loves me may be replaced by a different, unloving "I" and be forced to live forever underground and unexpressed?'

I nodded, still smiling.

'The "I" that loves you would like to arrange things so that the whole rest of my life is fixed to guarantee the continued fulfillment of himself. But it would mean the permanent burial of most of the other "I"s.'

'But ego or no ego, there are *natural* desires and imposed actions. To come over on top of me and fuck would be a natural act; to follow the fall of a die and kneel in the sand to jerk off wouldn't.'

I maneuvered myself clumsily into a kneeling position in the sand and began to lower my swim-trunks.

'O Jesus,' Linda said. 'Me and my big mouth.'

But I smiled and pulled up my trunks. 'You're right,' I said, and moved myself over and lay my head naturally onto her warm, soft thigh.

'So what are your natural desires? What do you *really* want?'

Silence.

'I want being with you. I want sunshine. Love, caresses, kisses. [Pause] Water. Good books. Opportunities to practice the dicelife with people.'

'But *whose* kisses, whose caresses?'

'Yours,' I answered, blinking into the sun. 'Terry's, Arlene's, Lil's, Gregg's. A few others. Women I meet in the street.'

She didn't respond.

'Good music, a chance to write,' I went on. 'Good film occasionally, the sea.'

'I feel . . . Huh! You're not even as romantic as I used not to be, are you?'

'Not this particular me.'

'You love me deeply though,' she said, and I looked up to catch her smiling down at me.

'I love you,' I said holding her eyes with mine. We looked deeply and warmly at each other for more than a minute.

Then she said softly:

'Up yours.'

We watched a gull circling and swooping, and she started to ask something but stopped. I turned my head to press my mouth against the inside of one thigh. It was hot and salty.

She sighed and pushed my head away.

'Then don't spread your legs,' I said.

'I *want* to spread my legs.'

'Well,' I said, and buried my head between them and sucked in a firm hot fold of the other thigh. She pushed medium hard at my head, but I had one arm around her now and held fast.

Letting her fingers relax in my hair, she said:

430

'Some things are naturally good and others aren't.'

'Mmmmmm,' I said.

'The dicelife sometimes takes us away from what's naturally good.'

'Mmmmmm.'

'I think that's too bad.'

I broke my mouth hold and hauled myself up on an elbow alongside her.

'Was that crazy slavery deal I created with you a natural and good thing?' I asked.

She smiled at me.

'It must have been,' she said.

'Everybody is always doing what seems to them to be naturally good. Why is everybody miserable?' I unhooked her bikini top and slid it off her onto the blanket. A ridge of sand lay across the upper half of each breast. I brushed it off.

'Everybody's not miserable,' she said. 'I'm not miserable.'

'You were before you discovered the dicelife.'

'But that's because before I had a sex hangup. Now I don't.'

'Mmmmmm,' I said, my mouth filled with her left breast and my right hand holding the warmth of the other.

'The Die is good for getting you over certain hangups,' she said, 'but then I think maybe it isn't so necessary anymore.'

I unswallowed her breast, licked the taut nipple a few seconds and said:

'Personally, I think you may be right.'

'You do?'

'Certainly.' I untied the near side of her bikini bottom. 'I don't consult it about a lot of things,' I said. 'But when I'm in doubt, I find it nice to consult the Die.' I untied the far side of the bikini.

431

'But why bother?' Linda said. She had a hand now under my trunks and was pushing them down with the other.

'I consult the Die at dawn every day about whether I should consult it about everything during the day, about only the big things or not consult it at all under any circumstances. Today, for example, it told me not to consult it about anything.'

'So even your dicelessness is filled with the Die?'

'Mmmmmmmnnnnn.'

'So you're acting naturally today, huh?'

'MmmmmmMmmmmmm.'

'I hope you're enjoying eating the sand down there.'

'Mmmmmm.'

'That's nice,' she said. 'I like that. I'm glad you told me. I like to know that what you're doing is natural.'

I came up for air and said:

'Most things people do *aren't* natural the first time they do them. That's what learning is all about. That's what the dicelife is all about.'

'Mmmmmm,' she said.

'If we always limited ourselves to what was natural to us, we'd be midget dwarfs compared to our potential. We must always be incorporating new areas of human action which we can make natural.'

'Mmmmmm,' she said.

'Say that again,' I said.

'Mmmmmm,' she said. The vibrations were delicious.

'I hope the dice keep me with you a long time, Linda.'

'Mmmmmmetoommmm.'

'Ahhhhh,' I said, and burying my head, 'mmmmmm.'

'Mmmmmm,' she said.

'MmmmMmmmmNnnnn.'

'Uhnn.'

'..'

'.'

Chapter Seventy-three

Our Dice Centers. Ah, the memories, the memories. Those, those were the days: the gods played with each other on earth once more. Such freedom! Such creativity! Such triviality! Such utter chaos! All unguided by the hand of man, but guided by the great blind Die who loves us all. Once, just once in my life have I known what it means to live in a community, to feel part of a larger purpose shared by my friends and my enemies about me. Only in my CETREs have I experienced total liberation – complete, shattering, unforgettable, total enlightenment. In the last year I have never failed to recognize instantly those who have spent a month in one of the centers, whether I'd seen them before or not. We but glance at each other, our faces explode with light, our laughter flows and we embrace. The world will go steadily downhill again if they close all our CETREs.

I suppose you've all read in one place or another all the typical mass-media hysteria about them: the love room, the orgies, the violence, the drugs, the breakdowns into psychosis, the crime, the madness. *Time* magazine did a fine article about us entitled objectively: 'The CETRE Sewers.' It went as follows:

The dregs of mankind have found a new gimmick: motel madhouses where anything goes. Founded in 1969 by a naïve philanthropist Horace J. Wipple under the guise of therapy centers, the Centers for Experiments in Totally Random Environments (CETREs) have been from the first unabashed invitations to orgy, rapine and insanity. Based on the premises of dice theory first expounded by quack psychiatrist Lucius M.

433

Rhinehart (*Time*, October 26, 1970), the Center's purpose is to liberate their clients from the burdens of individual identity. Those arriving for a 30-day stay in a Center are asked to abandon consistent names, clothing, mannerisms, personality traits, sexual proclivities, religious feelings – in brief, to abandon themselves.

The inmates – called 'students' – wear masks much of the time and follow the 'Commands' of dice to determine how they spend their time or who they pretend they are. Ostensible therapists often turn out to be students experimenting with a new role. Policemen ostensibly keeping order are almost always students playing the game of policemen. Pot, hash and acid are rampant. Orgies go on every hour on the hour in rooms fancifully called 'The Love Room' and 'The Pit' – the latter being a totally blackened room with mattressed floor into which students crawl nude at the whim of the dice and where anything goes.

The results of this are predictable: a few sick people feel they're having a marvelous time; a few healthy people go insane; and the rest somehow survive, often trying to convince themselves they've had a 'significant experience.'

In Los Altos Hills, California, last week 'significant experience' meant arrest for Evelyn Richards and Mike O'Reilly. The two were having a dice-demanded love feast on the lawn of Stanford University's Whitmore Chapel, and townsmen and police were not amused.

Stanford students, frequent visitors to the Hills' CETRE, are bitterly divided on the Dice Center. Students Richards and O'Reilly claim their hangups have disappeared since their three-week trip in the local Center. But Student Association President Bob Orly probably spoke for most of the students when he said:

'The desire to rid yourself of your personal identity is a symptom of weakness. Mankind has always disintegrated when he has followed the call of those who urge him to give up self, ego and identity. The people lured into the Centers are the same ones who get lured deeper and deeper into the drug scene. The dicelife business is just another way of slow suicide for those too weak to try a real way.'

At week's end, Palo Alto Police staged their second raid of the year on the Los Altos Hills Center, but netted nothing but a box of pornographic films, possibly filmed at the Centers. Manager Lawrence Taylor maintains that the only reason he regrets the raids is the favorable publicity it gives the Center

434

among the young. 'We're having to turn away a hundred applicants a week. We don't want to seem exclusive, but we just don't have the facilities.'

A team of *Time* reporters discovered that friends and relatives of CETRE survivors are uniformly upset with the changes which have occurred in their loved ones. 'Irresponsible, erratic, destructive' was the way nineteen-year-old Jacob Bleiss of New Haven described his father after Mr Bleiss returned from the Catskill (NY) CETRE. 'He can't hold a job, he's not home a lot of the time, he hits my mother and he seems stoned half the time, only on nothing. He's always laughing like an idiot.'

Irrational laughter, a classic symptom of hysteria, is one of the most dramatic manifestations of what psychiatrists are beginning to label the 'CETRE sickness.' Dr Jerome Rochman of Chicago University's Hope Medical Center stated in Peoria last week:

'If I had been asked by someone to create an institution which would totally destroy the human personality with all its integrated grandeur – the striving, the moral questioning, the compassion for others and the sense of specific individual identity – I might have created CETREs. The results are predictable: apathy, unreliability, indecisiveness, manic depressions, inability to relate, social destructiveness, hysteria.'

Dr Paul Bulber of Oxford, Mississippi, goes even further: 'The theory and practice of dice therapy both in and out of CETREs is a greater threat to our civilization than Communism. They subvert everything which American society, indeed, any society, stands for. They should be wiped from the face of the earth.'

Santa Clara District Court Judge Hobart Button perhaps summed up best the feelings of many people when he said to students Richards and O'Reilly: 'The illusions that lead people to throw away their lives are appalling. The rush to drugs and to CETREs is like the rush of lemmings to the sea.'

Or the rush of rats into sewers.

Time was, within the necessary limits set by fiction, totally accurate. Over the course of two years five of their reporters went through a month-long stay at a CETRE. The bitterness of the article may partly reflect that three of their hirelings did not report back to *Time*.

435

Ever since money contributed by Wipple, myself and others to the DICELIFE Foundation permitted us to build our first Dice Center, our CETREs have changed people. They destroy people for normal functioning within the insane society. It all started when I realized that dice therapy worked slowly with most students because they always knew that other people expected them to be consistent and 'normal'; a lifetime of conditioning to respond to such expectation wasn't being broken by the partial and temporary free environments of dicegroups. Only in a *total* environment in which *nothing* is expected does a student feel the freedom necessary to express his host of minority selves clawing for life. And then, only by making the gradual change from the totally random environment of a CETRE through our 'Halfway Houses' to the patterned society outside can we make it possible for the student to carry over his dicelife of freedom into the patterned world.

The story of the development of the various centers and of our theory behind them will be told in detail in Joseph Fineman's forthcoming book *The History and Theory of Dice Centers* (Random Press, 1972). The best single rendering of how the centers work to change a man determined not to change can be found in 'The Case of the Square Cubed,' an autobiographical account by Dr Jacob Ecstein. Jake's personal story was first printed in *The See of Whim* (April, 1971, vol. II, no. 4, pp. 17-33) but it is to be reprinted in his forthcoming book *Blow the Man Down* (Random Press, 1972). But for a general background, the Die has suggested I quote from Fineman's forthcomng book:

A student can enter only for a minimum of thirty days and must first pass an oral examination showing he understands the basic rules of the dicelife and the structures and procedures of the CETRE. He is told to come to the Center with absolutely *no* identifying personal possessions; he may use any names he wishes while at the Center but *all* names will be considered false . . .

CETREs vary in their details. In the Creativity Rooms, the Die often commands a student to invent new and better features for our Random Environments and many procedures and facilities have been modified in this way, some changes remaining peculiar to a single Center and others being adopted by all. All CETREs are similar, however, to the original Corpus Die complex in Southern California.

Although each of the individual rooms in a Center has a student-invented name (e.g. the Pit, the God room, the Party room, the Room room, etc.) the names vary from Center to Center. There are workrooms (laundries, offices, therapy rooms, clinics, a jail, kitchens), playrooms (emotion rooms, marriage rooms, love rooms, God rooms, creativity rooms), and life rooms (restaurants, bars, living rooms bedrooms, moviehouse, etc.). He must spend from two to five hours a day working at various dice-dictated jobs: he waits on table, sweeps out rooms, makes beds, serves cocktails, acts as a policeman, therapist, clothing clerk, mask maker, prostitute, admissions officer, jailer, etc. In all of these the student is diceliving and playing roles.

At first we kept most of the key positions filled with permanent, trained staff members: at least half the 'therapists' were real therapists, half the policemen were real staff members, our 'admissions officer' 'real' and so on.

However, over our brief three-year history, there has been a gradual withering away of the staff. With carefully prepared structures and instructions we find that the third and fourth week students can handle most of the key roles as well as the permanent staff used to. The staff members vary their roles from week to week like the temporary students, who thus can't be certain at any time who is a staff member and who isn't. The staff members know, but *they can't prove it*, since anyone can *claim* to be a staff member. Whatever usefulness there is in having permanent, trained personnel in a CETRE rests in their having ability, not in their having 'authority.' [In our Vermont Center we experimented by withdrawing our permanent dicepeople one by one until the center was functioning without a single trained staff member – only transient students. After two

437

months we infiltrated permanent staff members back in, and they reported that everything was proceeding as chaotically as ever; only a small amount of rigidity and structure had crept in during the two months in which the 'state' had totally withered away.]

In our structured anarchy [writes Fineman] the authority rests with the therapists (called Referees in most Centers), and with the policemen, *whoever they may be*. There are rules (no weapons, no violence, no roles or actions inappropriate to the particular game room in which you are acting, etc.) and if the rules are broken, a 'policeman' will take you to a 'referee' to determine whether you must be sent to 'jail.' About half our 'criminals' are individuals who keep insisting that they are only *one real* person and want to go home. Since such role playing is inappropriate in many of the workrooms and playrooms, they must be sentenced to jail and to the hard labor of dice therapy – until they are better able to function in multiplicity. The other half of our criminals are students who must play out their roles of lawbreakers even if the laws they break are the strange ones of our Dice Centers.

[After entering structured anarchy, the student, armed with his personal pair of distinctive dice, proceeds from room to room, from role to role, from job to job: from cocktail party to a creativity room, from an orgy in the Pit to the God room, from the madhouse to the love room to the little French restaurant to working in the laundry to acting as jailer to male prostitute to President of the United States and so on at the whim of his imagination and of the Die.]

The Pit, although justly notorious, is mostly used by students in their first ten days at a Center. It is useful for persons with deep-seated inhibitions regarding sexual desires and activities; the total darkness and anonymity permit the inhibited student to follow dice decisions he could never follow otherwise. One woman, fat and ugly, spent three straight days in the Pit, coming out only to eat, wash and use the bathroom. Was she different at the end of her three days? She was unrecognizable. Instead of a slump-shouldered, eye-avoiding lump, she carried herself proudly, looked at everyone electrically and oozed sexuality.

The Pit is also helpful in breaking down the normal inhibitions about sexual contact with members of the same sex. In a totally dark room, who is doing what to whom is often ambiguous, and one may be reveling in caresses which turn out to be by someone of the same sex. Since ('anything goes') in the Pit one may be the unwilling participant in a sexual act which at first horrifies and disgusts but which, one often discovers, neither horrifies nor disgusts when one realizes no one will ever know.

[In the Pit our students often learn that, in the immortal words of Milton in his great sonnet to his blind wife, 'Those also serve who only lie and wait.']

At first there was no money in any of our CETREs, but we soon relearned that money is more basic perhaps than sex as a source of unfulfilled selves in our society. We now arrange that upon entering, each student receives a certain amount of real money to play with, the amount chosen by the Die from among six options listed by the student. He begins with from zero to three thousand dollars, the median amount being about five hundred dollars. When he leaves he has to cast again from among the same six options he listed when entering to determine how much his bill for his month-long stay will be. When he leave she can take out any money he has saved, earned or stolen, less, of course, our randomly determined bill . . .

Students receive wages for the work they do while in the Center and these wages are continually fluctuating so as to encourage students to work at certain jobs that need to be done.

Students who begin broke have to beg or borrow money for their first meal or else sell themselves to play some role for someone at a price. Prostitution – the selling of the use of one's body for the pleasure of someone else – is a common feature of all our Centers. This is not because it is the easiest way to obtain sex – sex is free in a variety of easily obtained forms – but because students enjoy selling themselves and enjoy being able to buy others. [It's perhaps the very essence of the capitalist soul.]

During the last ten days of his thirty-day stay the student is free to go out and eat and live in the Halfway House, a motel located near the CETRE and staffed partially by our CETREs [maybe], but mostly by the normal owner, a sympathizer, but not necessarily a dice person [maybe]. Until one of our students suggested such Halfway Houses, students were having trouble going from the freedom from expectation within the Center the limitedness of expectation out in the society. [Living in a motel in which a sexy wench is *maybe* a dicestudent who knows she is role playing and maybe a normal one-role girl who only partly knows it, has proven to be an excellent method of transition.

The surly waiter is maybe 'real,' the great writer is maybe a writer and so on.]

The student has moved from a world in which everyone knows that everyone is acting to one in which only a few realize that everyone is role playing. The student feels much freer to experiment and develop his dicelife when he knows there are a few other students around [maybe] who will understand, than he could feel in the normal world of rigid expectations.

We hope that a student comes to have two profound insights while staying at the motel. First, he suddenly realizes that perhaps he's actually at a 'normal' motel, that no other dicepeople are there. He laughs and laughs. Secondly, he realizes that all other humans are leading chance-dictated multiple lives even though they don't know it and are always trying to fight it. He laughs and laughs. Joyfully he wanders back out onto the highway rubbing his dice together, barely aware that he has left the illusion of a totally random environment.

Chapter Seventy-four

The writing of any autobiography involves numerous arbitrary decisions about the importance of events, and the writing about a dicelife by a diceperson involves arbitrariness multiplied to the nth degree. What should be included?

To the creator of the Dice Centers – the Die determined that I devote all of 1970 to their development – nothing is more important than the long, hard, complicated series of acts which resulted in the formation of Dice Centers in the Catskills: in Holby, Vermont; in Corpus Die, California: and, in the last year, elsewhere. At other times the sexual, love and writing adventures of my previous dicelife seem much more worth writing about.

In all cases, however, I faithfully consult the Die about how to proceed with each major section or event of my life. The Die chose that I devote thirty pages to my efforts to follow its November, 1970, decision that I try to murder someone, rather than that I write thirty pages about my efforts of that year to create the Dice Centers.

I asked the Die if I could throw in some letters from my fans and It said fine. Some dicestudents' experiences at the centers? Okay. An article I wrote for *Playboy* entitled 'The Potential Promiscuity of Man'? No, said the Die. Can I write in detail about my long, chaotic, unpredictable and often joyous relationship with Linda Reichman? Nope, not this book. Can I write about my ludicrous efforts to be revolutionary? No, said the Die. About the dice decision that I write a four-hundred-page comic novel about sex? Nope. Can I dramatize my troubles with the

441

law, my experiences as a patient in the upstate mental hospital, my trial, my experience in jail? Yes, said the Die, if there's room. And so on.

One thing I've learned in my miscellaneous career is that any good creating that gets done gets done *despite* my efforts at controlling the writing, not because of them. In so far as I'm the Dice Man I can write easily in almost any form the Die chooses, but as serious, old, ambitious Luke, I run into as many blocks as a rat in an insoluble maze. Obedience to the Die implies with every fall that rational, purposive man doesn't know what he's doing so he might as well relax and enjoy the fumbling Die. 'The medium is the message,' once said the noted psychic Edgar Cayce, and so is mine.

Walk on, I've learned. I let my pen and the Die do what my mind boggles at doing. The falling Die and moving pen think for themselves and the interposition of ego, artistic conscience, style or organization usually weighs things down. These inhibiting forces removed, the ink flows freely, space is filled, words are formed, ideas spring full-blown on the page like giants from dragons' teeth.

Of course, continuity is sometimes tenuous, content thin. Digressions proliferate like weapons in a peace-loving country. I may have to rewrite the thing seven or eight times. But *words are written*. To a writer this is fulfillment. Creativity or crap, it counts.

During my early dicewriting days I would often overcome a long writing block of three or four minutes by letting the dice choose from among a selection of random writing assignments. Every writer has a message which can be gotten said around any subject. Ask me to write about democracy, apples, garbage men or teeth, and I'll give you the Dice Man. So if the flow is dammed in the mainstream of my writing, I pick a creek, a pond, a puddle. With luck I have a flash flood in no time and am back in my Mississippi.

Even if my dice-determined flow is exceptionally good I may brood that it nevertheless isn't what *I should* have written that particular day. But we must come to realize that every word is perfect, including those we scratch out. As my pen moves across this page the whole world writes. All of human history combines at this mere moment now to produce in the flow of this hand a single dot:. Who are you and I, dear friends, to contradict the whole past of the universe? Let us then in our wisdom say yes to the flow of the pen. Or, indeed, should that great-granddaddy diceplayer of us all, History, so dictate, say no. But let us say yes to our no.

I've obviously got several thousand pages of life to report, just counting my life since D-Day, but the best I can do, my friends, is random bits and pieces.

I should note finally that since my life is one devoted to disintegration, those periods when the Die had me doing long-range conventional things like founding Dice Centers are less full diceliving than others. To develop my CETREs I had to be as square as the cube of a die. I had to hang my MD around my neck and bulldoze millionaires and mayors and town planning boards and other doctors every second of every day. Except for brief, anonymous sidetrips to various places to commit murder or rape or larceny or buy dope or help a revolution, I had to be straight as John Lindsay.

However, I sometimes enjoyed it. There is a bourgeois businessman in me that loves being given freedom to buy and sell, to practice public relations, to chair committees, to answer questions of reporters or public officials. The work of developing the CETREs went on too long for my residual self's taste, but I farmed out more and more of the control and the work to Fred Boyd and Joe Fineman and Linda (my God, without her dieing, we'd never have gotten *any* of the centers and our DICELIFE Foundation would be broke).

But though I've enjoyed living most of my roles, and enjoy writing about them all, they simply won't all fit in one book. Fortunately, I have faith that the Die will choose a good selection of events, and if It doesn't, the bored reader can simply flip dice a few times and let the Die choose a new book for the night.

Not my will, Die, but Thy will be done.

Chapter Seventy-five

Dr Jacob Ecstein reports that his own initial reaction to the playrooms of the Corpus Die Dice Center was one of profound disgust. He could see no sense whatsoever in the required emoting of rage, love, and self-pity. He found himself unable to perform the exercises. For rage he emitted a slight peevishness, for love a hearty bonhomie and for self-pity an utterly blank expression. He indicated that he didn't understand what self-pity could possibly mean. To help Dr Ecstein, a teacher (an actual, as contrasted to an acting, dice teacher) spat in his face and urinated on his freshly shined shoes. Dr Ecstein's response was instantaneous:

'What's *your* problem, buddy?' he asked quietly.

The teacher then went and obtained Miss Marie Z, noted television and screen actress who was in her third week of random life, to come and try to help Dr Ecstein express love. Dressed in a lovely, soft white evening gown and looking even younger than her twenty-three years, Miss Z, eyes glistening, hands held demurely before her, said to Dr E in her softest voice:

'Please love me. I need someone to feel love for me. Will you please love me?'

Dr E squinted at her briefly and then replied:

'How long you felt this way?'

'Please,' Marie begged. 'I need your love. I want you to love me, to need me. Please.' A tear glistened at the corner of one eye.

'Who do I remind you of?' Dr E asked.

'Of only yourself. I have needed your love all my life.'

445

'But I'm a psychiatrist.'

'Please don't be a psychiatrist anymore. For one minute, no, for ten seconds, for only ten seconds, I beg of you, give me love. I need so much to feel your strong arms around me, to feel your love . . .' Marie was close to Dr E, her beautifully formed bosom heaving with her passionate need to be loved, tears now wetting both her cheeks.

'Ten seconds?' Dr Ecstein asked.

'Seven seconds. Five. Three seconds, just three seconds please oh please give me your love.'

Dr Ecstein stood squat and tense and his facial muscles moiled and twitched. His face began to get red. Then, gradually, the moiling stopped and, white-faced, he said:

'Can't do it. Honesty. Trust. Don't know what love is.'

'Love me, please love me, please I'm – '

The teacher pulled Marie away and informed her that there was a request for her presence in one of the love rooms and she skipped off, leaving Dr E still unloving.

Since self-pity is the hardest emotion of all for emotionless people to feel, the teacher made no further efforts with the basic emotions and took Dr E to the marriage playroom.

'You have been unfaithful to your wife – ' the teacher said.

'What for?' he asked.

'I am only suggesting options. Let us say then you have been faithful to her, but – '

The teacher was interrupted by a short, slightly fat, middle-aged woman coming in and marching up to Dr Ecstein and screaming in his face:

'You viper! You swine! You beast! You betrayed me!'

' – wait a minute,' Dr E stammered.

'You and that trollop! How could you?' She hit Dr E a

446

vicious blow on the side of the face, almost breaking his glasses.

'Are you sure?' he said, backing away. 'Why are you so upset?'

'Upset? The whole town talking about you and that cesspool behind my back.'

'But how can anyone know what never – '

'If I know about it, the whole world knows about it.' She hit Dr E again less strenuously and collapsed on the couch in tears.

'It's nothing to cry about,' Dr E said, coming over to comfort her. 'Infidelity is a minor matter, really nothing – '

'Ahhhhggg!!!!' she erupted from the couch, plowed her head into Dr E's stomach and sent him crashing over an easy chair onto a telephone table and wastebasket.

'I'm *sorry*!' Dr E screamed. The woman on top of him was scratching at his face and he rolled desperately away.

'You bastard!' the woman shouted. 'Cold-hearted killer. You've never loved me.'

'Of course not,' Dr E said, scrambling to his feet. 'So what's all the fuss about?'

'Ahhhggg!!!' she screamed and came at –

Later the teacher tried to suggest other possible options to Dr E.

'Your wife has been unfaithful, your best friend betrayed you, your – '

'So what else is new?' Dr Ecstein asked.

'Well, let's say your money has all been lost in foolish investment.'

'Never.'

'Never what?'

'I'd never lose all my money in any way.'

'Try to use your imagination, Jim. The – '

447

'The name is Jake Ecstein. Why use my imagination? If I'm in touch with reality, why leave it?'

'How do you know it's reality?'

'How do you know it's not?' Dr E asked.

'But if there's any doubt, then you should experiment with other realities.'

'No doubt in my mind.'

'I see.'

'Look, buddy, I'm here as an observer. I like Luke Rhinehart and want to look over his plant.'

'You can't understand CETRE without living it.'

'Okay, I'm trying, but don't expect me to use my imagination.'

Later Dr Ecstein was taken to the love rooms.

'What kind of love experiences would you like to have?'

'Huh?'

'What kind of sex experience would you like to have?'

'Oh,' Dr Ecstein said. 'Okay.'

'Okay, what?'

'Okay, I'll have a sex experience.'

'But what kinds interest you?'

'Any. Doesn't make any difference.'

The teacher handed Dr E the basic list of thirty-six possible love roles.

'Are there any that particularly appeal to you or any that you would prefer *not* to have as possible options of the Die?' he asked.

Dr E looked over the list: 'You wish to be loved slavishly by a – ' 'You wish to love slavishly a – ' 'You wish to be courted sweetly by a . . .' 'You wish to court sweetly . . .' 'You wish to be raped by a . . .' 'You wish to rape a . . .' 'You wish to watch pornographic films,' 'You wish to watch other people's sexual activities,' 'You wish to striptease,' 'To watch a striptease,' 'You wish to

448

be someone's mistress, a prostitute, a stud, a call girl, a male prostitute, happily married to – '

Most of the options gave the choice of alternatives for performing the sexual role with: a young woman, an older woman, a young man, an older man, a man and a woman, two men or two women.

'What's all this?' Dr Ecstein asked.

'Simply choose those you are willing to play, make a list and let the dice choose one for you to play,'

'Better scratch the "rape" and the "be raped". Had enough of those in the marriage room.'

'All right. Any others, Phil?'

'Stop calling me names.'

'Sorry, Roger.'

'Better throw out the homosexual stuff. Might hurt my reputation outside.'

'But no one in here knows who you are or ever will know.'

'I'm Jake Ecstein, damn it! I've said that six times.'

'I know that, Elijah, but there are five other Jake Ecsteins in here this week as well, so I don't see what difference it makes.'

'Five others!'

'Certainly. Would you like to meet some before you try your first random sex experience?'

'You're Goddam right.'

The teacher took Dr E into a room named Cocktail Party where a crowd milled and drinks were served. The teacher took a portly gentleman by the elbow and said to him:

'Jake, I'd like you to meet Roger. Roger, Jake Ecstein!'

'Goddam it,' Dr Ecstein said, 'I'm Jake Ecstein!'

'Oh are you *really*?' the portly gentleman said. 'I am too. How nice. I'm very pleased to meet you, Jake.'

Dr E permitted himself to shake hands.

449

'Have you met the tall thin Jake Ecstein yet?' the portly one asked. 'Awfully pleasant chap.'

'No, I haven't. And I don't want to.'

'Well, he is a bit dull, but not a young-man-with-the-muscles Jake. Him you must meet, Jake.'

'Yeah, maybe. But I'm the *real* Jake Ecstein.'

'How extraordinary. *I* am too.'

'I mean in the outside world.'

'But that's what I mean too. And so does the tall thin Jake and the young muscled Jake and the lovely young girl Jakie Ecstein. All of them.'

'But I'm *really* the real Jake Ecstein.'

'How extraordinary! I too am *really . . .*'

Jake passed up a love experience and got rid of his teacher and decided he needed to have a good dinner. He had read the center's *Game Rules* and knew as he ate in the cafeteria that the waiters might not be real waiters, that the guy slinging hash behind the counter might be a bank president, that the cashier might be a famous actress, that the woman sitting opposite him might be a writer of children's stories although she was apparently pretending, despite weighing close to two hundred pounds, to be Marlene Dietrich.

'You *bore* me, dahling,' she was saying, her chubby mouth manhandling a cigarette.

'You're not exactly dynamite yourself, baby,' he replied eating rapidly.

'Where are all the *men* in this place?' she drawled. 'I seem to meet only fruits.'

'And I meet only vegetables. So?' Jake answered.

'I beg your pardon. Who are you?'

'I'm Cassius Clay and I'll slug you in the teeth if you don't let me eat in peace.'

Marlene Dietrich relapsed into silence and Jake ate on,

enjoying himself for the first time since his arrival. Suddenly he saw his wife enter the cafeteria, followed by a teenage boy.

'Arlene!' he cried, half-standing.

'George?' she cried back.

Marlene Dietrich left the table and Dr E waited for Arlene to join him, but instead she sat down at a corner table with the teenage boy. Annoyed, he got up when he'd finished and went over to their table.

'Well, what do you think of it so far?' he asked her.

'George, I'd like you to meet my son, John. John, this is George Fleiss, a very successful used-car salesman.'

'How do you do,' the boy said, sticking out a thin hand. 'Pleased to meet you.'

'Yeah, well, look, I'm really Cassius Clay,' he said.

'Oh I *am* sorry,' Arlene answered.

'You've gotten out of shape,' the boy said indifferently.

Dr E sat down with them, feeling glum. He did so want to be recognized as Jake Ecstein, psychiatrist. He tried a new tack.

'What's your name?' he asked his wife.

'Maria,' she answered with a smile. 'And this is my boy, John.'

'Where's Edgarina?'

'My daughter is at home.'

'And your husband?'

Arlene frowned.

'Unfortunately, he has passed away,' she said.

'Oh great,' said Dr E.

'I beg your pardon!' said she, standing abruptly.

'Oh, ah, sorry. I was overcome with disturbance,' Dr E said, motioning his wife to sit. 'Look,' he went on, 'I like you. I like you very much. Perhaps we could stay together awhile.'

'I'm sorry,' Arlene said softly, 'I'm afraid people would talk.'

'People would talk? How?'

'You are a colored man and I am white,' she said.

Dr Ecstein let his mouth hang open and for the first time in his last nineteen years experienced something which he realized later may have been self-pity.

Chapter Seventy-six

Being an American born and bred, it was in my bones to kill. Most of my adult life I had carried around like an instantaneously inflatable balloon a free-floating aggression which kept an imaginative array of murders, wars and plagues parading across my mind whenever my life got difficult: a cabbie tried to overcharge me, Lil criticized me, Jake published another brilliant article. In the year before I discovered the dice, Lil was killed by a steamroller, an airplane crash, a rare virus, cancer of the throat, a flash fire in her bed, under the wheels of the Lexington Avenue Express and by an inadvertent drinking of arsenic. Jake had succumbed to driving into the East River in a taxi, a brain tumor, a stock-market-crash-induced suicide and an insane attack with a samurai's sword by one of his former cured patients. Dr Mann succumbed to a heart attack, appendicitis, acute indigestion and a Negro rapist. The whole world itself had suffered at least a dozen full-scale nuclear wars, three plagues of unknown origin but universal effectiveness and an invasion from outer space by superior creatures who invisibleized everyone except a few geniuses. I had, of course, beaten to a bloody pulp President Nixon, six cab drivers, four pedestrians, six rival psychiatrists and several miscellaneous women. My mother had been buried in an avalanche and may still be alive there for all I know.

Being an American I had to kill. No self-respecting Dice Man could honestly write down options day after day without including a murder or a real rape. I did, in fact, begin to include as a long shot the rape of some

453

randomly selected female, but the dice ignored it. Reluctantly, timidly, with my old friend dread reborn and moiling in my guts, I also created a long-shot option of 'murdering someone.' I gave it only one chance in thirty-six (snake eyes) and three, four times spread out over a year the Die ignored it, but then, one lovely Indian Summer day, with the birds twittering outside in the bushes of my newly rented Catskill farmhouse, the autumn leaves blowing and blinding in the sun and a little beagle puppy I'd just been given wagging his tail at my feet, the Die, given ten different options of varying probabilities, dropped double ones: snake eyes: 'I will try to murder someone.'

I felt acute anxiety and excitement combined, but not the slightest doubt in the world that I would do it. Leaving Lil had been hard (although I sneer at my anxieties now), but killing 'someone' seemed no more difficult than holding up a drugstore or robbing a bank. There was a bit of anxiety because my life was being put in jeopardy; there was the excitement of the chase; and there was curiosity: what person shall I kill?

The great advantage of being brought up in a culture of violence is that it doesn't really matter who you kill: Negroes, Vietnamese or your mother – as long as you can make a reason for it, the killing will feel good. As the Dice Man, however, I felt obligated to let the Die choose the victim. I flipped a die saying 'odd' I would murder someone I knew, 'even' it would be a stranger. I assumed for some reason that the Die would prefer a stranger, but the die showed a 'one'; odd – someone I knew.

I decided that in all fairness one of the people I might kill was myself and that my name should take its chances with the rest. Although I 'knew' hundreds of people, I didn't think the Die intended me to spend days trying to remember all my friends so that I wouldn't deny any of them the option of being murdered. I created six lists each with six places for the names of people I knew, I put Lil, Larry, Evie, Jake, my mother and myself at the top of each of the six different lists. For second names on each list I added Arlene, Fred Boyd, Terry Tracy, Joseph Fineman, Elaine Wright (a new friend of that period) and Dr Mann. For number threes: Linda Reichman, Professor Boggles, Dr Krum, Miss Reingold, Jim Frisby (my new landlord in the Catskills) and Frank Osterflood. And so on. I won't give you the whole thirty-six, but to show I tried my best to include everyone, I should note that for the last six on each list I made six general categories: a business acquaintance, someone I had met first at a party, someone I knew only through letters or through reading (e.g. famous people), someone I haven't seen in at least five years, a CETRE student or staff member not previously listed and someone wealthy enough to justify robbing and killing.

I then casually cast a die to see from which of the six lists the die would choose a victim. The die chose list number two: Larry, Fred Boyd, Frank Osterflood, Miss Welish, H.J. Wipple (philanthropic benefactor of the Dice Centers) or someone I had first met at a party.

Anxiety flushed through my system like a poison, primarily at the thought of killing my son. I had only seen him once since leaving so suddenly fifteen months before and he had been distant and embarrassed after a first leap into my arms of genuine affection. He was also the first diceboy in world history and it would be a shame . . . No, no, not Larry. Or at least let's hope not. And Fred Boyd, my right arm, one of the leading practitioners and advocates of dice therapy and a man I liked very much. His in-and-out relationship with Lil made the murder of either him or Larry particularly unpleasant; to murder Fred seemed motivated and was thus doubly disturbing.

Anxiety is a difficult emotion to describe. The colorful leaves outside the window no longer seemed vibrant; they seemed glossy as if being revealed in an overexposed technicolor film. The twitter of the birds sounded like a radio commercial. My new beagle puppy snored in a corner as if she were a debauched old bitch. The day seemed overcast even as the sun reflecting off a white tablecloth in the dining room blinded my eyes.

Still, there was a Die to be served. I prayed:

'Oh Holy Die,

'Thy hand is raised to fall and I thy simple sword. Wield me. Your Way is beyond our comprehension. If I must sacrifice my son in Thy Name, my son shall die: lesser Gods than Thee have demanded thus of their followers. If I must cut off my right arm to show the Greatness of Thy Accidental Power, my arm shall fall. You have made me great by Thy commands, you have made me joyful and free. You have chosen that I kill, I shall kill. Great Creator Cube, help me to kill. Choose Thy victim that I may strike. Point the way that I Thy sword may enter. He who is chosen will die smiling in the fulfillment of Thy Whim.

Amen.'

I dropped a die to the floor quickly, as if it were a snake. A three: it was my duty to try to kill Frank Osterflood.

Chapter Seventy-seven

From the *Bhagavad-Gita*

To Arjuna, who was thus overcome by pity, whose eyes were filled with tears and who was troubled and much depressed in mind, the Lord Krishna said:

Whence has come to thee this dejection of spirit in this hour of crisis? It is unknown to men of noble mind; it does not lead to heaven; on earth it causes disgrace, O Arjuna.

Yield not to this unmanliness, O Arjuna, for it does not become thee. Cast off this petty faintheartedness and arise, O Oppressor of the foes.

Arjuna said:

How can I strike, O Krishna, O slayer of foes? It is better to live in this world by begging than to slay another . . . My very being is stricken with pity. With my mind bewildered about my duty, I ask Thee to tell me that which I should do.

Having thus addressed the Lord Krishna, the mighty Arjuna said to Krishna: 'I will not kill,' and became silent.

To him thus depressed in the midst of two paths, Krishna, smiling as it were, spoke this word. The Blessed Lord said:

Thou grievest for one whom thou shouldst not grieve for, and yet thou speakest words about wisdom. Wise men do not grieve for the dead or the living.

Never was there a time when I was not, nor thou, nor these lords of men, nor will there ever be a time hereafter when we shall cease to be.

As the soul passes in this body through childhood, youth and age, even so it is taking on another body. The sage is not perplexed by this.

Of the nonexistent there is no coming to be; of the existent there is no ceasing to be. Know thou that that by which all this is pervaded is indestructible. Of this immutable being, no one can bring about the destruction. Therefore, O Arjuna, thy duty shouldst be performed.

457

He who thinks that he slays and he who thinks that he is slain; both of them fail to perceive the truth; no one slays, nor is one slain. Therefore, O Arjuna, thy duty shouldst be performed.

He is never born, nor does he die at any time, nor having once come to be does he again cease to be. He is unborn, eternal, permanent and primeval. He is not slain when the body is slain. Therefore, knowing him as such, thou shouldst not grieve and thy duty shouldst be performed.

Pick up thy die, O Arjuna, and kill.

(Edited for *The Book of the Die*)

Chapter Seventy-eight

I hadn't heard of Frank Osterflood in close to a year, and I genuinely looked forward to seeing him again. He had responded pretty well for a while to dice therapy first with me and then in a group with Fred Boyd. When he experienced the need to rape someone – boy or girl – as an arbitrary decision of the dice, it freed him from the great burden of guilt which had normally accompanied and magnified the act. And with the elimination of the guilt he discovered he had lost much of his desire to rape. I insisted, of course, that he had to *try* to carry through with any dice-dictated rape even though he didn't feel like it. He succeeded, found it a disgusting experience. I praised him for following the will of the Die, and he cut back drastically on the possibility of rape among his options and then eliminated it.

He enjoyed spending his money in random ways and then, much to my surprise, he married a woman as the result of a dice decision. Marriage turned out to be an apparent disaster. I had disappeared from the world at that time, but I heard from Fred Boyd that Frank had given up both his wife and the dicelife and was drifting again from job to job. Whether he was expressing his old aggressions in his old ways we didn't know.

I had no desire to limit my dicelife by spending it all in prison so advanced planning was called for. Interrupting my work at the Catskill CETRE for a week I went on a 'business trip' to New York. I discovered that Osterflood was living at his old apartment on the East Side – about four blocks from where I used to live. Ah, the memories.

He seemed to be working for a brokerage firm on Wall Street and was gone for nine hours each day. The first night I trailed him he went out to dinner, a movie, a discotheque and returned home alone and presumably read or watched television and then slept.

It's a rather interesting experience to spend an evening trailing a man you're planning to murder the next day; watching him yawn, become irritable when he can't find the right change for a newspaper, smile at some thought he's having. In general, Osterflood seemed rather nervous, I thought, tensed up – as if someone were trying to murder him.

I began to realize that murder is not as easy as it's cracked up to be. I couldn't loiter outside Osterflood's apartment a second consecutive night: my giant form was entirely too conspicuous. When and where to kill him? He was a big, muscular man, probably the only man on my original list of thirty-six that I wouldn't want to meet in a dark alley after I'd just fired a shot at him and missed. I had brought my .38 revolver I still possessed from my pre-dice, suicide-considering days, and I was pretty accurate at ten feet or less; I figured Big Frank would need a hole in the head to take him down. I also brought along some strychnine to help along in that way should the opportunity arise.

My main problem was that if I killed him in his apartment I would have trouble escaping unnoticed. Gunshots in East Side apartments renting for four hundred dollars a month are not especially common. His apartment had a doorman, an elevator man, perhaps a hired security man, probably no stairwell. To shoot Osterflood in the street or in an alley was also dangerous since although gunshots were there much more frequent, nevertheless, people usually had enough curiosity to look over at what was happening. I was simply too big to be anonymous.

I suddenly realized that living in New York City, Frank Osterflood – and every other New Yorker – lived year after year, without *once*, *ever*, being more than twenty feet from some other human being. Usually he was within ten feet of a dozen people. He had no private, isolated life in which he might be totally by himself and meditate and commune with himself and take stock and be murdered. I resented it deeply.

I couldn't afford to wait around; I wanted to hurry back to Catskill to continue developing the Catskill Dice Center, there to make people happy and joy-filled and free again.

Somehow I had to lure him away from the warren of Manhattan. But how? Was he interested in boys these days? Or girls? Or men? Or women? Or money? Or what? What was the hook that would drag him out of the cesspool of the city into the lovely, lonely autumn of the woods? How would I prevent his telling someone that he had seen me again, that he was going someplace with me? The only method that I could dimly see was to accost him as he returned from work, invite him to dinner and then lure him out of the city on some spontaneously combusted pretext and, on some isolated country road, miles from the nearest other human being communing with himself, shoot him. It seemed very messy and haphazard, and I was determined to commit a nice clean crime, without any sick emotions, without fuss, with dignity, grace and aesthetic bliss. I wanted to murder in such a way that Agatha Christie would be pleased and not offended. I wanted to commit a crime so perfect that no one would suspect anything, not the murdered, not the police, not even me.

Of course, such a crime would be impossible, so I

461

retreated to my earlier ideal that I should murder without fuss, emotion or violence and with dignity, grace and aesthetic bliss. It was the very least I owed the victim.

But how? The Die only knows. I certainly couldn't see how. I would have to have faith. I would have to get myself with Osterflood and see what turned up. I'd never read of an Agatha Christie murderer proceeding in quite this way, but it was all I could do on twenty-four hours' notice.

'Frank, baby,' I said the next evening as he emerged from his taxi. 'Long time, no see. It's your old buddy Lou Smith; you must remember me. Good to see you again.'

I pumped his hand as the taxi pulled away and, still hoping to prevent him from uttering my name within earshot of the doorman, I threw my arm around his shoulder and whispered that we were being trailed and began marching him away.

'But Dr – '

'Had to see you. They're trying to get you,' I whispered as we moved up the block.

'But who's trying – '

'Tell you all about it at dinner.'

He stopped about thirty feet from his apartment.

'Look, Dr Rhinehart, I . . . I've got an important . . . appointment this evening. I'm sorry, but – '

I had hailed another taxi and it careered over to our curb lusting after our East Side money.

'Dinner first. Got to talk first. Someone's trying to murder you.'

'What?'

'Get in, quick.'

Inside the taxi I got my first good look at Frank Osterflood; he was a bit heavier about the jowls than he had been before and seemed more nervous and tense, but it might have been his concern about dying. His hair was nicely trimmed and brushed, his expensive suit fit flawlessly, and he gave off the pleasant odor of some heroic after-shave lotion. He looked like a highly successful, well-paid, socially placed thug.

'To murder me?' he said, staring into my face in search of a jocular smile. I had glanced at my watch; it was six thirty-seven.

'I'm afraid so,' I said. 'I learned from some of my dicepeople that they're planning to murder you.' I stared sincerely into his face. 'Maybe tonight even.'

'I don't understand,' he said, looking away. 'And where are we going now?'

'Restaurant in Queens. Very good hors d'oeuvres.'

'But why? Who? What have I done?'

I shook my head slowly from side to side, while Osterflood stared nervously out at the passing traffic and seemed to flinch every time a car drew up alongside us.

'Ah, Frank, you don't have to hide things from me. You know you've done some things that . . . well, might upset some people. Someone, someone has found it's you. They plan to kill you. I'm here to help.'

He glanced back at me nervously.

'I don't need any help. I've got to go someplace at – at eight-thirty. Don't need help.' Tight-jawed, he stared straight ahead at the somewhat unartistic photograph of Antonio Rosco Fellini, driver of the cab.

'Ah, but you do, Frank. Your little appointment at eight-thirty may be your rendezvous with death. You'd better let me come along.'

'I don't understand,' he said. 'Since dice therapy with you and Dr Boyd I haven't, I haven't . . . done anything I haven't paid for.'

'Ahhhh,' I said vaguely, searching for my next line.

'Except my wife.'

'Where's this place again?' shouted back Antonio Rosco Fellini. I told him.

'And my wife has left me and is suing me and if I die she won't get a cent.'

'But those early days in Harlem, Frank. They may know.'

He hesitated and stared over at me wide-eyed in fear.

'But I'm leaving my money partly to the NAACP,' he said.

'Maybe they don't know that,' I said.

'Probably no one knows,' he said sadly. 'I just recently decided.'

'Ah, and *when* did you decide?'

'Just now, a minute ago.'

'Ahhh.'

We drove on in silence for a while, Osterflood twice looking behind us to see if we were being followed. He reported that we were.

'What's this appointment about tonight, Frank?'

'None of your business,' he answered quickly.

'Frank, I'm trying to help you. Someone may be trying to murder you tonight.'

He looked back at me uncertainly.

'I . . . I've got a date,' he said.

'Ahhhh,' I said.

'But it's a woman that I . . . that . . . she likes money.'

'Where are you to meet her?'

'In . . . er . . . Harlem.' His eyes flickered off hopefully at a bus stopped beside us, as if it might contain a plainclothesman or CIA man or FBI man. There were undoubtedly a few of each, but they were out of his reach.

'Does she live alone?' I asked. It was six forty-eight.

'Uh . . . Well, yes.'

'What is she like?'

'She's disgusting!' he spit out emphatically. 'Flesh, flesh, flesh – a woman,' he added.

'Ahh,' I said, disappointed. 'Do you think there's any chance at all that she might be involved in a plot?'

'I've known her three months. She thinks I'm a professional wrestler. No. No. She's horrible, but she's not – it's not her.'

'Look,' I said impulsively. 'Tonight the place for you to be is away from your apartment and out of public places. We'll have dinner in this out-of-the-way restaurant I know of and then we can all stay with this lady of yours.'

'Are you sure . . .?'

'If anyone is going to try to kill you tonight, you can depend on me.'

Chapter Seventy-nine

When Jake Ecstein was walking through a Dice Center one day he overheard a conversation between two people.

'Show me the best role you have,' said the first person.

'All my roles are the best,' replied the second. 'You can't find in me any piece of behavior which isn't the best.'

'That's conceited,' said the first.

'That's diceliving,' replied the second.

At these words Jake Ecstein became enlightened.

– from The Book of the Die

Chapter Eighty

It occurred to me on my drive to Harlem with Frank Osterflood after our uneventful dinner at an obscure restaurant in Queens that I might try to 'take him for a ride' to some dimly lit nowheres where mobsters drive to put other less successful mobsters away, but I didn't know any dimly lit nowheres, and besides, I was beginning to worry that Osterflood might turn his paranoic tendencies toward me and attack.

We arrived at the apartment house of Osterflood's 'date' at a little after eight thirty-four that evening. We seemed to be somewhere near Lenox Avenue on 143rd Street or 145th Street – I never did find out which. My victim paid the cabbie who looked resentful at being stuck in the middle of no-man's-land when he might be at the Hilton or Park Avenue. No one came close to us when we walked the thirty feet or so from the sidewalk to the door of the elegant and crumbling apartment building, although I sensed dozens of dark faces glaring at us in the deep dusk.

We clumped up the three flights of stairs together like a man and his shadow, I fingering my gun and Osterflood telling me to be careful of my footing. The sound of galloping horses and shouts came out of a first-floor apartment, high-pitched hysterical female laughter from the second floor, but from the third, silence. As Osterflood knocked, I reminded him firmly that my name was Lou Smith. I was a fellow professional wrestler. The incongruity of two professional wrestlers showing up to court a lady, one of them dressed with Brooks Brothers immaculateness and the other like a down-and-out hood escaped me at the time.

The woman who came to the door was a middle-aged fat lady with stringy hair, a double chin and jolly smile. She barely seemed a Negress.

'I'm Lou Smith, professional wrestler,' I said quickly, offering my hand.

'Good for you,' she said and walked out past us and waddled on down the stairs.

'Is Gina here?' Osterflood called after her, but she stomped on down unheeding.

I followed him inside, through a small entranceway and into a fairly large living room, dominated by a huge television set squatting against one wall directly opposite a long, Danish-modern couch. There was wall-to-wall carpeting, thick and soft and a pretty tan color, but badly spotted in front of the television set and the couch. The splash of running water came from a room off to the right, which, from the bulk of white I could make out, seemed to be a kitchen. Osterflood called in that direction:

'Gina?'

'Yeahhh,' came a high-pitched feminine voice.

While I was squinting at two photo portraits on one wall – they looked, so help me, like Sugar Ray Robinson and Al Capone – the woman came to the living room and confronted us. She was a young, full-figured, dark-haired woman, with the face of a child. Big, brown eyes exuded innocence, and her dark complexion was flawlessly smooth.

'What's this?' she said shrilly and coldly in a voice that, while high-pitched like a child's, had a 'what's-in-it-for-me?' cynicism that was totally incongruous with the child's face.

'Ah, this is Dr Luke Rh – '

468

'SMITH!' I shouted, 'Lou Smith, professional wrestler.'
I advanced and stuck out a hand.

'Gina,' she said coldly; her hand was lifeless in mine.

She moved past us into the living room and said over
her shoulder:

'You guys want a drink?'

We both asked for Scotch and while she was kneeling
and then standing before an abundantly supplied liquor
cabinet in the corner to the left of the television set,
Osterflood and I sat down on opposite ends of the couch,
he staring at the gray lifeless screen of the television set
and I at the brown leather miniskirt and tan, creamy legs
of Gina.

She came and handed each of us a nice stiff Scotch on
the rocks, staring into my eyes with that same incongruous
innocent child's face and saying coldly:

'You want the same as him?'

I looked over at Osterflood, who was staring down at
the rug. He seemed sullen.

'What do you mean?' I asked, looking back up at her.
She was wearing a tan, v-neck sweater that buttoned
down the front and her breasts balloonded out at me
distractingly.

'What are you here for?' she asked, not taking her eyes
off me.

'I'm just an old friend,' I said. 'Just here to watch.'

'Oh, that type,' she said. 'Fifty bucks.'

'Fifty bucks?'

'You heard me.'

'I see. It must be quite a show.' I looked back at
Osterflood, who still stared at the subliminal floor show
on the rug. 'I'll have to think about it.'

'I'd like another drink,' Osterflood said and, head
lowered, reached out his long, nicely tailored arm with
his glass and two ice cubes.

469

'The money,' she said to him without moving.

He pulled out his wallet and peeled out four bills of undetermined denomination. She ambled over to him, took the bills, fingered each of them carefully, then took his glass and disappeared back into the kitchen. She moved like a sleepy leopardess.

Osterflood said without looking over at me:

'Can't you stand guard outside?'

'Can't take the chance. The killer might already be inside the apartment.'

He glanced up and around nervously.

'I thought you said your date was disgusting?' I said.

'She is,' he said, and shuddered.

The disgusting flesh flesh flesh returned and fixed Osterflood his second drink and freshened her own. I was only sipping at mine, determined to keep my mind alert for the clean, aesthetic moment of truth. It was eight forty-eight by my watch.

'Look, mister,' Gina was saying in front of me again. 'Fifty bucks or out. This isn't a waiting room.' Her voice! If only she would never say a word.

'I see.' I turned to my friend. 'Better give her a fifty, Frank.'

He took out his wallet a second time and pulled off a single bill. She fingered it and stuffed it into a tiny pocket in her tiny leather skirt.

'Okay,' she said. 'Let's go.'

She walked over and turned on the television set, fiddling carefully with the dials and adjusting the volume quite high. When she moved away from the screen three young men were twitching away and playing loudly some rhythmic tune which was world-famous and which I almost recognized.

I was paying fifty dollars for this? No. Osterflood was paying. I relaxed.

'You want some hash tonight?' she asked Osterflood. He was brooding into his half-finished drink.

'Yes,' he said.

When Gina returned from the kitchen this time she had a small pipe, apparently fully loaded, since she handed it to Osterflood and he lit up right away.

He passed it up to her and she took a long toke and then sat down on the couch between us, leaning back and reaching out an arm to hand the pipe to me. I'd read someplace that the United States Marines found marijuana and hashish excellent aids to the performance of their duties, so I took a healthy puff and passed the pipe back to her.

After only about three or four puffs by each of us, the pipe seemed to have gone out, but after a few minutes, as I was watching a handsome, sincere American clobber a greasy Latin American type on the TV screen, the pipe appeared under my nose again nicely lit. As I passed the pipe back to Gina, holding the smoke on my lungs, I smiled at her, and her soft baby face and large brown eyes looked sorrowfully and innocently into mine. If only she doesn't talk. Was she Negro or Italian?

By the fourth toke of the second series I was really enjoying the rhythm of the deep inhale, the earnest American talking, frowning, driving his jet-powered jeep, then the blossoming beneath my nose of the gem-studded pipe, the inhale . . . As I passed the pipe back to her this time, I felt like smiling at her again, hoping she was enjoying the show too, and I watched with interest as she put the pipe in her mouth and Osterflood's hand bloomed into view just below her chin, clutched like an octopus onto one side of the v of Gina's sweater and then in slow motion flew away, sending the buttons in front popping off onto the living room rug like machine-gun pellets. Gina continued her inhale and handed the pipe back to me, her eyes focused on the ceiling. I looked at the pipe

471

pleasurably, examining the lacework of fake gems around the outside of the bowl, looked at the small, black, charcoal-looking lump inside, and took a pleasant, long toke. ABC, I now noticed, was presenting 'CIA in Action', a new adventure series, and when the commercial for Johnson's Baby Powder ended, two earnest Americans, one of whom I remembered seeing earlier, began talking about a Red plot in front of a backdrop of toiling peasants.

When I turned lazily to hand Gina the pipe she was sitting exactly as before, her head back against the couch and eyes ceilingward, but nude from the waist up. Her two breasts rose from her chest like two mounds of molded honey, with two neat circular sculpted crowns of brown sugar at the peak of each rounded, honeyed hill.

Without smoking she passed the pipe on to Osterflood on the other side of her. The pipe went flying off onto the living room floor on top of the buttons, the sweater and the bra. He had bashed at her hand.

'Get up,' Osterflood said.

Slowly, like a sated leopardess, she stood. I could see Osterflood now and he was staring at her bleary-eyed and without expression, neat in his soft, gray suit.

'You bitch,' he said dully. 'You cunt-caked bitch.'

I was smiling to myself without thought, leaning back and examining with aesthetic bliss the curve of Gina's right breast, which stuck out gracefully in front of her right arm like the prow of a boat nosing out from behind a cliff. An earnest American jawed aggressively with a greasy American just at the tip of the short bowsprit.

'You slut,' Osterflood said just a bit louder. 'You juicy-jointed sewer. Shitslitted slut. Slime-oozing whore.'

Gina was fumbling with the belt and then one side of her leather skirt and after a moment or two, the skirt dropped like a guillotine to the floor at her feet. She was now totally nude. A long lovely scar ran down the back of one thigh.

'You bitch!' Osterflood screamed, and he staggered woozily to his feet and wobbled uncertainly for several seconds. There was a scream from the TV screen and I glanced idly over to see one of the Americans pick up one of the peasants and throw him onto a manure pile where another peasant could be seen struggling ineffectually.

I turned back just in time to see Osterflood grab Gina's curly dark hair and throw her back onto the couch. She bounced once, in segments, and then sat quietly, her large brown eyes looking vacantly at the ceiling.

'Feces!' shouted Osterflood. 'Female feces!'

I smiled friendlily over at her.

'It's going to be a nice evening,' I said pleasantly.

Chapter Eighty-one

I have been a woman on hundreds of occasions: in my dicelife, group dice therapy and in our Dice Centers. I've usually enjoyed myself thoroughly. The only time I haven't enjoyed being a woman is when people have thought I was a man. For example, my experience with the Cleveland Brown defensive tackle (he used to be a truck driver – of Good Humor Ice Cream trucks) was at first unrewarding because he wanted me to be a man and I thought he was a man. Confusion of roles is always difficult.

I found that being a woman physically was more difficult than being one socially and psychologically. Sexually it was a big disappointment. I simply don't have the right equipment to enjoy being laid. It is much more pleasant in bed to play a passive 'feminine' role with an aggressive 'masculine' woman than with a real man. The pump of a penis in the anus is, to be precise, a pain in the ass. The feel of a nice hot prick moiling in one's mouth is certainly an experience that everyone should try, but is for me one of the minor sexual pleasures. The flood of hot semen into the mouth is pleasing enough if one takes any pride at all in one's work, but it is at best a psychological pleasure rather than a physical one. Choking on oversalted soup is not my idea of sensuous bliss, but I admit my limitations.

The appeal of being a woman – at least for me – lies in the freshness of the experience and in the passivity, the masochistic passivity I might even say. There is something basic in wanting to be dominated by a superior creature –

whether man or Die. Responding to men respectfully and passively has never been my majority nature, but the times the Die has ordered me to play a woman have uncovered the latent slave in me.

And certainly being a woman is absolutely basic for every man in our society. And vice versa for women. The human is built to imitate, and every male has stored within him a thousand female gestures, phrases, attitudes and acts which long to be expressed, but are buried in the name of masculinity. It is a tragic loss. Perhaps the single greatest contribution of our Dice Centers is that they create an environment which encourages the expression of all roles; it encourages bisexuality. One might even more honestly say *full* sexuality, were honesty one of our virtues.

I have been a woman on hundreds of occasions and I recommend that every other healthy, red-blooded American man be one too.

Chapter Eighty-two

Dicemasters train young people as well as old. Two Dicemasters each had a child prodigy. One child, going to buy bubblegum at the store each morning, would often meet the other going to the same place.

'Where are you going?' the first asked one day.

'I'm going wherever my dice fall,' the other responded.

This reply stopped the first child, who immediately went back to his Dicemaster for help. 'Tomorrow morning,' Jake Ecstein told him, 'when you meet that smart aleck, ask him the same question. He'll give you the same answer, and then you ask him: "Suppose you have no dice, then where are you going?" That'll fix him.'

The children met again the next morning.

'Where are you going?' asked the first child.

'I'm going wherever the wind blows,' answered the other.

This reply also stopped the youngster, who hurried back to his Dicemaster.

'Ask him tomorrow where he's going if there's no wind. That'll fix him.'

The next day the children met a third time.

'Where are you going?' asked the first child.

'I'm going to the store to buy bubblegum,' the other replied.

– from *The Book of the Die*

Chapter Eighty-three

'Daddy? Why do I have to brush my teeth every day?' the little girl asked.

'Try this new tube I've got for you, Suzie, and you'll never ask that question again.'

[Close-up of a big long tube of Glare Toothpaste.]

But I had to look away because Gina was kneeling on the floor, her hands tied behind her back with her bra, and Osterflood, with his pants and undershorts bunched at his feet but still dressed in white shirt, tie and suit jacket, was thrusting with his erect, pink weapon at her mouth, cursing her at every poke. I felt I was watching a slow-motion movie showing some huge piston at work, but some flaw in the machinery resulted in the rod's seeming frequently to miss the wide-open mouth which Gina, large-eyed and expressionless, was presenting. Osterflood's sword of vengeance against the female race kept sliding past her cheek or her neck or poking her in the eye. Whenever she would seem to have a good mouthful (she would close her eyes then), Osterflood would withdraw, raging, and thrust away sporadically, redoubling his curses. It wasn't clear whether he hated her more when she sucked him in or when he missed contact and bounced painfully off her forehead. In both cases he seemed like a movie director enraged because she, the actress, didn't mouth her lines correctly.

'Ahhhggg! How I hate you,' he yelled and lurched forward and collapsed onto the couch beside me. I smiled over at him.

He struggled sideways into a sitting position.

'Undress me, you disgusting, filthy hole,' he said loudly.

A cute, frightened peasant girl had joined the number-one earnest American and was pleading with him passionately about her corn crop. Without any apparent effort, Gina freed her hands and dropped the bra back onto the rug next to her skirt and sweater and the buttons and the pipe and came to the couch to undress him.

'Get me a drink,' he shouted to no one in particular as Gina tried to slide his pants over his shoes and off. She stood and said:

'Sure, honey. You want some acid?'

'I just want your ass, you sink!' he shouted after her.

'It's for the good of your country,' the firm TV voice said.

Osterflood's sword was melting into an arch at the moment but mine wasn't. My body was tingling all over pleasantly and I had to adjust my .38 and my other rod (semi-automatic), to make all continue tingling pleasantly. I wondered how Osterflood could keep his hands off those breasts and buttocks and I deeply resented all his talking and his abominable aim.

He gulped down the drink she brought him while she slowly untied and removed each of his shoes and the CIA man drove a tractor and then on her knees in front of him she removed his necktie, unbuttoned one by one the buttons of his shirt and – all in a slow-motion movie which I watched as if it were a faithful newsreel of the Second Coming – she had just managed to slide the second sleeve of his shirt down off his left arm (the peasants I could hear were cheering now and I glanced briefly to catch a glimpse of a forest of white, toothy grins), when Osterflood's huge, muscular arms loomed out, closed around her, his face plowed into her face and his mouth sunk into her mouth.

Gina groaned sharply and the way she twisted indicated he must be hurting her somehow.

'You bastard!' she snapped shrilly when she got her mouth free. She hit him as good a slap as she could from her close-up position, and he grinned and sunk his teeth into her shoulder. As she scratched at his back he toppled her backward onto the rug with a tremendous crash. When he raised himself off her to place his weapon into the disgusting cesspool, she got in a few blows at his face and then he was in and working.

There wasn't much to see: just Osterflood's big buttocks moving a few inches up and down as he plowed away at Gina's rich earth and her fingers splayed out on his back and occasionally changing position, as if she were playing chords. Gina was groaning, when Osterflood abruptly rose to his knees, flipped her over onto her stomach like a farmer working with a sack of wheat and fumbled with his weapon to reengage the enemy in her other cave. When he thrust himself into her and fell forward upon her Gina let loose a terrible scream. It corresponded so perfectly with gunshots from the screen that I looked back quickly to see a beautiful, frightened peasant girl with a ripped blouse clutching the arm of the number one earnest American and the peasant spies blasting away from behind a chicken coop.

Gina was fighting with her right arm to raise herself and twist Osterflood off and out of her, but he bore down, pulling her hair with one hand and controlling her right arm with the other. His professional-wrestler role seemed to be paying off.

'Bitchbitchbitch,' he gasped, and the American was dragging the beautiful peasant girl through a cornfield and bullets were shattering the kernels every which way and Osterflood was banging Gina's head against the rug and the American tossed a grenade and whomp! the chink peasants were splattered like fertilizer over the cornfield and 'Diediedie-bitchbitch,' Osterflood hissed and with a supreme thrust deep into her anus they both screamed.

An unearthly silence filled the room. The beautiful peasant girl was looking with most frightened eyes from the pieces of peasant to the earnest American. 'My God,' she said.

'Steady,' the deep voice answered. 'We've won this round, but there's always more of them.'

Osterflood rolled off his conquered foe with a grunt, his weapon still cocked, but presumably discharged.

Gina's hilly form lay quietly for a few moments and then she got to her knees and stood up. Although she was still facing away toward the TV set, I could see blood running in a tiny stream down the right corner of her mouth and something was smeared down the inside of one thigh. Slowly she moved off to the left and disappeared into what seemed to be a bathroom.

I was perspiring a good deal and a lady was smiling ecstatically as she held up her laundry and I found myself sailing over to the liquor cabinet and fixing three more drinks, adding mostly melted ice.

Osterflood was lying on his back when I sailed back again, but he sat up to take the drink I offered him. He stared wild-eyed at me.

'I'm going to be killed,' he said.

I'd forgotten all about that.

He clutched at my pants leg, spilling part of his drink on the rug.

'I'm going to die. I know it. You've got to do something.'

'It's all right,' I said.

'No, no, it's not, it's not. I feel it strongly. I deserve to die.'

'Come into the kitchen,' I said.

He stared wild-eyed at me.

'I want to show you something,' I added.

'Oh,' he said, and with a great effort he turned himself onto his hands and knees and staggered to his feet.

I flowed off behind his whalelike form toward the kitchen, and as he passed through the door in front of me I drew my gun from my pocket, raised it in a long endless arc up over my head, and then down with all my force onto the top of Osterflood's huge head.

'Wha'sat?' Osterflood said, stopping and turning, and slowly raising a hand to his head.

I gazed openmouthed at his erect, swaying, hulking body.

'It's . . . it's my gun,' I said.

He looked down at the black little pistol hanging limply from my fist.

'What'd you hit me for?' he said after a pause.

'Show you my gun,' I said, still gaping at his blank, bleary, bewildered eyes.

'You hit me,' he said again.

We stared at each other, our minds working with the speed and efficiency of lobotomized sloths.

'Just a tap. Show you my gun,' I said.

We stared at each other.

'Some tap,' he said.

We stared at each other.

'Protect you with. Don't tell Gina.'

Whn he stopped rubbing the back of his head, his hand and arm dropped like an anchor into the sea.

'Thanks,' he said dully, and moved past me back into the living room.

Two snake-eyed peasants were conspiring together on the screen, and I wandered over to the liquor cabinet and stared at the big photograph of Al Capone. Was it Al Capone? It was Al Capone. Robot-fashion I plucked three more fresh glasses from the neat stack there, poured in the dregs of ice from the bowl, and splashed some Scotch and water into each. I stirred them all idly with my finger, licked my finger and as a kind of dreamy afterthought, drew from my jacket pocket the envelope of strychnine and poured about half of it (fifty mg) into one of the drinks. I stirred it with my finger again and was about to lick my finger but thought better of it. I poured the other half of the poison into an empty glass, filled it from the pitcher of water and stirred it with my finger again.

'I'm going to die, whip me!' Osterflood was saying on his back from the floor. 'Beat me, Kill me.'

Gina had returned from wherever she had been and was standing over Osterflood, sweat glistening lightly on her chest and forehead. Her child's face peered down at him as at an interesting toad. Osterflood was groaning and writhing mildly on the rug. Then he stopped and said quietly,

'Whip me.'

Gina leaned down to her left and picked up her leather skirt and stepped into it, buttoning it loosely at her hips. She drew out the leather belt.

'Would you two like a drink first?' I asked, holding the three Scotch drinks on a tray before me.

Osterflood didn't seem to hear me, intent instead upon some inner light. Gina reached her free hand out and took one of the two harmless drinks and took a big swig from it.

'Frank, would you like – ' I began.

Whack!

The belt burst across Osterflood's thighs like a cannon shot. He grunted and turned over onto his stomach.

Whack! it came across his buttocks; whack! across the

482

back of his thighs. His powerful body arched in pain and then when Gina paused, collapsed trembling.

I noticed now a bloody gash on Gina's shoulder and blood mixed with saliva was still sliding from her lower lip. She looked down at Osterflood and in a single swift terrifying motion slashed the belt across his back. Three or four pinkish welt lines were now clearly etched on his body.

'Ahh,' I said. 'Is this part of the regular show?'

She stood without answering, breathing deeply, a single line of sweat now running from the side of her neck down in between her breasts, which rose and fell moistly.

'I'm dying, I'm dying,' Osterflood moaned. 'Beat me, please beat me.'

'You white pig,' she said in a soft voice. 'Fat man pig.' Thock!

I absentmindedly took a sip from one of the drinks and spat it out on the rug. Wrong drink.

A burst of applause flooded into the room and I glanced over to see a pompous little dictator parading down the aisle of an auditorium to the applause of formally dressed spics, or chinks, or gooks or greasies.

'Drink,' I heard a voice say.

Osterflood had gotten now to his knees and was reaching out an arm toward my tray. His eyes were unfocused and glittering.

I raised my free hand and Gina took from the tray a glass and handed it to Osterflood and he downed it at a gulp.

Holding the third drink in my free hand, I sighed. Osterflood had taken the wrong drink.

While Gina reached down to take another swig from hers, I returned to Sugar Ray and Al Capone and poured two more drinks. I marched back again with my tray of three and stood just beside and behind Gina.

'You're trying to kill me,' Osterflood said looking up at us from his knees. 'You shit-filled monster, you're trying to kill me.' He was staring at us glassy-eyed.

Gina looked down at him, her large brown eyes radiant and curious, and for the first time she smiled, slightly.

'Bad trip?' she asked quietly.

'I see it all now,' Osterflood shouted at us. '*You*'re the killer!' He began shaking his head and trembling. 'Now I see, now I see! It's *you!*'

The 'Thock!' that caught him across the face surprised both him and me, and he fell forward with a crash.

'Yes, yes, whip me, I deserve it,' he groaned. 'Hit me again.'

Gina looked down at him, the soft smile still on her face, and sweat running now from her forehead, chin and both heaving breasts.

She raised the belt slowly till her arm was perpendicular above her head and then dropped it in a lazy arc snapping the belt at only half-force across his back. Osterflood writhed nevertheless, and Gina's soft smile became a sneer.

I put my tray full of drinks on the couch and came over behind Gina, reached my arms around and enclosed at last in my hands those two marvelous mounds. They were hot and sweaty and firm and I grunted with pleasure. As I squeezed and pinched, and sucked at the salty sweat of her neck, I felt Gina lean back again and 'whack' across Osterflood's buttocks, and after a short pause another heaving motion and 'whock!' and Osterflood and I both grunted, although presumably for different reasons. Then Gina turned to me and we were two hot mouths endlessly exploring each other's watery, snake-bulging wombs. Although my hands had removed her leather skirt and were around her bulging buttocks and digging into every-thing they could, my world was soon composed of mouths, huge caverns of tongue-tangled flow of motion endlessly plunging and being plunged, biting and being bitten, rising and sinking, filling and emptying, and I felt something scratching at my leg.

'A drink,' Osterflood was saying. 'A drink, you fucking killer. One last drink.'

Reluctantly, I tore my hands away from Gina and dream-walked over to the couch and got him the desired drink.

Chapter Eighty-four

Dear Doctor Rhinehart,
   I love you. The Die said I should love you and I do. They told me to give myself to you and I will. I am yours.
                                                    Yours truly,
                                                    Elaine Simpson (age 8)

Dear Dr Rhinehart,
   In the case of Figgers vs. the State of New Hampshire, the defense for Mr Figgers has appealed the verdict of guilty of assault and battery on the grounds that the defendant was not responsible for his actions, having given up his free will to the fortunes of dice [sic], as recommended to him by his psychiatrist, a Dr Ralph Pleasant of Concord. Dr Pleasant has unfortunately abandoned a practice of twenty years and disappeared without a trace, but it is generally understood that he was a follower of a dice therapy first developed by you.
   Could you please write to us indicating whether in fact it is the general practice these days of qualified physicians using advanced modes of psychotherapy to recommend to their patients that they give up their free will to the fortunes of dice [sic]? In prosecuting Mr Figgers and attempting to defeat his motion of appeal we have been handicapped by our lack of knowledge of the latest advances in psychotherapy.

Sincerely,
Joseph L. Ting
District Attorney,
Humboldt, M.H.

Chapter Eighty-five

Osterflood was contorted on his hands and knees grunting incoherently and clutching at his stomach while the belt *whacked*! across his back twice more.

Canned hilarious laughter from the TV flowed hilariously across the room along the rug bubbling hilarious over Osterflood's twisted torso up Gina's long, sweat and semen-stained legs, over taut, dripping breasts, over my wet mouth drooling on her neck down my moisture-streaked chest and belly to bubble and reverberate hilariously at last in the endless sensuous roll and moil of my mighty oiled meat in the fold upon fold of Gina's molten, honeyed, holy-motioned, slow-rolling holy bowl. She was moaning now, holding the belt lifelessly at her thigh; I was growing and flowing in that holy motion of creation, my open hands sliding around her weary arms to enclose again her moistened round rubbery taut-tipped mounds.

A handsome, silly-looking man said:

'But I don't like sex!' and laughter roared out at us like the bray of an ass. Osterflood was mumbling about never doing it again and the little bitches and if only boys would something and beatmebeatme. He had drunk two-thirds of the glass of Scotch and strychnine I'd given him, but spit the rest out claiming it was poison.

I felt Gina's hand clutching at my balls and pressing herself back upon me and then she suddenly broke away, stepped over Osterflood as if he were a pool of vomit on the rug and got a straight-back chair, and placed it in the middle of the rug a few feet from him. I was tearing off the last of my clothes as fast as I could in a movie that always seemed to be in slow motion, but even before I'd finished or was even seated on the chair, Gina had guided the divine tool back into her, thrown her legs around me and, with a child's contented sigh, begun moving her boiling meat on my stiff bone.

One brief second she stared with wide brown eyes into mine and then her lips and mouth struck and we were engaged in two flowing worlds. Like midget octopi, my giant hands moiled and toiled at the great round rubber bowls of her buttocks and I squeezed and she churned and I pulled and she pressed and she rolled the folds of her vagina over me like waves and I tongued the back of her throat and she circled and I straightlined and she broke her mouth from mine and arched her head away from mine and said shrilly:

'Suck me, suck me,' and cupped her breasts out toward me.

I lowered my open mouth onto one and as I tongued and sucked and nibbled she moaned:

'I'm a woman! I'm a woman!'

'I know, I know,' I said as I moved from one mound of hot, salty honey to the next. She squeezed my head against her.

'Hard, harder,' she moaned.

I opened my mouth so wide I was afraid I'd never get it closed again and had a surrealistic vision of going through the rest of my life like a gaping fish and I drew all of one breast into my mouth as far as I could while I squeezed her other with both my hands pinching the nipple hard. Groaning, she pressed me tighter, shuddered, and began to pump her pelvis against me hard, and it flowed out of me at last, a molten roll of white womb-wetting foam, her fold opening and closing upon it swallowing with its honeyed tongues, her golden bowls rolling with my roll, filling where I rose, parting with my plunge, delirious, writhing, moaning, groaning done.

Or mostly done. I unswallowed her breast and managed to half-close my mouth and drew her warm soft body to mine and we churned at half-speed with each other, still enjoying the feel of it, my chin in her hair now, her lips and tongue idly tasting of the sweat of my chest and Osterflood was talking about dying dying dying and someone else was saying we could get there faster in a Ford.

We sat there for two or three minutes, Osterflood grunting, his face twisted occasionally into a horrible grin and the canned hilarious laughter blasting out at us from the television set like slop thrown out a tenement window.

Then I lifted Gina off me and walked over and collapsed into a sprawled sitting position on the couch wondering vaguely what time it was Agatha Christie time and how the great, clean, graceful murder, without fuss, emotion or violence, done with dignity, grace and aesthetic bliss was ever going to end. The handsome, silly husband was trying to explain to his pretty, silly wife why it was necessary to tell their teen-age daughter about the facts of life.

'If I thought it was bees, she can think it is bees,' the woman said and the actors paused to let the machine roar away its bubbled laughter.

Gina stood again now over Osterflood, the belt still in her hand – she hadn't released it from her hand since her first blow twenty minutes before. Osterflood was on his back, arcing it slightly, his feet toward the couch. He was grinning moronically, his eyes bulging and his cock stiff.

'I never meant to . . .' he was muttering. 'Nice boys nice girls . . . mistake . . . I'm sick, I'm sick . . . dying . . . see that now . . . NEVER AGAIN . . . be a good boy, Mommy, beat me BEAT ME.'

Gina stepped over him with one leg so she straddled his head and shoulders and faced his feet. She leaned forward a few inches and let a gob of spit fall onto his belly.

'Now, Joanie, there's something I must tell you tonight,' the husband was saying.

'Sure, Dad, but make it quick, Jack's coming with his motorcycle.'

Gina, smiling a child's soft smile, raised her arm and swept it down *thock*! the belt tearing across his thighs. Again she raised it – fascinating to watch the coil of her wet flesh, semen streaking the inside of her spread thighs, the breasts trembling as she hesitated at the top of the arc – and then *whack*! across his belly and extended rod. He screamed and vaulted his back, the grin still there, laughter from the television set spitting into the room like froth from a mad dog.

Osterflood's moans and mumbles were mostly incoherent now, and Gina rose and struck twice more with all her force, he now totally vaulting his back as if raising his stomach and thighs to embrace the hissing belt.

'Teenagers today are so violent,' the silly woman said to a silly woman friend as they walked their dogs.

Gina came back toward the couch, large eyes smiling at me, and took into her warm mouth my now boneless meat and sucked and chewed at it with good appetite. I smiled and stared stupidly at the image of two men on the screen, unearnest, silly men, talking earnestly about the horsepower of their earnest cars and of drag racing against their son's earnest motocycles.

Gina, her head bent back now, breasts trembling, had cupped my balls and buttocks with her hands and was forcing my now bulging, slimy, hot-tipped cock deeper into her mouth, pressing with her hands to force me deeper deeper plunging, a lady sword-swallower arching ever back deep to the throat moaning working me deeper,

490

then out, gasping blowing licking open and down down again swallow whole the great worn weapon of the much beloved foe down – fascinating, will my whole body be sucked up into her like a cartoon ghost by a vacuum cleaner? – down, her finger now in my anus, then she pulling me out of her mouth breathing me, tonguing me, sliding a long hard kiss along the length of me and then in again deep deeper . . . and up for air.

She twisted herself onto her back beside me on the couch, spread her legs, and, curving her head back again, directed me back into her mouth and to the base of her throat. The last thing I heard before her slimy thighs closed around my ears was the roar of motorcycles from the screen.

Gina was awash with semen and sweat and her own love juices and she used my head like a giant penis and pressed at her openings, squeezing with her thighs, writhing for something to enter her, burying me in the silken slime of her cunt until I felt I was drowning and broke myself free.

'We did it, we did it!' some male voice was crying from the television screen until the roar of other motorcycles drowned him out. Lowering my lips only to her clitoris I lengthened my hold on her buttocks to ooze my fingers into her rich openings, her cunt like a deep silken pool of the finest lubricants, her other a smooth, tight-fitting glove. I could feel Gina's hand around the base of my prick and occasionally enclosing my balls, and another hand around my buttocks and in my crack and another hand scratching hard at my back and shoulder until I wondered where she got her third hand and suddenly saw five inches from my eyes the twisted horrible grin of Osterflood, eyes bulging.

'Drink, drink,' he said and clawed at my shoulder.

I raised myself off Gina and tore my lower half out of

her mouth and marched off to the liquor cabinet to get that glass of water. When I marched back again Gina was standing beside Osterflood; he was slumped against the couch. She held out the belt to me as I approached.

'You want to try a few?' she said.

'No, no, I'm a pacifist,' I said. 'Thanks, anyway.'

She stepped to his back and raised the belt, but I told her to wait until I had given him the glass of water. He turned to me and stretched out a trembly hand for the glass, took it, raised it to his lips and began gulping. Sssssst *Thack*! The belt tore across the hand and the glass and water spilled to the floor.

'That wasn't very nice,' I said, wondering if Osterflood were immortal.

She smiled bright-eyed at me, like a schoolgirl who has just accomplished a particularly good trick with a jump rope.

'Save me, Rhinehart, save me,' Osterflood mumbled and clawed at my knees. But without Gina's striking him again he abruptly rolled onto the floor and vaulted his back. Gina smiled at him, but he stayed in his vaulted position; he was in another convulsion. As I watched, the belt fell lightly across my hair to my shoulder and Gina looped it so that she had me around the neck with the belt as noose and led me to the chair and forced me down into it.

She straddled me, lowering herself in little dips against the stiff cock which she maneuvered first against and slightly into one hole and then the other and then she slid over me, burying the cock deep within her. We rubbed now, and bit and clawed, and squeezed and pinched and sucked and laughter poured over us and Osterflood gurgled and choked and a voice said, 'So it isn't bees after all,' and I rose up and holding Gina tight to me by the buttocks I fell to a kneeling position on the rug and then forward on top of her she already coming in a frenzied pelvic pulsation sucking and biting at my shoulder and I rammed and Osterflood gurgled and I rammed at her rammed and rammed and rammed my mouth filled with breast and laughter flowing over us ramming ram and it ah flowed out hot ah molten wet lava pouring into her in ah in ah in and ram one more time GOOD AH ah ah good good good seeing Osterflood to my left beautiful grinning lying on his side knees drawn toward his belly his face beautiful twisted in its hideous grin his cock stiff his belly spilling his semen pools onto the rug his eyes open glassy, staring, fixed, unmoving, dead.

Chapter Eighty-six

The Die giveth and the Die taketh away. Blessed be the name of the Die.

Chapter Eighty-seven

Dear Dr Rhinehart and Company,

We are deeply indebted to you here at Fedel's for the fine catalytic effect your theory of the dicelife has had on sales and profits and on our lives. My business life had been giving me less and less satisfaction over the years. I had the usual ulcer and mistress, and I divorced my wife and took a dose of LSD or something and went to discotheques, but nothing helped: my profits and my indifference remained steady. Then I read an article about you in *The New Yorker* which I detest and never read, and located a follower of yours here in Columbus and I and my business haven't been the same since.

The first thing the dice told me to do was raise wages across the board thirty percent and write commending personal letters to everyone. Efficiency jumped forty-three percent that month (it dropped back twenty-eight percent the next). Then the dice ordered me to stop manufacturing conventional hats (the family product for sixty-seven years), but to make experimental hats. My designers went out of their minds in ecstasy. Our first line of hats (you may have read about them in *Ladies' Wear*) was the highly successful 'Boat Sombrero,' essentially a cowboy hat with a brim that tapers flush to the peak at the sides but flows out four inches in front and back.

Although our profits declined fifteen percent, our sales leapt twenty percent and I wasn't bored anymore. Our second design was the rainhat that looks like a Ku Klux Klan hood and is made of brightly colored plastic suitable for both sexes. It's not going well at all (except in the South) but all of us at Fedel's think it's great. My profits turned at this point into a loss, but the Die's will be done.

The Die then insisted we drop our number one money-making line of cheap men's expensive hats. Our retailers were appalled, but we were so engrossed in our third experimental design (the designer claims the Die made a key decision on it) that we didn't care. The 'pancake' or 'halo' (we haven't consulted the Die yet) is a disc-shaped headgear that works on the principle of the academic mortar board, but comes in a variety of colors, materials and shapes, although it is usually elliptical or circular. Our retail outlets are very skeptical, but have ordered so many on the basis of the success of the 'Boat Sombrero' that we're months behind in orders already.

We're deeply in debt, but our top designers and management personnel have all voluntarily taken fifty percent wage cuts in exchange for a share of the profits on our 'halo' line and we're going to survive. The Die last week ordered a designer of ours to design a hat that covers the whole body and although some of us are doubtful, he is going ahead with enthusiasm.

To think I used to design and sell the same type of hat year after year! Please send us all your publications, and thank you for your help.

Sincerely, yours,
Joseph Fedel, President
Fedel's Hats, Columbus, Ohio.

Chapter Eighty-eight

Professor Boggles at CETRE

Dear Luke,

I am a rational, linear, verbal, discursive, literary man and even your previous absurdities prepared me only minimumly for the shock of my first week in the Catskill CETRE. I dutifully expressed anger, played Hamlet, pretended to be a fool, acted like an enraged tiger; I even swished my considerable hips effeminately when the Die tried to turn me into a woman. However, I did all this in isolation; I saw to it that none of my role playing involved active interaction with other people. When other people attempted to impose their 'selves' on me I became cynical inside, no matter what I was halfheartedly doing outside.

A middle-aged woman grossly importuned me to seduce her and the Die dictated that I ought to respond favorably. I found myself slobbering on her neck and squeezing her expansive bosom but feeling totally detached. My phallus remained detumescent. After five minutes she huffed off to someone else.

My awakening came on the fifth day, in the creativity room. The Die had chosen for me the assignment to write four pages using a new language – one employing primarily words from known vocabularies but combining them in a new grammar, syntax and diction. I was to try to express real feelings. I sat for an hour and couldn't get past doodles. Then I finally wrote a sentence:

'Muckme piddles ping pong poetry.'

I liked the sound of it but the syntax was too regular. I wrote a second:

'Skinned. Skinniedup, baked. Stick a.'

That I felt was better, but lacking in verbs.

'Farceuncle midwoof floops on the cooch Harkening strayners at the dolor.'

I smiled to myself: I felt I was getting closer to truth.

'Missy-led clanker retchatches purr purr floops midwoof flushiting. I wunted crandy. Yo no crandy git, dabby sated. Yo knotted again, he replyed jobbily. Fluckit shushit. Hotbam mastar.'

But I was supposed to be expressing real feelings. How might I do that without being absurdly clear and trivial? I must proceed further, I thought:

'Mime a riter. A riter is sumun who rights. Words, wurts, worst . . . what too due? Fusshackle thought, ruddycup the blissbiz pronotions gaym, baby gone. Flat chance I have of whining a prize. Holy Muffer, merry of God . . . Ahhh.'

> Remaindered Redeemer, where dost thou go?
> Kink of the Whirl, you knot me so
> I ken not. Rash anality has deshitted me
> Of all my straineth. I beg you show me merdesee.

Yoose your head, your my-end, your braying! Your rashanality! He rashandill! (A reckoning crew will destroy us all.) Member, an hefull man is one who unjoys life, finds many playsures. He is a cheyeheld who nose nothink. Be rashanal and use sickology. But write, rite, right, reyet!

> Got is the kink of the Universe
> (Ice died for our since!)
> Got is the kink of the Whirl
> (He nailrows what is wide and free)
> God makes ridid what is fleshible
> (To him who hass much shall be piled)
> The seven deadly Since he names,
> The thinks we've done, we must do penitentiary for
> (Luff, Hee says, is oil)
> Got so luffed the whirl that he graved is unly beGotten son that those that bleaf he died for their since may have infernal life.

Ah, Luke, I wrote on and on, for two and a half hours I wrote all glorious nonsense and sense so interfused it will take my graduate students decades to decipher it all. It's beautiful. I felt so good the next fat female that bloated her boobs for Boggles was erected on the spot. Dear Luke, you are utterly amad and I your faithfool decipherpill.

Yours,

Gobbles.

Chapter Eighty-nine

[*Being a questioning of Dr Lucius Rhinehart by Inspector Nathaniel Putt of the New York City police regarding the unfortunate rigidification of Mr Franklin Delano Osterflood.*]

'It's good to see you again, Inspector Putt,' Dr Rhinehart said. 'How have you been?'

'Fine, thank – Sit down, Rhinehart.'

'Thank you. You've got a new couch.'

'You know why I've called you in?'

'No, I'm afraid I don't. Lost some more mental patients?'

'Do you know a man named Frank Osterflood?'

'Yes, I do. He was a – '

'When did you last see him?'

Dr Rhinehart pulled out a die, shook it in his cupped hands and leaned forward to drop it on the inspector's desk. After examining the results he said:

'About a week ago.'

Inspector Putt's eyes glittered minutely.

'You . . . saw . . . him . . . one week ago.'

'Yes, about then. Why? What's Frank up to these days? Nothing serious, I hope.'

'Please describe your meeting with him.'

'Mmmmm. I remember I ran into him purely by chance on the street near his apartment. We decided to go to dinner together.'

'Go on.'

'After dinner, he suggested we go visit a girlfriend of his in Harlem. So we went.'

'Go on.'

'I spent a couple of hours with Osterflood with his girlfriend and then I left.'

'What took place at this girlfriend's place?'

'We watched some television. And, well, Osterflood engaged the girl in sexual congress and then I engaged her in sexual congress. It was a joint session you might say.'

'Did Osterflood leave with you?'

'No. I left alone.'

'What was he doing when you left?'

'He was sleeping on the living room rug.'

'What was Osterflood's reaction to this girl?'

'I'd say it was basically masochistic. Sadistic elements too.'

'Did the girl seem to like him?'

'She seemed to take pleasure in her interaction with him.'

'You say Osterflood was asleep when you left?'

'Yes.'

'Was he drunk?'

'Probably.'

'Was he in good health?'

'Mmmm. No. He was overweight, had eaten too much that night. Had digestive problems. Was exhausting himself in acts of atonement.'

Inspector Putt stared coldly at Dr Rhinehart and then asked abruptly:

'Who prepared the drinks for everyone that night?'

'Ahh. The drinks.'

'Yes, the drinks.'

Dr Rhinehart bounced the die on the desk a second time. He smiled.

'Mr Osterflood prepared the drinks.'

'Osterflood!'

'I found several of my Scotches unfriendlily watered-down, but the service was otherwise fine.'

The inspector's face and eyes became exceptionally cold as he stared at Dr Rhinehart.

'Did the Die tell you to murder Osterflood that night?'

'Oh I doubt it. But it's an interesting question. Let's see.' Dr Rhinehart dribbled the die a third time, and then looked up brightly at his questioner. 'Nope.'

'I see. I suppose that's the truth,' Inspector Putt sneered.

'It's what the Die told me to say.'

The two men looked at each other and then the inspector, tight-lipped, pushed a button on the side of his desk and told the detective who came to the door to 'bring her in.'

Gina entered, dressed conservatively in a knee-length skirt, a heavy blouse and an ill-fitting jacket.

'That's the man,' she said.

'Sit down,' said the inspector.

'That's him.'

'Hi, Gina,' Dr Rhinehart said.

'He admits it. See, he admits it.'

'Sit down, Gina,' the detective said.

'Miss Potrelli to you, fuzz-face.'

'Please briefly repeat your story of how the evening with Osterflood went,' said the inspector.

'This guy and Frank came to my apartment and I gave them both a fuck. This guy served the drinks. Osterflood began to act as if he'd been drugged and was getting woozy and this guy dragged him off.'

'Dr Rhinehart?' Inspector Putt said coldly.

'Mr Osterflood and I paid a social call on Miss Potrelli. Frank made us all several drinks while we watched television and engaged in sexual congresses. I left with

Frank lying on the floor with a blissful smile on his face. Where is old Frank, by the way?'

'He's dead, damn you,' said Gina.

'Shuttup,' said the inspector and then went on quietly: 'The body of Frank Osterflood was discovered on November 15 in the East River under the Triborough Bridge. An autopsy has revealed that he'd been dead about two days. He was poisoned with strychnine.' He looked only at Rhinehart. 'You or Gina here – one of you – was the last one to see Osterflood alive.'

'Maybe he just took a midnight swim in the East River and accidently swallowed some water,' suggested Dr Rhinehart.

'The percentage solution of strychnine in the East River,' said Inspector Putt soberly, 'is still at acceptable levels.'

'But then I wonder what happened to him,' said Dr Rhinehart.

'Traces of strychnine have been found on the shelf above Gina's liquor cabinet and in the rug in front of the TV set.'

'How interesting.'

'You mixed the drinks!' Gina said shrilly.

'I did? No, my story is that Osterflood mixed them.' Dr Rhinehart scowled in concentration. 'Maybe a dice decision made him decide to kill himself in retribution for his sins. He showed certain masochistic tendencies.'

'You mixed the drinks and you left with him,' Gina said again shrilly.

'Not according to my story, Miss Potrelli. According to my story I left first and he left later.'

'Oh,' she said. 'You're a liar.'

'Let's just say we have different stories. This confuses the inspector and makes him uneasy.'

'There are already four other witnesses who claim that

they saw you leave with Osterflood, Rhinehart,' said the detective.

'Ahh, four! That shows initiative, Gina. It would be a shame to waste those witnesses.'

Dr Rhinehart retrieved his die from the desk and dropped it onto the couch beside his thigh.

'I left with Osterflood, Inspector.'

'Where did you go?'

'Where did we go, Gina?'

'You took a tax – '

'Shuttup! Get her out of here.'

Gina was removed from the room by the detective.

'We got in a taxi, I believe. I got off at the Lexington Avenue subway stop at 125th Street. I needed to relieve myself. Osterflood went on. He was quite drunk and I felt slightly guilty about leaving him with a suspiciously cheerful cabbie, but I was drunk too. I found a urinal near – '

'Why did you lie to us the first time?'

'Who says I lied to you the first time?'

'You've just changed your story.'

'Details.'

'Gina's witnesses exposed your lie.'

'Come now, Inspector, you know full well that her four witnesses are even less reliable than the dice, and that's going some.'

'Shuttup!'

'And besides, the Die told me to change the story.'

The inspector was glaring at Dr Rhinehart.

'You'd better consult your dice again,' he said. 'No cabbie in the city remembers picking up two big white men in Harlem that evening, or for that matter any evening in the last five years. You, as a doctor, would have recognized the symptoms of strychnine poisoning as different from simple drunkenness. We know Gina and her four witnesses are lying. We know you're lying. We *know* Osterflood was murdered at Gina's and never left there alive.'

Inspector Putt and Dr Rhinehart stared at each other.

'Wow!' Dr Rhinehart said after a while. He leaned forward on the couch, wide-eyed, attentive, interested, and asked intently: 'Who killed him?'

Chapter Ninety

Dear Doc,
   The Die told me to write you. Can't think of much to say.

                    Die bless you,

                              Fred Weedmuller,
                              Porksnout, Texas.

Chapter Ninety-one

A week after my interview with him, Inspector Putt announced to anyone who was interested that new evidence (undisclosed) indicated conclusively that Osterflood must have committed suicide probably. Privately, he informed friends and informers that it was clear he couldn't possibly get a conviction against either Gina or me. Gina wouldn't have murdered Osterflood so premeditatedly in her own apartment with another white man present, and strychnine, he noted, is not the usual mode of murder of 'abused Harlem whores.' Moreover, her four witnesses, while obviously they were lying, nevertheless would raise a shadow of doubt in the minds of a few radlib jurors.

Dr Rhinehart would be impossible to convict because no jury, radlib or one hundred and ten percent American, could be expected to understand Rhinehart's motivation. The inspector admitted he himself wasn't certain he understood it. 'He did it because the dice told him to,' the DA would proclaim and the defense attorneys would lead the general laughter which would follow. The world was changing too rapidly for the typical juror, no matter how American, to keep up. Moreover, even Inspector Putt was beginning to doubt that Rhinehart had done it, for, though he was certainly capable of murder, Rhinehart, if the Die had told him to do it, would clearly not have done such a debauched, confused, messy, unaesthetic, incompetent job of it.

Nevertheless, Inspector Putt had called me for one last

confrontation and had concluded a long lecture with the ringing words:

'Someday, Rhinehart, the law is going to catch up with you. Someday the furies are going to come home to roost. Someday the sins you are committing in the name of your dice games are going to be taken out of the bank. Someday, you will learn, crime, even in the United States, does not pay.'

'I'm sure you're right,' I said, shaking his hand as I left. 'But is there any hurry?'

So my dicelife went on. I gave the Die one chance in six that I do everything in my power to bring Osterflood back to life again, but the option lost out to another one-in-six shot: that I spend three days in mourning for Frank, and that I compose a few prayers and parables for the occasion.

On January 1, 1971, I had my third annual Fate Day to determined my long-range role for the year. The Die was given the options that (1) sometime that year I marry Linda Reichman, Terry Tracy, Miss Reingold, or a woman chosen at random (I felt that if I couldn't make a go of a dicemarriage with someone, then the nuclear family might be in danger); (2) I give up the dice for the year and begin an entirely new career of some sort (this no longer frightening option was inspired by Fuigi Arishi's article I had read that day on 'The Withering Away of the Die'); (3) I 'begin revolutionary activity against the estab-lished clods of the world, my purpose being to expose hypocrisy and injustice, shame the unjust, awaken and arouse the oppressed and, in general, to wage an unend-ing war against crime: namely, to smash society as radi-cally as I am trying to smash society in me' (I'd read a month or two before that Eric Cannon and Arturo Jones had formed an underground revolutionary group and the

508

memory that day made me feel heroic: I wasn't sure what my words meant that I *do*, but the ring of them made me sit proud on the living room rug where I was preparing to cast the dice); (4) I work during the year on books and articles and novels and stories about whatever the Die dictated, completing at least the equivalent of two books (I resented the bum job of publicity work that was being done for our Dice Centers and the DICELIFE Foundation and vaguely pictured myself coming to the rescue); (5) I continue my multiple activities in promoting diceliving throughout the world, the nature of my contribution to be determined by the Die (it's what I most felt like doing: Linda and Jake and Fred and Lil were all sporadically part of our diceteam, and the dicelife without other dicepeople is often lonely); and (6) I spend the whole year limiting my options to the duration of one day only, so that, indeed (to quote the inspired rhetoric of my '71 Fate Day), 'each day's dawning bring a new birth, while others ignore it and grow old.' (This last option fascinated me since I always find long-range options something of a drag: they tend to make me too patterned, even if it is the pattern of the Die.)

But the Die, testing me, tumbled down a 'four': that 'I work during the year on various writing projects.' Two subsequent dice decisions soon determined that I was to complete sometime during the year 'an autobiography of exactly 200,000 words' (so I've had this stupid thing barging in on my days most of the year) and that I worked on other Die-selected work when appropriate (namely when the Die and I felt like it).

Of course writing is hardly a full-time job and I continued randomly seeing my friends, working sporadically with Dice Centers and dicegroups, occasionally lecturing, whimsically playing occasional new roles, occasionally practicing my dice exercises, and generally leading a very enjoyable, repetitious, consistently inconsistent random sporadic unpredictable dicelife.

Then, naturally, Chance intervened.

Chapter Ninety-two

RELIGION FOR OUR TIME

presents

[The camera pans from one figure to the next of the five people seated on the slightly raised stage in front of the fifty or so people in the audience.]

Father John Wolfe, assistant professor of theology at Fordham University; Rabbi Eli Fishman, chairman of the Ecumenical Center for a More United Society; Dr Eliot Dart, professor of psychology at Princeton University and noted atheist; and Dr Lucius M. Rhinehart, psychiatrist and controversial founder of the Religion of the Die.

'Welcome to another live, free, open, spontaneous and completely unrehearsed discussion in our series about Religion for Our Time. Our Subject today:

IS THE RELIGION OF THE DIE A COP-OUT?

[Image of Mrs Wippleton.]

'Our moderator for today's program: Mrs Sloan Wippleton, former screen and television actress, wife of noted financier and socialite Gregg Wippleton and mother of four lovely children. Mrs Wippleton is also chairman of the First Presbyterian Church's Committee for Religious Tolerance. Mrs Wippleton.'

She bursts into a smile and speaks with enthusiasm.

'Thank you. Good afternoon, ladies and gentlemen. We are fortunate today to have a very interesting subject for discussion and one I'm sure you've all wanted to learn more about: the Religion of the Die. We also have a very

511

distinguished panel to discuss it. Dr Rhinehart [image shifts briefly to Dr Rhinehart, who, dressed totally in black with a heavy black turtleneck sweater and suit, looks vaguely ministerial. He chews on but does not smoke a large pipe throughout] is one of the most controversial figures of the last year. His papers and books on dice theory and therapy have scandalized the psychiatric world, and his readings from *The Book of the Die* have scandalized the religious world. He has earned from the American Association of Practicing Psychiatrists a Special Condemnation. Nevertheless, many individuals have rallied round Dr Rhinehart and his religion, some of them not in mental hospitals. Last year Dr Rhinehart and his followers began opening Dice Centers called Centers for Experiments in Totally Random Environments and thousands of people have gone through these centers, some reporting deeply religious experiences, but others suffering severe breakdowns. No matter how opinions differ, all agree that Dr Rhinehart is a very controversial man.

'Dr Rhinehart, I'd like to open our discussion by asking you our central question for today, and then asking each of our other guests to comment on the same thing: "Is your religion of the Die a Cop-out?" '

'Sure,' says Dr Rhinehart, chewing contentedly on his pipe, then he remains silent. Mrs W. looks first expectant and then nervous.

'How is it a cop-out?'

'In three ways.' Again R. chews wordlessly on his pipe, serene and satisfied.

'In what three ways?'

R. lowers his head and the camera pans down to see him rubbing something between his hands and then drop onto the small table in front of him a die; it is a six. When the camera pans back up to his face the viewer sees R. looking directly out from the screen. With a benevolent

512

glow, he holds his pipe steady and smokeless, looking at the viewer. Five seconds, ten seconds pass. Fifteen.

'Dr Rhinehart?' says a feminine voice off-screen. Image shifts to a serious Mrs W. Then back to R. Then to Mrs W., frowning, then to R., exhaling smokeless air from an open mouth. Then, uncertainly, appears the image of Father Wolfe, who looks as if he's concentrating on what he's going to say.

'Rabbi Fishman. Perhaps you'd like to lead off today,' says the off-screen feminine voice.

Rabbi Fishman, short, dark and fortyish, directs his words intently first toward Mrs W. and then to R.

'Thank you, Mrs Wippleton. I find everything Dr Rhinehart has said this afternoon extremely interesting, but he seems to be missing the chief point: the religion of the Die is a resignation from the status of man: it is a worship of chance, and as such, a worship of that which has always been man's adversary. Man is above all else the great organizer, the great integrator, while a dicelife, as I understand it, is a destroyer of integration and unity. It is a cop-out from human life, but not into the life of random nature as some of Dr Rhinehart's critics have maintained. No. Nature, too, is an organizer and an integrator. But the religion of the Die represents in a way the worship of disintegration, dissolution and death. It is anti-life. I find it another sign of the sickness of our times.'

[Camera pans smoothly back to Mrs W.]

'That's very interesting, Rabbi Fishman. You've certainly given us much food for thought. Dr Rhinehart, would you like to comment?'

'Sure.'

R. stares again serenely out at the television audience, benignly chewing on his pipe. Five seconds, ten, twelve.

'Father Wolfe,' says Mrs W.'s high-pitched voice.

'My turn?'

513

[Image of round, red-faced blond-haired Father Wolfe, looking at first uncertainly off toward Mrs W., then staring into the camera like a prosecuting attorney.]

'Thank you. The religion of the Die is, no matter how Dr Rhinehart may try to weasel out of it this afternoon, the worship of the Antichrist. There is a moral law, er, a moral order to the universe which God created, and the surrender of one's free will to the decisions of dice is the most outrageous and complete crime against ah God that I can imagine. It is to surrender to sin without raising a fist. It is the act of a ah coward.

'*Cop-out* is too mild a word. The religion of the Die is a crime, against ah God and against the dignity and grandeur of man created in ah God's image. Free will distinguishes man from ur God's other creatures. To surrender that gift may well be that sin against the Holy Spirit which is unforgivable. Dr Rhinehart may be well educated, he may well be a medical doctor, but his so-called er religion of the Die is the most unh poisonous, unh obnoxious and satanic thing I have ever heard of ah.'

'May I comment on that?' says R.'s voice from off-screen, and his image appears, wordless and relaxed, staring out, obviously not intending to speak a single further word. It is as if the channel had been switched every time his face appears on the screen.

Five, seven, eight, ten seconds pass.

'Dr Dart,' says a subdued female voice.

Dr Dart appears: young, dynamic, handsome, cigarette smoking, nervous, intense, brilliant.

'I find Dr Rhinehart's performance today rather amusing, and perfectly consistent with the clinical picture I have formed of him through a reading of his work and through discussions with people who have known him. We can't understand the religion of the Die and the peculiar way it is a cop-out unless we can understand the *pathology* of its creator and of its followers. Basically, as Dr Rhinehart himself has acknowledged, he is a schizoid. [The image on the screen becomes that of Dr Rhinehart, benignly looking at the viewer, and remains through the next part of Dr Dart's analysis.] Dr Rhinehart's alienation and anomie apparently reached such a degree that he lost a single identity and became a multiple personality. The literature is full of case studies of this schizoid type, and he differs from the typical case only in the large number of personalities he is apparently able to adopt. The compulsive nature of this role playing is masked by the use of the dice and by the mumbo-jumbo religion of the Die created around it. The pathological pattern of aliena- tion and anomie is common in our society, and the significant number of people influenced by the religion of the Die manifests the appeal of a verbal structure to mask and support the psychological disintegration which has taken place. [Image of Dr Dart reappears.]

'The religion of the Die is not so much a cop-out as it is, like all religions, a comforter, a confirmation and, one might say, an elevation of the psychological debilities of the individual who embraces the religion. Passivity before the rigid God of Catholicism or Judaism is one form of cop-out, passivity before the flexible and unpredictable God of chance is another. Both can be understood only in terms of individual and group pathology.'

Dr Dart turns back to Mrs Wippleton. Her image appears, serious and sincere.

'What kind of nonsense is that about the rigid God of Judaism?' says Rabbi Fishman's voice from off-screen.

'I'm just reporting commonly accepted psychological theory,' Dart answers.

'If anything is pathological,' says Rabbi Fishman darkly from the screen again, 'it's the sterile pseudo-objectivity

515

of neurotic psychologists pretending to understand spiritual man.'

'Gentlemen,' interposes Mrs Wippleton with her best smile.

'Catholicism is not the elevation of man's debilities [comes Father Wolfe's voice and then face] but of his spiritual grandeur. It is the insect minds of psychologists –'

'Gentlemen –'

'Your defensiveness interests me,' says Dr Dart.

'Our subject today,' interposes a beaming Mrs Wippleton, 'is the religion of the Die and I for one am anxious to hear what Dr Rhinehart has to say about the charge that his religion is schizophrenic and pathological.'

[The image of Dr Rhinehart appears, glowing, friendly, relaxed. Five seconds. Six.]

'I don't understand your silence, Dr Rhinehart,' says Mrs Wippleton from off-screen. Not a flicker of change in R.

'This is a typical symptom, Mrs Wippleton,' says Dr Dart's voice, 'of the schizophrenic in the catatonic state. Dr Rhinehart is apparently capable of going in and out of such states almost at will, a most unusual ability. In a few minutes he may be talking so much you won't be able to shut him up.'

Dr Rhinehart removes the pipe from his mouth and exhales a lungful of fresh air.

'But if I understand you correctly, Dr Dart,' says Mrs W., 'then you are saying that Dr Rhinehart has a form of mental disease which would normally be institutionalized.'

'No, not quite,' says an intense Dr Dart. 'You see, Dr Rhinehart is a sort of schizophrenic *manqué*, if I may coin a phrase. His religion has permitted him to do what most schizophrenics are incapable of doing: it justifies and unifies his splintered personality. Without his religion of the Die he would be a hopelessly babbling maniac. With

516

it he can function – function as an integrated, schizo-phrenic *manqué* of course, but function nevertheless.'

'I find his silence this afternoon senseless, rude and a cop-out,' says Rabbi Fishman.

'He is afraid to confront the unh American people with the enormity of his ur sin,' says Father Wolfe. 'He cannot answer Truth.'

'Dr Rhinehart, would you like to answer these charges?' asks Mrs Wippleton.

[The image of R. slowly removing his pipe, still looking at the viewer.]

'Yes,' he says.

Silence of five seconds, ten. Fifteen.

'But how?'

Dr Rhinehart is seen now for the second time leaning forward and rubbing his hands together and dropping a die upon the table next to the untouched cup of brown liquid. A close-up shot magnifies the result: a two. He reverts without a flicker of expression to his benevolent serenity flowing out to the viewers of the world.

Rabbi Fishman begins speaking and his face appears on the screen.

'This is the sort of imbecility which attracts thousands? It's beyond me. People starving to death in India, the suffering in Vietnam, our black brothers still with legiti-mate grievances, and this man, a *doctor* mind you, sits puffing on an unlit pipe and playing with dice. He's a Nero fiddling while Rome burns.'

'He's ah ah worse, Rabbi,' says Father Wolfe. 'Nero rebuilt Rome afterward. This man knows only how to destroy.'

Dr Dart speaks:

'The alienated schizoid experiences both himself and others as objects and is unble to relate to others except in terms of his fantasy world.'

517

'And we're not in his fantasy world?' asks Mrs W.

'We're there. He thinks he's manipulating us with his silence.'

'How can we stop him?'

'By being silent.'

'Oh.'

Rabbi Fishman speaks:

'Maybe we should talk about something else, Mrs Wippleton. I hate to see your lovely program ruined by a loony.'

[The image of Dr Rhinehart appears and is left there, eyes and pipe leveled at the viewer through all of the next bit of the program.]

'Oh thank you, Rabbi Fishman, that's thoughtful of you. But I do think we should try to analyze Dr Rhinehart's religion. It's what the sponsor paid for.'

'Notice he has no tics.' Dr D.

'What's that mean?' Rabbi F.

'He's not nervous.'

'Oh.'

'I'd like to answer your second question now, Mrs Wippleton.' [Father W.]

'Er, what's that?'

'Your second question was going to be "Oh my goodness, perhaps we should discuss why the religion of the Die attracts some people."'

'Oh yes.'

'May I give my answer now?'

'Oh yes, do. Go ahead.'

Father Wolfe's prosecuting-attorney voice snaps out from the same screen from which looks Dr Rhinehart.

'The devil has always attracted men through gaudy disguises ah, through bread and circuses ahh and through promises he cannot fulfill unh. I believe – '

518

'Wouldn't it be interesting if he never came out of it?' interrupts Rabbi Fishman's voice.

'I beg your pardon, I was speaking.' [Father Wolfe.]

'Oh he'll come out of it,' says Dr Dart. 'The permanent catatonic looks more tense but less alert. Rhinehart's obviously just putting on an act.'

'How can people be interested in such a nut?' asked Rabbi Fishman.

'I believe he's not always this way, is he?' asks Mrs Wippleton.

Father Wolfe says:

'He talked to me quite pleasantly before we went on the air, but I wasn't fooled. I knew it was just ah un trick.'

'Dr Dart, perhaps you'd like to comment on why the religion of the Die attracts followers,' says Mrs W.

'Look, he's exhaling again,' says Rabbi Fishman.

'Ignore him,' says Dr Dart, 'we're playing his game.'

Father Wolfe says:

'Mrs Wippleton, I must point out that you asked *me* to answer that question first and that I was rudely interrupted by Dr Dart before I had finished.'

[Silence. The image changes to Mrs Wippleton, who is sitting wide-eyed and openmouthed looking to her right.]

'Oh my God,' she says.

'Jesus H. Christ,' comes one of the panelists' voices off-screen.

[A loud crash and two or three feminine screams from the audience.]

'What the hell is this?'

'STOP THEM!'

[Bang.]

Mrs Wippleton, still openmouthed, is seen standing up and fiddling with the microphone at her neck. She tries a smile:

'Will the members of the audience please – '

'Ahhhhgggggh – ' a long scream.

'Shut her up!'

[The camera jerks a pan over the audience to locate two armed men, one white and one Negro, standing at the door behind the audience, one looking out, the other glaring at the audience. Then, for obscure reasons, the image of Dr Rhinehart returns, removing his pipe, exhaling air, and returning it to his mouth to chew on it.]

'Has Bobby got the elevators?'

'Are we on?'

[Bang, bamtwang.]

'What if they got Bobby?'

'Stay in your seats! Stay in your seats! Or we'll shoot!'

'Are we on?'

'Go ask Eric what's – '

Bambambambam.

'LOOK OUT!!'

[More gunshots bang away and Rhinehart disappears and is replaced by an armed man falling (clutching his belly). Two men with pistols fire past the audience at something. One of them falls forward with a groan. The other stops shooting, but remains looking off intently.]

'Are we on?' comes the masculine voice again.

[Dr Rhinehart's benign face is again the image on the home screen, but not centred, since the camera which happens to be on him and happens to be being transmitted has been deserted by the cameraman, who is sitting quietly now in the audience trying to look natural, which, since everyone else in the audience looks terrified, makes him stand out like a nude at a funeral.]

'All right, Charlie, get your camera aimed over here; our boys in the control room will do the rest.'

'Where's Malcolm? He was going to introduce Arturo.'

'He's a . . . he's a . . .'

'Oh. Yes.'

'Ladies and gentlemen, Arturo X.'

On the screen Dr Rhinehart looks out as always.

'Am I on?' says someone's voice.

'Is he on?'

Dr Rhinehart exhales.

'Where's Eric?'

'What the hell's the matter with you guys in there?' shouts someone.

[The image shifts to a shot of Rabbi Fishman's feet, which are wrapped around each other, and then to Arturo X, who is standing tensely with his back to the camera looking off at the control room.]

'You're on,' comes a muffled shout.

Arturo turns to face the camera.

'Black brothers and white bastards of the world – '

A gray-flanneled arm and white hand appear around his neck; the face of Dr Dart is seen tensely beside and behind that of Arturo.

'Drop your gun, you, or I'll shoot this man,' Dr Dart says toward his right.

'Inside the control room there, you!' shouts Dr Dart. 'You! Throw down your gun and come out with your hands up.'

Arturo's face begins to show less strain, and the viewer becomes aware of Dr Dart's face taking on a strangled look. A long black-suited arm and huge white hand are seen now firmly around his neck, and the face of Dr Rhinehart, still with the pipe in his mouth and still with the benign look on his face, appears beside that of Dr Dart. Arturo breaks away from Dart and the viewer sees a gun in Dr Rhinehart's other hand sticking into the side of Dr Dart.

'What do you want me to shoot now?' an off-screen voice says.

'Shoot me,' says Arturo's voice.

[The image pans slowly from the sedate wrestler's pose of the two psychologists past the terrified and bewildered faces of Mrs Wippleton and Rabbi Fishman, past the empty chair of Father Wolfe, to Arturo, still gasping for breath, but looking intently and sincerely into the camera.]

'Black bastards and white brothers of the world . . .' begins Arturo. A pained, quizzical expression crosses his face. He says: 'Black brothers and white bastards of the world, we have taken over this television program this afternoon to bring you some truths they won't tell you on *any* program except at gunpoint. The black man – '

[A tremendous explosion from the rear of the studio interrupts Arturo. Screams. A single 'bang.']

'Fire!!'

[More screams, and several voices pick up the cry of fire. Arturo is staring off to his right and he yells: 'Where's Eric?']

'Let's get out of here!' someone shouts.

Arturo turns nervously back to the camera and begins speaking of the difficulties of being a black person in a white society and the difficulties of being able to communicate his grievances to the white oppressors. Smoke drifts across in front of him and coughs, which had come at isolated intervals, now come from off-screen with machine-gun regularity.

'Tear gas,' yells a voice.

'Oh no,' screams a woman and begins crying.

Bang. Bangbang.

More screams.

'Let's go!'

Arturo, glancing continually to his right and occasionally pausing, struggles on with his speech, staring, whenever he finds the time, sincerely into the camera.

'. . . Oppression so pervasive that no black man alive

can breathe without seeming to have ten white men standing on his – chest. No more shall we lie down before white pigs! No more shall we obey the laws of white injustice! No more shall we simper and fawn to – watch out over there, Ray! – There! – to . . . ah . . . white men anywhere. We have abjected ourselves for the last time. No white, no white – Ray! There! [Shots are being exchanged off-screen; Arturo is crouching, his face a tangle of terror and hatred, but he struggles on with his speech.]

'. . . No white can deny us again our right to be heard, our right to say that WE STILL EXIST, that your efforts to enslave us continue, and WE WILL NOT LIE DOWN FOR YOU anyMORE! Ahhhh.'

The 'Ah' at the end of his speech was a gentle sound, and as he fell forward onto the floor the last glimpse the Sunday afternoon television audience had of his face showed a look not of fear or hatred but of bewildered surprise. The shouts and groans and shots continued sporadically, smoke or tear gas floating across in front of the TV image of Dr Rhinehart, his pipe still emerging in its permanent erection from his mouth, and tears appearing in his eyes. The sound seemed sedate and repetitious compared to the earlier action and hundreds of viewers were about to switch channels when a boy appeared in front of the man with the pipe, long-haired, handsome, blue eyes glittering with tears, dressed in blue jeans and a black shirt open at the neck.

He looked into the camera with steady and serene hatred for about five seconds and then said quietly with only one partial choking spasm:

'I'll be back. Perhaps not next Sunday, but I'll be back. There's rottenness to the way men are forced to live their lives that poisons us all; there's a worldwide war on between those who build and work with the machine that twists and tortures us and those who seek to destroy it. There is a worldwide war on: whose side are you on?'

He evaporates from the screen, leaving only a smoke-smudged image of Dr Rhinehart, crying. He arises now and moves three paces closer to the camera. His head is cut off so that all the viewer sees is the black sweater and suit. His voice is heard, after a brief burst of coughing, quiet and firm:

'This program has been brought to your by normal, earnest human beings, without whose efforts it would not have been.'

And the black body disappears, leaving on the screen only the image of an empty chair and a small table with a cup of undrunk liquid and beside the cup a blurred white speck, like the compressed feather of an angel.

Chapter Ninety-three

In the beginning was Chance, and Chance was with God and Chance was God. He was in the beginning with God. All things were made by Chance and without him not anything made that was made. In Chance was life and the life was the light of men.

There was a man sent by Chance, whose name was Luke. The same came for a witness, to bear witness of Whim, that all men through him might believe. He was not Chance, but was sent to bear witness of Chance. That was the true Accident, that randomizes every man that cometh into the world. He was in the world and the world was made by him, and the world knew him not. He came unto his own, and his own received him not. But as many as received him, to them gave he power to become the sons of Chance, even to them that believe accidentally, they which were born, not of blood, nor of the will of the flesh, nor of the will of man, but of Chance. And Chance was made flesh (and we beheld his glory, the glory as of the only begotten of the Great Fickle Father), and he dwelt among us, full of chaos and falsehood and whim.

– from *The Book of the Die*

Chapter Ninety-four

We know from tapes made on recording devices hidden by agents of the IRS, FBI, SS and AAPP in the apartment of H.J. Wipple, the fuzzy-minded, deluded financier whose millions have helped Rhinehart's various diseased schemes, exactly what transpired the afternoon and evening of the Great TV Raid. Much of it is not relevant to Rhinehart's desperate efforts to escape the law, but a summary is valuable as an indication of the sick structures and values being developed by him and his followers.

Wipple's living room contains a pleasant overstuffed Victorian couch, an oriental desk with a French provincial chair, two Danish-modern chairs, an upholstered navy-surplus raft, a large boulder, and a ten-foot area of white sand on one side of the early American fireplace. The living room is thus furnished in styles ranging from early Neolithic to what J.E. has joshingly called Fire Island eternal. It is recorded that Wipple claims that everything was chosen by the Die. It seems probable.

A cube of Trustees meeting of the DICELIFE Foundation had been scheduled there for after Rhinehart's appearance on the television program. Such meetings occur in such random places and at such random times that few have ever been recorded. Present that afternoon were Wipple, an essentially conservative man whose keen capitalist mind has somehow been poisoned by the atmosphere of dicepeople; Mrs Lillian Rhinehart, who had recently passed the New York State Bar Examination despite allegedly casting a die to choose answers to several of the multiple-choice questions; Dr Jacob Ecstein, the

526

deeply compromised associate of many of Rhinehart's ventures, who is reportedly acting in an increasingly eccentric and irresponsible manner (he is up for a Special Condemnation from the AAPP); Linda Reichman, Rhinehart's sporadic mistress and incorrigible whore; and Joseph Fineman and his wife, Faye, both active dice theorists. Attendance varies at these meetings, since apparently trustees determine whether they will attend by consulting their dice.

These six people had all gathered at Wipple's by 5 P.M. that afternoon – an hour after the conclusion of 'Religion for Our Time' – but only Mrs Rhinehart appeared to have watched the program; she informed the others about what had happened. A long discussion of the possible consequences of Rhinehart's behavior took place, some of it sickeningly frivolous (e.g., Ecstein suggested they hide Rhinehart by burying him in the sand). While Miss Reichman made phone calls trying to find out what had happened to him, Wipple indicated repeated concern over the effect Rhinehart's association with such dregs as Cannon and Jones might have on the public image enjoyed by the DICELIFE Foundation, but he found little support from the others. Joe Fineman noted that since two green dice had been found in a prominent place near the bombing of the army munitions depot in New Jersey and Senator Easterman's attack in the Senate on Dice Centers and dicepeople, there had been a sudden flood of incompetent dice therapists creating stupid and dangerous options for dicestudents; he suggested that the FBI might be infiltrating and trying to discredit the movement. Dr Ecstein squashed this dangerous speculation by noting that dicepeople could do perfectly all right, discrediting themselves without outside help. He went on to suggest perhaps ironically that the DICELIFE Foundation issue a formal statement dissociating itself from

527

any and all bad acts of dicepeople throughout the earth and adjoining planets – to save the trouble of having to issue a new statement 'every other day.'

Miss Reichman and the two Finemans left the apartment at this point to try to find out at the television studio and from the police what had happened to Rhinehart; it was almost two hours since the end of the program and no word had yet been received from or about Rhinehart.

The discussion continued in our desultory manner among the remaining three, Wipple doing most of the talking. He complained that the Internal Revenue Service was trying to deny the DICELIFE Foundation its previously granted tax-exempt status on the grounds that the religion of the Die doesn't fall within the generally accepted continuum of religions, that their educational programs seem aimed at unlearning of generally accepted knowledge, that their scientific studies seem often to contain fictional material and fictional research as evidence (Ecstein remarked here, 'Well, nobody's perfect'), and that their nonprofit Dice Centers can't be conceived of as therapeutic in any traditional sense since their successfully treated dicestudents, as they themselves claim, are often maladapted and subversive of the society. When Mrs Rhinehart and Ecstein indicated a lack of interest in what IRS did, Wipple noted that he deducted three hundred thousand dollars a year from his income, which partly accounted for his generous contributions to the foundation. He added that according to the latest treasurer's report, prepared by a reliable diceaccountant whom the dice had permitted to be accurate, the foundation's failure to charge reasonable fees for presence at the Dice Centers, for group therapy, for their children's dice games and for their various publications was meaning a net loss of over one hundred thousand dollars a month (Ecstein commented 'Right-on!')

[*We beg in our verbatim report at this point* (*HJW behbourlivrm:* 4.17.71. 7.22.-7.39)]

'[The voice of Wipple] Sooner or later we've simply got to start getting some more income. Don't you people realize that other businesses throughout the country are cashing in for incredible amounts on Diceboy and Dicegirl T-shirts, green-dice sports shirts, cufflinks, necklaces, tie clips, bracelets, bikinis, earrings, diaper pins, love beads, candy bars! That dice manufacturers have quadrupled their sales in the last year?'

'Sure,' said Jake Ecstein. 'I bought a hundred shares of Hot Toys Co., Inc. at 2¼ about a year ago and just sold out yesterday at 68½.'

'But what about us?' Wipple exclaimed. 'Other dicelife games, selling for four times what we charge for ours and, you tell me, totally missing the whole point of diceliving, are making millions, while we sell ours for less than cost. And bars and discotheques with a five-dollar cover charge, are advertising dice-dice girls who strip at random, while our Dice Centers' Sodom and Gomorrah are practically free. Everyone's making money out of the dice except us!'

'That's the way the cubes cool,' said Ecstein.

'We keep giving the Die options to make us some profit and It keeps turning us down,' said Mrs Rhinehart.

'But I can't keep covering these losses.'

'No one's asking you to.'

'But the Die keeps telling me to!'

[The sound of Ecstein and Mrs Rhinehart laughing.]

'So far we're the only religion in world history that's losing money hand-over-fist,' said Ecstein. 'I don't know why, but it makes me feel good.'

'Look, H.J.,' said Mrs Rhinehart. 'Money, power. Diceboy T-shirts, green-dice love beads, the Church of the Die – everything people are doing with the dice – all are irrelevant. Diceliving is only our game to promote multiple game-playing, our theater to promote multiple theater. Profits aren't part of our act.'

'You're playing the saint, Lil,' said Ecstein. 'If we're beginning to take pride in our novelty, I'm for trying to loot the public.'

'I tell you we've got to do something about this IRS business or I'm through,' said Wipple. 'We must hire the best lawyers in the country to fight this ruling – to the Supreme Court if necessary.'

'It'll be a waste of money, H.J.'

'Still,' said Mrs Rhinehart. 'It might be educational to have the issues debated in the courts. "What *is* religion?" "What *is* therapeutic?" "What is education?" I'm fairly certain I could make a strong case that the IRS would be the last organization likely to have the answers.'

'I suggest we hire you to appeal the IRS decision,' said Ecstein.

'We need the best money lawyers can buy,' said Wipple.

'We need a dicelawyer,' said Ecstein. 'No one else woud know what he was trying to defend.'

'Dicepeople are unreliable,' said Wipple.

[Again there is laughter, in which a nervous guffaw of Wipple can be heard too. The buzzing sound of the interbuilding telephone is heard and Wipple apparently leaves the room to answer it.]

'I hope Luke's all right,' Mrs Rhinehart said.

'Nothing can hurt Luke,' said Ecstein.

'Mmmm.'

'What are you consulting the Die about?' Ecstein asked.

'I just wanted to see how I should react to news of his death.'

'What did the Die say?'

'It said joy.'

Chapter Ninety-five

It had been an interesting program, with significant talk, action and audience participation: a thoughtful dramatization of some of the key issues of our time. The sponsor would be pleased.

Such were not my thoughts as I choked and gasped and staggered out the door opposite the control room, through which I'd seen Eric pull the body of Arturo. In the hallway I tried breathing again for the first time in fifteen minutes, but my eyes, nose and throat still felt as if they were supporting carefully tended bonfires. Eric was crouched over Arturo, but when I knelt beside him to examine the wound, I saw that Arturo was dead.

'To the roof,' Eric said quietly, standing. His dark eyes were streaming tears and seemed not to see me. I hesitated, glanced at a die and saw I couldn't follow him but was to seek my own way. We could hear sirens wailing outside in the street.

'I'm going down,' I said.

He was trembling and seemed to be trying to focus his eyes on me.

'Well, go ahead and play your games,' he said. 'Too bad you don't care about winning.' He shivered again. 'If you want to find me, call Peter Thomas, Brooklyn Heights.'

'All right,' I said.

'No goodbye kiss?' he asked, and turned away to trot down the hall toward a fire exit.

As he began opening the window at the end of the hall, I knelt beside Arturo to check a last time for a pulse. The door opened beside me and a policeman with twisted face hopped grotesquely into the hallway and fired three shots down the hall; Eric disappeared out the window and up the fire escape.

'Thou shalt not kill!' I shouted, rising stiffly. Another policeman came through the door, the two of them stared at me and the first one edged cautiously down the hall after Eric.

'Who are you?' the man beside me asked.

'I am Father Forms of the Holy Roaming Catholic Church.' I pulled out my canceled AAPP card and flashed it briefly at him.

'Where's your collar?' he asked.

'In my pocket,' I answered, and with dignity removed the white clerical collar I'd brought with me to wear on the interview show but which the Die had vetoed at the last moment. I began to attach it around my black turtleneck sweater.

'Well, get outa here, Father,' he said.

'Bless you, I suppose.' I moved nervously past him back into the smoke-filled studio and with a lumbering gallop made it without breathing to the main exit in back. I stumbled to a stairwell and began staggering downward. At the foot of the first flight two other policemen were squatting on either side with guns drawn; another was holding three giant police dogs who barked viciously as I neared. I made the sign of the cross and passed them to the next flight downward.

And downwards I went, blessing the sweating policemen who surged past me after the villains, blessing the sweating reporters who surged past me after the heroes, blessing the freezing crowds which surged around outside the building, and generally blessing everyone within finger-shot or blessing, especially, myself, who I felt needed it most.

It was snowing outside: the sun shining brightly out of the west and snow swirling down at blizzard pace out of the southeast, stinging the forehead and cheeks to give my head a uniform system of bonfires. The sidewalks were clogged with immobile people staring dumbly up at the smoke billowing out of the ninth-floor windows, blinking into the snow, using their sunglasses against the glare of the sun, turning off their ears to the din of horns coming from the immobile cars clogging the streets, and finally pointing and ahh-ing as a helicopter swept away from the roof far above accompanied by a fusillade of gunshots. Just another typical mid-April day in Manhattan.

Chapter Ninety-six

Lil held herself against me for about fifteen seconds, snow falling from my head and getting tangled in her blonde hair. I was exhausted. Arms about each other, we turned and staggered down the hall toward the living room.

'Are you all right?' she asked.

'Probably,' I answered. 'But I sometimes get the impression the world is disintegrating even faster than I am.'

As we entered, H.J. arose from a chair and came over to pump my hand.

'Incredible show, Luke,' he said, blowing cigar smoke against my chest and placing a chubby hand reassuringly on my shoulder. 'Don't see how you do it sometimes.'

'I didn't plan any of it,' I said. 'Didn't know it was going to happen. When Eric asked me for tickets to the program, I thought he and his friends had become my fans. Hypocrites!'

'Not too good for our image, though. Did you consider that?'

'Mmmm.'

'Was anyone killed?' Lil asked from beside me.

I moved over to the couch and with a groan collapsed beside Jake, who, dressed in white T-shirt and black Bermuda shorts, smiled warmly at me. His feet were bare and his hair looked as if it had last been cut two months ago, by Edgarina.

'Yes,' I answered. 'Can I have something to drink?'

'Sure,' Lil said. 'What would you like?'

'Hot chocolate.'

'You're beautiful, Luke baby,' Jake said, smiling benevolently. Lil headed for the kitchen.

'Thanks.'

'It's the white collar. You on a religious kick again?'

'It's a disguise. People trust priests.'

'I'm a little high,' Jake said, still smiling blissfully.

'Or at least they trust priests a little more than they do dicepeople.'

'But not so high that it interferes with my brilliance,' Jake added.

'You're melting on my couch,' H.J. said, staring down at me.

'Oh, I'm sorry,' I said.

As I stood up, a buzzer sounded off from somewhere and H.J. hustled off to answer it while I brushed off some snow.

'Are the police after you for the TV show?' Jake asked.

'I would guess so.'

'You ought to consider changing your personality,' he said.

I looked back at him and he burst into a grin.

'You're melting on his rug,' he added.

'Oh, sorry,' I said and moved toward the hallway, where I met H.J. returning.

'The police are on their way up,' he said neutrally.

I drew out a die.

'I'd like to try to get out of here and think things over,' I said. 'Is there a way?'

'What's happening?' asked Lil, coming from the kitchen.

'You can go down the service stairs to the basement garage,' H.J. said.

'What's happening?' Lil asked again.

'Is there a car I can use?'

535

'My Lincoln Continental is there. I'll phone down and tell the man to have it ready for a friend.'

A loud knocking came from the end of the hallway.

'Be sure to make a note of the mileage,' H.J. said. 'For income-tax purposes. I consider this a foundation business expense.'

'I've got to run, Lil,' I said. 'I'll phone when I get wherever I go.'

I hurried off to where H.J. had pointed to the service doorway, exchanging a last wink with Jake. Outside the apartment I began creeping with all deliberate stealth down the service stairwell to the cellar, and from there I moved like a cat – a large cat admittedly – to the door leading to the underground garage. Slowly, so slowly that I felt a thrill at the James Bond cunning of it all, I opened the door and looked into the brightly lighted garage. Except for a sloppily dressed, but clean-cut-looking garage attendant leaning in a chair back against the wall near the entrance, the garage seemed empty.

It took me only five minutes to pick out H.J.'s big Lincoln Continental from the eleven other Lincoln Continentals: I finally figured out it must be the one standing ready to go near the entrance. I checked the license plate again and, with cool nonchalance, slipped open the front door and slid smoothly into the driver's seat.

A young man in his thirties, handsome and earnest, was sitting in front also.

'I'm sorry to disturb you,' he said.

'That's all right,' I said, 'I just came down to the basement for a breath of fresh air.'

'I'm John Holcome of the Federal Bureau of Investigation,' he said. He reached into his suit-jacket pocket and leaned toward me to show a little card that looked like my membership card in the AAPP. I squinted aggressively at it.

'What took you so long?' I asked.

He replaced his card in his jacket pocket, leaned back against his seat and looked into my eyes earnestly.

'After learning through certain means that you were at Wipple's, we had to decide what to do with you.'

'Ahhh,' I said.

'And traffic in Manhattan is clogged in several places tonight.' He smiled slightly at me like a bright student reciting a lesson. 'You're Dr Lucius Rhinehart,' he finished.

'That's true, I often am,' I replied. 'What can I do for you?' I sprawled back against my headrest and tried to appear relaxed. My forearm sounded the horn.

Mr Holcome's pale blue eyes searched my unearnest face earnestly and he said:

'As you may know, Dr Rhinehart, in the course of your television performance this afternoon you broke several state and federal laws.'

'I was afraid I might have.' I looked vaguely out the window to my left for the Lone Ranger or Dice Woman to come rescue me.

'Assault and battery on Dr Dart,' he said. 'Brandishing a firearm in a public place. Larceny of Dr Dart's gun. Resisting arrest. Aiding and abetting known criminals. Conspiracy to overthrow the government of the United States. Illegal impersonation of a cleric in a public place. Illegal use of a sponsor's time to give a personal message over public media. And infringement of twenty-three other FCC rulings regarding decorous and proper behavior on a television-media performance. In addition, we are aiding Inspector Putt in amassing evidence for a possible future prosecution of you on a charge of murder in the first degree of Franklin Osterflood.'

'What about hitchhiking within the city limits?'

'Conservatively speaking – and we had no time to check

this without computers – we belive that these various crimes would lead to a sentence of something in the neighborhood of two hundred and thirty-seven years.'

'Ahhh.'

'The government, however, believes that you are actually the harmless dupe of more important subversive forces.'

'Exactly.'

'We know, although we could prove otherwise if we wished, that you were not in on the conspiracy to raid the TV station.'

'Good job.'

'We also know that, should you plead insanity, you would be able to make a very strong case.'

Silence.

'Therefore, we have decided to make a deal with you.'

Silence.

'If you will tell us where we can find Eric Cannon, we will do one of two things: we will so arrange our charges that the most incompetent attorney in New York can get you off with only about three years, or – '

'Unnn!'

' – secondly, give you thirty minutes to get out of here and take your chances with the law in the future.'

'Ummmm.'

'This offer is contingent, of course, upon our actually being able to capture Cannon and his crowd where you direct us. It is also contingent upon the New York Police not locating and arresting or killing you before we do. Not being a party to our arrangement, they might make it impossible for us to lessen the charges.'

'Mmmm.'

He paused and looked, if possible, even more sincerely into my face.

'Where is Eric Cannon, Dr Rhinehart?'

'Ah! Eric?' I flipped a die onto the seat between us and looked at it.

'I'm sorry, Mr Holcome,' I said. 'The Die feels I ought to think about whether I betray Eric and consult It in an hour. It has asked me to ask you to give me until tomorrow morning.'

'I doubt you have that much time. And *we* may not have that much time. I will give you exactly forty minutes. After that we come to make our arrest. If you tell us then, we'll keep this place staked out until we've caught Cannon or not. You can tell us whether you want three years or thirty minutes to run. Otherwise it's four walls till doomsday.'

'I see.'

'Now if you'd like, sir, you can go back to Mr Wipple's apartment and meditate there.' He opened the door on his side and got out. The garage attendant materialized suddenly outside my door and looked in at me earnestly.

'Yes. Yes, it would be messy driving tonight,' I said and lifted my heavy burden out of the car. 'I suppose we may be seeing each other again.

'In thirty-eight minutes. Yes.' Mr Holcome smiled, and his earnest eyes beamed into mine their unremitting sincerity. 'Good evening, Dr Rhinehart.'

'That's your theory,' I mumbled and walked with little enthusiasm back the way I had come.

I climbed up the ten flights of stairs with considerably less stealth and self-esteem than I had come down them. It was getting to be a *long* day.

Lil was the one who came to the door to let me in.

'What happened?' she asked as we moved down the hall toward the living room.

'Red light,' I said.

'What are you going to do?'

I collapsed in total exhaustion on the couch. Jake was

539

seated in the sand in a half-lotus position, staring into the red glow of a fake fire in Wipple's early American fireplace and smoking lazily on a homemade cigarette. H.J. wasn't around.

'They've got mad Lucifer really running,' I said. 'Do you think, Lil, the Die intended you to remain married to a man whom it may ask to spend the next two hundred and thirty-seven years in prison?'

'Probably,' she said. 'What happened?'

I began telling Lil and Jake about my conversation in the basement and all the options I suddenly found myself confronted with. They listened attentively, Lil leaning against the boulder, Jake staring into the fire.

'If I betray Eric, it will seem,' I concluded wearily, 'I don't know, as if I had betrayed someone.'

'Don't worry about it,' said Jake. 'We never know what's good for us. Betrayal might be just what Eric's looking for.'

'On the other hand, two hundred and thirty-seven years in prison seems like an unduly long time.'

'The sage can fulfil himself anyplace.'

'I think I might feel confined.'

'Dicedust,' jake said. 'You'd probably discover a whole new universe in prison.'

'I'd like to try to escape from here, but I'm not sure there's a helicopter on the roof.'

Jake, crosslegged in the sand, staring into the red glow of the fake fire, smiled again like a child.

'Create the options, shake the dice,' he said. 'I don't know why you keep talking.'

'But I *like* you people,' I said. 'I'm not sure I'd like prison as much.'

'That's a hangup, Luke baby,' he said. 'You gotta fight it.'

'So give good odds for trying to escape,' said Lil. 'Or

good odds for hiring me as your lawyer. That'll keep you free.'

'I'm worried about my image,' I said. 'The Father of diceliving has an obligation always to shake true.'

'Dicedung,' said Jake lazily. 'If you're worried about your image you're neither a Father nor a child; you're just another man.'

'But I have to help people.'

'Dicesnot. If you think you gotta help people, you're just another man.'

'But I *want* to help people.'

'Dicepiss,' said Jake. 'If you *want* anything, you're just another man.'

'What's with these new obscenities?' I asked.

'Diced if I know.'

'You're being silly.'

'Not half as silly as you're being.' He beamed into the fake fire. 'Create the options. Shake the dice. All else is nonsense.'

'But *I'm* worried. It's *me* that may get two hundred and thirty-seven years.'

'Who're you?' Jake asked lazily.

There was a long pause and by now all three of us were staring into the red glow.

'Oh yeah, I keep forgetting,' I said, pulling out a green die, sitting up erect and becoming aware that I was sitting on someone's snow. 'I am

Epilogue

One day when Luke was being chased by two FBI men with .45s he came to a cliff and leapt off, just catching the roof to a wild vine twenty yards below the ridge and dangling there. Looking down, he saw fifty feet below six policemen with machine-guns, mace, tear gas canisters and two armored cars. Just above him he saw two mice, one white and one black, beginning to gnaw away at the vine to which he clung. Suddenly he saw just in front of him a cluster of luscious ripe strawberries.

'Ah,' he said. 'A new option.'

–from The Book of the Die

Luke Rhinehart's sequel to *The Dice Man* is also available from HarperCollins. The following is an extract from *The Search for the Dice Man*.

I might never have gone on a quest for my father if it hadn't been for an unexpectedly light rain in Iowa. I was long three hundred futures contracts of December wheat based on a forecast of torrential rains in the Midwest. I expected the heavy rains to ruin the harvest and raise the price of wheat. Unfortunately, the rains didn't fall mainly in the plain. They fell primarily on Cleveland, Chicago and Detroit, where very little wheat is grown. The price of wheat plummeted the next day and I lost about two million dollars for my clients. My employer called me in for a chat. My clients phoned me for chats. My employees and colleagues avoided me. The only people who phoned or dropped by were people who wanted to shoot me.

I'd lost big money for my clients a few other times, but somehow having to explain that 'I thought it was going to rain harder' was the sort of explanation that incites rather than soothes. And it didn't help matters that the rains that didn't fall mainly in the plains hadn't been my only recent miscalculation. For almost three months I'd been on what is charitably called a losing streak. If my indicators said corn and wheat were going up, corn and wheat immediately changed their minds and took a dive. If I took a long position in the stock market, some unexpected inflation report or mad Iraqi dictator would set stocks spiralling downwards.

For three years I'd been something of a trading hotshot – ever since at the tender age of twenty-five I'd accidentally made a name for myself. I happened to be short several stock market futures on that lovely day in October

1

1987 when the stock market dropped six hundred points. While all around me friends, colleagues and strangers stood shell-shocked at the monitors watching the value of their stock holdings nosedive, I stood beside them watching myself and my clients grow richer and trying desperately to repress giggles.

In the fickle ways of Wall Street, that day I made my name at Blair, Battle and Pike (BB&P). At dawn I'd been a mere associate trader, given minimum leeway to dabble at my own ideas for trading. At dusk I was a Vice President and Senior Trader.

Mr Battle, the firm's esteemed leader, knew that he would feel more comfortable being able to tell people that his Senior Trader had been right on that infamous day rather than wrong, so he adroitly changed Senior Traders. In the morning the previous Chief Trader, Vic Lissome, had been king and I merely a peon. In the evening Vic was sitting blank-eyed in a local pub wondering how the market could have clobbered him so badly, and I was humbly thanking Mr Battle for his confidence – and trying desperately to remember why I'd decided to go short those futures.

And from then until the summer of 1990 I'd been a consistent winner, but in the last few months I'd begun to lose money. So when my father began to intrude again into my life after a fifteen-year absence, it came at a time when I was in a vulnerable position – financially, socially and emotionally.

My troubles began when I arrived back at the office after lunch. On a Friday afternoon in September, trading tended to be on the slow side, and this Friday was no exception. Jeff Cannister, a short, dynamic fireplug of a man who always greeted me with shades of nervousness ranging from nail-biting tension to total panic, announced that gold had gone down over a dollar and a half in the ninety minutes I'd been gone. Jeff always managed to report such market movements as if my personal absence had led to the fall in gold – or the fall in the yen, etc – and that had I stayed in my office staring at my monitor I'd have held up the price and saved the firm money.

With Jeff tailing along behind, I continued to stride through the mass of open cubicles at which brokers and traders sat in various states of controlled frenzy. I was aware of how incongruous the two of us were, my tall and lanky frame towering over the squat Jeff so that backbiters, as I knew, sometimes referred to us as 'Mutt and Jeff'.

So gold had fallen slightly when I thought it was about to rise; at least it hadn't fallen through the floor, as wheat had done the week before.

'Any news to cause it?' I asked Jeff.

'Nothing I saw,' said Jeff. Despite his thick solidity, Jeff was totally unfit for the traumas involved in making and losing large sums of money in short periods of time. Still, he was good at what we did and I was happy having him as an associate trader – until he burned out, got hooked on coke, discovered religion or ceased to sleep. Then he'd have to be pensioned off – at the age of twenty-nine, probably.

'The grains are rallying now, especially beans,' announced Jeff gloomily – as if all over the country corn and wheat and soybeans were bursting upwards in a personal effort to thwart Jeff and his firm.

'Just maintain our stops and let me know if they get hit,' I said, flinging my suit jacket over the back of a computer monitor and throwing myself into my swivel desk chair.

As Jeff left I began examining my main monitor, which

had quotes on all the stocks, bonds and futures I was actively trading. My phone line buzzed.

'Yes?' I said.

'Hi, darling, I miss you,' came the lovely voice of my fiancée, Honoria, who also happened to be the daughter of the head of the firm, Mr Battle. Oh, I was a winner in those days.

'Hi, sweetheart,' I said, leaning back in my chair and smiling.

'Daddy's house guests this week are two inscrutable Japanese bankers, one of them with a conspicuous interest in sex. When the tall one first met me he was masterful and flirtatious and eyeing all the more protuberant parts of my anatomy, but when he learned I was a VP at Salomon Brothers and engaged to you he lost interest and spent the day with an old issue of *Playboy*.'

'Say,' I interjected, 'what are two Japanese bankers doing as Mr Battle's guests, anyway?'

'I asked Daddy that and he was strangely secretive. I think he may want them to invest in the firm.'

'Not likely unless they actually buy him out. He's not thinking of selling, is he!?' I added with a brief flash of panic.

'Of course not, dear. He's grooming you to become head of the firm as soon as he retires at the age of ninety-nine.'

I frowned at the thought of Mr Battle's longevity. 'You know,' I said, 'I'd just as soon not see any more than I have to of your father and these Japanese this weekend. Maybe we can spend the day on my sailboat.'

'No, no sailing, dear. When I want to be bored and seasick at the same time I'll let you know.'

'Oh, yeah, right.' Honoria only liked water that was as flat and predictable as concrete.

'However, we can take a walk down to the river. When are you coming?'

'On the early train tomorrow morning. And I'm really looking forward to being with you this weekend.'

'Me too, darling. Oh, oh, big call coming in, have to say bye-bye. I miss your cock.'

And she hung up.

Her abruptness was typical. She enjoyed wealth and style, but liked to mask her enjoyment by sudden small eccentric acts of rebellion which made her seem detached and cynical. She was really a sexually conservative woman, and her saying that she missed my cock was one of her tiny acts to *épater les bourgeois*. When we were actually making love she somehow rarely seemed to notice my cock.

After I replaced the phone I let my gaze wander to the photograph of Honoria and myself on the bookshelf beyond my desk and complacently admired the handsome couple we made: me tall, dark and broodingly good-looking – a sort of gangly Richard Gere; she slender, blonde, nicely proportioned, exquisitely coiffed, flawlessly complected, and rich – an elegant Cybill Shepherd.

From the first time I met her, about a year earlier, I loved being with her, loved exchanging Wall Street gossip and admiring each other's trading coups, loved telling people we were going to get married, loved calculating our yearly income. A check of all the technical and fundamental indicators rated Honoria triple-A – a definite 'buy'. I knew that I, a poor orphaned nobody, was lucky to be where I was, if only I didn't blow it.

I tipped back in my swivel chair and felt a little angry that no one seemed to appreciate what I'd accomplished since October 1987.

Up until that month – all through the 1980s – BB&P had made money the way most firms did – the old-fashioned way: by doing nothing. That is, they bought and sold stocks for other people and themselves, using all sorts of interesting theories or no theories at all, and despite all their efforts or lack thereof they made money.

For most of the eighties if you had money you made money. You bought a condominium – you were clever. You bought a stock, any stock, you were a genius. You bought a house, any house, you were sharp. It was an era when rich dumb guys finished first and richer dumb guys finished even firster.

Until October 1987, anyway. Then a funny thing happened. Almost everyone who for at least five years had been a genius was suddenly in one calamitous day a jerk. Seldom in human history have so many bright wealthy men awakened in just one day to discover such an unambiguous truth: that they were neither so bright nor so wealthy. Their clever condominiums became rather quickly empty and unsellable. Their genius junk bonds became ungenial junk bondage.

My self-congratulatory musings were abruptly cut short when my secretary marched into the room without buzzing. Although normally as cool and efficient as a computer, she looked at me this time as if the market had just dropped a thousand points and she thought it might be her fault.

'There are two gentlemen to see you,' she announced shakily. 'They say they're FBI agents.'

At first I felt nothing; I just stared back at her, tipped forward in my chair and lowered my arms from behind my head.

'FBI agents?' I echoed vaguely.

'They won't say why they want to question you.'

I looked up at Miss Claybell neutrally, but with my heart now pumping panic and my mind desperately searching for the crime I must have committed. But since I was compulsively honest in all Wall Street financial dealings, my mind was filled with unpaid parking tickets, with a nineteen-year-old Goldman Sachs broker trainee I had seduced and abandoned, a 1987 income tax return that contained several creative deductions.

'Should I show them in?' Miss Claybell asked, watching me with that bland composure that made everyone else at Blair, Battle and Pike seem slightly panicky.

I came slowly to my feet, still staring at her uncertainly. I had an urge to pace, but managed to hold my feet to the floor, although my upper body rocked back and forth and my right hand was wrestling with pocket change.

'Yes,' I managed. But as Miss Claybell turned to leave I realized a futures trader being questioned by federal agents was bound to arouse a lot of not totally favourable conjecture.

'And I want you to be present,' I added.

She hesitated, nodded, and then, leaving the door open, disappeared.

The two men who soon entered looked like slightly unsuccessful businessmen who'd come to try to sell me some penny stocks or a supplemental health insurance policy. They introduced themselves as Hayes and Macavoy. They sat down stiffly in the two extra chairs while Miss Claybell, memo pad in hand, stood unobtrusively – or as unobtrusively as someone who dressed like Queen Victoria could – near the door, which she gently closed.

The one called Hayes, a hollow-cheeked man in need of a shave, glanced briefly back at her.

'We're here to question just you, Mr Rhinehart,' he said. 'Your secretary can go.'

'She's staying,' I countered quickly. 'I want a written record of our conversation.'

Hayes looked so expressionlessly at me that it was like looking at a computer screen whose language I didn't know.

'Have it your way,' Hayes said. After the briefest of glances at Macavoy he cleared his throat and continued. 'Is Luke Rhinehart your father?'

That stopped me cold. Parking tickets, male chauvinism and creative IRS deductions all disappeared, and I was left with the image of the big smiling father I'd barely known.

'*Was* my father,' I said.

Hayes stared hard.

'You believe your father is dead?' he asked.

'No, I mean Luke Rhinehart was my father until he deserted his family over fifteen years ago.'

'I see,' said Hayes. 'And do you know where he is now?'

'No.'

'When did you last speak to him?' Macavoy suddenly interjected. He was a slender man too, but taller, gangling, younger than Hayes. He looked like a prematurely aged teenage hoopster.

'Ten years ago,' I answered.

'What was the occasion?'

'My mother . . . had been killed in a car accident a week earlier,' I said as calmly as I could. 'He called to ask if my sister and I wanted to come live with him.'

Hayes and Macavoy waited for me to go on.

'Well?' Hayes finally asked.

'It was the first and only contact I'd had with him since he'd disappeared five years before. I told him to go to hell.'

Hayes blinked once and then nodded.

'And you've had no contact with him since?' he asked.

'None.'

'But you've had contact with his followers.'

'They've occasionally harassed me, if that's what you mean,' I said irritably.

'How have they harassed you?'

'By showing up. By telling me how my father has transformed their lives. Or ruined their lives. By being assholes.'

Macavoy coughed.

'Didn't any of them ever bring you a message from your father?'

'No.'

'Or told you some of the marvellous things your father is doing?' There was a sarcastic bite in the question.

'Look,' I snapped, abruptly standing. 'I really don't want to talk about this. How can you possibly be interested in pursuing my father for the stupid things he did fifteen or twenty years ago?'

Hayes looked at me a moment and then exchanged glances with Macavoy.

'We're not interested in what your father did twenty years ago,' he finally said. 'We're interested in what he's doing right now.'

I hesitated.

'Right... now!?' I managed.

'Yes.'

'And ... what do you think he's doing ... right now?' I asked, sinking slowly back down into my chair.

'We can't go into that,' said Macavoy. 'Let me ask you this: has anyone been acting strangely around you lately?'

I stared at him a moment and then laughed.

'Everyone. All the time. What else is new?'

'I mean has anyone new come into your life that struck

9

you as odd?' the gangly hoopster persisted.

'No,' I said irritably. 'What are you driving at?'

'We have reason to believe that your father may try to get in touch with you,' said Hayes.

'I don't know what you're talking about.'

'Good,' said Hayes. He stood. 'But when you do, we want you to get in touch with us. Immediately.' He reached across the desk and handed me a card.

'May I ask why my father, after all these years, might now want to get in touch with me?'

Macavoy too now rose.

'He's your dice daddy,' Hayes said. 'Maybe the dice will tell him to.'

The Search for the Dice Man

Luke Rhinehart

Larry Rhinehart is the son of an infamous father – the renegade psychiatrist Luke Rhinehart, otherwise known as the Dice Man.

Luke became a cult in the seventies, inspiring thousands to follow him into the anarchic world of Dice Living, where every decision is made not by the self, but the roll of a dice.

Larry, however, is emphatically not a follower. He has grown up to have a great respect for order and control. A wealthy Wall Street analyst, all set to marry the boss's daughter, Larry has got life where he wants it. Until rumours begin to circulate about the reappearance of his long-vanished father – and Larry's carefully organized world begins to look a lot less certain.

By turns funny, moving, and wildly erotic, *The Search for the Dice Man* is a journey of the body and spirit never to be forgotten.

ISBN 0 586 21515 8

Violent Ward
Len Deighton

THE STORY SIZZLES AS L.A. BURNS

Mickey Murphy is a tough, tightfisted criminal lawyer with a seedy downtown office, a '59 Cadillac which is his pride and joy, a son at USC ('the University of Spoiled Children') and a grasping ex-wife determined to get to Hollywood.

Mickey's troubles *really* begin when Ingrid, his high school sweetheart, comes back into his life. She's now married to Zach Petrovitch, a self-made millionaire who buys into Mickey's law firm and thinks he's bought Mickey too. Mickey soon finds himself falling back in love with Ingrid and at the same time being suspected of a brutal murder.

As the glittering city simmers towards an explosion of violence, Mickey begins to feel the heat. Fast-paced, suspenseful, brilliantly observed, *Violent Ward* is vintage Deighton.

'A blistering read . . . The guessing game continues to the final page'
Time Out

'Cracking pace, building to a suitable twist-in-the-tail ending'
Yorkshire Post

'Deighton's ear for dialogue and eye for lunatic California are perfect'
Sunday Express

'Crime at its most entertaining, filled with lively dialogue'
Sunday Telegraph

'Superbly edgy. Entertaining, full of good one-liners'
Sunday Times

ISBN 0 00 647901 4

Divorcing Jack

Colin Bateman

'Richly paranoid and very funny' *Sunday Times*

Dan Starkey is a young journalist in Belfast, who shares with his wife Patricia a prodigious appetite for drinking and partying. Then Dan meets Margaret, a beautiful student, and things begin to get out of hand.

Terrifyingly, Margaret is murdered and Patricia kidnapped. Dan has no idea why, but before long he too is a target, running as fast as he can in a race against time to solve the mystery and to save his marriage.

'A joy from start to finish . . . Witty, fast-paced and throbbing with menace, *Divorcing Jack* reads like *The Thirty-Nine Steps* rewritten for the '90s by Roddy Doyle'
Time Out

'Grabs you by the throat . . . a magnificent debut. Unlike any thriller you have ever read before . . . like *The Day of the Jackal* out of the Marx Brothers'   *Sunday Press*

'Fresh, funny . . . an Ulster Carl Hiaasen' *Mail on Sunday*

ISBN 0 00 647903 0